TUCSON
SUNRISE AND SECRETS

A NOVEL BY

JAMES L. CONNOLLY

authorHOUSE®

AuthorHouse™
1663 Liberty Drive
Bloomington, IN 47403
www.authorhouse.com
Phone: 1-800-839-8640

This book is a work of fiction, people, places, events and situations are the product of the author's imagination. Any resemblance to actual persons living or dead or historical events is purely coincidental.

Published by AuthorHouse 11/26/2013

ISBN: 978-1-4918-3895-2 (sc)
ISBN: 978-1-4918-3894-5 (e)

Library of Congress Control Number: 2013921586

Any people depicted in stock imagery provided by Thinkstock are models, and such images are being used for illustrative purposes only. Certain stock imagery © Thinkstock.

This book is printed on acid-free paper.

This book is dedicated to my
loving wife Judy.

Jim Cooper was sitting in a very plush Country Club bar on the north side of Tucson Arizona with a life long friend David Ortiz. Jim had just left his job with a major computer company. He worked for a division that was essentially top secret and only worked on government projects. He had worked there for two years on a contract that paid extremely well and also had a huge signing bonus. Jim's contract was up and he turned down a two hundred thousand dollar bonus and a large raise to sign another two year contract. Jim was tired of the work and the government's involvement in the two wars.

Jim and David grew up together on the south side of Tucson in a very old Hispanic neighborhood. It's still referred to this day as a barrio. Jim's parents were killed in an auto accident when he was sixteen. He was an only child and had no other extended family he knew of. What little money there was went into a trust that he couldn't touch till he was twenty one. David's parents were appointed by the court to be his guardians till Jim became eighteen. By seventeen Jim had graduated early from high school with almost perfect grades. At the same time he and David had been involved in a lot of criminal activity mostly of smuggling small amounts of marijuana and booze in from Mexico. Law enforcement and the courts knew them well but never got enough to prosecute ether of them. The Judge finely told Jim to join the service or he would at the first opportunity make sure he served prison time. Jim wisely joined the army.

After boot camp he did a two year combat tour in Iraq. When he returned to the states the Army recognized his ability and experience in computers they offered him a promotion and a large bonus to go through a secret one year CIA computer school. He would have to reenlist for another four years as part of the deal. Jim loved computers and thought the school they were offering was a once in a lifetime opportunity.

It was funny the school was at Fort Huachuca Arizona witch is about sixty miles South East of Tucson and close to the Mexican border. Fort Huachuca is one of the biggest military centers for communications around the world.

That year was nice Jim and David saw a lot of each other. Jim helped finance David in opening a high end used car dealership. He and David also invested in land in and around Tucson. After finishing the school Jim went back to Iraq for a second two year tour working on intercepting, decoding, and some times blocking communications of the enemy. Jim also became very good in Arabic and many of the different dialects. After that two year tour they brought him back to Fort Huachuca in Arizona. They again offered him a much bigger reenlistment bonus and a promotion in rate to an E-8 Master Sergeant and he would be earning over twelve thousand a month. He would again go into a top secrete CIA school then serve another two year tour this time in Afghanistan. That tour ended up being four years. By the time it was over Jim was sick of the war and the fact of all the young people that were dying so big corporations could get rich. When his third enlistment was up Jim got out. Even though the Army offered him a huge amount of money he wasn't willing to do another eight years.

As soon as Jim was out he had an offer from a major computer company to work on a top secrete classified project of building the government small super computers that were at least six generations ahead of anything you could buy or build. The money was over double what the army was paying him plus a lot of benefits and a huge bonus for a two year contract. Jim already had a top secrete clearance and that made him more valuable.

The plant he worked at was in Tucson just out side the Tucson Airport. By the time his two year contract was up he was tired of all the spy crap he had been working on and decided he would quit. He had a very luxurious town house in a gated community, plus two Mercedes Benz that David had found him and they were both 2010's. One was an M-Class SUV and the other was the big S-Class luxury sedan, they were both silver.

Now back to Jim and David sitting in the bar at La Poloma Country Club. David is a member and lives in a town home there. David has become very successful in his used car business and he now has three large dealerships, one in Phoenix, Scottsdale and the original in Tucson.

David asked Jim "What are you going to do now that you're unemployed?"

Jim laughed and said "I have over four million dollars in banks, plus all the land that I own. I was thinking of getting a real estate license then after a couple of years move up to a broker with my own business. Then the more I thought about it I was only creating another job, and that's the last thing I want. I do want to buy and sell property but I will find a good broker to handle all the paper work part of it so I can enjoy the good life."

David said "That reminds me there is seventeen acres you and I bought a good ten years ago that a developer wants. I had our accountant Bill Stine look up what we had invested in it including the ten years of taxes and insurance we have paid. Bill said the price they have offered would give us our investment back plus one point eight million profit for each of us."

"How much do we have invested in it?"

David laughing said "We each have less than four hundred thousand invested in it."

"We do need to sell at that price. We should also make them absorb any Real Estate fees as long as were not using a broker."

"I will contact them and if there agreeable they can put it on paper. That also reminds me I ran into Hugh Hanson from high school. He is now a real estate broker and has his own real estate business up here on the north side of town and is doing very well."

"I haven't seen him in years. I will make a point to go over there and have a visit. I am going to need a broker. I will need to reinvest the profit on the land or I will end up paying taxes on it."

The waitress brought them both another drink. David gave Jim Hugh's business card. David said "Before we go I was thinking I have a date tonight for dinner with a beautiful young lady. She has a roommate that is also beautiful and not seeing anyone. Her name is Rachel. If I can put it together would you like to go out with Rachel, Becky and me?"

"That does sound like fun; you know I am not seeing anyone. As a mater of fact I haven't been out to dinner with a young lady in over two months, possibly longer. If you can put it together give me a call, it sounds like fun."

When Jim left the Country Club it was only a little after three, Jim decided he would stop by Hugh Hanson's office to say hello and talk about buying and selling properties. Hugh, David and Jim were all friends in high school. Then after graduation Jim was in the Army and he and David lost contact with Hugh.

Hugh had a very nice offices right on Ina Road no more then four miles from the Country Club. It was a large agency and not a chain. It was Hanson Reality and looked to have at least twenty agents. Jim gave his name to the receptionist and told her he was there to see Hugh. She asked him to have a seat and she would call him.

It was only minutes and Hugh was in the lobby to see Jim. They were both happy to see each other and went into Hugh's office and the young lady brought them coffee. Jim and Hugh spent almost a half hour catching up. Hugh was married and had two children. He had met his wife while going to the University of Arizona and they married right after graduation. Jim did tell Hugh he had a land sale coming up and would have a little over a million dollars he would need to reinvest and he would like to buy up high end real estate mainly single family homes.

Hugh said "The market is full of them; most investors are still scared to jump out there no matter how good the deal is. When you're ready I would like to sit down with you and see if we can come up with some properties you might be interested in."

"I would also like that. As soon as this deal is done I will call you and set up a time. I will call you weather this deal goes through or not."

That was about the end of there conversation and Jim was on his way home. Jim's town house wasn't far; it was off of North First Avenue in the foothills. It was a gated community and the grounds were very plush and the pools heated for year round use. There were also great running trails and Jim did like to run.

It was after five when David called and said everything was set up. He had arraigned tickets for a play at the Arizona Theater Company then for dinner they had reservations for the Azul Restaurant at the La Poloma Country Club. Tucson has no shortage of great restaurants. They would be picking up the girls at seven. David said he would pick Jim up at six thirty. They talked about what they would wear.

Jim still had time so he went down to the pool that is close to his town house. The association fees cover not only the three pools in the community but also a well equipped work out room and showers. Jim swam laps for a good half hour then walked back to his house to get ready for his date.

The hot shower felt good, the pool is heated but the March weather even in Tucson is cool. Jim wore a nice beige slacks with dark brown western boots and belt to match. The shirt was a very nice white long sleeve and a sharp dark blue blazer. Now to pull it all together was a great tie. Jim has a large high end wardrobe and enjoys dressing well. One of the many perks of having money. For jewelry he wore a gold Rolex President watch and on the ring finger of his right hand he wore a gold ring with a very high grade one caret plus diamond. Now to finish it all off he did two sprays of Calvin Kline's Obsession; he is ready.

I guess this is a good time to tell you a little more about Jim Cooper. He is now thirty two years old, single, stands six feet three inches tall and weighs a hundred and seventy pounds. Jim tries to work out at least twice a week and runs a good five to ten miles at least three times a week. He has been able to defend himself well since he was in grade school. The Army gave him advance training in martial arts and the use of fire arms. He tries to make sure he is not in situations that would require the use of any of those talents.

David arrived on time and was also dressed for the occasion. David is also a sharp dresser and likes his clothes. David is six feet tall and weighs about a hundred and sixty five pounds and like Jim was a good street fighter.

After a few minutes they left to go pick up the girls. David drove a nice black S class Mercedes. David uses a dealer plate and has his choice of high end cars to drive from his dealerships. That is part of the fun for him. David has worked hard for many years to build his businesses and now is very rich and like Jim invests in land in and around Tucson.

Jim and David did stop and buy flowers for the girls. They made it one bouquet and very generic. The girls were ready and all of the introductions were done. They were both very pretty girls, some where in there twenties; it was hard to tell. Becky, David's date asked it they had time for a glass of wine?

Jim said "That sounds very nice; how about you David?"

"It does sound nice; let me help open it."

Both Becky and Rachel were nurses and worked at the University Hospital in Tucson and had been room mates for over two years. They were both outgoing and fun. The play David had tickets for was a comedy and at the Arizona Theater Company in down town Tucson. The drive was only about fifteen minutes and fun. The tickets David had were great seats and the play was funny. During the intermission they had a glass of Champaign and talked with some of the other guests. David knew a lot of people there and was introducing the girls and Jim. David is involved in the arts in Tucson and the University. The girls were having a good time as were David and Jim. David and Becky had dated a Number of times in the past few months and enjoyed each others company, but neither of them seamed to be looking for anything serious.

At the Country Club they also had valet parking. The restaurant was very nice and the Mater D was very attentive to make sure David and his guests were seated at a table with a great view. A very lovely young waitress was right there to take there drink orders. David suggested Champaign and they all thought it sounded nice. Drinks and dinner were great and the waitress was very attentive. Jim did get her name it was Sue. After dinner they had coffee and talked a while. The girls both had to work a shift in the morning so that was about the end of the night. They took the girls back to there home and all said good night. Jim even got a kiss on the cheek.

On the drive back to Jim's house they talked about the sale of the land. David said he would call tomorrow as soon as he had an answer.

Friday Morning March 12/ 2010 Tucson, Arizona

It was nine thirty in the morning and Jim was on the phone with David Ortiz. Jim had already run a good hard ten miles shaved showered and made his bed. David said he had the offer on the land they were selling and needed Jim to stop by and sign for his part of the sale. David told him he would be at the Tucson dealership any time after eleven. Jim said he would be there.

Jim decided he would treat himself to a nice breakfast at his favorite Café downtown. There is an old hotel called the Congress Street Hotel that has a great Café that Jim loves to have breakfast at when he is in town. It's a short drive after the rush hour; that's two times in the day Jim tries to avoid driving around in Tucson.

The waitress, Kay is always glad to see him and had coffee to him right a way. There are a lot of regulars that Jim has gotten to know over the years that also come in either before or after the rush. The Café is small and the tables are close together. Unless it's obvious your there with someone, you will probably share you table with someone. It's in most cases a nice way to meet people.

While Jim was eating he called his friend Hugh Hanson the Real Estate Broker and made arrangements to meet with him around one thirty in the afternoon. He also wanted to meet with his Accountant Bill Stine after breakfast so he also called him.

Breakfast was good and fun; Jim paid his bill and as always over tipped Kay. He was on his way to meet with Bill Stine. Bill not only takes care of all of Jim's taxes but also handles all his set bills like his association fees, utilities and housekeeping charges for his condo. He also handles all the taxes and expenses on the property Jim owns. They got coffee and sat in Bill's office. Jim told Bill he had quit his job and was going to just spend his time playing with Real Estate. Bill ran a quick spread sheet of the properties Jim owned and there income plus the income of the properties he and David owned together. After all the expenses were deducted Jim was still making over twenty two thousand a month and surely didn't need to work.

Jim laughed and said "I could say that I would cut back on my fancy living, but I haven't spent any money on just fun for a Number of years. I also plan to change that."

They spent about half an hour going over his accounts and redirecting some incoming payments. They said there goodbyes and Jim was off to see David at the dealership and go over the sale of the land and sign the paperwork.

David was there and glad to see him. They went into David's office and went over the sale. It was fairly cut and dry and a cash deal. David would take the papers back to them but first wanted Jim to stop with him and have a drink and talk. Jim followed David to a nice restaurant close to the dealership that had a bar. Once they were settled and had there drinks David said "I wanted to talk about the other night."

Jim said "That was nice and I had a good time with Rachel and Becky; they are both nice girls."

David started laughing and said "I think all of us had a good time, but I want you to tell me about you and the waitress."

Now Jim was laughing and said "I hope the girls didn't pick up on that, but yes there is something fascinating about her. As a matter of fact I have a meeting this afternoon with Hugh Hanson to talk about Real Estate and

I was thinking of inviting him and his wife to dinner at that restaurant in hopes I might get a chance to talk with her. I do really want to spend some time with Hugh and meet his wife."

Jim was still laughing and said "It even sounds stupid to me but I have to do it."

Now they were both laughing and David said "I don't think the girls picked up on it, but they don't know you as well as I do. I did need to know and I wish you luck."

They finished there drinks then David was off to do his thing and Jim was off to meet with Hugh Hanson.

Hugh was there and waiting for Jim they went to Hugh's office and he had a young man bring them coffee. Jim told Hugh the land sale he had told him about was now in escrow and would close in the next two or three weeks and that would leave him with a little over one point eight million in capital gains he would need to reinvest.

Hugh said "from our last conversation I understand you are looking for large investments that no one wants to take a chance on right now. I went and looked up all the Real Estate you have under just your name not including what you and David own together. I was amazed at how much you have amassed over the years. Then I started to look for things you might be interested in. As I was going over everything I knew was on the market I remembered a conversation I had with a friend of mine named Ed Morton, he is the property manager for the Catholic Diocese of Tucson. I have listed and sold a lot of Real Estate for them. Mostly they were properties that have been willed to the church. Now the Diocese as I am sure you know, have been liquidating a lot of properties trying to raise operating capital. Ed told me they have a forty plus acre estate with a ninety five hundred square foot home and three guest houses on it and all the amenities you would expect to go with it. This all sits at the base of the Catalina Mountains and is bordered on the north by the national forest land. Now here is the strange thing, they want a quiet private sale and don't want to list the property."

"How much are they looking to get out of this thing?"

"The only figure I got out of Ed was ten million and that was just in the conversation. If it's something you're interested in you have sixty some acre's on the east side of Houghton Road that I have a buyer for that would bring you over ten million."

"Well I can't say you didn't do your homework. Talk to your friend Ed and see if we can get a look at this. Now there is another thing; I would like to ask you and your wife Sharon out to dinner tonight at the La Poloma Country Club."

"That sounds like fun, let me call her."

Sharon also thought it would be fun. They arrange to meet at the Country Club at seven.

When Jim left he headed to the Country Club and met with the Mater D. Jim palmed him a folded up hundred and checked if Sue was working that night then arrange to have them seated in her section. His work was done and he decided a workout followed by a swim would fill up the rest of his afternoon.

After he workout, swam, shave and shower he was trying to decide what he would wear for the evening. Suddenly Jim was laughing he was feeling and acting like a kid who was trying to figure out how to impress a pretty girl.

A little before seven Jim was at the La Poloma Country club waiting on Hugh and Sharon. When they arrived Jim was pleased to find Sharon was a very nice and out going lady who dressed fairly conservatively and was pretty; they made a nice couple. Hugh did the introductions then they went to the restaurant. The Mater D said good evening Mr. Cooper your table is ready; may I show you the way. Jim thanked him as he palmed him a folded up hundred. The waitress Sue was right there and said hello. Jim said "Hello Sue, it's a pleasure to see you again." Sue smiled as she took there drink orders. Sharon asked Jim if he was a member of the Country Club. He explained he wasn't but had been there a Number of times with a mutual friend of his and Hugh's named David Ortiz who was a member.

Hugh explained to Sharon that he, Jim and David all went to high school together and were good friends. And after high school Jim went into the army and David opened up a high end used car dealership in Tucson and now also has one in Phoenix and one in Scottsdale. "He has done very well."

Sharon asked Jim what he did. He explained he was just speculating in Real Estate and trying to enjoy the good life. Hugh added that Jim had spent a long time in the Army and most of it overseas. Jim said I actually was in the Army twelve years and spent four years in Iraq and four years in Afghanistan then I contracted for two years at an engineering company here in Tucson.

Sharon smiled and said "There seems to me that there is a lot more to Iraq, Afghanistan and the engineering company then you are saying, but I won't ask".

Sue the waitress returned to the table and asked if they would like another drink. Jim looked at Sharon; smiled and said it sounded good to him. Hugh just laughed.

After Sue left the table Hugh told Sharon that he and Jim were going to look at a large estate that the Diocese of Tucson had at the base of the Catalina's. He said to Jim "I talked with Ed Morton this afternoon and arraigned to see it in the morning at nine o'clock if that works for you."

"Tomorrow morning would be great the place sounds like something we should at least see."

Hugh said "While I was talking to Ed he told me the Diocese has twenty four hour security on this place and it is staffed five days a week with house keeping and landscaping people."

Sue the waitress had brought there drinks and captured Jim's complete attention. After she had left the table Sharon said "As long as the two of you are going to talk business at the dinner table then I think I should at least be invited to see this estate with the two of you."

"I think you're right on both points; that was rude of us and I think you should accompany us. What do you think Hugh?"

Hugh was laughing really hard but did get out that he did agree and would love to Sharon come with them.

They did get dinner ordered and they had a great time and got to know each other. There waitress Sue was very attentive and they had coffee after dinner. While they were drinking there coffee Sharon said "Why don't Hugh and I go out to the lobby and wait for you so you can have the opportunity to talk with the waitress. She is quite beautiful and charming."

Now Jim was laughing hard and said "Again you are right; thank you that would be nice."

They finished there coffee then Hugh and Sharon went out to the lobby. With a smile Sue came over to the table with the bill and said "Your friends are very nice and perceptive. My name is Sue Taylor and yes I am single and not attached. I already know you are Jim Cooper and have at least three nice friends I know of."

Jim was laughing and said "I would like to ask you to lunch somewhere that you would feel comfortable and at any time you would like."

"Jim why don't you give me your Number and I will call you some time tomorrow. Will that work for you?"

While laughing he said "That is much nicer then all the scenarios I had running through my head and thank you for making this so easy. He gave her one of his cards then paid the bill including a hundred dollar tip.

Once in the lobby they were all laughing and Jim told them how easy Sue made it for him. They talked a few minutes then made arrangements to meet at Hugh's office at eight thirty in the morning.

It wasn't quite ten yet and Jim didn't want to go home; he also didn't want to stay at the Country Club. There was a nice club on the south side of town that Jim and a lot of the people he had worked with would go to Friday nights after work. Jim decided he would go there, have a drink and see who was there.

That late at night it was a quick drive and there was a Number of people he knew that were there and glad to see him. He got a drink and sat at a table with six of his friends from where he had worked at. He stayed a good hour then went home.

Saturday Morning March 13/ 2010 Tucson, Arizona

It was six in the morning and Jim was up, shaved, showered, dressed and ready for the day. He decided to drive downtown again and have a light breakfast at the Congress Street Hotel Café. He wasn't meeting Hugh and Sharon till eight thirty and he liked the Café. The waitress Kay was glad to see him and said "Two days in a row how nice."

"I quit working and now have no set agenda, so hopefully I will be seeing a lot more of you."

"Well good; we like you."

Jim enjoyed his breakfast and talking with some of the regulars then was off to meet with Hugh and Sharon.

Hugh and Sharon were already there and had coffee ready. Hugh said "I have talked with Ed and the entrance to this place is off of Campbell north of Skyline he said it just looks like a driveway coming off the street, he will meet us there at nine."

It was no mere then seven to ten minutes from the office so they enjoyed there coffee and talked about the land that Jim owned that Hugh wanted to sell to his developers. Hugh thought it could bring over twelve million even in today's market. Jim's concern was if he did sell it he would need to reinvest the lion's share of it right a way. Hugh said "Well let's go see what Ed has to show us."

The drive was quick and they took Hugh's vehicle. Up toward the end of the road sat a full size late model Buick and a gentleman standing beside it. They were blocking a small paved road that had a sign saying privet property no trespassing. He looked to be in his fifties thinning hair and a well worn suit and looking as if he was trying too hard to look conservative. They all got out and Hugh did the introductions. Ed Morton was very nice and wanted to make it clear that the Diocese had inherited the estate in a will and wanted to discreetly sell the property; first they needed the money and secondly they didn't want any connection to the person who left it to them then lastly they didn't want the Diocese to have any connection to any property of such opulence. "So what I am asking of all of you is to be discreet about what you see here."

They all agreed then followed Ed up the drive. About three hundred feet up was a turn around area a guard house and a large steel gate. The gate opened and the guard waved the two cars through. After a good quarter to a half mile a huge home that could have been a hotel came into view. Sharon said "I can't believe this; it's like something out of the movies."

The house was two stories built in a Mediterranean style with white stucco walls and a rustic red colored tile roofs and a lot of arches. The grounds were beautiful and landscaped like a resort. They walked up three steps to the entry that had two massive doors that were ten feet tall and made of a dark polished wood. The entry room was about fifteen feet wide and twenty feet deep with beautiful tile floors the North wall of the room was windows from floor to ceiling witch was eighteen feet high. The main house was built in a U shape with the open end pointing north giving it an unobstructed, up close view of the Catalina Mountains. In the center of the U was a huge court yard with a built in pool that extended into a room of the house. It was a huge room with a fire place and two different sitting areas, parts of the floor were cut out and had trees planted in it with there own watering system in that room the walls were thirty feet high with open beams and a good part of the roof was sky lights that would open. The wall that looked out to the court yard was all glass with large doors that opened into the court yard. There was also a large consort grand piano. Out in the court yard there was a very large built in Jacuzzi that looked to be big enough for at least eight people. The grounds were very lush with a lot of palm trees and fountains. Everything was professionally done. The second floors had balconies that looked out to the center court yard and also had a great view of the mountains to the north. They spent almost two hours going over the property and the houses. The main house was a little over ninety five hundred square feet plus a detached five car garage. The three guest houses were each nineteen hundred square feet and each had there own walled in patios with built in pools and Jacuzzis. There was also a large warehouse for storage of all the maintenance equipment plus three small SUV's the security people used. It also had an office inside that had monitors for surveillance cameras that covered the property. Another strange thing was that all four homes were completely furnished with very high quality furniture and art that was worth a lot of money just by it's self. Another building on the property was a forty three hundred square foot building that looked like it was for meetings, two sides of it was almost all glass. It was one large room plus a completely furnished kitchen and four large restrooms and one projection room with all the state of the art electronics still there. The ceiling in the main part of the room was at least thirty feet high and domed, there were twelve marble incased pillars that supported the whole span. In the center was a huge marble table that would seat thirty people.

They all thanked Ed for showing them the property and assured him that what they saw would stay private. Hugh also told Ed he would call him.

They had spent over two hours looking over the estate and on the ride back to Hugh's office they were all quite. As they got out of the car Jim said to Hugh "Go ahead and have you developers put an offer on paper for the Sixty acres off Houghton Road then we can talk about what we saw today."

Sharon started laughing and said "I am sorry but are you really serious about that resort."

Now they were all laughing and Jim said "I have done crazier things before but nothing that big. Let's see what Hugh comes up with."

They all said goodbye and Jim left and drove to the down town section and stopped at the Congress Street Hotel bar ordered a drink, paid for it and tipped the young lady bartender then went and sat at a table and was thinking of the estate he had just looked at. The whole thing was worth at least thirty to forty million and it had to cost at least seven to ten thousand a month to operate. He started laughing because he already knew if it could be put together he was going to do it.

Jim's phone rang and when he answered it he was pleasantly surprise because it was Sue Taylor from the restaurant. Sue said "Good morning Jim. If you would still like to buy me lunch I will meet you at a small Café located on the back side of the Congress Street Hotel in down town Tucson at one thirty, if that works for you.""I do know where the Hotel is and would love to buy you lunch."

"Good then I will see you at one thirty."

Jim closed the phone and again started laughing. The young lady behind the bar said "You're really having a fun Day."

"With any luck it should get a lot better."

Jim finished his drink gave the young lady a fifty and a smile then left. It was only eleven fifty and he had some time to kill. He took a ride to the south side of Tucson and into the Barrio that he and David had grown up in. Things always change but the Barrio will always be a place of security for Jim, a place where he can get his bearings and remember what is important in his life. After a while he headed back toward town and his lunch date.

Jim planed it so he would show up just on time. As he walked through the door he saw Sue sitting at a table looking very cute. As he walked over to her table Kay the waitress said "Will this is quite the surprise not only two days in a row but now twice in the same day."

Then she looked at Sue and started laughing and asked her "Is this the guy you were telling me about."

Sue was laughing and said "This is him."

Now the three of them were laughing then Kay said "I have known Jim as a customer for over a year and he appears to be a nice guy. Sorry Jim but that's the best I can do. Now can I get you some coffee?"

"Thank you Kay that also would be nice."

"Please sit down Jim. Believe it or not that was a nice compliment coming from Kay; she is very observant of people and wouldn't say that if she didn't think it was true."

"This all seems strange to even me starting Monday night when I meet you; I found you fascinating but wasn't in a position of saying anything. So when the opportunity of a business dinner with Hugh and Sharon came up I made sure it would be at your restaurant and we would be seated in your section. The funny thing was that Sharon saw through my little plan and suggested they would wait for me in the lobby."

Sue was laughing and said "That was nice of her."

"Well it gets weirder; when you called me this morning I was sitting in the bar of this Hotel having a drink. Then to have you be a friend of Kay's is almost too much."

"So who is Jim and why would he be sitting in the Congress Street Hotel Bar in the morning."

Kay brought Jim's coffee and asked if they were ready to order. Jim said "Would you give us a minute Sue looks like she may be ready to leave."

Sue said "I would like the chef's salad with the dressing on the side; ranch would be nice."

"Salad does sound good and balsamic vinegar for me please. Thank you Kay."

"Now for Jim; I am thirty two, single, never been married and was born and raised in Tucson on the south side. David, who you know, has been my best friend from the time we were in grade school and I even lived with his family for over a year. At the age of seventeen I went into the Army and stayed for twelve years a little over eight of that was spent overseas now for the last two years I worked for an engineering company here in Tucson up till Monday. My contract was up and I chose not to renew it. That was why David and I were out celebrating my being unemployed. That was a blind date David and his girlfriend set up for me. She was a very nice young lady. Since I was in high school David and I have invested in land and properties some times together. I have decided to now spend my time speculating in Real Estate. That brings us to Hugh and his wife Sharon. Hugh also went to school with David and I and we lost contact after high school, Hugh went on to become a Real Estate Broker and has his own company we only reconnected this week and were looking at properties to buy and some of mine to sell; and so dinner last night. We talked about a property he knew of that we wanted to see this morning. Sharon said if we were going to be rude enough to talk business at dinner then she also wanted to see the property with us this morning. We spent over two hours looking at it and it would be a major purchase and a lot to think about. That brings us up to me sitting in the bar having a drink."

"So now it's back to me. I am twenty five and am a graduate student at the University of Arizona and am working on my master's degree in art. I am not only a friend of Kay's but we shear a condo we rent by the University. Kay is also a student at the University. Now I was born in Oregon and my Father worked with a large computer company then was hired away by

IBM and we moved to Tucson. Later on they transferred to Colorado and I stayed here."

Kay brought there food to the table and said "I see you're both still here. That's a good sign." They all laughed and Sue and Jim enjoyed there lunch and talked for over an hour.

"I think were at the point that lunch is over and I am not at the point I want to say goodbye. I would like to ask you out to dinner tonight and so it wouldn't be too much to ask could we invite Kay and who ever she would like to bring. It will be my treat."

"Kay just ended a not to nice relationship and is not looking for anyone to date."

"Then let's ask Kay to join us; it might be the right thing for her."

"Now you're making it hard for me to say no."

"I am trying my best."

Sue laughing said "Let's ask her."

Jim motioned to Kay to come over to the table. She brought the bill and asked how things went. Jim said "I am at the point I asked Sue out to dinner and was hopping you would join us; that I think will push the deal over the top."

"Well how fancy."

Now Sue was laughing really hard and Jim said "Money is not a concern so it can be as fancy as you want."

"Sue gets to see fancy four nights a week but not me, so I want fancy."

"Then fancy it will be; we can put it at least one star fancier then Sue see's at work. Now all I need is a time, address and phone Number."

Sue was still laughing as she wrote out her address and phone Number then said "Would eight o'clock be ok?"

"Yes; so thanks to both of you and I will see you at eight."

He gave Kay the money for the bill and a fifty dollar tip and left feeling great. The ride home was fun, before he got to the house he thought it would be a great idea to go up to the Westward Look Resort and make arrangements at the Gold Room to have the table he wanted for eight thirty that evening. The Maître D was there and he and Jim made all the arrangements for the evening before leaving Jim palmed him two folded up hundreds as he said "Thank you."

Now it was time to go home change and go for a good run. While he was running he was thinking of all the things that have been happing since he quit his job on Monday. There was nothing he was having second thoughts about even the huge estate he was looking at wasn't scary it was exciting. And Sue, even with the small amount of time he had spent with her she was a lot more then even he had hoped for. The biggest part he was happy and having the time of his life.

At eight o'clock Jim was at the door of the girls condo with two bouquets of the proper flowers for a first date. Sue answered the door looking beautiful and immediately started laughing at the two bouquets of flowers. She gave him a small kiss and asked him in. Kay also liked her flowers and thanked him. Jim said you both look beautiful, and I should start by thanking the two of you for accompanying me tonight. To be honest this whole week I am having the time of my life. So let's go see if we can put smiles on the two of you."

Jim had driven the big S class Mercedes and held the doors for the ladies; they both loved it. The drive to the Westward Look went quickly and as they drove through the gates Sue said "And so five stars." Jim smiled as he pulled up to the front door. There were people there to open the doors for the ladies. As they walked in Kay said "Well done."

The Maitre D said "Good evening Mr. Cooper your table is ready for you and the ladies. If you will allow me I will show you the way."

It was easy to see the girls were impressed and happy. The table was one of the premier tables set so they would have a panoramic view of a large part of Tucson. Sue said "The food could be terrible and this still would be wonderful."

"Hopefully the food also will be nice. Would you ladies like to start with some Champaign?"

"Yes, Champaign does seam to be the proper drink for here, thank you."

Dinner was all that Jim hoped it would be. The girls were having fun and the food was fabulist. They all felt relaxed and got to know each other. They finished Dinner with coffee and the girls couldn't resist the deserts. Jim asked what else he could do to entertain them for the evening. Kay said "The music there having at the hotel tonight isn't too crazy and the girl singing is really good."

Sue asked if Jim had ever been to the Congress Street Hotel Club. "I have, even as old as I am and as Kay said some times the music is good and some times it's terrible. But the young people that show up are fun and for the most part there is no trouble. If you ladies like that can be our next stop."

Sue was laughing and said "I can honestly see you there; even being as old as you are. So let's make it our next stop."

Jim paid the bill and tipped there waiter two hundred as he thanked him. By the time they reached the entrance the vale service had brought up there car and opened the doors. As they were driving out of the resort Sue said "They definitely lived up to there five star rating, that was wonderful; Thank you."

Kay said "I also need to say thank you that not only lived up to fancy but went all the way to opulent."

Jim started laughing then said "I am the one who needs to say thank you to the two of you. I am having the best time. But I do need to disagree with Kay on the opulent part of tonight. The Westward Look is beautiful and deserves its five star rating but this morning I looked at a property that was definitely opulent. I have never seen anything like it. It's funny, that was the property that Hugh and I were talking about last night, so again it is connected to Sue because that was the only reason I invited them to dinner so I would have the opportunity to meet you. That also worked out because I enjoyed meeting his wife and we really did have a nice time."

"So you're a buyer of opulent properties?"

"Not normally, but I do own a lot of Real Estate in and around Tucson. This place is something special and I am sure there is nothing like it in this state. If I ever get to the point that I have it in escrow I would love to have the two of you come see it while I do my inspection. It has a twenty four hour security force that patrols the estate so we can't get in till then."

"Well that's a pretty big caret to dangle for a second date."

"Let's just call it an invitation and not a date. That way there are no strings; I know for myself I don't like people to attach strings on things."

Jim found decent parking and they walked to the club. It was after ten thirty and they were busy. Kay knew a lot of people there and it wasn't hard for her to get a table that the three of them could join. The band was playing and a young lady was singing and was very good. Kay said "That is Jan the young lady I told you about."

Jim said "She is very good and has a great voice, she needs a much better band or orchestra behind her and she could be great."

Jim got the waiters attention and ordered a bottle of Champaign Three glasses and a round for everyone else at the table. He palmed the waiter a twenty and said this is for you to get you started. The waiter smiled and said "That works."

Jim smiled at Sue and asked if she would like to dance. She smiled and said "I would, thank you."

As they got to the dance floor the song ended and they then started with a slow dance. Jim softly kissed Sue on the cheek and said "I really am having a good day."

The three of them had a great time with each other and the people at the table. It was almost twelve thirty when the decided to call it a night along with most of the other people. The band had changed and so had the music.

As they walked out there was an altercation when three bad boys were pushing around two young gay men and calling them names. The leader of the little pact hit one young man knocking him down. By then Jim was in the middle of it and quickly laid out the three bad guys. The big mouth leader was quickly on his feet and pulled a knife and took a swing at Jim who grabbed his hand breaking his wrist then his arm. Once he had him back on the ground Jim dropped with his knee onto the man's chest breaking at least two ribs. He then put his boot on his throat and quietly said "If I ever have to deal with you again I will kill you." Then he said "You other two cowards get up and get this piece of shit out of here and don't ever come back." He next picked up the knife stepped on the blade and broke it off then helped the two young men up and asked if they were all right.

They were and said "Thank you."

Jim said "I am sorry you had to deal with that is there is any thing I can do to help?"

The one young man said "You could make them replace my shirt that was the last new thing I bought before we got laid off."

Jim started laughing and said "I am Jim Cooper and here is fifty to cover the shirt, and my card. Call me next week and maybe I can help."

The young men were laughing by then and they introduced themselves as Steve and Frank.

Jim apologized to the girls and told them it would be better if they all left. On the way to the car Sue said "We see another side of Jim."

"That's not a side of me even I like to see. I have been scared like that and in a position where no one would or could help. I couldn't let that go on."

Kay said "I know both of those guys and they really are nice. I hope they weren't hurt."

On the ride back to the girl's house they went back to having fun. Jim walked them to the door and asked Sue if he could call. She gave him a small kiss and said "Please do."

Tuesday Morning March 16 /2010 Tucson, Arizona

Jim was up early and went for a good five mile run before he shaved and showered. He had spent part of Monday with his Accountant Bill Stine making sure he would be reinvesting all of the profits from the sale of the land he and David had in escrow. Then they looked at what Jim had invested in the land that Hugh was looking at selling for him. Jim was surprised in how little he really had in the land. The books showed he had over eight million invested but in reality it wasn't much over four million. He told Bill he would call as soon as he had any news.

Before Jim could leave for breakfastSue called and said that she and Kay had tonight off and would like to cook dinner for him if he was available. Jim laughing said "There is nothing I would rather do then to have dinner with the two of you. Would it be alright if I brought some wine?"

"Wine would be nice. We will be looking for you around seven."

Jim thought that wasa nice start to the day. He was meeting David for breakfast at a little restaurant close to his house. As Jim pulled into the parking lot there was a current model bright red Corvette sitting by the front door with a dealer plate on it. David was already sitting in a booth with his coffee and a copy of the morning paper. Jim knew he was checking the car adds for his dealership and all the others. Jim sat down and said "Good morning David; I can see you're keeping a low profile."

"That's a nice car; you would look good in it. As a matter of fact that cute young waitress might be impressed by it."

Jim started laughing and said "I am surly not looking for a girl that would be impressed by a car. And as for as that cute young waitress, we went out Saturday night and she just called this morning and invited me over tonight so she and the young lady she rooms with can cook me dinner."

"Well a second date for you, she must be special; good luck my friend"

The waitress brought Jim coffee and refilled David's. They both ordered breakfast. They talked about business and how money was tight on the market. David said there were a lot of high end cars coming on the market at really good price. They were the cars that normally never saw the secondary market and still a lot of dealers were scared to jump on them. He had picked up thirty in the past two months and was in no hurry to resale them. Jim told David he had been working with Hugh at looking at properties and had met his wife Sharon who was very nice; they made a nice couple.

David told Jim the buyers on there land wanted to close as soon as the title company could get there part done. "We may be closing this next week they already have architects working on the sight plan." Breakfast came to the table and it got quite.

As breakfast came to a close David was off to the dealership and Jim was going to the County Records and see what he could find out about the estate at the end of Campbell.

After almost an hour of going through County records all Jim could find out is that the property was held in trust by a corporation out of Richmond Virginia that had control of it since 1957 before that it was three different parcels of land. The ownership was transferred to the Catholic Diocese of Tucson in June of 2009. The corporation that controlled the property was DBS Properties with a P.O. Box in Richmond Virginia. Jim was sure he would find that the corporation was dissolved in 2009. It didn't really matter who had owned it but it sure made him curious.

Before Jim left the County Records he got a call from Steve Hays, one of the young men from Saturday night. Jim told Steve he might have a business opportunity for him and Frank and would like them to put together a brief resume and then they could have lunch Thursday if that worked for them.

"That sounds great, what time and where would you like to meet?"

Jim said "How about one o'clock and some where nice that you guys like; it's my treat."

"Would the El Parador restaurant on Broadway be all right?"

"It sounds great Steve; I will see the Two of you Thursday."

On the drive home Jim stopped and found two great bottles of wine to take to Sue's then the next stop was the florist. Jim learned a long time ago all flowers have different meanings attached to them and young ladies knew them very well. Jim picks out his own bouquets and actually enjoys playing the flower game.

Once home he put the wine in the refrigerator and the flowers in water then changed to go running then to the pool. He needed to stay busy and not just think about Sue.

A little over half way through his run Jim got a call from Hugh. Hugh said he had in his hand an offer on the sixty three acres Jim owned on south Houghton Road and wanted to bring it over. Jim laughed and asked Hugh to give him an hour he also gave Hugh the address and guest code for the gate. Jim finished his run then quickly showered and dressed.

When Hugh arrived Jim asked if he would like a drink. Hugh said "That is a good idea this has been a busy day."

While Jim made the drinks Hugh said "I have a one sale listing agreement for you to sign then we can go over the offer."

"I must say you moved fast on this. The other property I told you about that David and I are selling should close next week; they also were in a hurry. David said they already have architects working on a sight plan for the city. Maybe these people know something we don't."

"I hope so because I love selling property."

Jim brought the drinks over and Hugh gave him a copy of the sales agreement. Jim red it over then said to Hugh "If you can bring this in to where I clear over ten million. I will give you ten percent instead of the eight you have listed in your agreement."

"Then I think we will both be happy with there offer, even at ten percent you will clear over eleven million six hundred thousand. Let's go over it."

The offer was clean with them putting up one million in escrow and wanting to close as soon as possible. It took a good twenty minutes to change the sales agreement and sign all the copies. Jim made them a second drink while Hugh put all his stuff away. Then they sat and talked. Jim said "Once we have a real closing date on this property I would like you to set it up with Ed Morton to let me with two assistants do an inspection on the estate I will make an offer for the ten million contingent on the results of what I find."

"Well I must say you are quickly becoming my favorite customer."

After another twenty minutes Hugh was on his way to set up the escrow account and notify his customers that there offer was accepted.

It was still early so Jim changed, got a towel and went down to the pool to swim laps.

It was almost seven and Jim was walking up toward Sue and Kay's front door. He was dressed casually in Levis, a nice long sleeve light blue shirt, with black western boots, a nice beige cord sport coat now to finish it off he had two sprays of Calvin Kline's Obsession. He had the flowers and vase in his right hand and the two bottles of wine in the other. He rang the bell and Sue answered the door. With a big smile she said "Wine and flowers, how nice. Please come in." Kay was in the kitchen and dinner smelled Italian. Sue said "You picked a nice wine; if you would open it I will pour us all a glass."

Kay loved the flowers and said "You sure know how to spoil a couple of girls."

"I have to admit I am trying."

Once the wine was open Sue poured them all a glass and they sat in the living room. Sue asked Jim where he lived. "I have a condo off of North First Avenue. It's a gated community and is quite secure. I was spending a lot of time out of the country, the last time stretched out to be four years but that part of my life is over."

Kay said "That must have cost a lot to leave the place empty for four years."

"Not really, the condo is paid for and the utilities and association fees are absorbed by my investment company."

Sue said "To change the subject did you hear from the two young men from Saturday night?"

"They called me this afternoon and we are having lunch Thursday; they seem to be nice guys and got a good recommendation from Kay; hopefully I can find them some work they like."

"So you're also an employment agency?"

Jim laughed and said "No but if I am going to start speculating in properties then I am going to need some help from people I can trust to do things as I want, it's hard to explain."

Kay went in to check on the dinner and Sue and Jim sat and talked. They ate about eight o 'clock and it was definitely Italian and good. Jim and Sue did the dishes and the three of them had a fun evening Jim left about eleven after making sure he could call Sue. He got two kisses on the way out and the one from Sue was interesting.

It had been a great Tuesday as Tuesdays go.

Thursday Morning March 18 / 2010 Tucson, Arizona

Jim was up early and went for a run; he did a strong ten miles then he shaved, showered and dressed casually. He was meeting David for breakfast at the Congress Street Hotel Café. He was hoping that Sue's room mate Kay would be working.

When Jim arrived David was already there with a copy of the Morning paper. Kay was working and came over to the table with coffee for Jim and to refill David's. She said "I told David it's been a longer time since I have seen him. I will give the two of a few minutes."

David said "I am ready if Jim is."

Kay took there order then Jim said "I was going to call Sue but I didn't know when a good time would be."

Both Kay and David started laughing then Kay said "You will need to call to find out." As Kay walked off laughing David while still laughing said "You are acting like your back in high school."

Jim now laughing said "I almost feel like that; I will call her."

They were talking about David's car business and the price of the used car market. David said "The price of high end cars has stayed solid but the retail market for the average cars is really soft. At the last two auctions in Phoenix I have picked up sixty two high end luxury cars and put them in my warehouse in Phoenix, everyone is scared to bid on them it was almost like stealing them. Maybe we should put you into Mercedes SL 500, something sporty the ladies would like."

"I like the two vehicles I have. Speaking of things that would impress someone, I am looking at an estate that would impress the Queen of England."

Kay brought there breakfast to the table and while they were eating Jim told David about the estate and how close he was to putting it into Escrow. By the time he finished the story both He and David were laughing. That was the end of breakfast. David left and Jim paid the bill, over tipped Kay and thanked her.

Once at the car Jim called Sue and they talked a good twenty minutes. Sue was working Thursday, Friday and Saturday nights. Jim said "This is kind of a gamble but you look to be in great shape and I am thinking you're most likely a runner. If I am right would you like to go running any morning and then breakfast?"

Sue was laughing then said "You must be good because if I am not a runner that is a big gamble. But you're right I am a runner, and love to run. Let's go running in the morning, you tell me what's not too early for you."

"How about I come over at six in the morning and you decide where you would like to run and how far."

"I will be looking for you at six and thanks for calling."

Jim had a list of things he needed at the store and decided this was a good time; he had nothing to do until one o'clock. Just before Jim was ready to leave the store he got a call from Hugh who told him he had a closing date on the sixty three acres set for Wednesday afternoon. Jim said "How about I come over to your office at let's say, ten thirty in the morning and we work out an offer on the estate that the Diocese has."

"You know I would love to; I will see you in the morning."

Jim took his groceries and went home. After he put everything away he fixed himself a drink then sat in his recliner and pondered all the things that had transpired in the last two weeks. The two biggest things were Sue then the estate. Some how they were all connected. There was also some kind of force that was drawing him to the estate.

At one o'clock Jim was at the El Parador Restaurant. Steve and Frank were there waiting. They all said hello and were taken to a nice table. Jim asked if they would like to start with a drink. That kind of made the two boys a little more at ease. They all ordered a drink and Frank gave Jim the short resume's they had made up. Jim quickly looked over them and was happy to see that they both had been working for the last three years at the Hilton El Conquistador Resort setting up for special events and conventions. They had been laid off due to business slow down almost two months earlier.

There drinks had come to the table while he was reading the resumes. Jim said "I will assume you both receiving unemployment."

The boys said they were and were enjoying the time off except for the lack of money.

"Let me tell the two of you what I am into and what I was thinking."

The waitress came back over and asked if they would like to order. They all ordered lunch and another round of drinks while they were waiting. Jim explained that he bought and sold property in and around Tucson and had since he was in high school. But now he was going to only do that and was thinking he would need help in fixing them up and moving things around. He would need help in having his own people help over see what workers were doing and making sure things were done properly. "I was thinking to start with I could pay the two of you by the job. It would be cash and wouldn't interfere with you're unemployment. Then we could all see if it could work into something that would have a future for the two of you and be an asset to me."

The boys were excited about the idea. There drinks had come to the table. Steve said "It sounds a lot like what we were doing at the El Conquistador. We both did a good job at making sure things were done correctly and on time."

"I care more about things done correctly and not damage then the time it takes."

They talked a while and lunch came to the table. After they ate they ordered coffee then Jim told them a little about the estate he was looking at buying. They were all laughing about it. Jim paid the bill and over tipped the waitress. As they walked out he gave Steve and Frank each a hundred dollars and said he would keep them up to date on what he was doing. That was the end of lunch.

Friday Morning March 19/ 2010 Tucson, Arizona

Jim was up by five and got everything ready to meet Sue at six o'clock and go running. "He laid out the clothes he would change into for breakfast and the rest of his day.

He rang Sue's door bell right at six o'clock. Sue was dressed in a cute set of sweats and had on a well worn set of high end running shoes and best of all a great smile. She said "Would you like to run along the Reito River? I usually like to run five to ten miles, I am not sure what you're comfortable with."

"I love to run ten miles when I have the time. Let's just do what feels good then I will go home shower and dress and would like to take you to breakfast."

"I would enjoy all of that. Let's go."

They had a great slow run and talked most of the way they did a good seven miles and Jim was telling Sue he was putting an offer in on the property he had told her and Kay about and if they accepted it he would like to set a time where both she and Kay would be available to do the inspection with him. Sue started laughing so hard they had to stop running. Once she gained control she said "Are you serious about buying something that big?"

"Yes and as I said I would like you and Kay to look at it with me. It will take a good three hours and maybe longer. But it should be fun and afterwards we could all go out for some good Mexican food."

"I would love to see it and I am sure Kay would. We can ask her when we get back to the house and figure out a time."

Back at the girls Kay was up and had coffee made. They talked and agreed on a time of Saturday or Sunday mornings if Jim's offer was accepted by then. Jim finished his coffee then was off to shave shower and dress for breakfast.

It wasn't long and he was back at Sue's door. Sue looked very cute. She stands about five six and a hundred and ten pounds. Her hair is short and blond. She is what Jim would call petite and beautiful.

"So where are you taking me for breakfast?"

"As beautiful as you look it should be somewhere nice. How about the Starr Pass Resort; I haven't been there in over a year and that was business and not much fun."

Sue gave him a small kiss and said "Then let's go to Starr Pass and try and make it fun this time."

Star Pass was also very nice and they were seated to where they overlooked part of the golf course. Coffee and a juice cart quickly came to the table. After they had coffee and juice Sue said "I find you very pleasant and a lot of fun to be with but I am not sure of what your interest in me is. So why don't you try and tell me where you are coming from and what you're looking for?"

"I must say you are up front, and for the second time have made it easy for me to say what I want to. To start with from the moment I met you at the La Poloma Resort I have been fascinated by you and I am not talking about you're looks, Witch I do find wonderful But the whole perception of you. I also must admit I am in strange territory because I have never had this feeling about anyone before. Now with the short amount of time we have spent together the feelings I have for you have only grown stronger. Now for the immediate future I would like the two of us to get to know each other and see if this go's anywhere. If that's agreeable with you then we can just relax, have fun and get to know each other."

Sue smiled and said "I like that; let's order breakfast."

Breakfast was ordered and they were both more relaxed. Jim asked Sue about her art and what she was doing with it.

Sue's whole face lit up when she talked about art and her involvement in it from the living arts all the way to computer generated graphic arts. She told him working at the La Poloma Resort paid her more then she could get working in her field and gave her the time for school and to be active in many art projects in Tucson. She also played the piano and was part of the Universities Orchestra in her sophomore year. She started laughing and said I also twice played back up for the singer Jan at the club we were at the other night. I love to play but don't like to perform."

Breakfast came to the table and looked good. While they were eating Sue said "So you must be rich if you're trying to buy an opulent estate."

Jim smiled and said "I guess I am. I have made a lot of money both in the military and the last two years working for the engineering company and have never spent any of it. I didn't really own my own car till almost a year ago. Let me give you a quick run down about my money. When I was in high school David and I smuggled marijuana and alcohol across the border and sold it to bars and clubs around town. Law enforcement knew it but couldn't catch us and we never had any money. I remembered from the time I was a kid my Father and other adults would talk of all the big properties and developments that were just years ago a bunch of desert that could have been bought for almost nothing. I convinced David to join me in saving all are monies then with a lot planning invest it in Real Estate that we were sure would be valuable in the future. In high school we had our own investment company and no one knew of it. I finished high school early and a Superior Court Judge assured me that if I didn't join the service and change my ways he would at the first opportunity make sure I served prison time. The Army looked pretty good to me at that time."

Jim was now laughing and said "Now for me to buy that estate Hugh has arranged the sale of some acreage on the South East part of town that will give me more then enough cash to pay for this and still end up with a lot of cash. Even the condo I live in is one of my investments. I must say there is an irresistible force that is drawing me toward this estate and you. This all started when I decided I was done with just working and wanted a different life."

Sue sat back in her chair, smiled and said "First of all thank you for answering my question and second when you were talking about the Estate I suddenly had a feeling that I knew you're offer will be excepted and you will end up with it. The feeling is so real that it's almost scary. Now I am getting excited about seeing it."

Breakfast was over and they went back to Sue's. Jim thanked her for the morning and said he would call as soon as he heard anything. As he was leaving he got a nice kiss.

Jim was barely on time to meet Hugh at his office a young man brought them both coffee and Hugh said "I talked with Ed Morton at the Diocese yesterday and told him I expected to have an offer on the property to him by noon today. He will be waiting and have the people necessary to make a decision on it also available today."

"I have thought about this a lot and will offer them the Ten million cash they were looking for and I have a few things I want to make sure of: first is that everything that is now on the estate goes with the sale. Second I want to make sure that all water and mineral rights go with the property. If all that is agreeable with them I would like to do my inspection tomorrow or at least by Sunday. It will be me and two assistants. I brought with me a certified check for one million dollars to open an escrow account."

"Enjoy you're coffee this will take about fifteen minutes then you're signature."

It wasn't but twenty minutes and Hugh was on the phone with Ed Morton telling him he was on the way over with an offer. Once outside Jim called David and asked if he could get away for a drink. David asked if He wanted to do lunch. "No but you're welcome to eat."

David was laughing and said "Come over to the Dealership and I will drive."

Once he and David were on there way to the Country Club David said "Tell me what is going on."

"Let's get a drink first then I will tell you about my day."

As soon as they had a nice table and there drinks Jim told David all about his day starting with the run and all the way to making the offer on the estate. David was happy to see Jim that taken with someone, and he did like Sue. Now the property sounded exciting and he knew if Jim thought it was a good risk then it was. They had two drinks and talked for over an hour.

Once he was back at his condo Jim realized he was thinking more about Sue then the estate. It was after two when Hugh called and said his offer was accepted and he was in escrow. He also told Jim that Saturday morning would be fine to do his inspection. Jim told him he and his people would be there at nine in the morning.

Jim right then called Sue before she was on her way to work. He confirmed that he would pick up her and Kay at seven in the morning for breakfast. Sue was excited for him and said they would be ready.

Jim decided to go work out then call it a day.

Saturday Morning March 20/ 2010 Tucson, Arizona

Jim was up early shaved, showered and dressed. He had to pace himself he didn't want to be too early arriving at Sue's.

When he rang the bell Kay answered the door and was excited about the day to come. She said Sue would be right out. Sue come into the room looking very cute as did Kay. Jim made sure to tell the both of them. Kay said "I hope you're going to take us somewhere fancy for breakfast."

Sue was laughing and Jim said "I think that is a good idea we have plenty of time. How about Ventana Canyon Resort they should have a nice breakfast."

Kay was laughing and Sue said "Were spending a lot of your money on just fun."

"Fun is not over rated, and I have collected a lot more money then fun so let's enjoy it."

Ventana Canyon of cores was lovely and they were treated like royalty. Kay said "I wouldn't want to live like this all the time, but once in a while this is wonderful."

"Well I am honored and happy to be the one to bring the two of you here."

Juice and coffee were brought to the table right a way. After they ordered Jim said "I have a favor to ask the two of you. Included in this purchase is all the furnishings and art. I believe all the pieces of art are originals. The two of you are more knowledgeable then I am about art. So while we are inspecting all of the property I will give both of you a pad and pen and if you would be so kind please make notes on anything you see. I can tell you I am really excited and there seems to be something very mysterious about this place."

The girls were ready for the adventure. Breakfast came to the table and looked great and the conversation slowed down. After a few minutes Kay started laughing and said "I am having a problem picturing that place being more glamorous then the places you have taken us to, and then the fact that you are going to buy it."

Jim started laughing and said "I saw so much so fast when I was there that I can't begin to remember even part of it. There is one huge room that has trees growing in it and a swimming pool that extends out into the court yard. I can hardly wait to see all of it."

Sue said "What are you going to do with this place once you buy it?"

Jim was again laughing and said "I don't know. If you have any ides while we are there write them down on you're pads."

They finished breakfast and had more coffee while they talked and laughed a lot. It was time to leave and Jim took care of the bill and waitress. It was eight thirty and time to go to the estate.

They arrived a little early but the guard at the gate was expecting them and told Jim there would be someone at the house who would open anything they wanted and show them how everything worked. He could hopefully answer any questions he had. Jim thanked him and they headed up the road. The girls were being quiet till suddenly they came over a hill and the house was visible. Sue said "Shit this is a hotel. I can't believe someone just lived here."

"Hang on it only gets better."

There was a gentleman who looked to be in his fifties who introduced himself as Tim and said he was there to answer all the questions he could and assist them all he could.

Jim introduced himself and the ladies as his assistants. Then said they would like to start with complete tour of the estate.

As they walked through the front doors the girls both took a deep breath but didn't say a word. They spent over three hours going over the estate and making a lot of notes. Tim was a great help and answered a lot of questions. Tim supplied Jim with a list of all the companies that took care of the estate along with there numbers and the contact people. Jim thanked him for all his help and palmed him a folded up hundred as they left.

Once in the SUV Jim said would the two of you like to get some lunch and a drink? Then we can relax and talk."

Kay said "I must say that Resort we just looked at is the definition of opulence. I have never even seen anything in the movies that measures up to that. It's obscene."

Both Sue and Jim were laughing and he said "You may be right."

They went to a very up scale restaurant on Ina Road. None of them were hungry so they got a table and ordered drinks. They all brought in there notebooks. Sue said "The art in the houses and the meeting room all are originals or great fakes; and I am sure they are worth in the millions, and the furnishings, Rugs and that consort grand piano in the pool room is unbelievable. It's like Kay said I could never have imagined anything like what you have show us today."

There drinks came to the table and they all relaxed and started talking about the notes they had all made. After about forty minutes and a second drink Jim said "I still don't know what I am going to do with the place, but it is too good of a buy to pass up so I am going to buy it. I will sign off on the inspection later today. I really do appreciate all of your impute; it is a big help. Now I need to figure out something fun for a nice thank you."

"Well I don't know about Sue, but I have used up my supply of fancy clothes. You and Sue can keep that in mind while you figure out you're plans."

Sue was again laughing really hard then said "I think I am done for today, I have to work tonight."

He took the girls home and again thanked them for there time and input. His next stop was Hugh's office. Hugh had the closing on Jim's acreage set for Friday and said Ed already had the title company working on the estate and hopefully they could close on that also Friday. Hugh said "Theses will be the largest and fastest two sales I have ever made."

"Well Hugh this will be my two biggest and fastest moves also."

They finished all the paper work on the inspection and Hugh called the title company and said he would bring over the papers right a way. He also called Ed Morton at the Diocese and told him everything was approved.

Jim went home and then for a run so he could think. There was so much to the estate he had looked over today. Everything had been planed so well and the workmanship was beautiful and they had looked after the finest details. But there was something that didn't fit and he couldn't put his finger on it. He still hadn't seen the whole estate and felt like it was holding secrets of not only the past but that would also affect the future. Or maybe the whole secretive thing about the original owner of the property and the fact that the Diocese didn't want to be connected to the property in any way has him looking for shadows. In any case he finds himself transfixed on the property. But it's not much different then how he feels about Sue. Sue is so different then any woman he has known. She is not only beautiful but not pretentious and seems to be at ease around anyone. He would need to find things to keep himself busy.

Tuesday Morning March 23/ 2010 Tucson, Arizona

It was a little after seven and Jim was having breakfast with David at the La Poloma Country Club. During breakfast they were talking about business, Sue and the estate Jim was buying. Jim asked David if he would keep an eye out for a late model Isuzu box truck with a power lift gate. David told him he would find him a nice one; there were always some at the Auctions.

Jim's phone rang and it was Sue. She said "I been hoping you would call, then I remembered this is 2010 so I decided to call you and ask if you would like to come over for coffee?"

"There is nothing I would rather do; how about twenty minutes?"

"Twenty minutes would be nice."

As Jim closed his phone David said "So I guess that's the end of breakfast." He was laughing as he said "Go, I will handle the bill."

Jim only laughed as he left. There wasn't much else to say. He was really happy that Sue had called and he was on his way.

It had only been fifteen minutes when Jim was at Sue's door. When she opened it she had that beautiful smile and looked absolutely radiant. Jim just stood there taking all of her in. Sue asked "Are you alright?"

"I am not sure; you look absolutely wonderful and it just seems to stun me every time I see you."

"You're sweet; please come in. The coffee is almost ready and I made us some scones, I hope you like them."

"I have been trying to pace myself I didn't want to become a nuisance."

"Let's just try and be open to each other about our feelings, if I thought you were a nuisance I would have said something. I actually find you quite interesting you're good looking, single, never married, rich and not gay. Now I think that just by its self seems quite rare."

Jim was laughing and said "From the time I met you at the restaurant I was infatuated by you. David picked up on it and I hoped the girls didn't; they are very nice. And again I have to thank you for making it so easy on me the next night I had no idea what to say."

"I thought you were cute and didn't want to make it too hard on you."

Jim's phone rang and it was Hugh who told him he had arranged to have the closing on Jim's acreage at nine in the morning Friday then at eleven the closing on the estate. Jim said it sounded perfect. The Diocese had arranged to have the security stay on for that day and show Jim and his people how everything worked. Jim thanked Hugh and told him he would be in touch with him.

As soon as he was off the phone he told Sue about the plans for Friday. Sue asked what he was going to do with the place. Jim started laughing and said "I think I will move into the place. I have hired the landscaping company to continue with the up keep and I don't think I need the Security force. I have David finding me a Box truck and will have the two young men from the club move me then work for the estate."

Sue was laughing and said "You will be living in a resort all by yourself."

"But I will have a great sound system and a heated pool. It would be a great place to have a party. Also while we are talking I have arranged to have a helicopter fly me over the entire estate. Would you like to go with me?"

"That would be great; I have never been in a helicopter. When are you doing this?"

"I would like to do it tomorrow or Thursday. I left it open so we can work it around your schedule."

"You are sweet; anytime tomorrow would be great. Why don't we start with a run then breakfast at the Congress Street Café? During breakfast you can tell me how safe it is to fly in a helicopter."

The coffee and scones were good and they sat and talked till almost eleven.

Jim spent the rest of the day making arrangements to have the power transferred to his name and the bills sent to his accountant. He talked to the boys Steve and Frank, and had them lined up for Friday afternoon, Saturday and Sunday. David had located an almost new 2010 box truck like Jim wanted. It only had eleven thousand miles on it and was still under warranty. One of the banks David deals with had it in repossession. David would have it taken to his shop and gone over. Jim also had arranged to have the helicopter ready for ten in the morning. It was a small helicopter with a clear plastic bubble as the body. It would seat three including the pilot. They were much nicer then the ones Jim had flown in while he was overseas, plus no one would be shooting at this one.

Jim was meeting David at four o'clock in the bar of the La Poloma Country Club. Jim was the first one there and got a nice table with a view of the golf course. The waitress was right there. Jim ordered a drink and said he had someone joining him. It was about ten minutes till David arrived. He ordered a drink then told Jim they were closing on there property at nine Thursday morning and it should be funded by Noon. Jim was happy about that he would get around two point two million His accountant would have to show that one point eight of that got invested in the estate. Between this sale and that of his acreage after he paid for the estate it would still leave him with additional three point five million cash on hand.

David said "I looked at that truck. It's a 2010 Isuzu V6 with an automatic transmission and A/C. Everything is in perfect condition including the lift; it even came with a cargo tie down system and moving blankets. I will have it ready for you tomorrow after noon. And yes, I will have the plates transferred. Just tell me how you want it titled."

"Let's put it under Cooper investments. I will have Bill Stine get with you on the payment and he will also take care of the insurance. This is going to be fun."

"Well while you're having fun Becky and I are going to spend the weekend in Las Vegas. Were leaving Friday morning and probably will be back sometime Monday."

"Have fun and don't loose the dealerships."

"You know me, if the odds aren't in my favor I don't want to play."

The two of them sat and talked a good hour before leaving. Jim was going over to the club where his friends he had worked with stopped after work. A friend named Larry had called earlier and said they missed him and about eight of them were stopping it was the birthday of a friend named Mat. That was always a reason to have a few drinks.

Jim arrived a little after five thirty and the club was busy. They had three tables pushed together and everyone was having fun. There were ten of them and three were ladies who had worked at the company anywhere from five to twelve years. They were good employees and a lot of fun. They told Jim he and his cute butt were missed. The guys didn't think Jim had a cute butt so it must be a case of perception. They had all ordered a lot of different snacks. After a good two hours the party broke up and Jim called it a night.

Jim had set the alarm and was up early. He set out what he was going to wear for the day then dressed in his running gear. He was meeting Sue at six to go running and was looking forward to the day.

Sue was ready and looked great. They ran for a good hour and a half and were walking and talking at the end. Jim got a small kiss as he left to go home and shave shower and dress for the day.

When Jim picked up Sue she looked really cute. She wore Levis, with boots and a very pretty blouse. She also had a jacket that matched the boots. Jim did make sure to tell her how cute she looked.

When they got to the Congress Street Café it was nice that Kay was working. She got them coffee and juice right a way and asked Sue if she was feeling any better about the helicopter. Sue said "I don't think so; I have never been in a helicopter or even in a small plane."

"Our pilot is named Bob and I met him through David. Bob has his own corporate jet and has flown both David and myself a Number of times. He flew both jets and helicopters in Viet Nam. Now today Bob will have a small helicopter that seats three including the pilot it's the kind with a plastic bubble as the body and will give us a great view. I will also take a lot of pictures. It will be fun it's like the sports car of helicopters."

"Well I wanted a life in the faster lane, so I guess were going flying."

"I am sure you will love it"

Breakfast was fun and with a lot of laughing, then it was off to the airport to meet with Bob. They went to the small terminal on the west side of the Tucson International Airport it is the one private aircraft use. Bob was there and had the helicopter warmed up and ready to fly. Sue thought it looked awfully small to fly in. Bob assured her it was very safe. Jim showed Bob on the map the area they wanted to look at and told him he had notified the security people they would be flying over it today.

Just like Jim and Bob had told Sue, she loved it once they were off the ground. She was amassed as they flew over the city. Once they got to the property they were all impressed, as they flew over the main house. Bob asked "Who in the hell lives here?"

Jim laughing said to Bob "Starting Friday I will be living here."

Now Bob was laughing and said "Maybe I should double what I am charging you."

"The main house is nine thousand five hundred square feet and there are three guest houses and a large building for meetings this all sits on forty seven acres. I would like to fly over all of it. It's all fenced and there should be jeep trails where the guards patrol the boundaries."

"This is quite a fortress. What are you into now?"

Jim while laughing said "Nothing except real estate. This was just too good of a deal to pass up."

Sue said "The Mountains are beautiful when you are this close. Some of those cliffs must be at least a five hundred foot drop."

Bob said "Check this out under that cliff there is a covered patio with furniture on it. This is unbelievable; they have somehow run electric to it. It has lights and speakers. There are no wires so they must have run it underground all the way up there. Now that is hard to believe."

"The view from there at night must be breath taking."

"Some time after Friday we should come up and check it out."

There were trails that went around the whole property at least as high as they could get. The place did look like a resort complete with running trails and tennis courts. After a good half hour of flying around they returned to the airport. Jim paid and thanked Bob for the ride and the rental of the helicopter. He then asked Sue if she would like to stop and have a drink. Sue thought even though it wasn't noon yet it was still a good idea. They went back to the Congress Street Bar.

Once inside the young lady behind the bar recognized both Jim and Sue. She told Sue she missed her playing the piano. Sue thanked her and they ordered drinks. Sue said "That estate is so huge and beautiful it seems a shame it's hidden away where no one can appreciate it."

"I think you're right; there must be a thousand things it could be used for and I am not thinking of businesses. You are involved in the arts and the university. Try and think of some uses for it; things that are not connected directly to the university so that they don't have a say in it."

"If you're serious then it would be a lot to think about."

"Something outside of me is driving me toward this place and I know it's not about me reselling it. I don't want to live in this place like some kind of recluse hidden away in a huge estate. Like you I believe it should have a purpose and be enjoyed by many people; so I am open to any ideas. This whole thing should be fun."

Sue was laughing and they stayed and talked a good forty minutes then he took her home and thanked her for coming with him. Sue had to work that night and Jim had a lot of details he needed to take care of; one being the truck.

The truck was everything David had said, Jim signed all the paper work and was going to leave it at David's lot till Friday. Bill Stine had already taken care of the payment with David. Jim and David went and had a drink and talked about all the things going on. David and Becky were taking there relationship to the next level with the trip to Las Vegas for the weekend and they were both a little nervous about it. David was getting serious about Becky but wasn't sure how she felt.

Jim said "If anyone can empathize with you it's me. I am totally infatuated with Sue and am trying my best not to rush her. All I can say about Becky is that she is not only beautiful but a lot of fun to be around. That was the only time I have met her. I guess it's like the old saying goes; give time, time."

"Well I hope we both have an exciting and fun weekend."

On the way back to his house Jim stopped and bought some boxes, tape and paper so he could start packing some of his things.

Thursday Morning March 25/ 2010 Tucson, Arizona

Jim was up early and pumped up about the day, he decided to start with a good run before he shaved and showered. He was meeting David for breakfast then they were going to close on the first property at nine.

Breakfast was at the La Poloma Country Club, David likes to be seen there a lot; it's good for business.

At the same time Sue and Kay were sitting in there kitchen eating breakfast and talking about Jim. Sue was telling Kay about the helicopter trip around the estate and that there was also a helicopter landing pad on the estate. She also told Kay what Jim said about the use of the estate. Kay thought that would be interesting but really wanted to know what was going on between Sue and Jim. Sue was laughing and said "I was only interested in knowing him and having someone fun to date. Now I am not sure, he fits the image of everything I have ever imagined for the perfect guy. He is good looking, the right age, in good shape, a non smoker, never been married, not gay and as a bonus has money. There is also something mysterious and exciting about him. Also he is not pushy and willing to give this thing time."

"Well as the third party in this I think the two of you look good together."

They both had classes and Sue was working in the evening. By the time they were done with breakfast they were both laughing.

Jim and David did the closing on there property it took only a good twenty minutes the checks wouldn't be ready till some time in the afternoon. David gave Jim the keys to his truck and told him the registration and insurance papers were already in the glove box and it was ready to be picked up in the morning. David then left to go to his car lot and Jim went to a U-Hall store to buy three wardrobe boxes and some additional smaller ones, the Boys would need them in the morning. He also stopped and bought a nice hand truck the kind with the inflated tires. Jim would leave all his furniture, dishes and bedding. The estate was complete with all that stuff. He would continue to pack his personal stuff and let the boys pack, move and unpack the rest of what he was taking.

Jim made arrangements to meet Steve and Frank at the Congress Street Hotel Café for breakfast at seven. They would pick up the Box truck at David's lot then go to Jim's Town house so they could pack everything while he went to the closings on first the property then the estate.

Hugh called and said that everything was already set if he wanted to close today on the land. Jim liked that idea and they set the time for two o'clock.

The closing went quite quickly; the other side had already closed in the morning. The title clerk said she could just hold the funds for the closing in the morning then just give Jim a check for the difference if he liked. Jim thanked her and said it would make things easier. Hugh and Jim were stopping for a drink then Jim needed to stop at the title company from the other closing and pick up his check.

Once they had there drinks Hugh asked Jim what he was going to do with the estate. Jim while laughing said "I am moving in tomorrow as soon as the title is registered. I have already started packing and have two young men and a truck lined up for the morning."

Now Hugh was laughing and said "You will be lost inside that place. Also I was contacted by one of the security people who said he had been with the estate for over ten years and would like to talk to you about staying on. The security company is letting five people go after you take over. His name is Jerry Stevens; I called the head of the security company and they gave him a high recommendation. I wrote down all his information for you, and he will be working tomorrow."

"Thanks Hugh I was thinking about keeping one person for during the day, I will talk with him."

"Now for tomorrow if you like we can close at ten in the morning and the Diocese will close right after us and you should have the keys by noon."

"That will work for me; then by tomorrow night I should be enjoying my own pool."

"That reminds me; Sharon said after you get settled you need to invite us over along with Sue; she would like to meet her."

"We will have to do that; it would be fun. I am working hard at not scaring Sue off, I really do like her. You're a lucky man Hugh; Sharon is quite a lady she seems to know what people are feeling. That's quite a gift my friend."

Before Jim went home he stopped and picked up his check for his portion of the land he and David had sold. David had already been there and picked up his. Jim stopped at his bank and made a deposit and checked that he had a lot of cash on him to cover expenses for the weekend and money to pay Frank and Steve. Now it was time to go home and start packing again. He would also put tape on all the stuff he wanted the boys to move. Jim was really getting excited about moving and was wishing Sue was there to shear the excitement. He was thinking he never felt alone before he met her but now he does when she is not around.

Friday Morning March 26 / 2010 Tucson, Arizona

Jim was up early and it was cold out but he was so pumped he needed to start with a good run. Jim did a hard and fast eight miles then shaved and showered putting everything in his suitcase.

It was nice when he got to the Café Kay was working he told her Steve and Frank were joining him it was moving day. Kay was laughing and said "You will be all alone in that mansion."

"You and Sue are always welcome. When the two of you are off we should order some pizzas. We could also invite the boys and anyone you would like. I think it would be fun."

"You should talk with Sue; I like the idea."

Steve and Frank came to the table and everyone said hello. Kay got them all coffee and juice. After they ordered Jim told them what the plan for the day was. Frank said he had experience driving large trucks and would do the driving. Jim explained that he had tagged everything he wanted to take including the art. Breakfast was fun; Jim was trying to explain the estate to them and they were all laughing. After he had paid and tipped Kay they were off to David's dealership to pick up the truck. David had put a good lock on the back and included the keys on the rings he had given Jim. The town house was the next stop once the boys were planning out everything they were going to do. Jim left them and went to Hugh's Real Estate office.

They still had a little time so they had coffee and talked. Jim told Hugh he probably wouldn't be buying any additional properties for a while. Hugh laughed and said "You still have at least five million in extra cash sitting around."

"I think this property may be eating into a lot of that. But I still can't wait to get in there. I forgot to tell you how great the fly over in the helicopter was. That place even has its own helicopter landing pad and tennis courts. It was quite impressive."

After about twenty minutes Hugh drove them over to the Title Company for the closing. Like most of them it went rather quickly and the title clerk had a certified check ready for Jim on the balance left over from the sale of his land. She also said the Diocese was closing in about twenty minutes then she would send someone directly to the County to register the sale. That way he could have possession in two hours or less. Jim left her his card and she would call him.

On the way back to Hugh's office Jim called the boys to see if they needed anything. They told him they were doing fine and were busy. Jim thanked Hugh and before he left the parking lot he called Sue and asked if she would like to go out for some coffee. She said "No, but if you would like to come over I will put on a pot here."

"I like you're idea a lot better I will be there in about ten minutes."

When Jim arrived Sue really did look cute. She had on no makeup and her hair wasn't done. She was wearing an old sweat top and shorts. Jim said "You really do look cute, I love it."

"You really do want some coffee."

"Not really, but I really did want to see you."

"You're sweet. I have been thinking about you last night and this morning. This is you're big day, your closing on big estate today."

I closed on the land I was selling yesterday and have already closed on the estate this morning. The other side; the sellers should be closing as we speak. Then the Title Company needs to take it to the County and have it registered. I should have the keys in two hours."

Sue poured the coffee then said "So now you are going to move over there."

"I all ready have Steve and Frank at my house packing what I am taking and putting it in the truck."

Sue started laughing and said "You have them packing and moving you while you have coffee with me."

"I think it will work out well. They want the work and I am sure they will have more fun and do a better job without me looking over there shoulders. I even bought a nice fifteen foot box truck with a power lift on the back to make it easier plus I am leaving almost all the furniture and kitchen stuff. I will sell it all with the town house or give it away."

Sue was again laughing and said "It sounds so strange to hear someone say they will just get rid of there furniture because they don't need it anymore. You live in a different world then I do."

"It's funny that you say that because I don't see myself that way. I know only too well the value of money and things. Even the priority some people give it. I have had the benefit of both not having it and having it. It can make a lot of things easier and can buy a lot of shiny things. But it in it's self can't make you happy. David, his Mom and Dad and my friends are the only family I have left and none of them care if I do or don't have any money. My town house and all the stuff in it is only where I lived most of the time; it wasn't a home. I had everything looking nice and made my bed every day but never had any friends over there. I have done a lot of different things in my life but for the most part have been alone. So now I am changing how and why I live. I can't change the world but I can change what I do in it and like I told you I think this estate will be a big part of it. This should be fun."

"I must admit I love to watch and listing to you talk about it; you're excitement is contagious and I start picturing of all the things it might be. You also talk about something that is drawing you to this place. I don't know if it is you or there really is a power but I am also feeling the pull. I want you to know all about me and what it is that I do with the arts; it's becoming important that you know. Now I don't know how to explain that either."

"You don't need to explain it, I understand and we can make this fun. I don't know Kay's and your schedule but it would be fun if the two of you would come over when ever you could. Steve, Frank and I should be there any time after twelve. And if there is any one the two of you would like to bring that also would be nice."

"I will talk with Kay and we will figure out a time."

While they were talking the lady at the Title Company called and said everything was registered and he could pick up the keys. Jim was excited and Sue laughing gave him a small kiss and said "Go have some fun I will see you later."

Jim pick up all his papers and keys then went to the town house. The boys, Steve and Frank almost had everything in the truck they were laughing and said "The way everything in your house was so meticulous, especially your clothes we were thinking you were maybe gay."

"No it's just twelve years in the Army. Also Gay people don't have a monopoly on good taste."

Now they were all laughing. Steve said "You are leaving some beautiful furniture."

"When you see where I am moving to I think you will understand. The place is huge and comes complete with all the furnishings and art. As soon as we finish here the new place is close. We can take Ina road over to Campbell then north to the end of the road. After a good forty five minutes they were done. They did one final walk through to make sure they hadn't missed anything Jim wanted to take. He would leave his car in the garage for now.

Frank Drove the truck and Steve followed behind it. They followed Jim in his SUV it was a short trip and the guard at the gate was Jerry Stevens. They introduced themselves and Jim told Jerry he would like to talk with him a little later. By the time they reached the front of the house the boys were in awe of the place. Jim took them on a quick tour and showed them the master suite where everything would go. Steve said "Both Frank and

I studied art in college and I have never seen anything close to this. There is a fortune in just the art I have seen hanging on the walls, this is better then a museum."

"I am thinking there are a lot of things I can do with this place. I would hope there is some of it the two of you might be interested in. We can talk later but right now I need the two of you to unload and unpack my stuff; I need to meet with and talk to a lot of people right now.

The boys went to work and the first one Jim wanted to talk with was Jerry Stevens the security man. They talked a good half hour and came to an agreement for Jerry to stay on as the security five days a week eight to four. He would be working for Jim's investment company. Jerry also introduced Jim to the lady that had been handling the house keeping for the last seven years. After about an hour they had set it up so Mrs. Jacobs would start a company. The company then would clean the estate three times a week. She was going to keep three of the girls as her employees.

By the time Jim got back to the boys they had everything unpacked and the boxes broken down and back in the truck. They were sitting in the master bedroom and had some of Jim's CD's going in the sound system. Frank said "You have some really good music and this sound system can go to any part of the house and courtyard. It can also be controlled from any location with the remote. I have again never seen anything like it."

"Let's take the box with all the liquor down to the room with the pool and we will have a drink and talk."

There was a wet bar there and a small refrigerator with an ice maker and ice. The glasses looked to be crystal; they were all laughing. The drinks got made and they sat by the pool. Jim said "There is even more to this estate then you had seen. It has three guest houses that also have there own pools and Jacuzzi's and there is a large building for meetings. It is over four thousand square feet with a large kitchen and rest rooms. There is also a large warehouse with a security office in it. That is where we will put the truck. There is also tennis courts and helicopter landing pad. I bought not only the estate but also everything in it. I am sure you can see that I will need some help with running this place. I have hired the security guard to work the week days eight to four. After that the place has video, motion and heat sensor alarm systems. I also have house keeping coming in three days a week. Now for the two of you if you're interested I am going to need help in first doing a complete inventory of everything in this place both written and video. And while we are doing that and finding our way around the place I would like the two of you to join Sue, Kay and myself in thinking how I could put this place to a good and fun use for people in the Arts."

"You're talking about a job someone would dream up. I can't speak for Frank but I would be interested."

"I can speak for myself and I also am interested. I can't wait to see the whole place."

"Let's finish our drinks then walk around."

Just then Jim's phone rang and it was Sue. She and Kay wanted to come over and Kay wanted to bring Jan the young lady that was singing at the club. Jim said "I would love to have the three of you come over. I already told the guard at the gate you may show up; so come on."

"We should put the truck in the warehouse then Frank and I should take off."

"Let's put the truck away and I will pay the two of you for today. Then after that why don't the two of you stay, it's Sue, Kay and Jan the young girl that sings at the club are coming over and the two of you know all of them; it should be fun."

Steve said "I will play bartender; you have a nice selection it should be fun."

"After we put the truck away we should check the cupboards and pantry and see what else they left us."

The truck got put away and Jim paid Steve and Frank they were also coming back in the morning. Steve was going through the cupboards of the bar in the pool room. He said this bar is completely stocked with all top shelves. It also has a selection of twelve bottles of wine. I bet this place has a wine room."

Frank came in and said "The pantry is full of the basic staples and they all have current dates on them. There is also a fully stocked wine room. This place is becoming scary like the people that were living here just left."

Jim heard the front door bell ring he was sure it was the girls. It was the girls and they were excited. Sue said "The guard knew my name and was expecting me. I have never been anywhere that had a guard at the gate especially one that knew my name."

Kay said "Let me introduce Jan Burns, you heard her sing at the club."

"High Jan, I am Jim Cooper and I indeed did hear you sing that night and enjoyed it very much. I believe your singing will be taking you many places in the future. It's a pleasure to meet you. How about we all go to the pool room Steve is playing bartender."

Kay said "This place still blows my mind and I can't believe you're going to live here by yourself."

Steve and Frank were having fun with the sound system and some of Jim's CD's. The bar was beautiful. Steve asked what everyone wanted. He said "We have a great selection of wine or mixed drinks; No beer."

The girls thought wine would be the appropriate drink for the afternoon. Frank said "The water in the pool is seventy two degrees and from what you have said no one has been swimming in it for over a year at least and probably longer."

"Being that I don't know how to cook we all should have a pizza and swim party when you're all available. I am sure a party is another thing this place hasn't seen in a long time."

"Do you mind if I give Jan a tour of the estate?"

"That would be nice of you; don't forget and take your wine with the two of you."

The boys were centering there attention on a large television on one of the other seating area's. Sue said "You seamed to pick up on Kay and Jan right a way. I only started to notice on the drive over here and I am still not sure they see it themselves."

"It will be fun to watch; they both seem to be excited and happy. So now let's talk about Sue. I would like to do a pizza and swim party some time this weekend but I also would like to ask you out on a date next week. I was thinking Italian then go dancing if you like."

"I would love to go on a date with just you; Italian and dancing sound like fun. I will know my schedule by Monday morning. Now while all the other kids are playing how about you and I take our wine and walk around this estate of yours?"

They told Steve and Frank they would be walking around for a short while. They refilled there glasses and were off. "Steve and Frank seam to be nice guys I hope they work out to be what you're looking for."

"As you know I gave them a complete free reign on the moving and as I thought they did a better job of it then I would have. I have a feeling this will work great for them and me. Let's start with the kitchen and see what they left for dishes and utensils. The boys said the pantry was full of nonperishables. They also said they were all up to date as if they kept the stock rotated. Things like that are scary."

"The whole idea of this place even existing is scary. The idea that someone would have the money to build, furnish and maintain something like this is scary. Also to be honest the fact that you have enough money to pay cash for this and operate it makes you a little bit scary to me."

Now Jim was laughing and said "I am the last thing in the world you should be scared of, and for buying this I thought I was at best only paying a fourth of what I believe this place is worth. But after our inspection and what I have seen since then I believe I only paid maybe a tenth of what this is worth. But to be honest the fact that it does exist and all the secrecy stuff about it fascinates me. Now if you change that word scary to exciting this will be a lot more fun."

Sue laughing gave Jim a small kiss and said "Let's go to the kitchen and have some fun."

The kitchen was large and beautiful Sue said "They have four different kinds of ovens; I don't even know what there all for. They also have two huge cook tops."

"I only made sure they had a microwave being a bachelor that's all I know how to use."

"Oh Jim look over here, there are three different sets of china, and they all look expensive. These people must have had people come in and cook and serve them, this is like something out of a Novel. Everything I see in this place is way over the top."

"You're right about everything here being beautiful, but I wonder if they had any fun. For some reason I don't believe they did. I want this place to be fun and have some kind of a purpose. I am thinking you and your friends will come up with some ideas on how to make that happen. I am hoping the pool party will be a start."

"Let's go back and see if all the other kids are back together."

When Sue and Jim got back to the pool the boys and the girls were sitting on the edge of the pool with there feet in the water and drinking wine. Steve said "We found plastic glasses; there sitting on the bar if the two of you want to join us."

Sue was laughing and said let's join them, but I need to leave by four; I am working tonight."

"Go ahead and sit down I will change the glasses."

They all sat around and talked till three thirty. Everyone was having fun and Sue told the others what Jim had said about the estate and wanting it to have a purpose. Jim loved the looks on all there faces.

After the girls left Jim and the boys decided to again meet at the Congress Café for breakfast at eight o'clock. Frank and Steve cleaned up before leaving.

On a table in the entry room there were five remotes, they were all numbered to match one of the garage doors. Jim put his SUV in the garage. The garage was huge as garages go there were five electric roll up doors there was also room in front of each vehicle for a work bench and cupboards above it for storage plus a large section at each end for storage. There were also utility lights and water hoses that hung above each work bench. It was quite a garage.

The next thing Jim did was to take his keys and go through the house and make sure everything was locked up. The security guard had already checked all the other buildings before he had left. Once everything was locked and the alarm was set Jim changed into his swim suit he next change out the music to some Pink Floyd, Nora Jones then fixed himself a drink and went swimming.

Saturday Morning March 27 Tucson, Arizona

Jim was up early and decided to go for a run on some of the trails he had seen from the helicopter. It was below freezing and still fairly dark the trails were in great shape and the views were breathtaking especially as the sun started to rise.

When Jim arrived at the Café he was pleased to see Sue sitting with Steve and Frank. Kay was working and had coffee to Jim by the time he sat down. Sue said "I had a feeling you would be here this morning so I caught a ride with Kay."

"There is nothing I can think of that would make me happier. Let's have breakfast then if you like you can come with us. I would like to go through everything on the estate and make a video recording of it; first of all so I know what I have but also for Insurance purposes."

"If you like we could stop at my place I have some books on art that may help identify and put a value on some of the art you have."

"That would help a lot. I will call the guard and tell him the two of you will be coming in ahead of us. I will also give him a list of people that will be coming and going so you won't need to stop when you come over also I will give each of you the code for the gate for when the guard isn't working. This should be a fun day.

Kay took everyone's orders and said "The three of them were talking about the pizza and swim party and decided it should be on Sunday because they were all off work."

"That settles it the party will be on Sunday, and don't forget your swim suits; there are plenty of towels at the house.

Breakfast was fun and they all talked about the day to come. Jim also told them all too please invite anyone else they would like to be there. The boys liked that.

On the drive over to Sue's Jim suggested she might want to bring her swim suit then after they finished there work the two of them could go swimming. Sue took his hand and said "That would be fun."

The boys were already there and had made up a list of things Jim would need for the party Sunday. Jim told them he would give them the money and they could pick up whatever they thought would help make it fun. The filming of everything went rather quickly with the boys help. Sue was taking pictures of all the art and keeping notes on each piece. It was Jim's digital camera and he could download it to his computer print copies then attach the notes to each picture.

By one o'clock they were done. Jim had paid the boys and gave them money to buy whatever they needed for the next day. He also gave them the code to the front gate.

As Jim closed the front door he turned around and Sue said "I think its time for wine and swimming but first I would like a kiss."

"Then a kiss you will have."

It was a fun afternoon. After they went swimming he and Sue sat and went through the art books she had brought and tried to find some of the art that was all around them. Before it was time to take Sue home they had identified twenty seven pieces.

On the drive back to Sue's house Jim asked if she would like to start tomorrow with a run then breakfast. Sue was laughing then said it sounded like fun. By the time he left Sue's he had a date for six thirty. On the way home he was thinking about what a beautiful body Sue had. It was like she was a gymnast; she had the abs and everything.

After he returned to his house Jim got his laptop fixed himself a drink and sat in the pool room and went on line to try and locate information on his art collection. After a couple of hours it was time for some music, a second drink then to go swimming.

Sunday Morning March 28/ 2010 Tucson, Arizona

Jim was up early and ready for a run with Sue. Before he could leave the house his door bell went off and when he answered it he was pleased to see Sue. "I decided it would be fun to run the trails on your property."

"I think that is a wonderful idea. Let's get started I ran some of them yesterday and the view is great."

The run was fun and neither of them pushed it the views of both the city and the sunrise were again wonderful and not wasted on either of them. Toward the end they were walking hand in hand they had not only seen rabbits and coyotes but they got a good look at a bobcat. Sue said "This is a special oasis that someone has created and it's sad to think that they never really shared or enjoyed it. There are many different groups that would love to have the use of that huge meeting room. This is a very creative environment."

The run was fun and ended in a nice kiss. Sue went home to shower and dress for breakfast and Jim did the same then left to pick up Sue. When Sue came to the door she was beautiful and Jim did tell her so. "So where are you taking us for breakfast on this special day."

"I was thinking about La Poloma unless you would rather not."

"I have never been there as a customer; I think it's a great idea I would be pleased to accompany you."

It was only minutes and they were at the La Poloma Resort. They were taken to a very nice table and the gentleman didn't seem to recognize Sue. Now the waiter was much more observant and said good morning to Sue. Sue said good morning and introduced Jim. Coffee and a juice cart were quickly there. While they were drinking there coffee Jim said "you do look quite radiant this morning and I am hoping I have at least a small part in that."

It's funny that you mention it because I think you do. I find my self quite attracted to you. Now I think we should order before the whole staff is over here."

Jim was laughing as he motioned for there waiter. They ordered quickly then Jim was talking about what he had found on line and what they had listed as the last time some of the pieces of art had sold for and the dates of the sales most of the ones he could find were last seen in public over fifty years ago. They were listed to be in private collections with no location available.

"This private resort of yours is becoming stranger by the day; I can't wait to see what we find today."

"I am for one very optimistic about what the day may bring. As far as the estate goes each day I find my self believing that place I holding some big secrets, some of them connected to the past and some that will affect the future. I have no idea what they are or how it is holding them but it is part of what is drawing me to the place."

"Now you're starting to sound like you're moving closer to scarier then exciting. Let's go back to talking about the pool party."

There breakfast came to the table and looked good. While they were eating sue was smiling and said "We are the main topic of conversation among the staff."

Jim leaned over kissed her and said "Now they have something to talk about."

Sue smiled and said "I liked that kiss."

Breakfast was fun and they talked and laughed a lot. When they were done Jim paid the bill over tipped Phil and thanked him.

Sue already had everything she needed for the party in a small over night bag. Jerry Stevens was already on duty. Jim stopped and told him of the guest that would be coming over and asked if there was any thing Jerry needed. Jerry thanked him and told him he had reviewed all the tapes from the night before and everything was fine.

Once at the house Jim parked in the garage. Sue noted it was an awfully big garage. As soon as they were in the house Sue asked Jim where he thought the secrets would be. Jim laughing said "In all the old movies it was almost always the library. And there is something about this library that doesn't seem right. Let's go look at it again; yesterday I only filmed all the books very slowly, I never even looked at the titles."

They were off to the library. Sue looked around then found a seat on one of the leather couches and slowly scanned the room. After a few minutes she said "You're right and I think it's the wall by the fire place. It sticks out unlike the wall on the other side of the fire place; do you think it just because of the fire place?"

Jim looked at it and walked around and viewed it from different angles then said "I think you're right, it's almost two inches wider and there is no reason it wouldn't be the same as on the other side."

They both walked over to that section of wall and looked it over. Jim was looking at the floor to see if there were any marks that would show that the wall was not secure to the floor or ever moved. After a few minutes he said "I don't see any signs that show this section moves but I still think you're right. We will need to leave this for another day of playing Indiana Jones."

Sue was laughing really hard then quickly gave him a great kiss that he returned. Sue smiled and said "I guess we are past that hurdle and I loved the kiss."

Jim hugged her and kissed her on the forehead and said "You make me so happy."

They heard Frank yelling come out where ever you are. They were both laughing as they came out of the library.

Steve and Frank had two young men with them named Troy and Jared they both seamed to be nice young men. The boys had picked up an assortment of chips and two nice vegetable and fruit trays. They also had bought a case of Champaign and two cases of soft drinks. Steve said "There will be no problem fitting them all into those huge refrigerators of yours."

Frank asked Jim what kind of wine he would like them to bring out. Jim smiled and said "Whatever you think our guests would like. Remember this is all about having fun. The boys got busy making it a party. It wasn't long till Kay and Jan showed up. Now it was a party, Frank was playing bartender and Steve, Troy and Jared had found Jim's music and was having fun with the sound system. Jim was going up to his room and change into his swim trunks. Sue grabbed his hand and said "I will come with you and also change."

Kay while laughing kissed them both on the cheek and said "Don't be too long."

Once up stairs Sue quickly took her clothes off kissed Jim and said "You better put your swim suit on while you can."

As he was putting on his swim suit he watched Sue put on a small two peace suit and a matching cover up she was beautiful. Before they went back down Jim gave her a great kiss and a smile.

Back in the pool room it was a party Frank got both Sue and Jim a plastic glass of Champaign then joined the other three boys in the pool they loved the idea of swimming out to the court yard. Kay and Jan were sitting on the couch close to the pool Kay was telling her about the large building with the big table. Jan asked Jim if he had decided what he was going to do with the place other then live in it. Jim told her he was hoping between all of them they could come up with some ideas and he didn't want it to be a business or connected directly to any particular grope. "I was thinking it would lend itself to the world of the arts. Now all of you have a lot of involvement with a large spectrum of the arts, so come up with some ideas; nothing is off limits."

Suddenly the room was quiet. Then Sue started laughing and said to Jan "If I play the piano would you sing something for us?"

"I would love to; let's see if that thing works."

It was back to being a party again. Frank was freshening up everyone's drinks while Sue was checking out the piano. Suddenly Jan said "There is a panel in the floor and when I opened it there are sixteen hookups for microphones and instruments. You could have a whole band in here."

Frank said "Behind the bar there is a complete mixing board. You have a nightclub here."

Sue was laughing really hard then said "You now have your own private nightclub; I love it."

Everyone was laughing and the guys were checking out the sound system. Steve figured out that it could support its own speakers and would also feed into the main sound system for the house.

Sue started to play the piano and Jan started singing. She sounded much better then she did in the club and everyone in the room knew it including Jan. Kay was totally into it and Jan and by the looks form Jan she was totally into Kay. By the end of the song Kay was so pumped she ran up to Jan and gave her a great kiss that was returned. Everyone one was clapping for the two of then so Jan kissed Kay again. Sue started playing the piano again and Jim went over and sat on the bench with her. The party was really going everyone was getting in the pool.

He said "Thank you for playing; you really are very good and I love piano music. Also Jan is very talented and sounds much better then when she sang with that band. She has great potential.

"You pay a lot of attention to people and what is going on around you. Maybe you have come up with what you are going to do with me."

"I am totally infatuated with you and am thinking I have fallen in love with you. I am trying not to scare you away; I know this money thing is a problem for you but if you give me a chance I hope you can see the real me. The money is nice but I am a lot more then that. So to answer your question I am going to try and hang on to you the best I can."

"Give me one of those nice kisses then let's go swimming with the other kids."

Later in the afternoon Steve told Jim he would order the pizzas then would meet the delivery out by the road. He smiled and said "I still have a lot of your money."

While Steve and Cory were getting the pizzas Frank and Jared were fixing a large salad then brought plates and all the accessories out to the pool room and set up a buffet. When everything was together with the pizzas Jim said "This is like a restaurant; thank you."

The afternoon and evening were fun; they got Sue back to playing the piano then Jan again singing. They all came to agreement that Jan sounded much better without the band. The time came when Jim said "If there is going to be any more drinking you all need to consider staying the night here. There as you all know a lot of bedrooms or a guest house if you prefer."

The boys all looked at each other then Steve said "We guys will take one of the guest houses if you don't mind."

"That's great; you know where the keys are when you're ready. Also take what ever you need with you."

Kay and Jan were laughing then Jan said "We will take one of the bedrooms."

Sue kissed Jim and said "I know where I want to sleep."

It wasn't long and they were all sitting in the Jacuzzi Drinking wine. After a while they were heading to where they were going to spend the night. Sue kissed Jim and said "Take me up stairs and make love to me; I want to spend the night in you're arms."

Monday Morning March 29/ 2010 Tucson, Arizona

Jim was the first to wake up and decided to wake Sue as he had always dreamed of being woken. Neither of them was done with the night before. The shower was big enough for four people with many shower heads. Sue has as Jim sees it the perfect body and he couldn't keep his hands off of it. They were both laughing and having fun.

When they dressed and went down stairs there were notes taped to the coffee pot. One was from Kay and Jan thanking them for all the fun and they would talk later. It had two kiss marks on it. The second was from the boys; they also thanked Jim for the party and said they had cleaned up and talked with Mrs. Jacobs who said she would handle all the beds and what ever else that needed attention. Sue was laughing and said "Your staff seems to have everything under control. Now you can take me home."

"We should take you to breakfast; you need to keep you strength up."

"Then you can take us to the Congress Street Café; I want to see Kay. I should also tell you I have a class at ten o'clock."

"That's all very doable and if after your class if the rest of your day is open I would like to invite you to come over and we can continue our treasure hunt from yesterday."

"Now you're cheating again; what girl would turn down a treasure hunt."

While laughing he said "I have to admit I am trying as hard as I can, plus it wouldn't be much fun without you."

Sue gave him a small kiss and said "Take me to breakfast."

As soon as they walked in the Café Kay saw them and with smile ran over hugged and kissed them both and said "I am happier then I have ever been in my life. That was one hell of a party."

Jim laughing said "It was for me also and I know how you feel."

Sue kissed them both and said "Let's go sit down before we have to invite everyone to the next party." They were all laughing.

Breakfast to say the least was fun. Jim had Sue back home by nine twenty. She said she would call him after class then come over.

On the drive back to the house Jim was wondering how David and Becky's weekend had gone; he was hopping for them it was as good as his. As Jim got to the gate Jerry was there and said he had reviewed the security tapes for Saturday night and Sunday and everything looked as normal. But already this morning there had been a gentleman come by form an insurance company wanting to see Jim. Jerry had him leave his card. Jim told him the sale of the estate is public knowledge and there would probably a lot of people like that and if there was anyone that would be coming over that he wanted to see he would notify Jerry in advance.

Once in the house Jim looked for Mrs. Jacobs but she had already finished her work and was gone. There was note stating she had also done the guest house. Jim was impressed. He fixed himself a drink then walked out in the courtyard and was looking at the mountain; it was a beautiful close up view. He could also see the covered patio at the base of one of the cliffs. He was hoping Sue would stay and they could drive up there and watch the sunset and the lights to the city come on. He suddenly realized he was just standing there thinking of Sue, last night and this morning. She was everything he had ever hopped for and there was still so much more to her he wanted to know. He walked to the end of the courtyard and he could see the huge meeting building. Just the fact that it was there meant that someone had regular meetings but who were they and what was it about?

It was eleven thirty when Sue called and said she had just left the university and was on her way up. That put a smile on Jim's face.

When Sue arrived she was laughing and said "It still is fun to arrive and have a guard smile and call you by name; it's like being in a romance novel."

Jim gave her a small kiss and said "You're making my life like a romance novel and I am enjoying every minute of it. If you're ready for a treasure hunt we should start with a glass of wine or a drink."

"A glass of wine sounds good."

They took there wine to the library with them. Jim had on some nice Sade CD's. The area Jim thought was out of place was part of the book shelves that went from floor to ceiling except for the huge dark wooden casing at the top and bottoms. They started slowly removing the books from the area while inspecting everything. After a time Jim could see where a section of it was some how moveable. They sat and drank some of there wine and Sue said "The idea of what could be behind there really has me excited."

"I am thinking there is some kind of electric switch that will open and close that section. So we need to think where we would hide such a switch."

Sue started laughing and said "This is so much fun; let's refill our glasses then sit here and figure it out."

They got there wine then were sitting on the couch looking at the portion of the wall that was the book cases and the rock fire place. The fire place was built into the rocks it wasn't an insert with fake rocks it was all solid. Every so often one or the other would get up and go check where they thought a switch could be hidden then they would laugh and end up hugging each other. Suddenly Jim said "The last place you thought might be it, I think is correct. Think of it. It's the perfect location and being that it is part of the casing of the other bookcases it would need to be a stiff enough switch that it wouldn't be activated when someone was dusting or polishing the woodwork."

They both got up and went to the wall; Jim pushed the section of wood hard and suddenly it moved and the noise of an electric motor started then that section of the bookcase Started to rise up into the wall leaving the upper and lower casings still in place. Jim and Sue just looked at each other in amazement. When it came to a stop the only thing there was a closet four feet by four feet and about seven feet high. They went over and looked inside. Jim said "The floor opens and there is a latch to hold it in place. Also look at the ceiling there is a hook that can be used to raise or lower thing. We have a basement."

"Are we going to go down inside there?"

"You know we are; this is starting to get exciting. Let me get a couple of flashlights."

Jim quickly came back with two of the small LED flashlights then opened the floor and secured it with the latch. There was a ladder built into the wall going down. As soon as Jim was a short way down he found a light switch and as soon as he flipped it a large room was illuminated below him. It looked to be about twenty five feet square; making it a little over six hundred square feet. Jim went down with Sue close behind him. Sue said this is scary; it's like something out of a spy movie. Look at all the computers, storage cabinets and five big safes."

"You're right about it looking like something from a spy movie. There are some big secrets being held down here and I can't wait to find out what is inside those safes."

The safes stood at least six feet tall and had front doors like a gun safe would, only these were deeper and looked to be secured to each other.

"How can you get them open without people finding out about this place?"

Jim smiled and said "With some very basic equipment I can open them. I need to write down a little information on each of them then I will get what I need. I also can't wait till I can get into that computer; I think what is in there and the safes will answer most of our questions about this place and what went on here. Let's go back up and close all of this back up and replace the books."

Once back up Sue was laughing and asked "Am I going to be invited to accompany you when you crack the safes? I am working tomorrow night."

"It wouldn't be any fun being a safe cracker without you there. Would you like to go to an early dinner with me then we could dress warm and go up to the patio we saw from the helicopter and watch the sunset then the lights of the city come on for us."

"You do know how to put together a romantic evening. I would love to do all of that."

They decided on Mexican food. Jim changed clothes still dressing casually in Levis, a nice long sleeve shirt and black western boots. Then it was off to Sue's so she could change. She also wore Levis and a cute blouse. She brought a heavy jacket, scarf and gloves. They went to a really nice Mexican restaurant that had good food. Jim asked Sue if she would like to start with a Margurita. Sue thought that was also a good idea. Dinner was great and they talked about all the possibilities of what could be in the safes. Jim said "Think of it, when this guy died I bet he was the only one who knew of the basement, otherwise the safes would have been opened and the computer system would have been removed. We most likely are the only two people alive that know of the basement and what is in there. Also I would like to keep it that way if you would."

"A secret; will that will be hard, but I do understand and it will stay between us."

"I have a feeling there are secrets in there that could put us in danger if anyone knew we had found the room."

"Now you're moving from exciting back to scary. But now I am hooked and want to see what's in there. I can now understand what drives treasure hunters and I love the feeling."

"In the morning there is an electronics store that handles the equipment I need to open the safes. The computer system will be harder but that is my area of expertise. I believe that is where the secrets will be."

When they left the restaurant the sun was already low in the sky. Jerry the guard had already left for the day. They first stopped at the house and Jim got a jacket, a small blanket, a bottle of nice wine and two plastic glasses. "Nice idea I like both the blanket and wine."

The drive up to the covered patio took only minutes. There were nice chase lounges and chairs, the padded covers were in a large plastic container big enough to be a casket. It did keep them dry and away from bugs and spiders. Jim had one of the small flash lights and did check for any snakes; there were none.

The colors of an Arizona sunset weren't wasted on either of them. As the colors were fading the lights of the city were starting to show. Between the show and wine there was a lot of kissing going on. After it was dark and the city was completely lit Jim asked Sue if she would again spend the night. With a nice kiss she said "I can't imagine going home right now; I would love to spend the night."

It was almost seven when they got back to the house and Sue called Kay to tell her she was spending the night. Jim was opening another bottle of wine when Sue walked over to him laughing and said "Kay won't be missing me tonight; Jan is staying with her. Why don't we get undressed grab a towel and take our wine to the Jacuzzi."

"You come up with some wonderful ideas."

Tuesday Morning March 30/ 2010 Tucson, Arizona

Jim and Sue were up early and in the shower acting like a couple of teenagers. Jim said "If Kay is off this morning why don't you call and invite the two of them to breakfast; we will find somewhere fun."

"She is off today and that would be fun, I will call her as soon as I am out of here but that will take at least two more kisses."

Sue called and the other girls loved the idea; they were all laughing.

Once at Sue's she was going to change and put on a little make up. Kay and Jan were almost ready. They were all in Levis and nice tops and all looked beautiful. Jim made sure he told them so then asked if Star Pass Resort would be alright with them. They all while laughing said it would be.

It was a twenty minute drive but it was beautiful morning and they were all having fun. The dinning room looked busy for a Tuesday morning so Jim asked the young man at the door if he and the ladies could get a table looking out over the golf cores as he palmed him a hundred dollar bill. The young man said "Indeed I can sir; if you would give me a minute."

They were quickly taken to a table with a great view. Coffee and a juice cart were quick to come to the table. Kay laughing said "That worked."

"I just didn't want our seating to be a problem."

Sue kissed him and said "Thank you."

After they ordered Kay and Jan were talking about clothes and not going anywhere fancy because they had all used up what they had in evening dress. Sue suggested they could all wear the same clothes because they were about the same size. Jim said "I have a fun idea, when the three of you have time I will take all of you shopping at the fancy ladies shops at the mall. I will be the sugar daddy and cover the cost and the only rules for the three of you is you can't look at price tags. It should be a blast for all of us."

The three girls were silent for a moment then Sue said "Do you realize the kind of money you are talking about?"

Jim laughing said "I do and we will include shoes, purses and Hats if you like. I do have the money and it would be fun. So what do you think?"

There breakfast came to the table and everyone was quite then all the girls started laughing and said it would be fun and they would be crazy if they didn't do it. While they were eating they would start laughing then stop for a minute then another one would start. The meal was fun to say the least then the girls started talking about what they wanted to get. They were laughing so hard there sides hurt. Jim paid the bill thanked there waitress and tipped her a hundred and fifty. That made one more very happy girl.

On the ride back to the girl's house they figured that the next day at noon they would all be free; Kay had to work from six in the morning till eleven then they needed to have Sue back to her house by four because she had to work that evening. They all three had classes Thursday and Friday and Sue was working Wednesday, Thursday, Friday and Saturday nights. They left Kay and Jan at the house then Jim and Sue were off to the electronics store so Jim could buy what he needed to crack the safes in his basement.

When they arrived the store had just opened and the manager and two young men that worked there were the only people in the store. The manager was named Terry. Jim told him what he wanted and what power level he wanted it to work at. Terry laughing asked if he was a safe cracker. Jim told him this was close to it; Sue almost laughed. They went over a Number of things and found exactly what Jim wanted. Terry said "If there are any electronic devices monitoring what you will be working on you may want a scanner that would not only notify you of its existence but would also help you locate it. It will run a tight ban on a range that will show you anything from a GPS transmitter to listing devices all the way to devices that will receive signals from cell phones."

Terry brought one out and they went over the booklet that came with it. The device wasn't much bigger then a cell phone and would give both a audible and visual alert and also show where in the ban the signal was telling the operator what kind of device was activating it.

Jim bought that also along with two sets of starlight binoculars and a device that would temporally scramble any signal while Jim tried to locate its source Terry said "I also have inferred heat activated monitors that can be hand held if you might think it could be useful."

Jim laughing said" I don't think I am at that point yet but if I get there I will be back.'"

Jim had spent a lot of money and they both had a fun time. On the way to the estate Sue was reading the book on the scanner. After a bit she said "This is like the spy stuff they talk about on those silly TV crime shows. I didn't think they really had stuff like this. So why do you want it?"

"I was thinking if there are any GPS devices attached to that computer I would like to know about it before someone else knows that it has been turned on. I may sound paranoid but I sure don't want to find it out after the fact.

"You really do believe there is something sinister about what is down there. I am also getting the feeling that you believe our government has something to do with it."

"You young lady are very perspective. Who else but our government has the power and money to finance a place like this estate? I was thinking of some rogue off shoot of the CIA. No one really knows what they do and they have such huge amounts of discretionary funds they can spend and not be accountable to anyone. Then Homeland Security came along. This could be something they just wanted to go away and not exist any longer."

"Your mind works different then anyone I have ever met. I could have never come up with that scenario and can't believe you did."

"It has a lot to do with what I specialized in for many years; I had top secret clearance and worked with a lot of stuff even I didn't believe. It got so bad I no longer wanted anything to do with it. Then I worked a private company that built secret computers and programs for our government and I also got tired of all there lies and spy shit. That was my real life and it is over with. I am not saying it was all terrible; It was exciting, I learned a lot, met a lot of nice people all over the world but I learned a lot of what we did was cover up and a lot of young people died that didn't need to."

Jerry was at the gate when they arrived they stopped and said hello and talked a minute then it was to the house and the library. Jim was putting together the stuff he had bought to open the safes. Sue asked if she should open a bottle of wine and get two glasses. Jim smiled and said "If I can get a kiss before you do that it would be nice."

"You can have your kiss and if we had the time, any thing else you might want."

Now Jim was laughing and said "So safe cracking comes first."

Sue gave him his kiss and was laughing as she went to get the wine. Jim had his listing device put together and hooked up to its battery pack and a speaker headset. When Sue returned with the wine Jim had the bookcase open and the trap door to the basement open. Jim locked the door to the library then he and Sue took there wine and toys down to the basement. Sue poured the wine while Jim hooked up his listing device to the first of the safes it had a microphone that was part of a suction cup that stuck to the face of the safe close to the combination. He put on the headset then slowly turned the combination then said this should be easy. He had a pad of paper and a pin and started to turn it till he heard a sound then wrote down the Number. He would then turn it in the other direction and write down the Number of the next sound. After about seven minutes of doing this the safe unlocked. Sue sat down on the floor with him as he opened the door. The safe was full of like shoe boxes only they were a foot and a half square and a foot deep and under them were bars of gold. Sue said "Oh my God, someone will be looking for all of this."

"I don't think so. Let's put the boxes on the table. There were ten of the boxes and they weighed something like thirty plus pounds each. The bottom of the safe was full of gold bars both ten and twenty pound bars. The final count was thirty of the twenty pound bars and forty of the ten pound bars a total of a thousand pounds. Jim put the gold back in the safe then sat back with Sue and the wine.

"I don't care what you say this is scary; people don't just have piles of gold sitting in there house."

Jim started laughing and said "After seeing this, spending money on a shopping trip doesn't seem to be that big of expenditure."

Sue was trying not to laugh and said "You're not funny. What do you think is in the boxes?"

Jim gave her a kiss then said "Let's go look." Sue opened the first box and it was full of Euro bills. Jim wasn't sure but thought the domination was close to our hundred dollar bill. There were two boxes of them then eight boxes of American hundred dollar bills all in ten thousand dollar bundles. Each box was two million dollars. That with the Euro money was twenty million in cash. Sue was laughing and said "I have never seen so much money. What are you going to do with it?"

Jim was also laughing then said "Spend it I guess; will you help me?" They were both laughing then Sue gave him a big kiss. Jim said that was nice; we still have four safes to go but they can wait."

Sue started laughing, pushed Jim onto the floor and gave him a big kiss then said "We should get started on the next safe; I need to be home by four."

Jim went through the same procedure and had the second safe unlocked and had written down its combination. He looked at Sue and asked if she wanted to open it. Sue was laughing and almost jumping up and down. She said "You know I do."

Her hands were shaking as she took the handle and slowly pulled it open. She said "Oh my God there are more of those gold bars in the bottom of this one."

There was what looked like the same amount and sizes of gold bars that were in the first safe. This safe had shelves and was full of a lot of different size boxes. Jim said "Let's open the boxes one at a time. You pick the first one you want to open."

Sue picked what looked like a large cash box that was heavy and took it over to the table and opened it. Inside were a lot of black leather pouches with leather draw ties. Sue opened a bag and with a scared look on her face emptied a good two pounds of sapphires on to the table. They were all cut into beautiful stones from what looked like one to fifty carats. "Oh Jim this is really getting scary; I have never heard of such wealth. I am scared to look in the other pouches."

"Have a drink of your wine then we will open the next pouch. Those are beautiful stones and I love the color; it's such a deep cobalt blue."

Jim put the sapphires away then handed Sue the next pouch. It also weighed a good two pounds. Sue opened it and poured out a huge amount of large rubies again all cut and polished. They both started laughing. Jim said there are still three pouches to go and the bottom one looks three times the size of the rest. The next bag was all beautifully cut diamonds that were all ten to thirty carats. Neither of them had seen diamonds that big.

They took a break sat down and drank some of there wine and talked of the treasure and laughed a lot. Sue said "I am still having a problem imagining someone wanting this kind of wealth and then it just being hidden under a house."

"The money, gold and gemstones are just ways to diversify ones wealth. I am sure we will also find bearer bonds and stock certifies. This isn't just some man's wealth this is part of someone's power. Let's open the next pouch at this rate we will be lucky to get this safe gone through before I have to take you home I will wait till you have the time before I open the others."

"Ok then that is the end of the wine and we do need to get busy."

The next pouch was emeralds, again over two pounds and all large beautifully cut and polished stones. Jim put them back into there bag then took out the last and much bigger pouch; it was a good ten pounds. Again they were all cut diamonds only smaller; one to ten carats and again they looked to be high quality stones. Jim put all the pouches back into the metal box and set it aside. Then they started taking out the other small boxes. There was a good twenty pounds of beautiful Jewelry Everything from necklaces with matching ear rings to many rings all the way to bracelets and a diamond and gold Tierra. Sue said "This is the kind of Jewelry Elizabeth Taylor had; only a lot more of it. This is crazy."

"I was thinking how you could make a lot of this look much better."

"You are as crazy as this person was. I need you to hold me and kiss me."

They still kept finding boxes of jewelry and expensive watches both for men and women. Jim found a gold Rolex watch that he really liked so he put that on. It was almost three before they finished going through that safe. Sue went up to get herself a Coke while Jim returned everything to the safe and locked it up. He had kept out a hundred thousand dollars from the first safe. He figured he would take fifty thousand with him for the girls shopping trip. He closed up the basement and he and Sue sat on the couch. They talked a bit then it was time to take Sue back to her house.

After Jim left Sue's he called David. He hadn't heard from him since he left for Las Vegas. When David answered he was laughing. Jim said "I want to hear everything; if you're available I will buy you a drink at La Poloma."

Still laughing David said "I will make myself available; I do need to talk to you. Give me twenty minutes."

Jim was on his way to La Poloma and was thinking how much he was missing Sue. He got himself a drink and waited on David.

When David arrived he did look happy. They got a table and David ordered a drink and a second for Jim. As soon as the young lady left the table David said "I can't believe how happy I am. We didn't get back to town till mid morning. Becky is all I ever hoped for in a woman and we had the best time. Neither of us particularly likes Vegas but there is a lot to do there and we did it all. I am going to give it a little time then I think I am going to ask her to marry me."

"That's great and I am happy for you. I also like Becky; she is not only beautiful but has an outgoing personality and is funny. This is great."

They sat and talked about Becky and David the car business and what kind of house David thought Becky would like. Jim started laughing and told David he and Becky needed to come over and see the estate he had bought and they should arrange it so Sue would be there. David started laughing and said "Let's get another drink then you can tell me about you and Sue."

As soon as the waitress left the table Jim said "I am so in love with Sue I can't stop thinking of her. She spent the last two nights with me and surpasses my wildest dreams. I would like to marry her today but it's been so quick I am afraid I would run her off so I also need to wait."

"Well my friend God has been good to the both of us."

Jim went back to the house and parked in his garage before he could get in the house his phone rang and it was a friend from where Jim had worked named Larry. After they said hello Larry said he needed to talk to Jim somewhere private. Jim asked where he was. Larry was on the east side of town by Wilmot and Speedway. Jim said "There is a coffee shop in the shopping strip on the North East corner of Swan and Grant I will meet you in twenty minutes."

Larry sounded scared. He is a good guy and smart, he supervises a section of the production line for the computers they built. Jim was in the part where they wrote the programs that operated it. Larry like Jim made great money and was single only Larry liked the fast life, the showy cars, jewelry and parties.

Jim arrived first and waited in his car for Larry who wasn't far behind. They both got a coffee then found a table that would give them some privacy. Larry said "Thanks for coming I will be quick about this. I just found out today that the fed and there drug task force is coming after me. I sold ten ounces of cocaine to one of there undercover agents and they are going to get an indictment then arrest me and try to use me to go after my suppliers. If I did that I would get killed. Now they haven't even gone for the indictment yet so I have a little bit of time. I have a passport and am going to leave the country and disappear but I have two problems I am hoping you will help me with. This isn't the only stupid thing I have done, the other is I have over the past year successfully removed and assembled a complete one of our computer systems and have it at my house. I need two hundred thousand and to get rid of that computer. If they find it I will be in prison for the rest of my life. Can you help me?"

"If you can successfully get out of the country and disappear you will need to be gone a Number of years. If you go before they go for there indictment they may never do it. Also I don't know how much money you have but you will need a lot to stay that long and you will also have to start keeping a low profile. I will give you three hundred thousand as a gift and tell you a place to leave the computer. Have it with you in the morning and I will call you. I am sorry you have gotten yourself in this mess and Larry I do wish you the best. Keep my Number incase you ever need it. Now let's get out of here."

"Thanks Jim this really is a big help and I will note this as a wake up call."

As soon as Jim left the coffee shop he went to the nearest Wal-Mart and bought a small gym bag, a box of latex gloves and two prepaid cell phones then used one to call David. When David answered he didn't realize it was Jim right a way. Jim told him it was a new phone and he needed to see David right a way. David was at the dealership and Jim was on the way.

As soon as Jim got there they went into David's office. He told David the whole story and what he wanted to do. David made a few calls to his Phoenix store and made arrangements to have a used Chevy van and a driver to be at his Tucson dealership by eight o'clock in the morning. Jim used David's yellow pages and found an older self storage place on the south west part of town that was inside the boundaries of the barrio that Jim and David grew up in. Jim called them and asked if they had two ten by twenty foot units close to each other that were for rent. They did and gave him a price. Jim told him he was from a Phoenix company named Vantec Electrical and they were doing a job close to them and would need the units for a month and a half but they would send an employee in the morning to rent them for two months. When all the arrangements were completed David was laughing and said "I love this it's like the old days."

David called an old friend of theirs and asked him to have people from the Barrio watch the storage place and the neighborhood around it for any undercover police or feds between eight and ten in the morning. It would be arranged. David also arranged to have a set of stolen license plates for the van. There work was done and he and David arrange to meet early for breakfast.

When Jim got home it was after six he first opened the box of gloves and put a pair on then used a wet dish cloth to wipe down the handle of the Gem bag; it was the only place on it he touched. Next he got the scanning device he had bought that morning then with it and his gloves on went down into the basement opened the first safe and took out three hundred thousand dollars from one of the boxes they hadn't touched. While he was there he scanned the whole room and got no hits; that was good. He put the money in the gem bag then locked everything back up and closed the room.

He was hungry but too pumped to eat he fixed himself a good double got out some cheese and crackers left over from the party and went to the pool room, turned on some nice music, sat down and had some of his drink. He did believe Larry was being straight with him but couldn't afford to take any chances. Even if Larry had been recording everything they said there was really nothing that would directly link Jim with the computer. Jim would be in the van with his scanner so he could secretly scan Larry and the computer for any GPS transmitters.

As he sat there with his drink he was thinking how much he wanted to tell Sue everything that was going on. He finished his drink and snacks then called it a night.

Wednesday Morning March 31/ 2010 Tucson, Arizona

Jim was up early and decided he would start with a short run. This was going to be a busy day. He shaved, showered, dressed and met David for breakfast by seven. David had already talked with the driver out of Phoenix and he would be on time and had already put the stolen plates on the van. David had talked with the man from there barrio and he had his people all set with the surveillance of the storage facility and neighborhood and would be in contact with David who would be in contact with Jim on one of the new prepaid cell phones.

They enjoyed there breakfast and talked mostly of the two girls. They then left for the dealership Jim gave David two thousand dollars for the men in the barrio and another two for his people. David said "You know you don't have to do that."

"I do know that. Another thing we need to do after this is all over with is talk about money."

"Money is something I always like to talk about."

When the van arrived at the dealership Jim went over everything he wanted the driver to do. His name was Hector and he was sharp. As they left the dealership in the van Jim called Larry and told him to go to a convenience store on South Sixth Avenue just south of Ajo Road and wait for him. Once at the storage facility Hector went in and rented the two units and paid cash for the two months. Jim was surprised that the place didn't have a video system and the gate was open between seven in the morning till seven at night.

As soon as Hector was back in the van and Jim had the unit Numbers he again called Larry and told him the address and unit Number of the storage unit. He told him there would be a gym bag there for Larry and that Larry was to leave what he had in the unit and to use the lock that also would be there to lock the unit as he left. Jim gave him directions then closed the phone.

Jim put the gym bag and the lock inside the unit and closed the roll down door. He and Hector placed the van in front of the second unit with its door rolled up so that Jim with the rear door of the van ajar would be able to scan Larry and the computer for any kind of GPS transmitters.

After a good fifteen minutes Jim could see Larry in the same car as yesterday coming down the row of units looking at the Numbers. He stopped directly in front of the unit Jim had given him the Number of then looked around especially at the van then opened the unit and went inside. After only a minute he brought out the bag then opened his trunk and unloaded three boxes and quickly put them in the unit. He then closed and locked the pull down door. Larry was quickly in his car and on his way out of the lot.

Jim had gotten no hits off of Larry or the boxes he unloaded so he and Hector with gloves on unlocked and opened the unit then loaded the boxes into the van. Jim again scanned everything while Hector closed the unit back up and didn't lock it. David called and told Jim no one had come into the neighborhood except the one car and it was now gone. Jim thanked him, then he and Hector left for the dealership.

Once back they put the three boxes in Jim's SUV then changed the plates back on the van. David paid Hector and Jim thanked him then Hector was on his way to Phoenix and Jim was on his way to the house.

Jerry was at the gate and Jim said hello then drove to the house. He quickly unloaded the boxes and put them in the library. He looked over what he had and as Larry said it was a complete set up of the computers they produced at the company. The only thing that was missing were serial Numbers on any of the units or there components. Jim wondered how Larry ever got that stuff out of the building.

Jim opened the basement and took all his prizes down then locked everything back up. It was only a little past ten and he was expecting Sue to call after all today was the big shopping trip.

It was eleven when Sue called and said Kay was home and they including Jan would be ready when he got over there. Jim told her he would be there in a few minutes.

As Sue answered the door she gave Jim a nice kiss and said "I missed you last night."

They all looked nice and as if they were ready to go shopping. Jim suggested they might want to leave there purses at home so they could use both hands. They were all laughing but thought it was a good idea.

As they were leaving Jim asked if the Foothills Mall would have what they were looking for. They all thought it would be a good place to start. They started in one of the nicer stores that had evening wear in petite sizes. The girls all had big smiles on there face. Jim tipped the lady at the counter and told her he was the sugar daddy for the afternoon and the young ladies would need a lot of assistance. He did tell her the rules were that no one could look at the price tags. She was laughing along with the girls then said "Let's get started I have never done this before."

They were all having a good time and the girls were modeling the outfits for Jim. He finely went and found a large cart to buy that he could push and it also was to where he could hang there garment bags. They shopped till three thirty and did five stores. Jim was having the best time.

They loaded his SUV including the cart; it folded down. The girls had gotten two very dressy outfits each then a lot of sporty clothes and a ton of shoes, purses and a couple of hats each. Jim did tell them that he loved the hats on them.

By the time they got back to the girls house Sue needed to get ready for work. Jim asked if she would like to run and do breakfast in the morning. Sue kissed him and said "I would love to do that; how about six in the morning and you pick me up."

"I will be here at six."

Jim did get three kisses as he left; not a bad afternoons pay. By the time he reached the house Jerry the guard had already left. He went in and fixed himself a drink then walked out into the court yard the days were getting longer and the hint of spring was in the air. He was hungry then remembered there was left over pizza in the refrigerator. He would microwave the pizza and watch the news on his huge television.

Thursday Morning April 01/ 2010 Tucson, Arizona

Jim was up early and had on his running gear, made his bed and laid out his clothes so he could shave shower and dress to go to breakfast after there run.

Jim was on time for there run and Sue looked great and was happy. They did a good seven to eight miles and were at a walk as they returned to Sue's house. As they were almost to her house Jim said "This is April fools day and after breakfast I would like to talk to you about some idea's I have. They say in love fools rush in where wise men fear to go; so this may be the perfect day."

"Wait while I shower and dress. We can get a coffee on the way over to your place and talk before breakfast. And you're right this may be the perfect day."

It didn't take long and Sue was ready and looked beautiful with little or no make up. They stopped at one of the drive through coffee places then went up to the house. Jerry hadn't started yet. Once in the house they went to the pool room and sat on one of the couches. Jim said "I would like to start this with an idea and would like it if you would let me complete the whole thing before you comment on any of it."

"I think I can do that if it's not too long."

"Thank you. Now to start I think you know how I feel about you; so that is a given. What I would like to do is make it so we both have more time to get to know each other. My idea is to have you quit your job and I will make you an employee of my investment company with a signing bonus of a hundred thousand and a salary of seven thousand a month and all your benefits including a late model SUV. This would give me a chance to know more about you and your interest in the arts. You would still go to school and we will work around your schedule. Now so you don't feel trapped and unable to walk away I would like to give you two million dollars in cash to put away. It would be yours with no strings attached. Now I know that sounds like a lot of money, but you already know how much money I have and I believe there is more to be discovered. Now this isn't anything you need to decide on right away but I would like you to think about it."

"You are the strangest person I have ever met. You have thought about this a lot and I do appreciate you thoughtfulness. Now as for being in love with you; I am. Now is that how I want to spend the rest of my life well like you said I am also not sure. April fools day is perfect for this. I do accept your offer. Let's have breakfast at La Poloma and I can resign at the same time. Working last night and just thinking about you was terrible. It's like you can see inside my thoughts. Give me a great kiss then take me to breakfast."

They were both happy as they left for breakfast. Jerry was at the gate and waved as they left. On the ride to the Country Club the two of them were acting like kids. Sue said "I feel so free; like I never have before. It's a funny feeling and I don't know how to really describe it."

"You don't have to describe it to me because I feel it also. Let's do something fun tonight; just because we can."

"There is an art show at the Tucson art museum tonight. It's a cocktail party and the opening of a new exhibit. There are a lot of people I would like you to meet."

"Wouldn't we need an invitation?"

"I am always on there list but I will call ahead and advise them of who will be accompanying me."

"That would be fun and I would like to meet some of your friends. Let's do dinner after that."

"I will wear some of my new clothes."

When they got to the resort Jim waited while Sue went and resigned her position. It was early enough for them to change there schedule and bring in a different waitress for that evening. As Sue returned to the lobby she was all smiles and said "They were very nice and I feel great."

"Good let's get some breakfast; we will have a busy day in front of us."

In the dinning room all the staff knew Sue and they did get extra nice treatment. That made Sue feel good and Jim happy. Breakfast was fun and they both felt closer to each other and they could relax. Jim paid the bill and over tipped the waitress.

On the way to the car Jim said "It's still too early to call anyone so let's stop at The Super Wal-Mart and I will buy two large briefcases then go to the house and get the two million. I also need to tell you the rules of cash. You can't deposit large amounts of cash into any bank account without them notifying the government the federal guideline is Ten thousand in any one month period or if the bank thinks the deposit is suspicious. The safe Number seems to be not over five thousand in one month. So what I will ask you to do with this is get the largest safe deposit box your bank has to offer and put one million of this money in it. They will tell you that you can't put cash in a safe deposit box. But in reality they don't see what you put in there. Now my accountant will give you two checks for fifty thousand each. You can deposit one in your savings account at your bank. The other check you can use to open a checking, savings and another large safety deposit box at a different bank then you can put the second million in that box. Also you can get an automatic deposit set up with either bank so your pay can be automatically deposited each month."

"This having money sounds complicated."

"You will have to pay taxes on the hundred thousand and taxes will be deducted from your salary. Now for the two million when ever you take any of that out of your safe deposit box you will have to list that as income and pay taxes on it."

"Well the government and I still will be happy."

They found two inexpensive brief cases then went to the house, opened the basement and then put a million dollars in each of the two cases. Sue asked what the boxes of stuff were that Jim had put in the basement. "I am not sure of exactly what I have there; but we will find out some time after we finish the safes and there computer. Now let's lock this up and I will call my friend and accountant Bill Stine and make sure he is in the office."

Jim made his call and told Bill he and Sue would be right over.

On the way over to Bill's Jim was telling Sue how Bill handles all his business accounts and pays all his regular bills. "You seam to have everything in you're life all lined out."

Jim while laughing said "That's one of the great things about you. Ever since I have met you all of that in some ways has changed; the things that are important to me are completely different. I never knew I could be this happy. I am not saying the money is not important but it is a way down the list where it should be."

Bill really liked Sue and put everything together for her including a direct deposit of her salary. It wasn't but a half hour and they were on there way to the branch of the bank Sue used. She put one of the fifty thousand dollar checks into her savings account she then opened a large safe deposit box and fit one million into it. A block down the street was a Bank One branch. Sue opened a checking and savings account with the second check and also got a large safe deposit box. The whole thing took a good half hour but it was done. Jim asked Sue if she felt any different now that she was a millionaire. Sue laughing said "I feel exhausted, take me back to your house and let's have a drink."

Back at the house Jim fixed them both a drink and they went to the pool room. "I don't think the money thing has sunk in yet but like earlier I feel freer then I ever have. I do know that it's you that makes me feel that way."

"After we rest up would you like to go back to safe cracking?"

"You know I would love it. The whole idea of looking at things no one else even knows exists is in its self addicting. I guess that is why people spend so much time and money looking for sunken treasure. It's the Indiana Jones thing."

"If you want to make us a second drink I will open up the basement."

When Sue brought in the drinks Jim closed and locked the library doors then they took the drinks down into the basement. "You still have to go through all the cabinets; they cover the one wall floor to ceiling. I bet they also hold secrets."

"Time will tell. We will start on them after the safes."

Jim had his equipment hooked up plus his pad and pen. He had a harder time with the third safe it took a good fifteen minute but it did unlock. Jim looked at Sue and said "It's your turn if you want to."

"You know I can't help myself; I want to open it."

Sue opened the door and said "Again the bottom is filled with gold. It looks like the first two. This is so crazy. This safe had more shelves and they were full of boxes that had names of different corporations. Jim opened a couple of them and they both were full of bearer bonds. They kept opening the boxes and they were all the same. There were thousand's of them. Jim said "I am sure the value of theses will be more then all the gold we have found so far. There is so much wealth here that it is looking quite sinister.

Hopefully between the next two safes and the computer we can find out who this person was and what this is all about. Let's put this all back and open the next one."

"I would like it if you would take a break then hold and kiss me."

"That is a great idea."

There was a lot of holding and kissing then they sat on the couch, finished there drinks and talked about all that they had found so far. After a good twenty minutes they returned to the safe cracking.

The forth safe again had the bottom filled with the gold bars. The rest of it was full of American hundred dollar bills. They also were in ten thousand dollar bundles then wrapped in vacuum sealed clear plastic bundles that looked to be a million dollars each. There were ten of those bundles. Jim said "Well I don't think I will run low on cash or gold. Let's open the last one."

The fifth safe also had the bottom filled with the gold bars it looked to be the same as the others there were also four more of the plastic wrapped bundles. But this safe had three boxes that held CD files. There looked to be about thirty some discs between the three boxes. Each disk was only identified by a series of Numbers written on it with a black marker. These were files for the computer and Jim hoped they would hopefully answer some of his questions.

"Well Mr. Rich man, this means I can order dessert tonight."

"Yes you can. Let's reopen safe Number two and find some nice jewelry for you to wear tonight."

Sue started laughing and said "I have never worn anything like is in that safe. I wouldn't know how to act."

"I can't think of anyone in the world that I would like to see that stuff on other then you. And if you just act like yourself it will be perfect."

"You better kiss me again I am afraid I am going to wake up."

They found a beautiful necklace and matching ear rings that were made up of ruby's and diamonds. It looked beautiful on Sue and yet still petite enough not to over power what she was going to wear. She kissed him and asked if he was going to put them on her after she dressed. "I was hoping you would let me."

"Why don't you take me home then come over about six and bring them with you. You have me feeling like Cinderella; I hope this doesn't end at midnight."

"Trust me the only one that could end this is you."

With the help of a lot of kisses Jim got her back to her house. He then went home to figure out what he wanted to wear.

When Sue walked in the house she saw Kay and ran over and hugged her and said "My whole life has changed today and all my feelings and my head are spinning around. Let me tell you what has happened."

Sue told Kay the story of her day leaving out everything about the basement. They talked and laughed for over an hour then Kay helped Sue put together what she was going to wear then helped her do her nails. Sue picked a ruby red polish and lipstick. After she showered she did her hair a bit on the wild side and Kay loved it. They also talked about Kay and Jan. Kay told her she had never felt as happy as she did with Jan and they were getting closer to the point of moving in together. Sue told her if that was the case she would do what ever was necessary to make sure it worked out for her. By six Sue was ready.

Jim showed up looking good and carrying a beautiful bouquet of flowers. Sue said "You sure know your flowers and I do love them."

"They really looked better until I saw them next to you. I also brought something I would like to give to you and to have you wear tonight."

Sue went to say something but Jim had the box out and open before she could. He said "I would like to be the one to put them on you."

Kay gasped and Sue started to tear up. Jim quickly kissed her on the cheek and said "That will rune your make up. I do want to tell you that I love you."

"This really isn't fare but thank you and I also love you."

She gave him a nice kiss then hugged Kay and said "This really is quite a day. We need to go before I start crying."

Kay said "Neither of you are going anywhere before I get a picture of the both of you."

"I think Kay is right."

Kay did get the pictures and there were no tears. Then with two kisses from Kay they were off to the party.

On the way Sue said "We only agreed that I would wear this stuff tonight; not that they would be a gift. These are worth a fortune and having them is scary."

"I was thinking of there value this afternoon and realized there only value to me was seeing them on you. Now for the scary part, you can keep them in your safe deposit box or in my safe and they like everything else have no strings attached to them. If you do fall in love with me I would like it if it's just me, so I also don't want this stuff to be part of the equation."

"Ok then let's go to this party and have a great night."

When they arrived they did have valet parking and when Sue got out of the car a lot of heads turned. She did look stunning. They got a glass of Champaign and mingled with the other guests. Most of the people they came across knew Sue and she was introducing Jim. Sue also knew the artist that there work would be part of the new exhibit. Suddenly Jim saw David and Becky who were walking over to greet them. They were all laughing and David did all the introductions. They had all of cores met before but it made it nice they all got another glass then with the rest of the people went in to view the exhibit. Sue was introducing David, Becky and Jim to the different artist as they went through the exhibit. David also knew a lot of people there. They were having a fun evening. Jim invited David and Becky to join Sue and him for dinner afterwards. David said I have reservations at La Poloma unless Sue would rather not.

"I have never been there for dinner and would love to go."

"They are your reservations but I asked so this is my treat."

David laughed and said "When someone offers to buy my dinner; I let them."

After another half hour the party was slowing down so they called for there cars and were going to meet at the Country Club. On the way Sue said "This should be fun; I was to be working this shift. Like last night I would have been thinking about you."

"You can't believe how happy I am that instead of working, you will be here with me."

They met David and Becky in the lobby then went to the dinning room. The Mater D greeted them then took a double take at Sue then gasped. Sue with that great smile said "Hi Randy"

They were seated and treated like they had the President with them. They all loved it and knew it was because of Sue. While they were talking Sue explained she had resigned and was now working for Jim's investment company. Jim made it clear that Sue was more then an employee. Becky and Sue were talking about the exhibit and Sue's connection to Tucson's art community. During the evening they talked about Becky's work at the University Hospital and Sue's working on her Master's Degree in Art.

The evening was great both the service and food were over the top and the best part was the girls really seamed to like each other. Jim got the bill and over tipped everyone. They all had a good time and Jim again invited them to come up and see the new estate when they could all be together.

When Jim and Sue were on there way out of the resort Sue undid her seat belt and was all over him with kisses. Jim was laughing and had to stop the car. Sue said "Thank you; I have had the best time tonight. Now let's go back to your place take off these clothes and get in the Jacuzzi."

Jim was kissing her back and said "Let's add a bottle of Champaign to that."

The ride back to the house was quick and once inside there was a trial of clothes leading into the pool room Jim did stop and get a bottle of Champaign and plastic glasses. They were both laughing and kissing in the Jacuzzi. Sue said "Everyone I talked to there eyes would go to the jewelry I was wearing."

"You did make them look special."

Sue was laughing and said "I do love you."

Sue did spend the night. She did have classes in the morning but not till ten thirty. They decided an early run, swimming then breakfast would be a nice start to the day.

Friday Morning April 0 2/ 2010 Tucson, Arizona

Jim and Sue had the perfect morning even the shower was something special. He had Sue back at her house a little after nine thirty.

After Jim was back at his house he first put Sue's jewelry in one of the safes in the basement. He next called the boys, Steve and Frank and asked if they had some time that they could come over. They were available and said they would be over in about thirty minutes. He went up to make the bed and pick up and was surprised, Mrs. Jacobs had already been there and the room was perfect. Jim laughed, she was like a ghost; he never saw her but everything was always done.

He went back down and fixed himself a drink while he waited for the boys.

When he answered the door the boys were laughing. They told Jim that Jerry had remembered them and there names. They had never been somewhere where they were greeted by name. Jim smiled and said "Let's go to the pool room. Would the two of you like a drink?"

"Let me make them; I like to play bartender."

"The reason I wanted to talk with the two of you is I have decided I need help to run this place. I have Jerry for security during the day Monday through Friday, Mrs. Jacobs and her crew for the housekeeping and the landscape people for the yards and the pools. Now what I was thinking of was to have the two of you to oversee the entire estate. You would have to work with Jerry so you would know the whole security system and be able to monitor all of it if necessary. There is a lot of electronic surveillance so I don't think we need twenty four hour live guards. Let's talk about money and the possibility of the two of you moving up here and taking one of the guest houses."

Now the boys were really excited. They all had a second drink then talked for a good two hours and switching to coffee. They talked about everything they could think of that might come up including the boys having company and even parties. Jim did make it clear no hard drugs would be tolerated for them or there guests. Alcohol and grass were fine but kept under control. All the guest houses had pools and Jacuzzis but the boys wanted the house they had stayed in, they loved the view. They worked out the money then got Bill Stine on the phone and he got all the information he needed and also put them on the medical insurance. The boys had there own cars and Jim told them they would have the use of any of the SUV's that were there for the security people and also the box truck for moving. He also told them anything of there's or anything out of the house they didn't want to use they could store in the warehouse. They were still talking when Sue came over.

Jim was explaining to Sue what they were doing. She was excited for them then told the boys that she also was working for Jim's Company. She smiled and said "I am an employee with benefits."

They were all laughing and the boys said they would start moving the next day then they said goodbye and left. Sue gave Jim a Kiss and asked what they were going to do. "I was thinking first the cabinets then I would like to start on the computer. Would you like coffee or a drink first?"

"The drink sounds nice. Also I am glad you're going to have the boys living here. The thought of you being out here all by yourself, and as scary as this place is; I will feel better that they are here with you."

"With time and a lot of luck I hope I won't be out here alone forever."

Sue while laughing kissed him and said "Time answers most questions."

They played around a few minutes then went to the library, locked the door then opened the basement. They started with the large cabinets; Jim had a cordless drill and quickly drilled out the locks on the first two. As he opened them he was shocked to find a rather large arsenal of weapons. There were eight M16 automatic rifles with fully loaded clips in them, eight assault style 12 gage shotguns fully loaded and eight 9mm semi automatic hand guns. They all looked to be Government Issue and from the Vet Num era. There was also a large amount of ammunition and extra clips. "Don't tell me this isn't scary. Who the hell were these people?"

"I don't know but this place has a lot of secrets that we haven't even come close to. I am hoping the CD files we found for that computer will answer a lot of our question. Let's keep looking."

In all the other cabinets they found every type of spy equipment you could think of all the way to thermal imaging cameras that were a lot more suffocated then what the spy store had. In one of the tall cabinets they found all the blueprints of everything that had been built on the property and the basement and the entry from the library weren't part of the prints.

"Let's get a drink and talk."

They locked the library and went to the pool room. Jim fixed them both a drink and as they sat there he said "With everything we have seen down there we haven't found anything that is of a personal nature. There are no pictures of people or just little stuff we all have around us to some degree. Even working in a war zone I had stuff around me that was personal. I have the feeling if we had the place checked for finger prints the only ones they would find would be ours."

"You're right I was also thinking something was wrong but couldn't put my finger on it. That place is too sterilized. We haven't even seen anything that was hand written. That is scary down there."

"I think we are only seeing the tip of this iceberg. The computer is the next thing I want to do but that will be another day."

"Then why don't you lock up the basement then we can go swimming. I don't have my swim suit if that's ok."

He kissed her and said "I love looking at your body. I will be back in a few minutes." Sue was laughing as he left.

They spent a couple of hours in and around the pool enjoying each other Jim had made a pot of coffee and they talked about a lot of things including Sue's parents. She said "I told my Mom all about you and your estate. She was telling me to be careful of you."

"If I was your mother I would have been on the first plane out here to make sure you're all right."

"Well I am glad you're not my mother for a lot of reasons. Now why don't we get dressed go over to my place and I will cook you dinner."

"See if Kay and Jan would like to join us if you like."

"That would be fun; let me call them and see what they have planed."

Sue called and the girls loved the idea. They had planed to go out that night to a club by the university and asked if Sue and Jim would like to go with them. They thought it was a great idea. Jim shaved showered and dressed before they left. They stopped at the store and bought what Sue needed to make dinner Jim also got some nice wine and flowers. Sue kissed him and said "You are a romantic at hart."

Kay and Jan were happy to see them and it was an instant party. Sue was fixing pan fried shrimp with a skinny looking spaghetti type noodles and it all covered in a sauce. She said it was a recipe a friend of hers that cooked at The Olive Garden gave her. They also had a great salad and hot French bread. Dinner was great and they all had a good time and finished dinner with coffee. While they were talking Kay said she and Jan had decided to live together and see how this all worked out. Sue was happy for them and asked when they planed on doing it.

"Jan is living at home and I wanted to talk to you about our arrangement here. I don't want to leave you in a bad situation."

"Don't worry about the rent with my new salary I can afford to pay the whole thing."

"I am happy for the two of you and have an idea. There are two of the houses on the estate sitting empty. If the two of you like you are welcome to live in one of them. Steve and frank are moving into the third one. And will be working there. Now for the other house I would like to offer it to Sue. Now I will have Bill write up agreements so everyone feels secure about the living arrangements."

"So you want your girl friend living next door."

"That does sound bad and I apologize. What I really wanted was to ask you to marry me."

Jim got down on one knee took Sue's hand and said "Sue Taylor would you marry me and let me love you for the rest of your life?"

Sue was totally shocked and looked at Kay and Jan then back at Jim and said "You by far are the craziest person I have ever met. It must be catching because I do love you and yes I would love to marry you and love you for the rest of my life."

Kay and Jan were screaming and Sue through her self into Jim's arms and gave him a great kiss witch he returned. There were a lot of kisses and hugs going around.

"I need to call my Mom."

"Ok but I need one more kiss first. I can't believe you said yes. You have made me the happiest man."

Jim got his kiss then Sue grabbed her phone. Kay brought Jim a bottle of wine to open and was so happy she was almost dancing. While Jim was opening the wine Jan walked over and kissed him on the cheek and said "I am so happy for you."

"I am also happy for you and Kay. I really would like it if you and Kay would think about my offer; we would love to have the two of you as neighbors."

"It's like Sue said you are a strange man. And for one I would love to live out there so let's see what happens."

Kay had the wine poured and Sue was still on the phone with her Mom and laughing really hard. She said "My Mother is threatening to get a ticket and come out here."

Tell her I will arrange to have a limousine pick her and your Father up and have them flown out here on a private jet. They can stay in the guest house; I would love to meet them."

Sue was laughing so hard she couldn't talk so she just handed the phone to Jim. "Hi Mrs. Taylor I am Jim Cooper and I meant what I said; I would love to meet you and Mr. Taylor so why don't we do this?"

"Sue said you were a strange man and you are definitely living up to that and I don't know what to say."

"I won't rush you so why don't the two of you figure out when would be a good time and let Sue know. But I also want to assure you I do love Sue and want to marry her."

Jim with a small kiss gave the phone back to Sue. She talked with her Dad and told them both she loved them and couldn't wait to see them.

When she was off the phone she pushed Jim down on the couch and jumped on him kissing him and said "I do love you and I do want to see them."

Kay said "Why don't the two of you give us a kiss then take off. We will handle the clean up."

They got there kiss then Jim and Sue were on there way. Once in the car Jim said "As soon as we get to the house I need to call David and tell him."

"Why don't you call him and invite him and Becky over then tell him."

"You are so smart; I love the idea."

Jim called David and as luck would have it he was at dinner with Becky. Jim told him it was important and they needed to come over. They agreed and Jim told him to call a few minutes before he got to the end of Campbell and Jim would meet them at the driveway. It was only minutes and he and Sue were at the house. Most all the outside lights automatically come on at sunset also some of the interior and some of the courtyard lights come on at the same time. The house does look very dramatic as you drive up. It took a lot of kisses to get in the door.

Jim found two nice bottles of Champaign in the refrigerator; he put them on ice and got out four glasses. Sue said "This should be fun I like both David and Becky and if David hasn't seen this place it will blow his mind.

"The big deal tonight is the fact that you said yes and that is much more important then this place. I can't believe I asked you so soon; then I was scared I was chasing you away."

"I have to admit I was shocked that you asked, but deep inside me I wanted to marry you. I wanted a life in the faster lane and I didn't want to be tied down. It's funny because being with you has never given me that feeling. Actually I feel freer then I ever have."

"Would you like a glass of Champaign while we wait?"

"No let's wait on them, but I would like another kiss."

It wasn't long when David called and said he was just crossing Ina Road. Jim told him to drive slowly and he would meet him at the driveway. Jim was excited and Sue said she would wait at the house.

By the time Jim got through the gate and to the road he could see David's car. Jim flashed his lights then turned around and started back up the drive with David behind him. He pushed the button on the remote and the gate opened and David followed him through. Once in front of the house David and Becky got out and David was laughing and said "You bought a hotel.

Sue was waiting for them at the door and said hello to Becky and David. Jim said this is great but come in I have something more important to tell you. Neither David nor Becky could believe it as they walked inside Jim led the way to the pool room then said "Today I asked Sue to marry me and by the grace of God she said yes."

David was really excited and gave Sue a big hug and a kiss on the cheek and said "Welcome to the family."

Becky also hugged and kissed them both. Sue had opened a bottle of the Champaign so Jim poured them all a glass. They had a toast to the engagement. They all sat and Jim told them the story of his proposal. They were all laughing then Sue told them of her phone call to her parents and what her mother said. They were all having fun and the second bottle of Champaign got opened. Becky asked Sue if she could see the house. Sue with a big smile said "We should all take a tour."

They spent a good hour going over the main house and the court yard where they could see the three guest houses and the huge meeting room. Jim also explained about the warehouse and the electronic mentoring office inside it plus the tennis courts and helicopter landing pad. Sue also mentioned the covered patio at the base of the cliffs and what a beautiful view it had of the sunset and the city lights.

The four of them worked there way back to the pool room and Jim put on a pot of coffee. They talked and laughed for another hour and a half before David and Becky left.

As they watched David's car go down the drive Sue kissed Jim and said "Why don't we lock this place up and move this party up to your bed."

Saturday Morning April 03/ 2010 Tucson, Arizona

Jim and Sue were awake by seven but weren't quite through with they started the night before. Sue said "Tell me last night wasn't a dream."

"It wasn't and you did say yes. I know because I am the happiest man in the world."

"Ok then kiss me and let's get a shower then you can take me some wear nice for breakfast."

At breakfast they were talking about Kay and Jan moving to one of the houses. Jim reminded her that she needed to talk to her Mom about when they would like to come out. Sue started laughing and said "I really do want them to come out and meet you. They are very concretive and I am sure they have never been in a privet Jet. And this place for sure will be a culture shock to them."

"I don't want to shock them; remember I am trying to make a good impression on you're parents."

"Just be yourself; the person I fell in love with. I want them to get to know the real us. That includes me; while there here I would like to stay here with you. They can stay in the guest house."

"I do love you and so it will be. As soon as the boys get settled we can have them move the rest of you girls."

"Sometime today I would like to go home and if you don't mind I will pick up the things I need for right now and if it's all right with you I will move them over to the house."

"You know I would love it, but don't forget you said you would marry me."

They were both laughing as they finished breakfast. Before they could leave Steve called and said he and Frank wanted to come over and look at the guest house again so they would know what they wanted to bring. That would be great and I will have a set of keys for you and keys to the Box truck.

After they were back at the house Jim put on a pot of coffee and Sue called Kay. She was at work and would call Sue after she was off. Sue then called her Mother and they talked for almost forty five minutes. When she was done she was laughing and said "She will call me back with a date after she talks with my Dad. She wouldn't commit till after I told her I was moving over here today."

Now Jim was laughing really hard then kissed Sue and said "You do know what buttons to push. I am sure that your Dad will be ready to leave today. I know I would."

"I think you will make a great father. That will be one of the big conversations we will have."

By the time the boys showed up Jim had put together a set of keys to the house they would be using plus a set for the box truck and the warehouse. The first thing he told them was that he and Sue were engaged and he would need them soon to move her plus Kay and Jan would be moving to one of the other guest houses hopefully during the week and he would need them to also help them. Steve and Frank were excited about all the news especially about Sue and Jim. They congratulated Jim and were happy for Sue. Steve said there friends Jared and Troy were going to help them. Jim told them to have fun.

Jim said "I would like to get an engagement ring today. Have you thought of what you might like?"

"I would like to have a ring, but to be honest I have no idea; could we just go look at some first then talk about it?"

"Let's lock up and go look; it's after ten and they should all be open."

They started at a large Jewelry wholesaler in down town Tucson. They looked at a lot of different settings and Jim wanted a high quality ten caret diamond. The gentleman told him the stone alone would be over thirty thousand. Sue said "I don't want you to spend that kind of money for a ring."

"If you like I have bags of beautiful diamonds and also hundreds of beautiful rings. Would you like it if we first looked at them? We can have any combination of stones and settings made up."

"If you add a bottle of wine to that offer, it would sound like a lot more fun then this is."

Jim went back and thanked the gentleman and said they might be back. Then it was back to the house with a purpose. Sue picked out the wine while Jim opened the basement.

The jewelry was in the second of the safes. Sue poured the wine while Jim got all of it out. They spent over an hour going through every bit of it again. There were three rings that Sue really liked and they all had large diamonds in them. To Jim one of them was perfect for Sue; the stone was a little over ten carats but in that setting it looked petite on Sue. It would need to be sized down to fit properly. Jim said let me put all this away, lock up and then we will go and get it sized right a way."

Sue kissed him and said "I love you."

They went back to the same gentleman they had talked to before. Jim told him he had a ring that Sue liked but it needs to be sized. Sue put out her hand to show him the ring. He looked at it and said "It does need to be sized."

He took the measurement of her finger then looked at the ring and said "The quality of this diamond is at the top and it looks to be eleven carats plus; this ring has never been worn or sized before. If you have ten to fifteen minutes I will size it right now. Feel free to look around and there is coffee by the wall."

"Thank you we will."

"That must be a very valuable ring."

"Remember its only value to me is to have it on your hand."

"You do know the right things to say to a girl. Let's look around and see if they have anything that comes close to what you have."

They were having fun while they waited. After about ten minutes the gentleman had the ring ready. He gave it to Jim and said "I am sure you want to put it on the young lady."

"I do and thank you."

Jim paid, tipped and thanked the gentleman then asked if they bought loose diamonds. "We have a buyer who travels all over the country and oversees buying diamonds. What do you have to sell?"

"I have a large quantity of high quality stones that are from one to ten carats."

"What would you call a large quantity?"

"I don't have an exact weight but it is over ten pounds."

"Well that is a very large quantity. Please take my card and if and when you are interested in selling any of them we definitely would be interested."

Jim did take his card and again thanked him. As soon as they were out the door Sue through her arms around his neck and laid a great kiss on him and said "I love my ring and Kay should be home by now and I would love to show it to her."

"Then let's go see Kay and on the way let's pick up a nice bottle of wine."

The trip to Kay's was like a party in itself. At the liquor store they ended up buying two cases of assorted wines. Sue of course knows her wines very well; she had also taken classes on it for working at the resort.

Both Kay and Jan were there and they both loved Sue's ring. Jim opened the bottle of wine they had brought in and Kay got four glasses so he could pour it. They had a toast then Sue was telling them about the conversation she had with her Mother. They were all laughing and the girls agreed Sue should receive an answer by the end of the day. They sat and talked about many things then Jim asked if they had decided on his offer of them moving to one of the houses. Kay said "There is still two more months after this one on the lease. We also need to look at what you would want for rent."

"I am sorry I didn't make myself clear. First Sue can give my accountant the information on the lease of this place and he will handle that. Second I will have him write you up an agreement so there will be no rent on the house. Utilities, pool care and landscaping will also be taken care of. I also have a large P. O. Box we all can shear. As I told you the boys are moving to one of the other houses as we speak and will be available to move the two of you by Monday if you like."

Sue was laughing then hugged Kay and said "If the two of you are ready to take the jump we would love to have the two of you as neighbors."

Kay Kissed Jan and said "I am ready if you are."

Jan kissed her and said "I have been ready for a long time. Let's move."

By the time they got back to the house they could see the boys and the box truck were at one of the houses. Jim unloaded the wine while Sue was taking her things up to the master suite. There was an abundance of mirrored closets in the dressing room. Sue was putting things away while Jim brought up the rest of what she had in the SUV. Jim kissed her and said "Only having my clothes in there was quite lonely; you make me complete."

It wasn't long and the sun was going down. Jim said "At Swan and Skyline Road there is a nice restaurant that among other things has a great hamburger and batter dipped fries."

Sue was laughing and asked how many thousands of calories that was.

"We can go running in the morning, plus you can get a salad with that."

Sue kissed him and said "let's go."

While they were eating he said "I have a membership to a gem and enjoy working out. I was thinking if you would like it if we could take the office that is adjoining the pool room and put in work out equipment. The desk would easily go into the library; I don't think we need an office in there."

"I also like to work out. I keep a locker at the university gem. But working out here would be wonderful"

"We need to go on line and decide what equipment we want. I know the owner of the gem I belong to and we could talk with him and possibly have him order what we want and have him install it. I still want to keep my membership because at times I like to use a trainer. If you like we can get you a membership also."

"Let's look at the place first before I decide that."

"We will try and do that tomorrow or at least Monday."

"When we go to the house take me swimming then to the Jacuzzi."

"I will also open us a nice bottle of wine to go with that."

Sunday Morning April 04/2010 Tucson, Arizona

Jim and Sue were up early and out for there run the trails were marked for the distance you had gone from the house and they were on track for a good ten mile run. As they reached the house Sue said "So what were you thinking about no the way back? It was obvious you were in deep thought."

"You really are good. I was thinking about the basement and all the things we found. Outside of what may be on the computer and the CD files there is nothing personal in there. And we know no one could have been in there to have cleaned it out. So that has me thinking there is more to that basement then we have found."

"You really think there are other rooms down there based on that feeling?"

"Think of it; whoever built this thing wasn't hampered by money and if he went to that much trouble why would he only build one room. I also believe he wouldn't risk having a second entrance to the basement. If I am right the access to the other room or rooms would be through the wall that has cabinets from floor to ceiling."

"You really are the strangest person I have ever met. Now you have me thinking you're right. What could this be about? Why would anyone need all this secrecy, and what could be down there?"

"I don't know but I see the boys outside there house let's stop and say hello."

Steve and Frank were excited to see them and were thrilled with there new home. Frank invited them in for coffee. The house was in perfect order and everything was in its place. Steve said "We left all our furniture there. We were renting the place from a friend so we told him he could now rent it furnished and he was happy with that. When ever Kay and Jan are ready to move just let us know. We didn't break down the boxes so it should go rather quickly."

"When you do move them if either of you see things they need or that should be replaced I will give you enough money to just go out and get it. Like with the two of you I would like them to have everything they need to make them feel at home."

They enjoyed there coffee and talked a good twenty minutes before going to the house.

"Would you like to shower and dress and I will take you to breakfast."

"Well you take me to the Congress Street Café?"

"I will take you where ever you want to go. Also your Mother should call this morning; I actually thought she would have called last night."

They were both laughing as they got in the shower. It was a fun shower.

As Sue knew would be the case Kay was working and glad to see them. When she had the chance Sue told Kay she would have the boys call her Monday morning and they also had the boxes to move both her and Jan. Kay was almost giddy and couldn't believe it was all real.

They did have a fun breakfast. Then the next stop was the Gem on the Northwest side of town. It wasn't far from where they lived. Jim introduced Darrel the owner to Sue and told him what they wanted. Sue was surprised how nice and clean the place was. She also liked it that they did also have a separate women's section; not mandatory but available. They decided what equipment they would like to have at the house and Darrel told them they could buy less expensive equipment for there house because what he had was of a commercial grade. Jim thanked him but wanted it so they could quickly change the machines depending witch one of them were using it. Before they left Jim had given Darrel a deposit on the order and also signed Sue up with a membership.

On the way to the house Sue asked if they were going back to treasure hunting. "Would you like to?"

"You know I would and I know you want to as bad as I do."

"If there are any kisses and a bottle of wine included then I think it's a great idea."

"There could be a lot more then kisses and wine if you like."

"Then I think we will be treasure hunting."

It didn't take long and they were in the basement with there wine and doing a lot of kissing. "Ok Indiana Jones; let's see if you're right."

"I have come to the point that I know I am right. The challenge is to find the way in. We know the cabinets can't rise up and I wouldn't think they would go down so I believe they would open in. I believe that the two larger ones with the guns will be the way in. So let's think where the switch would be. And let's keep in mind it will be different then the one that opened the basement."

"You seam to know what this person was thinking when he had this built. And you're thinking that computer, the CD files, money, jewelry and gold were just a ruse to send anyone who got that far in the wrong direction. If that is right then they are willing to spend at least a couple hundred million dollars just to protect what ever this is all about. My God Jim if that is true we must be in big shit. Is it just me that is getting scared?"

"I think you're starting to get into there head also. I also agree with you about it being scary. But we must remember the two of us are the only ones that know about this. I am sure there are other people involved in what ever this is, but I also believe none of them know about this. And I think now you like me have to know about all of it; there is no way either of us could close that door now. Were both hooked and need to go wherever this takes us."

Sue hugged and kissed him then started laughing and said "You're right I have to know. So let's have some of our wine and figure out where that switch would be and what it would look like.

They sat on the floor across from the two open cabinets that held the guns and drank some of there wine. After a good fifteen minutes Jim started laughing then kissed Sue and said "I have it." He got up and went over to the second cabinet; the one that held the Shotguns and hand guns. The hand guns hung on L shaped brackets that stuck out from the back of the cabinets. He said "For some reason I know it's the third bracket."

By now Sue was on her feet and standing next to him. Jim took the gun off the bracket then he slowly turned the bracket to the left. The whole insides of the cabinet along with the guns and ammo started moving back then suddenly stopped and started moving to the right of the opening. Sue had hold of Jim's arm and said "I am so scared I can't move; I can't even run."

"It's not being scared; you're just so excited, and you don't want to run. Let me get my flashlight and find the light switch."

Right inside the opening was a panel with a Number of switches. Jim started turning them on then he and Sue went through the opening. They both just stood there looking around in silence for a good five minutes.

"This is a lot more then just some insane billionaire. And your description of me just being excited is a way off base. I am scared for the both of us."

"I have to admit this goes far beyond my wildest imagination. This all is part of something huge."

They were standing in a room that looked to be fifty by fifty feet with twenty large steel posts supporting the ceiling witch was reinforced concrete along one wall were stacks of gold bars five, ten and twenty pound bars then huge stacks of gold ingots that were marked fifty pounds. There were also stacks of silver ingots. Sue said "This looks like Fort Knocks. Also look at all the computer stuff and monitors. That section looks like it something out of the Houston space center."

"This equipment is state of the art, and no more then four years old. It must be connected to a dish to get satellite access. This goes way beyond what any company or individual wood have. This must have a connection to the government on some level."

As they went through the room they found stacks of military type ammo boxes. There looked to be a hundred or more of them. All of them they opened were filled with gold coins of three different types and weights. There were some file cabinets with some records that went back to the fifties and a lot of files that were on the old floppy discs.

In one section of the room there were enough supplies and beds for at least four people to stay down there for a couple of months. There was even an electric toilet that would incinerate the waste.

"I bet that the electrical power created by the solar panels we saw from the helicopter can be directed from down here to power this place. Let's stop and have some wine before we go through all the cabinets and lockers."

When they got back up in the library Sue's phone showed a miss call. It was from her Mother. Sue started to laugh and said "Let's take our wine out to the pool room and then I will call her back."

When Sue called back her Mother asked where she had been because her phone said she was out of the area. Sue told her that parts of the house have poor reception. Her Mom said they could come out for a few days on either Wednesday or Thursday.

Jim talked with her and said he would have a very nice lady named Darleen call her Monday with all the arrangements. Her Mother Helen while laughing told Jim that Mike Sue's Father wanted to fly out there yesterday. Jim laughing said "I also can't wait to meet the both of you."

He said his goodbyes and while they were both laughing gave the phone back to Sue. Sue talked and laughed a good fifteen minutes with her Mom. When she was done she jumped on Jim and was kissing him and laughing. She said "My Mom is really happy for me and my Dad is acting like he never considered the fact that I would get married. I can hardly wait to see them and I am sure you will like them."

Jim got a small canvas briefcase and inside he had a personal phone directory. He said "Darleen is a travel agent and a good friend of mine. She will set it all up including calling them."

"It's Sunday shouldn't you wait till in the morning."

"Darleen works out of her house and doesn't care when I call."

Jim called and they talked a while, he told her about Sue and that they were engaged and the people that she was flying out from Colorado were her parents. He also asked if she would use Bob and his plane. Jim gave her Bob's current Number and asked if she would tell him it was for Jim and that they were Sue's parents. Darleen said she would handle it then call him and confirm the arrangements and what time they would be at the house.

After he hung up he said "It will be only hours after they leave Colorado till they will be here at the house. I hope they will stay a while."

"This is all like a dream; why don't you kiss me so that I know it is real."

They sat and talked a good half hour then Jim asked if she wanted to go back to the treasure hunting. Sue laughed and said "We both know that we have to. The more we look the stranger this place gets. Let's see how far we can go."

The first lockers they opened had clothing all folded and wrapped in units that were a complete change. There were also packages of toiletries to match having four people living there. The next five lockers were again Full of Hundred dollar bills wrapped in plastic bundles that looked to be a million dollars each. There best count was fifty bundles. None of the cabinets in this room had locks on them. They found a lot of supplies then Jim found what he was looking for. It was a well organized set of CD files they were again numbered only this time each one had an X behind each Number. Jim told Sue the X was probably to make sure they didn't accidently get mixed up with the CD's from the other room.

"You think the computer and files out there are all part of a decoy so that no one would look for this room?"

"As crazy as that sounds I do believe that."

They also found an electric hoist with a cable and hook that could be used to bring things in or out of the basement. There also was a small cart and cargo nets to bring heavy things over to the entrance. "This means whoever lived here moved everything into this basement himself."

"That's right. But remember he had over forty years in witch to do that. Now should we get my equipment then see if this computer system has any unwanted transmitters on it?"

"I guess that is the only place we are going to find any answers."

Jim got his scanner and the device to jam any signal coming out of the computer. It took only minutes and he was ready and started to turn on each of the components one at a time. As he suspected there were no unwanted signals. It was only minutes and he had a name; a Mr. Robert P. Christenson. The computer system was hooked up to its own secure Wi-Fi so Jim went on line using his Yahoo account then goggled the name Robert P Christenson and got a few hits but none of them appeared to be this guy. He went to a Number of different search engines and again no results. He sat back and said "That could be a phony name. Let me put in the first of the Numbered CD's and see what it tells me because all the document files on this unit are empty."

Jim put the first of the CD's in and opened it up. It for sure was a list of what each of the other CD's had on them. The first twenty seven CD's were all international banks and monetary funds. The next twenty two were different countries. The list went on and showed there were a total of two hundred and seventy six CD's.

"What do you think this is all about?"

"Just looking at the lists I would say it's about money, Oil and politics."

"Why would you think politics?"

"Oil is just another form of money like gold, silver and cash. Money the size of this is only a tool for power, and that means politics on a world wide scale. One of the things on the list is CD's and DVD's of the meetings that were held here and there dates. I hope the DVD's show who was in attendance at the meetings and who they represent."

"I don't know if that is good or bad but we have gone this far."

"Let's leave this for another day, shut this down and lock this place up. We don't want to miss another of you're Mothers calls. Plus we need to get some dinner."

"If were going to live here we should go grocery shopping."

"Couldn't we get the boys to do that?"

"No we can't. I bet you have never been shopping for groceries or cooked a real meal."

"I have made scrambled eggs with ketchup on it and toast."

"Before my parents get here we will go shopping."

"After dinner tonight would you help me bring my car over here? I left it at my town house."

"Does moving the car come with extra benefits?"

Monday Morning April 20/ 2010 Tucson, Arizona

Jim and Sue were up early and went for a good run then showered and dressed for the day. As they were leaving for breakfast they saw the boys getting the box truck out of the warehouse. Jim got the keys to one of the guest houses then stopped and talked with the boys. He gave them the keys and three thousand dollars so they could buy the girls anything they thought they might need. Steve smiled and told them they would handle it.

While they were at breakfast Darleen called and told them Sue's parents would be at the house Wednesday around eleven. She also said she included a nice tip for Bob and the Limousine drivers both coming and going. Jim thanked her and told her to include a five hundred dollar tip in the bill for her. He then told her to figure out a vacation for her and a friend, any where she wanted to go and he would pay for it plus a thousand dollars spending money. Darleen was laughing and said "I do love you and will talk to you later."

Sue was laughing and Jim said "I don't think she believed me."

"Eat your breakfast little boy I have a feeling this will be a busy day, plus we need to go grocery shopping."

"Some where in this busy day I need some one on one time with David; I am going to bring him in on some of this money stuff but not the basement and all that stuff. I need him to start to revive our personal defense force. It is organized and can reach anywhere I need it to. I am hopping I won't need it but I will feel better if it is in place."

"Are you talking about the mob and gangsters?"

"No these are people who David and I have relationships with; the first is all the people who are part of our Barrio. They are connected to David and me as we are to them. If any of us are in trouble or need help, the rest will do all that they can. That includes sharing there connections. There is a network of people around the world that will get you what ever you need and do what ever you need done for a price. There not people you can go out and hire, you need to have a connection that they can trust."

"You're talking about a criminal underground. How would you ever be able to contact such people?"

"You need to be one and have references that they can trust. There are no contracts that you can sue someone over it's all done with a handshake but it is binding. Remember when I was a teenager David and I were in the business, we both made sure we never lost our contacts; it's part of the macho thing of being a Home Boy. It's a term that's demands respect where I grew up."

Sue started laughing and said "Let's not take my parents over to the Barrio while they are here; it's going to be enough for them to just get over you."

Now they were both laughing and that was the end of breakfast.

When they got back to the house Jerry was at the gate. Jim told him who all was moving to the estate including Sue and between him and Sue they had every ones phone Numbers. Jim also told Jerry that Sue's parents were coming in Wednesday about eleven in the morning and would be arriving in a limousine. Jim also asked Jerry if there was anything he needed. Jerry told them he was good and that he had reviewed all the security for the weekend and it all appeared to be normal.

As soon as they were in the house they went to the library locked the doors behind them and opened the basement. Jim took one of the briefcases they had bought and put a million dollars in it then looked at Sue and said "I should blow his mind" then took out a twenty pound bar of gold and put it into the briefcase.

Sue was laughing and said "I would love to have a picture of his face when he sees that."

Jim called David and said he needed to talk. David said "What the hell let's meet at the bar in the Country Club. How about fifteen minutes?"

As Jim was going out the door they saw the boys in the box truck coming up the drive with Kay and Jan right behind them. Sue kissed Jim and said "I will be over with them."

When Jim walked into the bar with his briefcase David was already there and had ordered them both a drink. Jim smiled as he held up the briefcase and said "You're going to like this; let's get a table."

Once they had there drinks and the waitress left the table Jim opened the briefcase and took out the bar of gold and handed it to Dave as he said "That's a little over three hundred and sixty thousand."

David started laughing and said "How much trouble are you in?"

Jim while laughing handed David the briefcase then said "None yet, but look inside that's a million in hundreds and both of them are just party favors. I am into something that has a lot of money the type neither of us have dreamed of. Like I said I am not in trouble yet but I believe there is something sinister about all of this. What I would like you to do with some of the million is use it to freshen up our connections with first the people in our Barrio then our connections with the rest of our old friends. If trouble shows up I may need all the help I can get."

"What about the gold bar?"

"That's just for you. I was going to bring you a fifty pound ingot but it wouldn't fit into the briefcase. David I have a lot of gold and money, neither of us will ever worry about money. I will give you all you could ever want."

David started laughing then said "You for sure are the craziest son of a bitch I have ever known. I have never seen a bar of gold like that and for sure not a million in cash. Let's get another drink then you can tell me what you can about this. I can see you're not ready to tell me everything you know yet and that's cool."

They got there second drink and talked for a good hour.

When Jim got back to the house Sue was over at Kay and Jan's new house and they were having a ball. Jim had brought over two bottles of wine and as soon as he walked in Jan came running over through her arms around his neck and said "Thank you; I am so happy." Then she gave him a kiss. Kay was right behind her with a hug and kiss.

"Thank you girls, but I think I am missing someone."

Sue was right there with a huge kiss then said "If there is anything else you think might be missing I will take care of that also."

They were all laughing and the wine got opened and they drank a toast to the new home for Kay and Jan. Sue said the boys went to pick up some stuff and said they would be back soon. The girls gave Jim a tour and said some of the art and things the boys were going to put in the warehouse.

When Steve and Frank returned Jim poured them some wine and they joined the party. After a time Jim suggested they all go out for dinner later. They all thought that would be a good idea and Kay said "That would nice because Jan and I need to go shopping for groceries."

"Before you go Steve and I picked up some things we thought the two of you should have. We will get them from the truck."

They all went out to the truck to help bring everything in. The boys had gone to one of the big Box stores and bought everything they thought the girls might need. There were a lot of boxes. Suddenly Kay started crying and said "You're all making me feel like Cinderella and I don't know what to say."

Jim hugged her and said "Kay your with people that love you and want you to be free to go after the things in life that fulfill your passion. So there is nothing you need to say, just let us all love you."

After a bit Sue said "My parents will be here Wednesday about eleven and Mr. I don't know how to cook has nothing to eat in the house. So how about all of you come with me to the grocery store. We can take Jim's SUV and we can all get what we need for all the houses. Jim can stay at home and work on his computers."

Jim kissed her and said "If you will all let me the trip can be my treat and if you like Steve and Frank can take the truck with you."

The girls both had Tuesday off and thought it would be fun. Steve told Jim he still had some of the money he had given him left over. Jim told him that he and Frank should use it to have some fun.

As they walked back to the house Sue said "I thought that would give you some time to play with the computers."

"Unless you have something else you want to do I would like to work on them this afternoon."

"It sounds like fun and while you're doing your thing I will go through all the other stuff in the cabinets."

They worked in the basement till after four o'clock then went to the pool room and Jim made them a drink then said "Just the little bit I have looked at shows numbered bank accounts all over the world with hundred's of billions of dollars sitting in them and this Robert Christenson has control of all of them; witch includes the account numbers, names and electronic addresses of the banks and best of all, the pass words."

"Are you saying that now you have control of them?"

"That's right and I am sure that is just the tip of what this is all about. I quickly scanned over some of the CD's that list the different countries and each one of them list the different corporations and Government departments in that country that are involved in this. It also gives the Number of the CD"S that further break down each company, there contacts, revenue they produce and what amount are embezzled and transferred to this organization. There must be thousands of people involved in this. Now everything I have looked at has no activity after June seventeenth 2008. Now that date matches with the last meeting they had here."

"You're thinking he must have been sick and dropped out of the Organization. But if that was true, why would he still have control of the bank accounts."

"You're going to love this. I am thinking that he like the rest of them was a thief. Now think of this, these people are embezzling over a trillion dollars a year from there countries and corporations and our Mr. Christenson was the head of all this. I am thinking the accounts I have found are his share plus I believe he was stealing from them. That would mean that no one but you and I know of the accounts."

"So now you're telling me you have not only hundreds of millions of dollars but hundreds of billions of them."

"I think so, but first I need to check the accounts and make sure the money is still there. That part might be difficult because I don't want them to be able to trace the inquiry to me."

"Can you do that even thou banks are secure sights?"

"Nothing is really secure. There are a number of ways I can do it. Now tonight after we are home from dinner remind me to tell you a story about the boxes of computer stuff that I put in the basement."

"There are a lot of things I would like you to tell me after dinner. We should have this conversation in the Jacuzzi with a bottle of Champaign."

They had all decided on the Olive Garden restaurant. The food was excellent and the boys were in a funny mood and had everyone laughing. They also told all the girls they should make a list of the things they wanted for sure so they didn't miss anything at the store. Sue said "Us girls do know how to shop."

The boys looked at each other then started laughing then they all started laughing again. It was a fun time. Jim got the bill and over tipped all the people that had waited on them.

On the drive back to the house Sue wanted to make sure Jim hadn't forgot the agenda for the evening. Once the Champaign was open and they were in the Jacuzzi and had exchanged the proper amount of kisses Jim told her about Larry and the computer and its accessories and what he with the help of David did. Sue sat there for a few seconds then said "The government and the company don't even know it exists?"

"If they did I wouldn't want any connection to it. But the cool part of this is it can go anywhere and bypass any security without a problem and will leave no trace that I was ever there. It has other very secret functions it will perform that nothing on earth will do. My main concern is that it is all there and that it is working. I will find that out while you kids are shopping."

They both started laughing about the boys telling them to make a list. The Champaign and Jacuzzi wasn't wasted on either of them. They had a beautiful night.

Tuesday Morning April 06/ 2010 Tucson, Arizona

Jim and Sue were up early and went for a good ten mile run. Then it was the shower before dressing for the day. There was still nothing to eat so it was off to breakfast. While they were eating Sue told Jim she had an early class both Wednesday and Thursday mornings and wondered if he would take her parents out to breakfast Thursday. Jim said "It will be fun, I will take them to the Congress Street Hotel Café; they will love it."

"Just don't take them to the Barrio; this trip will be hard enough on my Dad. I don't think he ever considered I would give up my independence to get married. He still thinks of me as a high school student."

"I can understand that. I probably would have hired a privet detective to check me out."

They were both laughing and Sue said "He may have. I wonder what they found on you."

"I am the kind of guy a girl would take home to meet her mother or a guy would let go out with his sister."

Sue was laughing and said "Finish your breakfast then let's go home and see the other kids."

At the house Jim had for her a set of keys and remote for the SUV plus a set of keys for the house. "I will be working in the basement and will have the library locked. Also here is five thousand to cover everything at the store and the rest you can keep on you. I will leave my phone up in the library so I can hear it."

"It's still strange to talk about money like this. Also is there anything special you want from the store?"

"I am good, but thank you for asking. Now give me a kiss and go have fun with the other kids."

Jim locked himself in the library, opened the basement then went to work checking out the system he had gotten from Larry. Jim was thinking of Larry and hoping he was doing ok. Larry was a little wild but all in all a good guy.

The computer and all its systems were complete and operating. Jim had checked each piece and there were no GPS or any other identifying transmitters. He hooked it up to the existing computer then started to check the bank accounts he had located. One by one they checked out and the money was still in all of them. Jim has an existing off shore account that has a little over two hundred thousand in it. So he got his account Number then transferred twenty two million from one of the accounts to his Numbered account then had it transfer twelve million to the account of his investment company in Tucson. By the time he had checked all the accounts he had found almost seven hundred billion dollars. He also knew that was only part of the wealth; there was also all the bearer bonds and he had no idea what they were worth.

About two o'clock Jim went to the pool room and fixed himself a drink. Sue heard him and came in from the kitchen kissed him and asked if he would fix her one. Jim did then told her what he had found and that he had moved some of it into his accounts.

"The thought of you moving that amount of money into your accounts is just staggering. What are you going to do with it all?"

He started laughing and said "I was hoping you would help me spend it."

"You're starting to scare me again. Won't the government come after you?"

"Bill our accountant will show it as income and I will pay quarterly taxes on it. The government will be happy to have the income. That way when we spend it, or give it away it won't bring us any unwanted attention. So tell me how shopping went."

Sue started laughing and said "I can cook you dinner and breakfast, but I have to tell you it was a great shopping trip. The boys had the girls and me laughing so hard we could hardly talk. The two of them should have there own cooking and shopping show on television. They were showing us how to check the sell by dates, how to select the proper brands, sizes and how to read all the nutritional information on each product. I am sure they both are gourmet cooks based on what they were buying. I have to say I am having a great day and am so excited about my parents coming out tomorrow. I need you to kiss me, hold me and tell me this is all real."

Jim did hold her and kiss her then said "I am the one who has to worry that you're not just a dream. I have never been so happy in my life and it has nothing to do with the money or this place; it's all about you."

"Come into the kitchen and I will fix us something light to hold us over till dinner. Otherwise I will tear your clothes off right here in the pool room."

"I will go with you but the alternative sounds pretty good."

The kitchen was fun and Sue fixed them a nice salad witch they enjoyed as they talked about her parents coming in and what they would do. In the end they decided to just play it by ear and make it fun.

Jim found out Sue did know how to cook. Lunch was light but very good. They sat with there coffee and talked for a while then Jim helped Sue with the clean up and dishes. Sue was going to make sure everything was ready for her Mom and Dad while Jim went back to his computers.

Wednesday Morning April 07/ 2010 Tucson, Arizona

Jim and Sue started the day with a run. She was excited about seeing her family. Jim suggested they go out for breakfast after they showered and dressed. "You have class this morning and your parents will be here around eleven."

Sue kissed him and said "I am so happy and this should be a fun day. My parents are going to love you."

Sue was off to school and Jim was thinking he wanted to return to the computers. Yesterday in the afternoon he had found some references to Libya and directly to Kaddafi and his son's. It led him to a Number of different restricted sights in Libya. He hadn't had time to go into any of them. He knew they would have to wait till after Sue's Parents had gone back home.

By ten fifteen Sue was home and excited. Jim told her he had talked with Jerry at the gate and he would call as soon as they left the gate. He kissed Sue and assured her everything was ready including the coffee it was ready to turn on.

It was a little after eleven when the call came in. Jim turned on the coffee as they went to the front porch and waited. It was only a minute till the white limousine came over the rise. Sue took a deep breath then kissed Jim quickly as the car was coming up to the house.

As the car came around the drive and came to a stop Jim and Sue left the porch and walked down the brick paved walk to greet Sue's parents.

The driver opened the door and the first one out was Sue's Mother, she looked to be in her fifties about five two, thin and very attractive. Her hair and makeup were well done and she appeared accustomed to dressing well.

There were hugs and kisses going on as her Father got out of the car. He looked to be six feet tall, a hundred and eighty to ninety pounds and in his late fifties with a much receded hair line. With a few more kisses and hugs Sue introduced Jim. The driver had there luggage out. So Jim thanked him, then they all took the luggage into the house.

Sue's parents like everyone else were in awe of the house but more then anything happy to see her. Sue showed them where the rest rooms were if they wanted to freshen up. Then they all went to the pool room. Jim offered them coffee or wine if they preferred. They all had coffee then sat and talked. After a bit sue offered to give them a tour of the house. Jim stayed in the pool room he figured it would give them an opportunity to talk with Sue alone.

When Sue and her parents returned they were all laughing. Sue's Mother Helen said "I have never seen anything like your house, this is beautiful."

Her Father Mike said "Sue told us you only recently perched it and all the fun the two of have had putting it together."

"To tell you the truth, moving from a town house to this place was quite a culture shock. The price on this was too good to pass up and I am sure with Sue's help we can put it to good use. Now I am sure the two of you have a lot of questions about me the same as I would, so feel free to ask anything you want. I should stare with the fact that I am madly in love with your daughter and will do every thing in my power to take care of her and make us a happy and fulfilling life."

"I think this is where I should tell the two of you that I am also in love with Jim and want to spend the rest of my life loving him."

Sue's Mother gave them both a hug and kiss then said "I still have a lot of questions but I can see in both your eyes and faces that you do both love each other. That was my big concern."

They spent the afternoon talking and getting to know each other. Sue's Father did have a lot of questions and was kind of shocked at some of the answers. Sue suggested they all go to dinner at the resort where she had worked and met Jim. Jim was laughing as he called for reservations. Helen wanted to know what was so funny so Sue told them the story of how she and Jim met. By the end of the story they were all laughing and Sue's parents had a better idea how the house was part of it all.

They took her parents and there luggage over to the guest house witch was ready for them including fresh flowers, refreshments and snacks.

Dinner at the La Poloma was Fun and Sue for sure was the star. Dinner as always was great and everyone seamed to have good time. Sue was explaining that her friend Kay and Jan had moved into one of the other guest houses and there were also two young men that worked for the estate and were also friends of all of them living in the third house.

On the way back to the house Sue suggested that she put some wine and glasses in a basket, and then they all drive up to the covered patio at the base of the cliffs and watch the sunset and the city lights come on. Her mother loved the idea so it was now a plan. While her parents stopped at the guest house Sue got the wine and Jim put on five CD's and set it so the music would be on up at the patio.

The sunset and city lights weren't wasted on any of them. Sue and her Mom were talking about the art in not only the house but also the guest house and the huge meeting building. Sue told them that on all of it she had researched it hadn't been seen in public sense the early fifties and was listed as being in a private collection. She told them that they have talked about loaning it out in small lots to the different art museums for exhibits then maybe donating it for permanent display.

Mike asked Jim what they were going to use the large meeting building for. Jim said "With Sue's involvement with all the arts in Tucson and the University there should be no shortage of groups we can make it available to. There is a lot we can support and get involved in. Sue has been doing a lot on her own and I also would like to be part of that."

Sue was telling them that there were great trails on the property for running or walking and that she and Jim ran three to five times a week. Mike said "Your Mother and I also go jogging at least three times a week. We have been doing it for over two years. We both ran in college then a lot after we were first married then with work running kind of went away but were back at it now."

"Did you bring your shoes and gear?"

"No we just brought enough to come out and rescue you."

They were all laughing and Sue gave him a hug and kiss then said "We can get you shoes and any thing else you need in the morning."

It ended up being a nice evening and by nine o'clock Sue's Mom and Dad were all settled in the guest house and Jim was fixing Sue and him a drink as she sat in the Jacuzzi.

Sue kissed him and said "Thank you for a wonderful day."

Thursday Morning April 08 / 2010 Tucson, Arizona

It was five twenty and Jim and Sue were out on a run. Sue said "I would like to invite Kay, Jan, Steve and Frank to have breakfast with my parents and us."

"I think that would be a great idea. Let's just call and ask them all when we get back."

It didn't take long and it was all arranged. Frank was driving Jim's SUV and the girls were riding with him and Steve. Jim called and made reservations with Ventana Canyon Resort. Sue's Mom loved the idea. They had been there for dinner years before but never for breakfast.

As expected from valet parking all the way to the dinning room the resort had made arrangements for the eight of them that were very nice with a great view. Jim was discreetly passing out folded up hundreds to insure that everyone was well taken care of. The extra attention was noticed and Helen asked if Jim was a member. He explained he wasn't and had only recently started exploring some of the fancier places in Tucson. He said "To be honest my favorite place to have breakfast is the Congress Street Hotel Café. That is where I first met Kay a year and a half ago. After ordering breakfast the main conversation was about the café and how they all met each other there. Jan was telling them how at times Sue played the piano at the club there while she sang. The boys were telling them how good Jan was with Sue playing back at the house. They all thought that would be fun for later in the afternoon.

Breakfast came to the table and the conversation slowed down. At one point Sue's Mom was telling Kay how much she liked the dress she was wearing. Kay said "I got this when I went shopping with a sugar daddy."

Sue almost choked then they were all laughing with the exception of Sue's Mom and Dad. Sue's Mom with a smile "Said this sounds like a story Mike and I would love to hear."

Kay and Jan were laughing and said "We would love to tell it to you."

Sue leaned over and gave Jim a little kiss and said "You have to admit it is quite a story."

They finished breakfast and everyone was having fun. Jim took care of the bill and people. As they got to the entrance the cars were being driven up and the doors were opened for them. Helen said "I have to admit I love all of this."

"We want you to have fun. Also this car is available for the two of you if there is any where you want to go by yourselves or to see old friends while you're here."

Mike said "Thank you, we will take you up on that."

When they were all back at the house everyone was going to freshen up then they were all meeting at the big room with the swimming pool. At the bar in that room there is a coffee pot and Sue had it working right away then Kissed Jim and told him how happy she was. There was time for a few more kisses before people started returning. The last ones there were the boys and they had a tray of light pastries they had baked from scratch. The three girls looked at each other then started laughing. Sue and the girls had coffee to everyone and a second pot started. Helen said loudly "Now I want to hear the shopping with a sugar daddy story."

They were all laughing then the three girls were telling the story and hearing it from there prospective was quite different. Sue was laughing so hard she had tears running down her chicks and was holding her sides. By the time it was don it was quite a story; a lot of it Jim didn't know. The boys had opened two nice bottles of wine then Kay started telling the story of Sue's first date with Jim at the café. It was funny and Helen loved all of it. The boys asked Sue and Jan if they were going to play and sing for them. Frank was playing bar tender and bringing around the wine while Sue and Jan were getting ready to play.

It made Jim feel good to see how happy Mike and Helen were to see Sue that happy. About two o'clock Sue's parents were going over to see some friends they hadn't seen since they had moved. Sue told them if they hadn't brought swim suits they should stop and get them for the pool and Jacuzzi. Her Mom told her they would. Jim asked the rest if they wanted to stay and go swimming. The boys were meeting up with some of there friends but the girls wanted to stay so the party went on.

By four o'clock the girls had gone home and it was back to Sue and Jim. They sat around the pool talking and enjoying each other Sue said "I am so glad I skipped my class this morning. Around seven Sue fixed a great salad for dinner. Jim did the clean up then put on some great music. At eight thirty Sue's Mom called and said they were back and had on the swim suits and robes. Sue asked them to come over and join her and Jim.

It ended up being a great day and night.

Friday Morning April 09 / 2010 Tucson, Arizona

Sue woke up Jim very early and said "Well you go running with me? I feel a great need to run hard and fast."

"I will love to go running with you; let's work it out to where we are at the patio by the cliffs so I can hold you while the sun comes up."

Sue gave him a great kiss and in minutes they were out on the trails running hard. It was cool to say the least but great weather to run. In the early morning the night predators are still out and they both love to get a quick look at them. There are always coyotes and some times they get a look at a mountain lion, black bear or bobcats. They did get to watch the sun rise with Jim standing behind Sue with his arms wrapped around her. The run back to the house slowed down to a walk at the end with them holding hands. Just as they got to the house they met Sue's parents as they were just starting out on there run. Jim invited them to stop by the house on the way back and the coffee would be ready. They liked the idea and said they would be there. Jim poured them both a cup then put the rest into a thermal serving pot then started a fresh pot. Sue said "We do have time for some serious kisses."

When her Mom and Dad came back they all sat by the pool with there coffee and talked and some where in the conversation Mike said to Jim "I know you have a great deal of money and you speculate in real estate, But isn't that awfully risky in these times."

Jim smiled then told them the story of how he and David started investing in high school and how they got the first moneys they invested. He told them the whole story except what he and Sue have found. He did tell them he owned outright over forty million in real estate around Tucson and Southern Arizona and had at least twenty million in liquid assets in both banks and bonds. He also told them that they also had more then enough income from the properties that it not only covered there expenses but provided a good income. "I can tell you this is not how I am accustomed to living but it is fun and we think this place can be put to good use."

Sue Gave Jim a small kiss then told them the story of how Jim hired her to come to work for his investment company and why he did it. She also told them about the signing bonus, salary and the two million dollars so she wouldn't feel like she was trapped. She was laughing then went on to tell them about the proposal. Now they were all laughing. Helen while still laughing said "Being money is not a problem why don't the two of you take us to the Café at the Congress Street Hotel for breakfast."

Sue gave her Mom a kiss and said "That will be perfect Kay is working this morning and it will be fun."

"If Kay is working we should invite Jan to go with us."

Sue kissed Jim and said "You are such a smart boy; I will call her right now."

Sue was making her call and her parents went back to there house to get ready. As soon as she was off the phone Jim said "We have plenty of time if you want to help me make the bed before we shower."

Sue with a big smile grabbed his hand and they ran up to the bed room.

It was almost nine when they got to the café; the morning rush was already over and Kay was thrilled to see them. Sue's Mom loved the hotel and café. They have a very diverse menu and everything is prepared with fresh ingredients. They had fun even ordering and Kay helped with explaining the different dishes. Breakfast was great and they all had fun even Sue's Dad was more relaxed and was talking with Jim about computers. Mike was impressed that Jim helped design and write programs. He was well aware of the company Jim had worked for and what they built. Jim paid, thanked and tipped Kay then Sue and Jan were going to give Helen and Mike a tour of the lobby, night club and bar of the old hotel.

Back at the house Jan thanked everyone then went to her house to get ready for her afternoon classes. They were sitting by the pool having coffee. Sue's parents were again going to visit some of there old friends for the afternoon so Jim asked if he could take them to dinner at the Westward Look Resort. They all seamed to like the idea and agreed on seven o'clock to be ready.

After Sue's parents were on there way Sue said she had been talking with a friend that also worked with the Arizona Theater Company and they were looking for a place to have a working sessions for two large up coming productions. They were looking for somewhere off sight to avoid all the interruptions. She said "I told them I knew of a place and would check and call if it was available."

"That sounds like a great idea. We can draw a map of how to get here then scan and E mail it too her. Also tell her we will provide Coffee and soft drinks then ask if there any other needs we can help with."

Sue kissed him then said "Let's do that right now."

It took no more then thirty minutes and it was all arranged for the following Wednesday morning at ten o'clock.

After that was done Sue asked if he wanted to work on his computers in the basement. Jim kissed her and said "Let's leave that stuff alone till after your parents go home. We need to enjoy them while we can, remember there leaving Sunday morning."

"Ok then give me some nice kisses and let's go swimming."

By eight o'clock that evening the four of them were setting in the Gold Room of the Westward Look Resort at one of the premier tables with a great view of the lights of Tucson. Helen said "I noticed you always have one of the best tables. Also when we returned this evening room service had been there changed the bedding and put in fresh flowers. This is much nicer then being at a resort."

"Sue and I want you both to feel comfortable and remember the house will be just sitting there so when ever you want to get away and come visit we both would love to have you come out."

"Mom and Dad we both feel that way so whenever the two of you want to get away please let us know."

"It would be nice, both your mother and I like to play golf and go jogging and it is a lot more fun to do it in Tucson in the winter plus we both have old friends we haven't seen in a long time. So the two of may be seeing more of us."

"We will get a membership at the La Poloma Country Club and put the both of you on it so all of there facilities and golf courses are available to you and your guests."

"It's hard to get past this money thing but I have to admit it does sound like fun."

Dinner was fun and both Mike and Helen were relaxed and were talking about all the fun they have been having with all there old friends. Dinner as always was great and everyone was happy with what they had ordered. They had coffee and talked a good half hour after dinner. Sue suggested that after they got home they should change then come over and enjoy the Jacuzzi with them.

Back at the house Mike and Helen went to there house to change. Jim said to Sue "I would like to get two of the ten pound bars of gold and one of the fancy necklaces out of the basement and you can give them to your Mom and Dad. We can tell them we have been playing Indiana Jones and have found some treasure and wanted them to have some of it. We also should ask them to keep it private where it came from."

Sue was laughing and said "I love it; they will go nuts. Let's hurry before they come back."

They were both laughing as they went through the jewelry. They found a great necklace that was made up of large Sapphires and diamonds. Sue said "This is the one for Mom."

They quickly changed and Jim opened a bottle of Champaign and got four plastic glasses then they waited for Sue's Mom and Dad. Sue was giving Jim kisses and telling him how much fun she was having. Soon Sue's parents were there and they all went out to the Jacuzzi with the Champaign. Jim poured them all a glass then said "There is something else Sue and I have been doing that we would like to share some of it with the two of you. I can't tell you all of it right now and would ask that we keep what we are doing private. I will let Sue explain some of it to you."

Sue was laughing and said "This is so exciting and fun; Jim with some of my help have been playing Indiana Jones and have found very old treasure. We both would like to give you both some of it so you can enjoy the excitement with us."

Sue got out and went over to the table where the towels were stacked and took the bars of gold and the necklace out from under the pile and brought them back to the Jacuzzi then gave them each a bar of the gold as she got back in. Mike said "My God; are they real gold?"

"Yes they are. This is only a small part of what is there and I am sure you can understand why we need to keep this privet at this point. Sue has something we thought Helen would like."

Sue was holding the necklace under the water then brought it out and handed it to her Mom. Helen looked shocked then said "I have never seen anything in my life like this. It must be worth a fortune."

Sue said "Let me help you put it on. It's like Jim says there only value to us is to see them make the two of you happy."

Mike said "This is crazy; how much treasure are you talking about?"

Jim said "I really don't know all of it yet and don't want to say how much we have already found. I will say that it is a lot and most of it will be given away to where it can be put to good use. We just wanted the two of you to enjoy some of the excitement that goes with treasure hunting."

Helen started laughing and said "I would like some more Champaign. This has been the strangest week I can ever remember. Just the thought of treasure hunting gets me excited."

Sue hugged and kissed her Mom and said "It is as exciting as you can imagine; some day we will show you things that are unbelievable."

Jim said "I could have just as easily given you fifty pound ingots of the gold. The ten pound bars are easier to handle. This information should make it easier to take money out of consideration when you are planning what you want to do."

"Like Helen said this has been quite a week but the only important part to us is that Sue has found the man she wants to marry and it appears that both of you love each other. So for me I can tell you I am quite happy. The house and treasure hunting are both exciting but not as important as the two of you."

"Thank you. Both Sue and I wanted the two of you to know all about us; even the part that we would like to keep private at this time."

Between the four of them they finished half of the second bottle of Champaign before they called it a night.

Sunday Morning April 11 / 2010 Tucson, Arizona

Sunday started with a run then breakfast with Sue's parents. The limousine was picking them up at ten o'clock. Mike and Helen as well as Sue and Jim were glad they had come out. The four of them had a chance to get acquainted and they all had fun. The goodbyes were said then as quickly as they had arrived the Limousine was going back over the hill and out of sight. Sue put her arms around Jim's neck and gave him a great kiss then said "Thank you I had a great time. I know it's early, but we should get a bottle of Champaign then go to the Jacuzzi."

"I think that's a great idea, then later this afternoon if you like let's go back to the computers in the basement."

Tuesday Morning April 13 / 2010 Tucson, Arizona

Jim and Sue were up early. Jim had spent most of Monday working on his computers going over the CD's they had found in the basement. Sue had set it up with her friend Betty to use the meeting building Wednesday. They were expecting twenty two people from the Arizona Theater Company. She had made up a map, scanned and E-mailed it and also asked the Boys to set up the room and refreshments for them.

Sue had fixed them something to eat then she got everything ready for school. She had three classes that day and a meeting. Jim did get a Number of kisses before she left for the university. He cleaned up the kitchen then went into the library locking the doors behind him.

Jim went to work on the computers leaving his phone in the library. It was after four when Sue called and told Jim she was home and wanted some kisses. Jim came right out and fulfilled her wishes. He locked the library and they went to the pool room to get a drink and talk of there day. Sue was exhausted but said she had a fun day. Some of her friends had noticed her ring. They decided to sit in the Jacuzzi and enjoy there drinks and talk. It came to the point when Sue asked Jim about his day. He explained he had spent all of it on the computer going through the CD's and most of it was about the Middle East and the enormous wealth and fortunes of the rulers who are plundering there countries. "I believe they are the real weapons of mass destruction in the area. Along with there families, businessmen around the world and many other governments they are a house of cards that is already falling apart."

"You're talking about Tunisia and Egypt?"

"They are for sure among them, but I believe the entire region of the Arab world are feeling the heat and afraid of the revolution that is coming."

"Well you have had quite a day, if you don't have plans for the evening we could get something light to eat then go down to the Arizona Theater Company. They are rehearsing a play and they would like to meet you."

"That sounds like fun. There is a nice bar and grill very close to the theater. It very casual and there food is good."

They both dressed in Levis but Sue still looked as if she had just come off of a photo shoot. Jim did make sure he told her how beautiful she looked.

They had a nice dinner then went to the theater. They were working on the rehearsal when Sue and Jim arrived. Right a way they stopped. Sue was excited to introduce Jim as her fiancé. Everyone was very nice and excited to meet him. It was obvious that Sue meant a lot to them and they enjoyed seeing her that happy. They spent over two hours watching the rehearsal and talking with some of Sue's friends. Jim was duly impressed with Sue and her knowledge of the theater. On the drive home Sue was explaining her involvement with the theater at both the university and working theatrical groups. It made a fun evening.

Wednesday Morning April 14 2010 Tucson, Arizona

Jim and Sue were up early and on a short run they only did four miles and were walking hand in hand on the way back. Sue said "The coffee should be ready, let's use the outside shower then set in the Jacuzzi and drink our coffee and you can tell me what you are going to do with all the information you have on all these people and governments."

"Are there going to be any kisses in all of this?"

"I would hope so."

"Then I think it's a great idea."

Once they had there coffee, were in the Jacuzzi and shared the appropriate amount of kisses Jim said "I have also been thinking about that. There is still a lot of information I haven't looked at yet and it will take weeks to look at it all. There is trillions of dollars involved in this but we already have at least hundreds of billions so I sure don't want any of there blood money. I did have the thought of taking all the money each leader and there regimes have hidden away then holding it in an account till that country has set up a stable government then I will return it to them. The same for all the corporations and businessmen with what they have stolen."

Sue was laughing and said "Are you a little upset with these people?"

"The whole world should be; they murder, torture and starve the people in there countries. I personally don't like there countries and for sure there type of governments. But I do believe the monies that have been plundered from there countries should be returned."

"Well this is turning out to be quit a conversation."

"This isn't something we need to rush into. I would though like to look through all the CD's and also see the corporations and people in our country who are part of this. I think they also should lose there money."

"You need to be careful, these are people who are ruthless and would kill you even if they thought you knew about this."

"Before I do anything I will make sure we would be the last people they would look at. Now let's forget them and talk about you and your art."

"The semester is almost over and I will have my Masters Degree in Art. I think we are close to the big conversation about you and me, and what we are going to do."

"This is something I have thought about and I am hoping you have. Let's go to the Congress Street Hotel Café have a nice breakfast and start this conversation. I would like to be part of all of your life."

"Give me a nice kiss, then let's shower and dress."

Once at the Café they were greeted by Kay and got a small table. Coffee and juice came right a way and they both ordered a light breakfast. "I would like to start this conversation by saying I would still like to be involved with buying and selling Real Estate. It's something I enjoy playing with but still won't be tied down to where we can't travel or be involved in other things."

"I would like to be involved in the arts, but like you said I don't want to be tied down with a job. I would like to be involved in all the arts and be able to travel. At some point I would like to have a family."

"I would love to have children with you. I think you would make a wonderful mother and we can have all the children you want. We both missed out on having siblings."

"It's funny I can see you being a dad and helping the children with school work."

"With you're knowledge and interest in art you could open a consulting company and do what you already are doing plus help people and different groups find funding for projects. Also you could arrange art showings that would promote new artist and for a draw you could add some of our collection to each of the displays. You can have all the funds you want at your disposal."

"Well that is something I never thought of. Would you help me in something like that?"

"I will always try and be where you need me and do what I can to help you."

Breakfast came to the table and looked good. While they were eating Sue said "This is a big conversation. I think I have more questions now then when we started."

"I think if we love each other these things will happen in a very natural way. Your consulting business has already started. Your first clients will be at the house later this morning."

"Lets finish our breakfast then you need to take me home and give me a lot of kisses."

When they reached the house it was funny the boys had made up very professional looking signs directing the people that would be coming in to an access road that would bring them to the parking area by the large meeting building. On the path leading to the entrance they had another sign saying **Welcome the Arizona Theater Co**. Sue was laughing and said "This is like a resort."

"Let's go inside and work on those kisses."

After the kisses they walked over to the meeting building and the boys were there and had set up a table with refreshments. It indeed did look as good as any resort would have set up for a group of that size. Both Sue and Jim told them how nice it looked.

Soon some of the people started to arrive and were shocked by how beautiful the place Sue had found them to have there meetings. Soon they had twenty six people there the one who seamed to be in charge was Betty. Sue introduced her to Steve and Frank and said they would handle any need they would have. Steve gave Betty a card with his Number on it and said they would be on the grounds. Sue also told Betty she and Jim would be at the house if they needed anything. Betty almost shocked said to Sue "You live here?"

Sue laughing said "Yes, this is Jim's home. When you are all through if you like I will give you all a quick tour."

"I would love to; I have never seen anything like this place.

"Then please call me when you're done here. Now we will get out of your way."

On the walk back to the house Sue had hold of Jim's hand and said "Thank you, now I can see all of this will just happen as it should."

"In the Morning we will have some business cards made up and talk to Bill Stine our accountant about setting up a business for you."

"You said our accountant?"

"Yes I did, and I also want to know when you are going to marry me. You can have any type of wedding you have dreamed of and we can go any where you want on our honeymoon. I really want you to take that jump from my Fiancée to my Wife."

Sue was laughing and said "Take me to the house, kiss me, open some wine then let's sit by the pool and talk."

As soon as Sue's requests were fulfilled she said "I should start this by saying I also want me to be you're Wife and not just you're Fiancée. As far as the weeding goes I don't want the weeding I dreamed of as a girl. I would like my parents to be here and the people we love. I would ask Kay to be my Made of Honor and I can't think of anywhere better then being married in that huge meeting room."

"I of course would want David as my Best Man and I would like to have a Priest or a Minister to do the ceremony. I don't go to church but I do believe in God."

"I also believe in God but don't go to church."

"There is an old Mexican Priest back on the south side of town who has always been special to me and someone I could talk to. Being neither of us is practicing Catholics I am not sure he will marry us. I will make a point of seeing him if that would be acceptable with you."

"I would love it. Now we need to talk to all the people we would like to be there then figure out a time. With all this money would you like a prenuptial agreement?"

"If I felt that way I never would have asked you to marry me. Well unless you're afraid I will squander your two million."

Sue jumped on him and started kissing him while they were both laughing.

It was after two when Betty called Sue and said they were done and all wanted to see the house. Sue was laughing and told her she would be right over. She kissed Jim and he said "If you like after your tour invite them to the pool room for a glass of wine."

Sue kissed him again smiled and said "I will."

Jim stayed in the pool room and gathered up enough nice wine then set out plastic glasses so he could play bar tender when they came to that room.

After about forty five minutes Sue came in with her friends they were all laughing and having fun. Jim was playing bartender and getting people wine. Sue was happy and laughing about living in a resort. Everyone was very nice and left after forty minutes. The boys came over and said they had cleaned up and closed the meeting room. Jim asked them to stay and have a glass of wine with them.

The day ended with Sue fixing a light dinner then having some Champaign in the Jacuzzi.

Thursday Morning April 15/ 2010 Tucson, Arizona

Sue woke Jim up early and asked him to go running with her. They did a good eight miles and watched the sun come up from the patio by the cliffs.

"Let's go out for breakfast, I know you have class this morning but this afternoon I would like to take the folder with all the pictures you took of the art that is in this house and the large building and go by the Tucson Art Museum and we can talk to them about putting some of them on display when they are having showings of new artist. They could help them have a bigger turnout. After we are done there I would like to open a membership at the La Poloma Country Club for us and your Mom and Dad."

"I like all of that; let's start with the shower and some kisses."

At breakfast Jim said to Sue "How would you like you're name to be after we are married? You can keep your name as it is, incorporate you last name in with mine or just take my last name."

"I want to take your last name. You know I prize my independence but I want to be your wife in name and in every other way. Being with you makes me freer then I have ever been."

"Then that is how it will be. When we get the membership at the Country Club we will put it under Mr. and Mrs. Jim and Sue Cooper."

"I like the sound of that."

Back at the house Sue was getting ready to go to her classes and Jim was going down to the basement and work on his computers. After Sue was on her way he left his cell phone in the library and locked the doors.

It was after two when Sue called and said she was home. He unlocked the doors and got some nice kisses then said "Let's fix a drink, close up the basement then go to the Tucson Art Museum. I made up a notebook with copies of the pictures you took of the paintings and with the notes you took."

"I know the director there, his name is Todd Butler. Let me call him and tell him we are coming over."

By three thirty Sue and Jim were at the Museum and Sue was introducing Jim and Todd. Todd invited them to his office. Jim explained that he and Sue had a fairly large privet collection of art that has not been seen in over fifty years. "I was thinking when the Museum was displaying the works of the newer artist it might be an extra draw to put a few of the older one's on display at the same time. I have a note book that Sue put together showing the pieces we have."

Jim handed Todd the notebook then he and Sue waited while Todd looked through it. The expressions on Todd's face were priceless. Todd finely looked up and said "This is one of the most fantastic collections I have ever seen; its value is in the hundreds of millions. You have this collection in Tucson?"

"Yes it's at our home. If it's something you're interested in we would love to have you and some of your people come out and see it."

Todd looked at Sue and said "I am amazed, plus I noticed the ring. Are the two of you married?"

"As soon as I can pin her down on a date we will be."

"Will congregations Jim and I am very happy for you Sue. This has turned out to be quite a day. I still can't believe the collection you two have and I definitely would love to see it."

Arrangements were made for Todd and six of the other people from the museum to come out to the house on Saturday morning. Sue was having so much fun with everyone she has known them all for years.

On the way home Sue was laughing and said "That was so much fun and they all are really nice people."

"It's too late to go over to La Poloma today, how about tomorrow after breakfast?"

"That would be fun, but right now would you take me home, fix us some drinks then we can sit in the Jacuzzi and talk about kisses."

It turned out to be quite an evening, Sue fixed a light dinner then they went to the upper patio and watched the sunset then the city lights come on.

Friday Morning April 16/ 2010 Tucson, Arizona

Sue was the first one awake and wanted to go for a run. It was a beautiful morning and they did a good eight miles. "Let's use the out side shower then sit in the Jacuzzi. If you would like I will take you to the La Poloma Country Club get us our membership then take you to breakfast."

"I like all of that. What else would you like to do today?"

"If your day is open I would like us to go to some of the art galleries in Tucson and also Tubac. On the way to Tubac we could stop at the San

Xavier Mission. I have always loved to go there for not only the paintings in the chapel but it has always been a place where I can meditate and find a special sense of peace. It's hard to explain but there is something special about the Mission."

"I also go out there a lot and what you said is also true for me. The best that I can explain it is that I feel some kind of magic. I have never told anyone but in the summer time during the monsoon season the sense of magic is almost overwhelming to me; it's very spiritual."

"I do love you. This is something I have never shared with anyone. After and during a monsoon storm the whole desert and especially the Mission are filled with the magic and it is spiritual."

"Kiss me then let's make this a special day."

Before they left for breakfast Jim took six hundred thousand dollars out of the safe in the basement and told Sue he would like to give five hundred thousand of it to the Mission as an anonymous donation to help with the ongoing restoration. Sue liked the idea.

It was a little after nine when they reached La Poloma and met with a Mr. Howard Welt the manager of the resort. Jim explained he would like a full membership for not only Sue and himself but also Sue's parents even though they would only be visiting part of the year. Jim gave David Ortiz as his reference. The whole thing took almost a half an hour and when it was complete Jim paid for the year's membership in cash. Jim then asked Sue if she would like to eat breakfast.

Howard walked them to the dinning room to introduce them as new members. Right away everyone was saying hello to Sue. When Howard realized who Sue was they were all laughing. Breakfast was special and fun, a lot of Sue's friends stopped by to say hello.

After they finished breakfast and were drinking there coffee Sue leaned over and gave Jim a small kiss then said "Would you take me to the Mission first then we can look at the galleries."

"I would love to take you to the Mission. Let me take care of this then we will be on our way."

The ride to the Mission was fun to say the least. Jim had the five hundred thousand in the second of the small briefcases. They first went to the chapel witch still overwhelms you with the beauty of the paintings the Indians did hundreds of years ago. After a good half hour they went to the office and Jim asked to see Father Duarte. The young lady asked if they would wait a minute and she would try and get him. It was only a matter of minutes when an older Hispanic Priest with white hair and a full white beard came out. He immediately recognized Jim and came over to say hello. Jim introduced Sue and told the Priest they were engaged and would soon be married. After a few minutes Jim asked Father Duarte if he would take a walk with them. While they were walking Jim explained he had a donation for the mission but he would like to keep it anonymous. "Well Jim unless you tell me who it is from it will be anonymous; so I guess it's not a problem."

Jim handed the priest the briefcase and said "I have something else we would like to talk to you about and it has nothing to do with this. Sue and I have talked about it and would like to ask you to perform our wedding. Now neither Sue nor I are practicing Catholics but we both believe in God. Is this at least something you would think about?"

"I don't need to think about it; I would be happy to marry the two of you. I have known you sense you were a boy and know you have a relationship with God. Now it is easy to see the love the two of you have for each other. Now Sue, I have seen you at the mission many times over the last five years and have seen the effect it has had on you. Remember nothing happens in God's world by mistake. When you two have a date set let me know and I will make arrangements to be there. Now go in peace."

Sue didn't say a word till they were outside, then she said "You need to hold me. That was one of the strangest things I have felt and I do mean felt. There has always been something spiritual here, but with you, me and the priest there I felt the presence of God being there with us."

"It's not just you, The Mission has always been special to me and I have felt his presence here from the time I was a boy. Hundreds of thousands of people from around the world come through here each year and only a few experiences the magic. You and I are very lucky. I personally believe one needs to have an open hart to feel it."

"Did you notice Father Duarte wasn't surprised to see me here with you. I have never met him before and don't even remember seeing him when I was here. Yet he acted like he expected us to be together."

Jim kissed her and said "God does work in mysterious ways."

They drove on to the town of Tubac. It's a small artist community in the middle of very expensive homes and a beautiful Country Club. Jim asked if Sue would like to have a drink at the Country Club before they started to look at the galleries. Sue said "I think that would be a good idea."

The country Club was Very nice and the bar overlooked part of the gulf course. While they were enjoying there drink Jim said "Unless there are pieces of the art that is in the house that you want to keep, I was thinking it would be nice if we found art we both liked and then slowly replaced what is there. I know what is there is very valuable but I would like the house to reflect us and not be a museum."

"I like the idea, there are so many great new artists out there and I also would like the house to be our home and part of us. Now give me a kiss and let's start making the rounds."

They spent till four o'clock going through galleries and only stopped because they were getting ready to close.

They spent the evening at home with Sue showing Jim how to cook they had a fun time and a good meal. "After we clean up would you like to invite the other children to come over for some wine and the Jacuzzi?"

"That would be fun; let me call them and see what they are doing and invite them."

They all thought it would be fun Steve and Frank were going out but not till later that night. The wine company and Jacuzzi were all great; Sue was talking about the people from the Tucson Art Museum coming out in the morning to see the art and of Jim's idea about putting some of it on display along with other exhibits to help draw a bigger response. Frank and Steve were really excited and said they would oversee the moving and care of the art if Jim liked. Jim and Sue thought that would be nice.

"While we are all together I would like to tell all of you that I have come into some large unexpected profits on a business deal and I was thinking all of you like Sue have student loans plus car payments and other bills. What I would like to do if you will let me; is to pay off any and all of these bills just to take some of the pressure off of you. I also need to say this all comes with no strings we both love all of you so please let us do that."

Kay said" This whole thing is so strange; it's like you have come along and changed all of our lives. Don't get me wrong it is great and I am happier then I have ever been and you have had a part in all of that. I just keep wondering why."

"Like Kay said this also has me overwhelmed."

"As the girls have said this is away over just a job to both Steve and I and it is kind of scary."

"I do understand what you are all feeling; the money thing is hard to get over. Let me first ask the four of you to keep this private. Now with that said I will tell each of you that I have more money then all of us could spend in our life times. So with that knowledge let's take money out of the equation. If there is anything that any of you need please say something to Sue or I. So let's get all the information on any loans or bills you have and we will quietly take care of them."

It was a fun evening and the boys were the first to leave then Jim and the girls were talking about the art and what they were going to do with it.

Saturday Morning April 17/ 2010 Tucson, Arizona

Jim woke Sue with kisses and said "Let's go running then watch the sunrise from the upper patio."

"I love the idea but want some more of those kisses first."

It was the start to a great morning Sue fixed them a nice breakfast while they talked about there friends from the art museum that were coming around nine o'clock Steve was going to open the gate at eight thirty and leave it open till after they left. Frank had gone to a very nice bakery and picked up some nice small snacks for the guests. Sue had made-up a thirty cup coffee pot and they had invited both the boys and the girls to also join them and the guests. It was a little after nine when the three cars showed up. Jim and Sue went down the walk to welcome them. Like everyone they were shocked with the estate by the time they got to the pool room they were almost speechless.

Sue took over introducing everyone including the Girls and boys. Almost everyone already knew Kay and some knew Jan. Steve and Frank automatically took over being the hosts and getting people coffee and pastries. Everyone had a million questions about the house and the rest of the estate. Jim told them some of the story that he had purchased the estate with all the art with it. Sue and I know the value of the art but would like the house to be our home and not a museum. So we have decided to slowly replace it with art we like. Most of this collection has been out of circulation for over fifty years and we don't want to see it go back into privet collections so eventually we would like to donate it to museums in and around Tucson. When you're ready we can take a tour of the art and Sue can share what she has been able to find out on each piece."

After an hour two of the people went back to the museum to get it ready to open at noon. The tour went on including the large building they called the meeting room. The boys and the girls offered them to look at the art that was in there homes. The boys explained there were six paintings that they had removed from there homes and they were stored in the warehouse. Jim suggested that that six might be a nice group that he could send over to the Museum for them to put on display when they had the opportunity. They all went back to the house and got more coffee. While they were talking one of the women named Cathy told Sue that a mutual friend of theirs named Ken Benton had been killed. They first thought it was a traffic accident but now the State Police believe the accident was staged to cove up a murder.

Sue was visibly shaken and started to cry. Jim was right there wanting to know what was wrong. Cathy told him what had happened and that she and Sue had know him through the University and he was also active in the arts. Sue had regained her composer and told Jim what a nice guy Ken was and that he was a good friend.

Todd and Jim exchanged Numbers and Jim said he would call him and arrange to have the six paintings delivered to the Museum.

After they had left both Sue and Kay thought a drink would be a good idea. Kay also was a friend of Ken and upset about his death. The boys made the drinks while the girls talk about Ken. When Sue met Ken he was in his last year of law school at the University and she was a sophomore. They along with Kay were involved with the performing arts. Even after Ken graduated and passed the bar he was still active in the Arizona Theater Company. Kay said "The last I heard Ken was an Associate working for a large Law firm in Phoenix. His Mom and Dad still live in Tucson."

"Ken was such a nice guy; I feel so sorry for his parents."

Sue turned to Jim and asked "Would you try and find out what happened to Ken; I don't think I can do it."

"I have a lot of sources and will start on it Monday."

The boys said they would handle the gates and make sure everything was locked up. They were meeting with some of there friends and it was Saturday night.

Jan and Kay stayed another forty five minutes then it was back to Jim and Sue. They decide to go for a swim.

They spent most of the afternoon around and in the pool. Sue was telling Jim more about Ken. Jim could tell sue was really feeling bad he suggested they go out for dinner somewhere low keyed. Sue kissed him and said "Thank you, that news took all the wind out of my sales. I have never had any of my friends die let alone murdered; that was quite a shock."

"I can get on the computer right now and find out about the funeral do you know when this happened?"

"Cathy never said and I didn't think to ask."

Jim had his laptop open and was already on line "Here it is Kenneth Benton. I am sorry the funeral was Tuesday morning at Holy Hope Cemetery."

"Let's shower; dress then you can take us out to eat. Then later would you hold me?"

"I love to just hold you."

Monday Morning April 19/ 2010 Tucson, Arizona

It had been a quiet weekend and Sue again wanted to start the day with a good run. The morning was cool and the sun rise wonderful. Jim suggested they have breakfast at the Country Club. Sue smiled and said "I like that."

During breakfast Jim told Sue that when they got home he would call Todd then arrange to have the boys take the six paintings over to the Museum. "Then I will go to our computers in the basement and see what I can find out about Ken's death. Would you like to do this with me?"

"I feel much better today thank you, and yes I would like to help you."

After there return to the house it wasn't long and the arrangements were made for the paintings and he and Sue were in the basement. Jim using the X computers went directly into the State Police files on the accident of Ken Benton. In Arizona the State Police are called The Department of Public Safety; they think it sounds more refined. The accident was reported at nine o'clock in the evening; it was a one car accident the vehicle had hit a concrete station of an over pass going west bound on interstate eight west of Casa Grand Arizona. The report listed his residence as a Phoenix address and his parents as next of kin.

"Let's see if we can find the investigation file on this."

It was only a matter of seconds and he was into the homicide file and started to copy the whole file. While it was printing page after page Sue said "If I wasn't sitting here watching this I wouldn't believe you could do this without them knowing anything about it. This is amazing."

"You young lady are one of very few people in the world that have ever seen this thing work. This is only one of its simpler tasks. I wrote many parts of these programs but I am still amazed to see it work."

Once the file was copied Jim got out of there system then shut everything down, locked up the basement and he and Sue took the copies to the pool room. "Would you like a glass of wine while we read through this stuff?"

"You get comfortable with your files while I pick us a nice bottle of wine and open it."

Jim sat on one of the couches and started to read the file from the start. Sue brought him a glass of wine and a kiss then sat and read each page after him. They were on there second glass of wine when they finished the file. They both sat there for a minute without speaking then Jim said "That wasn't just covering up a murder; that was a professional hit. If it wasn't for the transient under the east bound side of the overpass they may well have gotten away with it. Interstate eight I think is the least traveled interstate in the state. Its not a place you want to have a break down you could sit for hours before someone comes along. After reading this the first thing that popped into my mind was that old movie with Julie Roberts and Denzel Washington; the Pelican Brief. They killed a young lawyer because he saw something that put them in jeopardy."

"You think someone hired people to kill Ken and make it look like an accident?"

"That's what the State Police think; he worked for a Phoenix law firm; let me find the name. Here it is Sims, Brown and Lovitt. Do you want to just follow this story or do you want to get involved?"

"If what you and the police think is true we would be playing with some very dangerous people. I really liked Ken and hate the fact that someone just decided to take his life. I don't know."

"Take you're time and think about it. Remember we already are playing with dangerous people and I have tools that even the police don't."

"Let's have a fun day then you can take me out to the Country Club tonight for dinner; we both need to have some fun and smiles."

"Would you like spend the afternoon looking at some of the art galleries in Tucson?"

"That would make the perfect afternoon; let me freshen up then let's get started."

Tucson has an abundance of Art galleries some of them are cooperatives where many artist will have there studios together and run a common gallery. Jim and Sue had a wonderful afternoon and bought two paintings they both liked. They stopped in a small Café in the middle of the arts district and had a glass of wine. While they were talking they decided to call David and invite him and Becky to have dinner with them. Sue asked David if he would have Becky call her so they could plan what they were wearing. David while laughing said he would.

They took there two prizes home and went swimming then stayed out by the pool till it was time to get ready for dinner. Sue and Becky had talked and decided what they would wear for Dinner. Jim had called and made the reservations. It was still early and Jim asked if Sue would like to go early and have a drink in the bar first. Sue also thought it would be a good idea so they were off.

As they walked in the bar there was David and Becky sitting at a table. They were all laughing as they joined them. The waitress was bringing David's drinks and she took Jim's and Sue's order. While they were talking Jim told David that he and Sue had taken out a membership at the Country Club and used David as a reference. David was pleased and they talked of many things. As the time for dinner came close the girls went to the rest room.

As soon as they had left the table Jim handed David a piece of paper and said "That is the name and E mail address of an off shore bank the next set of Numbers is the account number then the next set is the pass word. I recently deposited twenty million dollars in it for you. You can slowly work some of it into your investments here with Mike's help. This is something I would like to stay between you, Sue and myself. If and when you marry Becky telling here is up to you.

"You say twenty million so easily I can't believe it."

"David I could have just as easily made it a hundred million. This is better then the lottery; with this you need to figure out how to show it as income to pay taxes on it."

"This is already one hell of a dinner my friend."

The young ladies returned then it was time to go to the dinning room. They were expecting them and very happy to see them; will mostly Sue. The service was over the top and the food great. The best part they all seamed to have a fun evening.

After they were home and getting ready for bed Sue said "Back to the conversation about Ken's murder; I would like to get involved. I can't just turn my back on someone having a friend killed. It would bother me forever."

Let's start the morning with a run then I will start finding out everything I can about Ken and the law firm he worked for.

Tuesday Morning April 20/ 2010 Tucson, Arizona

Jim and Sue were up early and on a good run. They showered and dressed then Sue fixed them a nice light breakfast. Jim opened the basement and started up the computers while Sue cleaned up after them. When Sue came into the library she brought cups and a thermos filled with coffee Jim locked the library doors they both left the phones in the library when they went to the basement. Jim first went into the law firm Sims, Brown and Lovitt they showed seven partners and twenty eight Associates including the late Ken Benton. Jim broke into there billing files to see what cases Ken had been working on. Jim printed the list of everything Ken had billed time on in the last two months. There were a lot of hours billed but most of them were consternated on only three separate cases. Jim stopped had some of his coffee and said to Sue "I think ken saw something he shouldn't; I doubt that it was something on the cases he was assigned to."

"I don't know how you would think of that, but it makes sense."

"Let's look at all the billing it should tell us the big cases the firm is working."

After an hour and twenty minutes and a second cup of coffee Jim said "There is only one really big one at least based on the hours billed and they are representing a corporation called Clifton Financial. I have never heard the name but they must be big to afford all the hours they are billing them. Let's look at the litigation and see what this is all about."

"While you're doing that I will open a nice bottle of wine and bring it and a couple of glasses down."

"If I can get a kiss first it sounds like a good idea."

After another hour Jim said "This Clifton Financial is in litigation with both the State of Arizona and the Federal Government and a lot of there regulatory agencies. There are at least three off shout smaller cases. This is all connected to the Palo Verde Nuclear generating Plant here in Arizona.

Let me have the X computer cross check and see if Ken billed any hours on any of these cases."

Sue had her chair right next to Jim and was watching everything. When Jim started the program the screen was a blur as the computer went through every file and cross checked every tenth of an hour Ken had billed in the last two month. When it was all done Ken had billed twenty two hours on two of the smaller cases.

"Well that's a starting place. I will need to go through the main case and see if I can find out what this is all about and who the big players are. That will be for another time; let's shut this all down and take that wine to the pool.

"I like that idea; I will take all of this up."

"It was a beautiful day and a lot of sunshine they swam for a while then laid in the sun and talked about what they had found on the computer. Jim said "I wonder if the police searched where Ken was living and weather they found his cell phone or his lap tops. There should have both a personal and a corporate computer. I also need to find out his cell phone Number and pull a record of all his calls for the last two months. I bet the police have already done that."

"It still hard to believe you can go into secure files like that and have no one know you were there."

"If the government ever found out I have this I would be in prison for life. Well more likely they would have me killed. They couldn't have the knowledge that this actually exist come out in open court."

"You do like to play with dangerous people, and I can tell that David is the same. I think that is part of what I saw in you that was kind of scary to me in the beginning. It was also part of the attraction."

Jim was laughing and said "One of the exciting things I first saw in you was a wild edge and that you were someone that was looking for a life in the faster lane. You were very reserved but your eyes gave it away."

"So you think I am the wild girl that will fulfill all you little boy fantasies."

"You my love have already surpassed all my fantasies both little boy and big boy ones. You are just as hooked on this bad boy stuff as David and I are. The thought of looking in places that we are not allowed to look turns you on."

"There are other things that turn me on if you have the time."

It was almost an hour and a half and they were back at the pool with there wine and smiles. "You have classes in the morning so how is your afternoon?"

"It's open if you have any suggestions."

"One of the more exciting things I have done is gliding I did a lot of it years ago but only twice in the last two years. I am a certified pilot and if I can arrange it; would you like to go gliding tomorrow afternoon?"

Sue was laughing and said "I have seen shows about gliding on PBS and it looks scary. Yes I would love to go gliding with you." With that Sue was all over him with kisses while laughing.

After a quick phone call they were set to go gliding at two the next afternoon. Sue said "I am so excited we need to do something tonight and I have no ideas of what."

"Let's see what Kay and Jan are doing and if they would like to go out to a fun dinner then to a club; just something to have fun."

"I love the idea I will call them right now."

It turned out to be a wonderful night and everyone had a great time Jim did remind them to get together all there outstanding bills and loans so Bill could have them all taken care of. By the time they got home all the girls wanted some Champaign in the Jacuzzi.

It wasn't long and they had all changed and were sitting in the Jacuzzi with Champaign and great music playing then Sue was telling the girls about them going gliding tomorrow. She was so pumped up and excited it made Jim happy just watching her talk about it.

As the night was finishing Jim got two more bottles of Champaign, one was for the girls to take home and a bottle for him and Sue to take upstairs.

Wednesday Morning April 21/ 2010 Tucson, Arizona

Jim and Sue were up early and on a run the sky was getting light in the East and before they reached the upper patio they got to see a mountain lion. He was beautiful and looked as if he had just come from a groomer. He stopped on top of a ridge no more then a hundred feet from them; it was like he wanted to show them just how magnificent he was. There were some clouds over the Rincon Mountains that just enhanced the sunrise. It was a great run.

"Let's go out for breakfast then we can skip lunch before we go flying."

"I would like to go to the Congress Street Hotel Café if you don't mind."

"You know I love to eat breakfast there."

"Well we still have time for a nice shower."

It was a great shower then they were off to the café. "What time do you think you will be home from school?"

"I am hoping twelve thirty. Also after Friday I will have completed everything for my Masters. Graduation ceremonies will be Saturday May 22nd. Also Kay and Jan also will be graduating."

"I know a great place to have a party. Are your Mom and Dad coming out?"

"I don't know we haven't talked about it. I would like them to be here."

"Call and tell them that. We can have Bob pick them up. Then while there here we could get married."

"You are such a smart boy. I love the idea and do want to marry you. Let's get to the Café I am so excited and hungry; I need to eat."

Kay was working and breakfast was fun. Sue was telling Kay they needed to talk about the wedding.

Sue was off to class and Jim went back to the basement and his computers.

By twelve o'clock Jim had everything closed up and was waiting on Sue to come home.

When she arrived she was still excited Jim told her they had time for a drink if she liked. Sue thought that was a good idea. Jim was explaining gliding and the thermals of air coming up from the desert floor. Sue had seen shows briefly explaining it but didn't know how you would know where to look for them. They enjoyed there drink and talking about there trip then it was time to go. The drive out there took almost forty minutes. They met the pilot of the plane that would take them up. He was also the owner of the glider. When they walked out to the glider it was sitting behind the plane already tethered to it. The glider was all white and very sleek looking. The wings were long, and it was tipped to one side. Sue loved the look of it. She was scared but ready to go. Once they were in and secured the plane was already running. As the plane started towing it someone ran along side to help keep the wings from hitting the ground but quickly they were moving fast enough that Jim could control keeping it balanced then suddenly they were in the air and flying. Once they were high enough Jim pulled the release and they were souring on there own.

The first thing Sue noticed was the silence. They were having a ball and Jim was showing her how to fly it. The thermals were great and they achieved great heights that allowed them to play with great turns and a lot of speed. After an hour of flying he asked Sue if after Friday she could take some time off. She said "Of course what do you have in mind?"

"Is your passport up to date?"

"Again I will say yes."

"If I can arrange it would you like to spend a week in Cuba?"

"Are you kidding; Cuba!"

"I have some really good friends there and they will arrange a visa for us. We can stay in the fancy hotels and they have great beaches and shopping."

"You have to be the wildest man I could ever have met. I would love to go to Cuba with you. You sure know how to make a wonderful day."

After another half hour they returned to the air strip with no problem. Once they were out of the glider Sue was all over Jim with kisses. In the car Sue said "Let's go to the Country Club and you can buy us a drink."

On the drive to the Country Club Sue had a hundred questions about Cuba and Jim's friends there; they were both laughing. At the Country Club Bar they got a nice table and ordered drinks. "What made you think of Cuba of all places?"

"Like I said I have friends there and have wanted to go there for years then this afternoon watching you living on the edge I knew you would love going to Cuba. It is legal but the government doesn't want people to support there economy. It's been sixty some years sense Castro and his Commonest government took over and they are better off then when the American puppet government and capitalist were plundering there country. It is a beautiful place and they have some great beaches."

They sat with there drinks talked and laughed and after a while Jim said lets keep this day going by asking the girls and boys out to dinner here then we can go to the club or some were."

"I love it; let me call them right now."

The boys already had dates and were going to a party. The girls loved the idea and the three of them were talking about what they would wear. Before they left Jim had made the arrangements for dinner at eight o'clock.

Back at the house Sue thought some Champaign and the pool sounded wonderful. They swam played and talked till it was time to get ready. When Kay and Jan came over Jim asked if they would like to start and stay with

Champaign for the night. The girls with big smiles thought that would be nice. They were talking about the wedding and that Sue and Jim wanted it to be after graduation. "Sue told me that the two of you will also be graduating. I would like it if the two of you would let us take care of any air fair, rental cars and lodging for any of your family or friends you want to be there. Again I know this money thing is hard to get past, but let's."

Jan said "I really would like my Mom to be here, so thank you and I will talk to her and let you know."

Kay said "My parents are divorced and my Mom is coming from California that would help with the finances, so again thank you."

"Good now that is settled after dinner would you ladies like to go to the club at the Congress Street Hotel, or do any of you have another idea?"

None of them knew who was playing that night but decided they all wanted to go then if they didn't like it they would go somewhere else.

At the Country Club the three girls were getting a lot of attention and loving every minute of it. After they were seated Jim ordered them Champaign. After it was poured Sue was telling the girls about Jim arranging a trip for them to go to Cuba for a week. Kay and Jan were both excited and wanted to know all about Cuba and how they thought about going there. The three of them were having a lot of fun talking of Cuba and what it would be like. They finely got dinner ordered and a second bottle of Champaign. After the waiter left the table Jim asked if Kay and Jan had passports and if they were up to date. Sue started laughing then gave him a big kiss. Kay was laughing and said "If you're a girl in college and want to dream, you make sure you have an up to date passport."

Jan looked shocked then said to Sue "Is he kidding?"

"You both will have finished your finals so there is no reason you can't go."

Kay kissed Jan and said "I would love to be in Cuba with you and we would be crazy to pass this up."

They were all laughing and having a better time then anyone else in the restaurant; dinner was very good and the service as always was over the top. Jim made sure he over tipped everyone.

On the way to the club Jim asked if they would all get there passports to him in the morning and he would call his friends and have them arrange the visas and there hotel for Monday, then he would call Bob and arrange for him to fly them out Monday morning. Kay asked "Are you talking about a private plane to fly to Cuba?"

"Bob has a late model Gulfstream 450 jet that seats twelve; it really won't be a long flight. Also don't pack much they have great shopping in Cuba."

Sue was laughing and Jan said "This is all like something out of a novel; people don't just say let's fly to Cuba on a Wednesday evening."

"Jan this is just as much fun for me. I spent most of my life working and not having much fun. Now sense I have met Sue all of that has changed; like you and Kay I have someone to share it with. Let's have fun tonight then tomorrow I will try and put this all together."

The club was busy but between the girls there was no problem finding a table to join. Jim ordered Champaign for them and around for the table. They had a Jazz group playing and they were good. After a couple of songs a member of the group came over to the table and asked Jan and Sue to join them for a few songs. There were a lot of people clapping as the girls went up.

They ended up doing four Numbers and the whole group was having fun. The audience was eating it up and gave them a standing ovation as they came back to the table. Jim switched to coffee and they partied till almost midnight. On the way back to the house they all decided to get there swim suits and meet at the Jacuzzi and keep the party going.

Thursday Morning April 22/ 2010 Tucson, Arizona

It was almost nine when Jim and Sue got up and to the shower. Sue made up Coffee and fixed a light breakfast with just fruit and melon while Jim made up the bed. After they ate Jim got his book with all his contact information in it and called the first of his friends in Cuba, a Chris Gutierrez. After some catching up Jim told him that he, his Fiancée and two other friends wanted to fly to Cuba on Monday on a private Jet and stay for a week at one of the high end Hotels on the beach where there was good shopping, also money was not a factor. Jim asked if he and there other friend Don Farrin could arrange visas on such short notice?"

"You're still a crazy guy and I love the part where you have a fiancée. I will call Don and put this together then call you back. I will need all the passport information on you and your guests if you can get that ready in the meantime. Don and I will be thrilled to see you."

"Now let me call Bob and see if we can arrange this for Monday morning."

"I can't believe you're really putting this together this quick. I will go over to the girl's and get there passports while you call Bob."

It took a couple of hours to get it all done Jim gave Chris all the information and he lined up two suits next to each other at one of the best hotels on a beach with great shopping all around it. Jim even lined up a Limousine to pick them up early Monday morning and take them to the private air field in Tucson.

When it was all done Sue said "Let's go for a good run I feel the need."

"That's a great idea. After we get back let's hit the outside shower then the pool with a bottle of wine."

They did a good eight miles then they swam before having a glass of wine. While they were sitting by the pool Sue suggested that she would fix them a big dinner if Jim liked. Jim kissed her and said "If you don't mind I would really like us to work on the computer in the basement. I have been thinking about you're friend Ken's murder and want to look through the investigators notes. For some reason I think there is something in the notes that will give us a lead. Then later I will take you out for some really good Mexican food."

"That would be great I really would like to get who ever had him killed. I will bring down another bottle of wine and some kisses."

Jim with his X computer found the senior investigator handling the case, his name was Bruce Tate. Jim looked through his notes one of the things he had done was to list all the calls sent and received by Ken's cell phone for the last two months before the murder. As Jim went through the Numbers there were two calls to the Phoenix Republic news paper. They were two weeks apart. The officer had contacted the paper but there was no way to find out what department or person he would have been calling. Jim asked Sue to go on the other computer and find out who the top reporters were and there phone Numbers while he was still going through the police files. At the end he could see they were at almost at a dead end.

Sue had come up with a list of reporters but said "If Ken had anything big and wanted to talk to anyone about it there is a team of investigative reporters that have handled the only big break through stories the Republic had in the last three years. There names are Hoyt Segal and Bill Mitchell. I have the papers Number and there extension."

"I need to get a new prepaid cell phone and call them from out of town. Would you like to take a quick ride to the towns of Eloy and Casa Grand? We can buy a Number of phones then call the reporters."

"Now you're starting to sound like a secret agent man. I would love to go with you."

"I know it sounds funny but if were going to play with the people who killed Ken I don't want us to show up; I will also ask you to wear a baseball cap with a white bill. If the stores have surveillance cameras they are always up high and so the bill of the hat will help cover your face and being white it will kind of bleach out what the camera sees. So don't look up."

"Ok Mr. secret agent man, you get what you need and I will use the rest room and get the hats."

It wasn't long and they were on interstate ten headed to Eloy first. It's a good fifty miles each way. Sue found a great classic rock station and they had a fun ride. They bought a total of six prepaid cell phones then in Casa Grand Jim called the Phoenix Republic and used the extension for Bill Mitchell and Hoyt Segal. Bill answered and Jim introduced himself as Jeff Black and said he was a friend that was looking into the murder of Ken Benton who had a connection to them and there paper. He went on to say that Ken was a lawyer who worked for a large firm in Phoenix and the subject he called them on was probably the reason he was killed.

Jim said "I can give you the dates and times of the calls but I am sure he used a fake name. I also believe this concerned something he saw at the firm that put him in jeopardy. Now I need to be up front with the two of you; any information you might have on this will also put the two of you and your paper in the same position. I have access to a lot of information that isn't public knowledge. Why don't you and Hoyt think this over and if you want to be players call me back at this Number. Also if you do want to play call me from a clean cell phone."

Jim closed the phone and asked Sue if she wanted to go home and have a drink. "Would you first drive down interstate eight to where they found Ken's body? I do know that wasn't where he died, but I would like to go there."

"It's not very far and I will be glad to take you."

It was a short drive no more then fifteen minutes. There were marks from where the officers had used spray paint to mark the position of the car. Based on the report Jim had read the witness was a good two hundred and fifty feet away. In his statement he remembered three people that staged the wreck. Two men and one woman they all appeared to be white.

There was a turn around under the overpass so it was only a few minutes and they were on there way back to Tucson and home. Sue with puffy eyes said "What could have been so important that they would have someone killed like that."

"There are only two reasons for murder like this; it's either hate or greed. I believe this one was greed. I think Ken came across something big and was trying to figure out a way to stop it. That's just a guess but I think I am right. I hope the two reporters want to play with us."

They went to a small Mexican restaurant on the south side of town Jim knew a lot of the people that worked there and enjoyed introducing Sue as his Fiancée. Dinner was as always great and they both had fun.

Back at the house Sue was talking with Kay about the morning. Kay was working early then the three of them had there last mandatory classes in the afternoon. Jim suggested they have breakfast at nine at the café and Jan should come with them. The girls all thought that would be a good idea. Plans were set for the morning.

Sue's next idea was the Jacuzzi and they only needed towels and some nice wine. Jim thought it was a good idea and it was.

Friday Morning April 23/ 2010 Tucson, Arizona

Jim and Sue slept in till seven then had a fun shower. Kay was already at work and Jan was going with Sue and Jim to the Café.

They arrived about nine thirty and Kay was happy to see them, Breakfast was fun as always it was slow enough so that Kay could spend some time with them. Most of the conversation was about Cuba and what they were going to pack. Jan was going to stay at the Café then go to the university with Kay when she got off.

On the ride back to the house Jim said "If you decide to do the consulting company and work with the art community you might think of hiring Kay and Jan to work with you. That would give all of you the opportunity of working in your fields and not having to worry about money. The company could also handle the benefits so they would have health insurance and any other things they may need."

"Like you I do love them and think it would be a wonderful thing. Let's wait till were on our trip to talk about it."

Sue was excited about her last classes and was making sure she had everything ready. After Sue was off to the university Jim fixed himself a drink then closed the library and went down to work on his computers.

The first place he went was into the secure system the law firm of Sims, Brown and Lovitt. Any large law firm has great security on there computer systems and this firm had a very complex security system. The X computer had no trouble compromising there system. The first place Jim went was the case of Clifton Financial, the senior partner handling it was Brian Lovitt. Jim read through the files trying to find out what it was all about.

After a good two hours Jim had a good idea what it was all about. The government was claiming that Clifton Financial who represented the major stock holders in the Valley Electric and Power Corporation. Witch operated three electric generating sights in Arizona, one being the Palo Verde Nuclear generating station in central Arizona. Of not only embezzling from Valley Electric but also from the stock holders they represented. Another offshoot part of this was a large Phoenix accounting firm named RC Rankin and Associates. If they were cooking the books they couldn't do it without the accountants.

As Jim was going through Clifton Financial he came across the name of the person in charge. It was one Gregory Booster; a name Jim had seen when he was going through the files that were hidden in the basement. It wasn't related to any thing really big but still big enough to be in there. It could be a coincidence but Jim didn't believe in coincidences.

It was four o'clock so he closed everything down and closed up the basement. When he checked his phones he had missed a call on the phone he had used to call the reporters at the Phoenix Republic. Jim fixed himself a drink then called them back. The phone rang twice then a voice said "This is Hoyt Segal, is this Jeff?"

"It is and I assume by calling me you have decided to play with this story."

"We have talked it over with both our editor and the publisher. If what we write looks too dangerous we have an apartment here at the paper. So tell us what you think this is all about."

"I have only started into this but to start with the reason that the Department of Public Safety has changed this investigation from being an accident to being a murder is that there was a witness who watched three people and a second car stage the wreck. Ken Benton was already dead. The three People were Caucasian; Two men and one woman. The DPS has a list of all the outgoing and incoming calls for the last two months on Ken's cell phone. Two of the calls as I told you were to your paper. Being you and Bill are the papers top reporters I am sure both calls were to the two of you. The firm Ken worked for was Sims, Brown and Lovitt. The biggest case the firm has is Clifton Financial verses the government. This also involves R C Rankin and Associates there Accountants. The one in charge of this case is Brian Lovitt. Now our young Associate Ken Benton was not part of this case but in the last month before his death he billed twenty two hours on a peripheral part of this that was connected to the Accountants."

"Well Mr. Jeff Black how is it you have access to all of this information; are you connected to law enforcement?"

"I am sure you know there is no Jeff black but the only way this will work is for me to stay anonymous. This way when you tell law enforcement your source is anonymous you won't be lying. The two of you might look into this action by the government it could be over a billion dollars and yes I did mean to say Billion. As I come up with something that you can put into print I will call. If you need to talk to me use this Number but I will be out of touch for the next week and a half. Take care."

After he hung up Jim sat back in the chair and had some of his drink and was thinking about the connection this might have to the stuff he had found in the basement. The name Gregory Booster was just hanging there and Jim kind of knew it was the same person.

When Sue came home she was excited about that being the last of her required classes and she had fulfilled all the requirements to receive her master's degree. After the appropriate amount of kisses she joined Jim in having a drink. "Would you like to go to the Country Club for dinner? We could also invite Kay and Jan if they're not already doing something."

"That would be fun, they also have completed all there requirements for graduation. I will call them and see if they would like to go."

The plans were made for the evening including reservations. While he and Sue were talking about her day Sue asked Jim what he had found on his computers. Jim told her about all he had found including the name of Gregory Booster. He also told her he had seen that name in the files that were in the basement. "You're thinking Ken's murder is some how connected to all the stuff you have found in the basement."

"So far it's just a name but I don't believe in coincidences. Also I got a call from Hoyt Segal one of the reporters from the Phoenix Republic news paper. The two of them along with there editor, owner and legal people have decided they want to go ahead with the story when we come up with something they can run with."

"You also had a busy day; let's take our drinks and go to the pool."

The pool turned out to be a great idea they spent the rest of the afternoon there till it was time to get ready for dinner. The girls all looked very pretty in there spring dresses and Jim made sure he told them so.

The Country Club as always was happy to see them and the Girls were getting more then there fair share of attention; they all loved it. Jim suggested they have Champaign and the girls also liked that. The conversation eventually went to what Jan and Kay were going to do after graduation. At a point Sue told them what Jim had suggested she do. She explained the consulting business she was going to start. She said "I was going to wait till we were on our trip to have this conversation but we are at that point now. What I would like to ask the two of you if you would like to work with me in the business. It will be something we can all do and still be involved in the arts. The company will give us all insurance and benefits we need and the pay will be more then enough to live however you want to. The company won't be for making money; actually it will be providing money and assistance to people in the arts that need assistance. This is something we can all think and talk about."

Dinner got ordered then the conversation was mostly about Sue's business and the trip to Cuba. Dinner as always was great and they finished with coffee. Jim told them there was live entertainment in the lounge if they liked. They all decided they would rather go back to the house and Jacuzzi with a bottle of Champaign.

Saturday Morning April 24/ 2010 Tucson, Arizona

Sue and Jim's day started with a good run then a better shower. Breakfast was light then Sue was going to work with Kay and Jan on deciding what they were going to pack for there trip. Jim locked him self in the library and went back to work on his computers.

Sunday Morning April 25/ 2010 Tucson, Arizona

The morning was like Christmas Eve and the three girls were like ten year olds. They were all fixing breakfast and laughing at everything. Jim was just enjoying it all. Breakfast was good and Jim did the dishes refusing all the offers to help; that also made the girls laugh. He did remind them that the Limousine was picking them up at seven in the morning.

Jim had arranged it so the boys would have the gate open early. They were also aware that Jim and Sue along with the girls would be gone for a week. He had left them extra money to handle anything that may come up; they also had his and David's phone Numbers.

The girls asked where they were going in Cuba. "When I was talking to Chris and Don I told them I wanted the best hotel we could get and it had to have great beaches. They picked a great hotel that is on the Cays. They sit on the Northeastern Coast. There are two of them; one is Cayo Coco and Cayo Guillermo. We have two suits at the Melia Cayo Coco. If you like I will pull it up on my laptop and display it on the big screens TV in the pool room."

The girls all loved the idea. In about ten minutes they all had coffee and were sitting in the pool room. Jim had the Hotels web sight up on the screen. They spent almost an hour looking at everything the hotel offered. They also went to a Number of sights that gave them a great deal of information on Cuba. It was almost eleven in the morning when Kay and Jan went back to there house. Jim said to Sue "Let's go to the basement I would like to take forty pounds of the gold coins with us for Chris and Don. I will also take them some cash; Cuba doesn't care how much money we bring in they only care how much we take out.

At four thirty Sue made them dinner using all the perishables she could so she could clean out the refrigerator before they left. It was a slow and fun evening and they both had there suitcases and garment bags sitting by the front door.

Monday Morning April 26/ 2010 Tucson, Arizona

Jim and Sue were up by five forty five and quickly in the shower Jim had shaved while Sue went down and turned on the coffee. The shower was short but fun. Kay and Jan were coming over with there luggage then having bagels and coffee while they all waited for the Limousine. Steve and Frank came over to see them off and to insure them they would look after the estate.

The limousine was on time and the big adventure started. On the way to the airport Sue was telling them of her conversation with her Mother; she had told her about the trip, graduation and that she and Jim wanted them to come out for not only graduation but they also wanted to get married that week. Sue was laughing through the whole story. Her Mom was excited and said they would be there.

When they arrived at the air field Bob and his beautiful Gulf Stream 450 was sitting there waiting for them. The limousine drove out on the tarmac up to the steps of the plane. Jim introduced Kay and Jan to Bob. The luggage was quickly loaded and once inside the girls loved the inside. None of them had ever been on a private Jet and didn't realize how luxurious it was. Bob showed everyone all the facilities and also told them there was a nice selection of soft drinks and wine in the refrigerator. The girls were having fun and were all excited.

The girls were talking about Sue's consulting company and how it would work. Sue explained how she had set it up for the Arizona Theater Company to use the meeting building on Wednesdays for the next four weeks. The boys were handling all the arrangements and that they had a charge account for everything they needed to purchase. Whale they were talking Jim went up to talk with Bob.

After about forty minutes Bob came to the back to use the rest room and get a soft drink. Sue with big eyes asked Bob who was flying the plane. Bob with a big smile said "It's on auto pilot but Jim is watching to make sure nothing goes wrong. I did tell him not to do any fancy moves or barrel roles."

The girls all thought Bob should go back up and fly the plane. When Jim returned Sue said "I am sure both you and Bob enjoyed that."

While laughing he said "The plane flies it's self, I just watch all the gauges incase we crash I can tell Bob what went wrong."

"You think you're real cute. Why don't you get us all a glass of wine because where're all on vacation."

While he was getting them all wine Jim told them they were stopping in Mexico and some one would come aboard and stamp there passports then when they went to Cuba they would only look at them but not stamp them. That way there wouldn't be any big deal with Customs when they returned.

They landed at a fairly large international airport on Cayo Coco Both Chris Gutierrez and Don Farrin were there to meet them along with a small shuttle bus from the Hotel Melia. One of the Cuban customs people came aboard and checked there passports and welcomed them to Cuba.

The luggage got unloaded and they said goodbye to Bob he was picking them up the next Monday morning. On the ride to the hotel Jim was doing all the introductions and was really happy to see his old friends. After they got registered Jim paid for the week and also exchanged two thousand dollars into Cuban money. He then asked Chris and Don to come with them to the suite before they all went and had a drink. The girls all loved the hotel and the suits; they both were like bungalows and had there own private back yards with Jacuzzis.

Once they were all together in the room Jim told Chris and Don he had brought them both a present. Jim opened both his and Sues suitcase and got out two small leather bags the size of men's shaving kits then said "I need to start by telling the two of you I have made an unseemly amount of money and I would like it if the two of you would let me share a small amount of it with you."

With that said he handed each of them one of the leather zipper bags. When they opened them they took out a fist full of hundred dollar bills then a hand full of gold coins. They both looked at Jim then Don said "What the hell are you into?"

Jim laughing said "Nothing but Real Estate, but I have made a lot of money. There is fifty thousand in cash and twenty pounds of gold coins in each case. The two of you know you will always be family to me; so let me do this. Now let's all go have a drink and talk."

The lounge was beautiful and had a great view of the beach. While they were having drinks Don and Chris were telling them about Cuba. They told them the crime rate in Cuba was very low but if they wanted to go into the big cities or out of the tourist areas they would take them. They all had something to eat and a fun afternoon.

After Chris and Don went home Jim and the girls went back to there suits and changed into there swim suits, cover ups and beach shoes; grabbed there towels and headed for the beach. The water was warm and the beach pristine. This resort was an adult-only and very popular with the younger crowd. Most of the guest were European and like the staff mostly spoke English. Jim and the girls all spoke Spanish. Jim spoke it quite fluently along with Russian, Arabic and French. They spent a couple of hours at the beach then decided to check out the shops in the hotel. The afternoon went quickly and they all got clothes that would be fun at the hotel and for just hanging out. The hotel had three great restaurants that went from fine dinning to just nice non formal restaurants. There was also one bar and three night clubs in the complex. They all decided they would just do dinner and call it an early night.

Tuesday Morning April 27/ 2010 Cayo Coco, Cuba

Jim and Sue slept in till eight o'clock Cuban time. There was a three hour difference from Tucson time. There were a lot of kisses and fun; even the shower was fun. Sue called over to the girl's suite and Jan answered and said they were dressed and ready for breakfast.

At the restaurant they were seated outside and it was beautiful. The food was great and they were all hungry. After they ate they sat with there coffee and talked. Kay and Jan were going to walk around the shops and beach and just spend time with each other. Jim made sure they had enough money with them.

Sue said "Let's take our coffee and sit by the pool then would you tell me about you, Don and Chris? I know there is much more then all of you just being friends."

"I definitely do want you to know everything about me, and Don and Chris are a part of who I am." They spent a good two hours sitting by the pool, after an hour they switched to mixed drinks.

Don and Chris were part of the same squad as Jim. In the first years of there deployment to Iraq they each had saved the others life's in combat some of witch was hand to hand. Jim told Sue everything including all the people they each had killed. By the time there two year tour was up they had lost over half of there squad. Don and Chris were done with the Army and weren't going to reenlist or go back to combat duty. They both kept there American citizenship but lived most of the time in Cancun Mexico and Cuba, they have homes in both places together. They have two rather large ships and unofficially supply Cuba with a lot of necessities that help a lot of people. He thinks they each have a family in Cuba but have never said anything about it, so he doesn't ask. The war emotionally damaged both of them. "We have always kept in contact with each other and I hope we always do."

"Thank you for sharing them with me. I have always wondered how people can serve in combat then just come back to the life they had before, I can't imagine the horror the three of you went through."

"Let's jump in the pool cool off then change and go looking for some art that we both like; something that will remind us of out trip."

"I love the idea, let's get wet."

The week went really fast, the four of them did so many things all the way from Salsa lessons to snorkeling and jet skiing. On Saturday night Chris and Don took them to the Café Taberna, a nightclub in old town Havana. They spent a good three hours there and they all had a better understanding of what Salsa music and dancing was all about. They all had a good time and spent a lot of one on one time with each other. On the flight back they each had a second suitcase. Sue and Jim had three paintings and Kay and Jan had two.

Jim had the same limousine take them home. Jim and Sue helped Kay and Jan take there luggage and paintings to there house. It was nice the boys had fresh flowers in both homes.

Once Sue and Jim were back at there house Sue asked if the pool and Champaign could be on the agenda. Jim gave her a great kiss and said "It sounds perfect to me."

The boys had left them a note saying everything was ok and they would talk to them tomorrow.

Tuesday Morning May 04/ 2010 Tucson, Arizona

Sue and Jim were up early and on a run. Sue said "There is no ocean out there but it's great to be home. Would you take me to breakfast?"

"Breakfast sounds great. Let's go to the Country Club and let them pamper us."

Sue was laughing and said "I will pamper you baby."

At breakfast they both were pampered and truly were happy to be home. "On the flight back yesterday I was thinking about your friend ken, the law firm and there accounting company. I have a lot of ideas and different places to look and unless you have something else you want me to do I would like to work on the computers."

"You're going looking for the connection to them and what's already in the basement. I know you are aware of how dangerous these people are so I won't say to be careful."

Jim worked in the basement up to five o clock except for a few rest room breaks and a few drinks. He found this Greg Booster was not only an employee of Clifton Financial but also showed up on the payroll of the accounting firm in Phoenix. Jim had his X computers do a search through the other Arizona corporations that were on the CD's in the basement and found him also listed on three of them. He wasn't in a prominent position in any of them. It took a little while but Jim found this Greg Booster was just mussel with a suit. They listed him as head of security in two of the corporations. If it was the Mafia he would be a soldier. Jim already knew in his mind this Greg Booster was the one that killed Ken Benton but he was just doing what someone told him to do. Jim wanted all of them.

After he had shut up the basement he asked Sue if she would like to have a glass of wine and sit in the Jacuzzi. She thought it was a good idea. While they were having there wine Sue told Jim she had spent some time with Kay and Jan talking about The Consulting Company. Jim suggested she used a generic name for the company. After some discussion Sue came up with Catalina Consulting and for a logo to have a shadow outline of the Catalina Mountains as a background on any business cards or stationary. Jim thought it was a great idea and told her he would have there accountant set it up as a corporation and they would put four hundred thousand in it as start up money. Sue was excited and was going to design the business cards and stationary.

Sue wanted to make dinner and to have Jim help. They really did have fun and fixed a nice dinner. After they clean up the kitchen Jim wanted Sue to come up to the upper patio and watch the sunset with him. "Ok let's run up then we can walk back and you can hold my hand.

Wednesday Morning May 05/ 2010 Tucson, Arizona

Jim and Sue were out running as the sun was coming up they did a good eight miles and were having a good time. As they were getting close to the house Jim asked Sue if her morning was open and if she would go to breakfast with him. "Well sir it just happens my morning is open and I would love to have breakfast with you."

Jim kissed her and said "Let's go to the Country Club I have some ideas I would like to run by you."

"I also have some ideas for our shower that you might like."

Sue was right and it was a wonderful shower then they were off to the Country Club. Once they had there coffee and ordered Jim said "One of the things I would like to do this morning is go over and see our accountant Bill Stine and have him set up the corporation for your business. I also would like to start investing some of the money I have transferred into real estate. Would you come with me to meet up with Hugh Hanson our broker?"

"I think all of that would be fun; now what else is there you wanted to talk about?"

"You're really good. The other thing is Ken's murder. I know the people who had him murdered even the one that did it but I can't prove it. What I can and want to do is to expose some of what they were into and leak it to the State Police and the news paper at the same time. Now while they are upset I will take all the funds out of the account of this Greg Booster and make him believe this lawyer Lovitt is setting him up."

"You think you can turn them against each other without any proof and the news paper will run the story."

"I think I can come up with enough proof to expose the conspiracy between Clifton Financial, there Accountants and the law firm of Sims, Brown and Lovitt. Along with that I will show how it was necessary for them to take Ken out of the picture because he was the one who exposed this evidence. Then at the same time I expose them I will empty there bank accounts both corporate and personal. After that we can watch the shit fall where it will. So what do you think?"

Sue just sat there a minute then said "You really think you can do that and have no one know it was you."

"When it's all said and done Ken Benton will be the hero that in reality he truly was. Then we will find a place to put there money to good use."

There breakfast came to the table along with fresh coffee and a smile. Sue thanked the young lady then looked at Jim and said "I don't even know what to say."

"Let's enjoy our breakfast then if you like we can talk about it; there is no hurry."

Toward the end of breakfast Sue started laughing really hard then said "You by far are the strangest man I have ever met, I don't know how you could ever come up with that solution to such a complex problem."

"It's easy you inspire me."

Sue got up kissed Jim and said "Finish you're breakfast then we have a lot of people to see."

They had a lot of fun with Bill there accountant and got him started in putting together Sue's Corporation. Jim also wanted to discuss him expanding his Real Estate holdings buy a good thirty to forty million. Bill also suggested that Jim get a good Law Firm of Attorneys one that included a good Real Estate Attorney. Bill had a few suggestions that Jim might check out. Jim thought it might be a good idea to keep a good firm on retainer.

Before they left Bills office Jim called Hugh Hanson his Broker and asked if he had time for him and Sue to stop over and talk. Hugh told him of cores; he was his favorite customer. They both laughed and said they would be there in twenty minutes.

On the drive over there Sue said "Maybe I should call the boys and remind them the people from the Arizona Theater Company would be using the Meeting Building today."

"That's there job and it's our job to expect them to do it. So let's not call."

"You're right, thank you."

Hugh was glad to see them and had a young man bring them all coffee in his office. Hugh was glad to officially meet Sue and they laughed a lot about the first time they met. Jim did tell Hugh that he and Sue were engaged. Hugh congregated Jim and told Sue his wife Sharon would really be happy to hear that. And suggested they all go out to dinner when Sue and Jim were available. Sue said "I would enjoy that and would like to meet Sharon."

"Why don't you talk to Sharon and see what would be a good night for the two of you then give me a call. I also would like that and it is my treat. Now let me tell you the other reason I am here. First I would like to increase my real estate holdings and I am looking for large properties and land around Tucson. I know there are a lot of speculators like me that are now wanting to unload there inventory. Also if you would look over my existing holdings we can sit down and look at the ones I am willing to consider selling or trading. The estate is not on that list but the town house is and it can go furnished."

"It looks like you are going to continue being my favorite customers."

"Oh another thing I am looking to set up a relationship with a top rated law firm with among other things a good Real Estate Attorney. Do you have any you would recommend?"

There are a lot of good Real estate lawyers out there, but the only Law firm that I could recommend is Walker, Burwell and Alistair. Stewart Walker is one of the best if not the top Criminal Lawyer in the state and Paul Burwell is a great Real Estate lawyer. I think Alistair is into Corporate Law. I hope that helps."

"It does and thanks Hugh. Don't forget to call us after you talk to Sharon that would be fun."

As they left Hugh's building Jim asked Sue if she would go with him to talk with David. "Of cores I would, that should be fun."

"You do have to remember it's a guy thing, so to talk we need to meet for a drink."

Sue was laughing and said "You're both little boys, but it should be fun. So call him."

David was available so they met at the bar in the Country Club. Sue and Jim were the first to arrive so they got a table and ordered drinks. David arrived before the waitress left the table so he also ordered after saying hello to Sue. They did some small talk till the drinks came to the table and the waitress left. Jim said "I have some work I need done in Phoenix, but first let me tell you what this is all about and the type of people we will be dealing with."

Jim went through the whole story including how dangerous the people were that they were dealing with. He did leave out everything that had to do with the basement or the other people. By then they were into there second drink. Jim gave David the list and also told him to make sure he insolated himself from the people he had doing the work and that right now he only wanted photos and general information on all of them and on the Greg Booster guy he also wanted photos and names of who he hung around with. "Remind your people this guy is dangerous and we don't want any contact." Jim handed David an envelope and said "For expenses."

David was laughing and said "You know I am like you and get off on this shit. It's been a long time sense we played with anything fun; except the little thing with your friend."

"If I can pull this off and take down these people and there corporations I will take a lot of money and make you rich."

"You have already given me more money then I could spend."

"But if you marry Becky you will need to cover her shopping and don't forget about shoes."

They were all laughing and Sue said "Becky and I should go shopping with our sugar daddies and show the two of what spending money is all about."

"Talk to Becky; I am game. So David what do you think?"

"I would be scared to say no."

After there time with David they headed to the house. Jerry was at the gate and they said hello. The people from the Arizona Theater Company were there in the meeting building and the signs were again out.

"Come swimming with me. Then after the appropriate amount of kisses tell me your time table on this thing."

After they changed Sue brought ice tea out to the pool room then after they got in the pool and exchanged the proper amount of kisses Jim told her he was hoping to have everything ready to the point he could raid Greg Boosters bank accounts first thing Monday morning and set him off on his friends. Then later in the day have the documents delivered to the state police and the news paper at the same time. "I almost forgot I will also raid all the bank accounts of Clifton Financial, there Accounts and the Firm of Sims Brown and Lovitt. These withdrawals will also include all there officers and partner's personal accounts and certificates of deposit. Altogether it should be quite a substantial sum of money."

"These people are going to try and kill each other; there will be a war on the streets of Phoenix."

"It may bring about a small amount of justices and at the same time save the tax payers some money on prosecutions. Remember they were the ones who didn't care about spilling blood."

"You're right but this still scares me."

"It is scary to me also and I will try and make sure none of this comes close to us. Now let's enjoy the pool and each other then before its time for your theater people to leave you could get dressed and go over and talk with some of them. That will give you the opportunity to mention the consulting company you have started and what you plan to do with it. You could get some good input and it would get a lot of people talking about it."

"You're such a smart boy; at the same time you will be in the basement working on your computers."

Jim kissed her and said "You have a key."

It was almost five when Sue came down into the basement and gave Jim a kiss and said "When you get where you can quit let's go up and I will fix us something to eat and open a nice bottle of wine."

"While you open the wine I will shut this down and lock it up for the night. After dinner if you like we could walk up and watch the sunset and the lights of the city come on for us."

"I like all of that; this is starting to sound like a romantic evening."

Jim and sue were on an early run and it was beautiful out. By the end of the run they were walking hand in hand back to the house. "How about I fix us a nice breakfast then you can lock yourself in the library and work on your computers. While we were running I could tell that is where your mind was."

"You only think you know that."

Sue was laughing and said "You may fool all those other people my love but you don't fool me. You're such a little boy."

"Well breakfast sounds good."

It was almost five when Jim shut down all his computers and locked up the basement. When he walked out of the library Sue was there with a kiss and said "Use the rest room, then come to the pool room and I will fix you a drink."

Jim did get his drink and a few more kisses. "While you were working in the basement I was talking with Becky and Sharon and we girls have planed to have you guys take us out to the Gold Room at the Westward Look Resort. They accompanied by David and Hugh will meet us here at seven so Sharon can see the house. Our dinner reservations are for eight thirty. Oh yes; the Maitre D did reserve us a table with a view."

"I must say I love all of that, but did you plan anything for us later in the evening?"

"If you can handle it tonight could be life changing."

"I will make sure I pace myself; I wouldn't want to miss a minute of this. Now could I have a couple more of those kisses?"

Becky and David were the first to arrive followed closely by Sharon and Hugh. The girls were really having fun. Once in the pool room Jim asked if they would all like a glass of Champaign. The girls all thought that would be the appropriate drink for the evening. While he was pouring the Champaign he did tell the ladies how beautiful they each looked. Sharon loved the house. She had only seen it during the day when Hugh and Jim first looked at it and like them could hardly remember what she saw. In the evening light with all the different accent lights on it took on a whole different dimension. They were all having fun and Sue was explaining what they were going to do with most of the art; that conversation got into Sue's new company Catalina Consulting and its purpose. Both Sharon and Becky were interested in that.

David had driven a large sedan so they all went with him on the short drive to the Westward Look Resort. Sue had everything arranged and they were treated like celebrity's all the girls loved it and Jim was handing out a lot of folded up hundreds. The food and service was great and the six of them were having a great time. Somewhere in the conversation Becky asked Sue how there trip to Cuba was. Sharon's eyes got big and she said "You guys went to Cuba?"

Sue was laughing and said "We had the best time and even took lessons for Salsa dancing. Cuba was wonderful and we went with another couple."

Dinner was over and the girls wanted to go back to the house and hear about Cuba and what made them think about going there. Jim got the bill and tip and David's car was waiting for them with the doors open when they came out.

Back at the house Jim got everyone something to drink and Sharon and Becky wanted Sue to tell them about Cuba. They all had a fun time and it was after eleven before there guests left.

Jim locked everything and with a switch in the house closed the gates. Sue said "Pour us some of that wine, get rid of those clothes and let's go to the Jacuzzi."

"Thank you that was a wonderful evening you put together."

"Well I also had a great time, I really like Becky and Sharon; especially Becky. Sharon and Hugh are really nice but very concretive. Now Sharon really gets excited about all the things we do and really liked the idea of Cuba and Salsa dancing."

"They are a really nice couple and I am glad you invited them. Now for David and Becky I know he is head over heals in love with her and I think they would be a great couple."

"Becky is madly in love with David and I think tonight was good for both of them."

"Well I am madly in love with you and can't wait till we are married. Now why don't you tell me the rest of you're plans for the night?"

Friday Morning May 07/ 2010 Tucson, Arizona

Jim and Sue were again up early and on a run, they were going to breakfast at the Congress Street Hotel Café then later Sue was going to the university and Jim was going to a couple of office supply stores to buy pre punched paper, extra ink for the printers and some notebooks. He didn't want to get everything at one store. He also wanted a box of latex gloves so when he complied all the information on his bad boys and there corporations none of the papers or notebooks would have any fingerprints on them. He then was going to work in the basement. He wanted everything ready to go by Sunday morning.

Before Jim went to the basement he called David to see if his people in Phoenix had anything yet. David reported that they had located all the people and had photos of them all. David said "This guy Booster has two guys that he is tight with and they hang together a lot. Now you told me there witness of the killing said it was two men and a woman. Now one of Boosters friends has long hair he wears it in a pony tail. I had them get a lot of pictures of the three of them. I will have them for you in the morning."

"That's great David; now if I can put this together right these people should be shooting each other some time Monday morning."

It was after five when Sue came down to the basement and asked Jim if he would like a drink and something to eat. "If there are a lot of kisses with that I would love it."

Jim locked up the library used the rest room then he and Sue sat in the pool room caught up on there kisses then he told her what he had found and how he was going to try and get this all ready for Sunday morning. He asked what she had done. With a big smile sue said "Kay Jan and I made sure everything they needed for graduation and everything I needed for my degree was all in line, then we worked on our design for our business cards and stationary. We then had them all printed including the stationary and envelops. We even took some of it over to Bill Stine and he loved it.

Now I need you to help me figure out the money and benefits thing for Kay and Jan."

"Sounds like you had a good day and I will be glad to help you with that. Would Monday be alright with you?"

"Monday would be wonderful. Now come to the kitchen and I will fix us something to eat so you can get back to you're computers. Then when you're done for the night we can have some wine and spend some time in the pool and Jacuzzi."

In the end it was a nice night.

Saturday Morning May 08/ 2010 Tucson, Arizona

Jim and Sue had set the alarm so they could be out and running early enough to be at the upper patio and watch the sunrise. They wanted to make sure they had some private one on one time knowing today would be busy. The sunrise was beautiful and they got to see a lot of the desert wildlife. They were meeting David for breakfast at seven and he would have all the information and pictures his people in Phoenix had put together.

Breakfast was to be at the Country Club but the shower was one they would both remember for a long time.

David was on time and as soon as they had coffee and juice they ordered. When the waitress left David gave Jim an envelope with all the photos that the Phoenix people had taken along with all the information they had gathered. Sue also wanted to see the pictures. They talked till there breakfast was served. Jim told David he would need one of his trusted people to deliver a package Sunday morning to a reporter at the Phoenix Republic News Paper. "How about the two of us go up there early Sunday morning and oversee this thing, I have a second package that will need to be delivered later in the day to a detective at the State Police. Another thing this morning can you have one of your people in Phoenix go to a bank and get change for two hundred dollar bills, have him get all twenties and to put them in an envelope with only touching the two outer bills. This is important we don't want any of our fingerprints to show up or any prints that would connect the bills to Tucson. David this is all connected to something really big and bad and none of us can afford to have any piece of this touch us."

"Well when you get back in the game its big time; I love it. You know anything you need, will always be there."

"I have always known that. How about you pick me up at six in the morning and drive something that will blend in."

Before they left they all talked about the night before and how much fun they had. On the way home Sue said "I will be on the estate all day so if you need anything call me."

It was four thirty when Sue came down in the basement and gave Jim a kiss and told him he needed to take a break. "You're right I could use some more kisses and a drink."

"You use the rest room and I will fix the drinks."

They sat in the pool room and enjoyed there drinks. "I have a good four to five hours of work before I have this all ready. If I don't have enough proof in there they will be scared to print it and I want it in the Monday morning edition."

"You don't need to push yourself, it's your schedule and you can just change it."

"This is really going to sound weird, but this isn't my schedule there is something inside of me that is telling me it needs to be tomorrow. I don't know how to explain it to you, or me but it's real and I have to do it."

"This all goes back to the Mission, the Priest, The estate, treasure, Ken and you and me. You need to hold me because I know what you're saying is real."

"Let's have a second drink then I will go back and put this thing together."

"Would you like something to eat?"

"I am too pumped to eat; I will get something in the morning with David. You know it's a guy thing." They were both laughing and Jim went back to work.

While Jim was in the Library he called and talked with Hoyt Segal and told him about the story that would be delivered to the two of them in the morning and they would need to have it in the Monday morning edition because the State Police would also have the same information delivered to them Sunday. Jim did tell Hoyt that he and Bill should stay off the streets starting Monday morning because things will be breaking loose.

It was a little after eleven thirty when Jim closed up the basement. He had two gym bags that held the two notebooks a lot of money and latex gloves. Sue said "I opened a nice bottle of wine and have it and towels out by the Jacuzzi."

"Let me put this by the front door and get out of these clothes."

It was a wonderful night and there was no talk of bad guys or money.

Sunday Morning May 09/ 2010 Tucson, Arizona

Jim and Sue were up early enough to enjoy each other both in and out of the shower before they dressed. David was on time driving a nice silver four door Buick with current Arizona license plates. Jim had his bags and they stopped on the way to the freeway and each got Café Mochas for the trip. Before they had breakfast Jim wanted to make sure the first notebook was delivered. The drive up was fun and Jim was telling David all the shit these people were into. He didn't tell him about the basement or any of the other shit he had found.

David was telling Jim he was going to ask Becky to marry him sometime this next week and if she says yes he wanted them all to go out some where nice for dinner. "I won't say anything to Sue, but I know she will also be excited. Sue and I really do like Becky and I am sure she is in love with you."

They were met at David's Phoenix dealership by a nice looking young man. Jim called Hoyt Segal and told them the package would be delivered in fifteen minutes to the frond door of the news paper an that he and Bill would need to show identification to get it.

"Bill and I will be at the front door with a security guard because the paper is closed today."

"That's great; fifteen minutes."

David and Jim followed the young man and parked where they could watch the delivery. Everything went as planed. "Ok my friend Phoenix is your area so find us somewhere nice and I will buy us breakfast."

"I just happen to know a great place and we can start breakfast with a Bloody Marry."

Jim was laughing and said "Why not."

David did find a nice restaurant at a very nice Resort in Scottsdale. They did start with a Bloody Mary and Jim explained the next delivery would be to the detective at the State Police and he wanted a third party that wouldn't have any knowledge of either of them. "I have the detective's personal cell phone Number and I will call him and arrange the delivery. That is why I wanted the money to be from Phoenix with no finger prints on it. The worst scenario would be that they would detain the person that delivered it and check the money he was paid for fingerprints and question him about who had him deliver it. I honestly don't believe that will happen but we still need to do it."

"When you're ready to set it up I have the people and it won't be a problem."

Breakfast was served and they both enjoyed it then had some coffee. Jim was explaining to David that he was having Hugh find properties he could buy and sell so he could have Bill start showing some of those millions as income and he would pay taxes on it. Then he said to David "You also need to start investing in things that you can sell so Bill can start showing profits so he can move some of these millions into your accounts. I need to tell you when this thing we are working on is done I expect to pull out Hundreds of Millions of Dollars. And as I told you before I already have hundreds of millions and you will have all that you want."

"We need to get out of here and if we are just wasting time I will take you over to my warehouse and show you some of the cars I have stashed."

"That sounds like fun; let me take care of this."

Jim and David did have fun at David's warehouse. The place was huge and David had almost a hundred cars inside of it. Some of the cars were David's private collection. He had a Ferrari, a reproduction A/C Cobra, Three older collector Corvettes and three other old mussel cars. "David this is something you like, you could redo this warehouse then Buy and sell collector cars for cash then show millions in profits that you could pay taxes on. You could also show a couple of extra millions in profit on your dealerships."

"Now that you mention it I have a perfect piece of land in Tucson that I would love to build a great warehouse on. It would be something I have always dreamed of having. This money could be fun."

At two o'clock Jim called Detective Bruce Tate of the Arizona State Police on his private cell phone. Jim gave his name as Jeff Black and explained the evidence he would turn over to him, and gave him information on the murder of Ken Benton and told him that the motive was to keep Ken from exposing a huge criminal enterprise. He also told him the two men and one woman his witness saw was in fact three men and one had long hair that he normally wore in a ponytail. They made arrangements for the drop to happen within ten minutes of the call.

The third party made the drop with no problem and Jim and David saw the whole thing.

Before they left Phoenix Jim called Hoyt and Bill at the paper and asked if they were going to get the story in the morning paper. Bill said "This story will be the headline and the front page. None of us can believe the documentation and photo's you have on this story. I don't know who you are or where you got this stuff but it is gold."

"Do a good job on this and it just may be the tip of a huge story that will rock more then just this country. Have fun guys and stay safe."

The ride back to Tucson was fun; David was pumped mostly about asking Becky to marry him but also the fun they could have with the money. Jim called Sue when they were about an hour from the house.

David just dropped Jim off and went on. Sue was waiting with some kisses then wanted to know how everything went. "Let's get a drink and sit in the pool room then I will tell you everything."

The drinks got made and with a few more kisses Jim told Sue the story of his day up till then. "Now some time this evening I need to empty out all there accounts I can, then move the money around to where they can't trace its final destination. I have written a Number of programs to help me expedite doing that but it will still take from two to three hours."

"It's Four thirty now so if you want to start I will fix us something light for dinner and bring it down there. That way when you're done we can relax in the Jacuzzi and pool."

By the time Jim shut down his computers he had taken one billion eight hundred and twenty six million and change out of thirty three different accounts that belonged to the bad guys corporations and them personally.

Sue said "I opened a bottle of wine and put it and some towels out by the Jacuzzi. Why don't you get rid of those clothes and come out with me; then you can tell me what you have done."

Once in the Jacuzzi and after the appropriate amount of kisses Jim said "Starting some time early tomorrow morning the shit should hit the fan. Tonight I took one billion eight hundred and twenty some million from there corporations and personal accounts. The news paper will name the three of them as the ones who had Ken killed to keep him form exposing them and there fellow conspirators in this huge conspiracy to defraud the government and the stockholders of Valley Electric and Power Corporation out of Hundreds of millions of dollars."

"You took over one billion dollars and you don't think they will be able to trace it."

"Yes I did and no they won't have any idea of where it went."

"Ok I believe you, but just incase we should have a really good time tonight."

They did have a really good time.

Monday Morning May 10/ 2010 Tucson, Arizona

Jim woke up Sue a little after six and said "Let's take a nice run then go to the Country Club for breakfast, after that we can come home and monitor the news."

"I like all of that except the part about the news; it scares me thinking how this will all play out."

"Maybe they will do to each other what I can't have the law do. I know they murdered Ken but I don't have enough direct evidence for the court system to get a conviction. Hopefully whatever happens this morning will resolve that."

They did a nice five mile run followed by a fun shower.

At breakfast Jim said "We need to pick a date for our wedding and make our plans. Graduation is the end of next week and you did say you would marry me."

"Yes I will marry you. Let's get past today then we will make this happen."

Breakfast was fun and the talk was about the wedding, family and friends. Not a word about murder or the news.

Once back at the house Sue put on a pot of coffee and Jim turned on the television in the pool room. He went to the Cable News Channel. They were already talking about the on going stories coming out of Phoenix Arizona and in ten minutes they would be going to continuous coverage from Phoenix. Jim's phone rang and it was David who told Jim he had someone bringing down four copies of the Phoenix Republic and as soon as he had them he would be over. Sue came in and Jim told her what was coming on and that David would be bringing over copies of the paper as soon as they arrived. They got there coffee and made themselves comfortable and waited for the story to start.

When they came back from commercial break they said they had an ongoing breaking story coming out of Phoenix Arizona that started this morning when the Phoenix Republic News Paper published its morning edition with a headline story involving the states largest power supplier Valley Electric Power Corporation witch is owned by Clifton Financial of stealing hundreds of millions of dollars from its investors, customers, the State of Arizona and the Federal Government. It also names there accounting company R C Rankin and there law firm Sims Brown and Lovitt. This story started to come to light when a young Associate Lawyer named Ken Benton tried to expose this conspiracy then was murdered to keep him silent. The murder was staged to look like an auto accident and if it wasn't for a witness and a sharp detective from the State Police Bruce Tate they may have gotten away with it. Now the paper goes on to name three of the top executives who were involved in the murder and another two men that were accomplices. The paper also goes on to show each of there Pictures and list there affiliations and all the banks, account Numbers and the staggering amounts of money they each have deposited; these banks are both in and out of our country. The article also states that The State Police also received a copy of this report some time Sunday.

There are other reports this morning in Phoenix that the bodies of Attorney Brian Lovitt and that of David Rankin have been found and witnesses have stated that the third executive Greg Booster and his two associates were responsible and at this time are still at large. We have news people on the seen of the shootings and are trying to get comments from any of the law enforcement agencies involved in the investigation. Stay tuned after commercial break we expect to have live coverage from the seen of the shootings.

"Well you have one hell of a story there. What do you think that Greg Booster is doing right now?"

"I am sure he and his two friends are in total panic right now and are looking for all the money they can scrape together. I don't expect them to last very long; I just hope no law enforcement or innocent people get hurt in this thing."

The Cable News was back and had so many different stories going on they couldn't keep up. They were trying to get interviews with the reporters that broke the story and also with the Detective from the State Police. No one seamed to want to talk right now. There was an abundance of people at the shooting scenes that wanted to talk. It was funny how the stories of what they saw varied. The news media was now at the point of connecting all of this to the Government's original case against the Power Company. "It won't be long and all the talking heads will tell us what this is all about."

It wasn't long and David came over and they talked about the morning developments. David assured them the people who were doing the work for them in Phoenix were totally blind to who they were working for and also liked it that way. "I am sure after this morning there even happier."

Jim told David the amount of money he had taken from them and that he had it out of the country. "Some day we will all figure out what to do with it."

The conversation went to Sue and Jim getting married and it was going to be soon. Sue opened a nice bottle of wine then after a while David said he was going to propose to Becky this week. Sue said "When she says yes we all need to celebrate and go somewhere fun."

David with a concerned look said "Lets wait and see if she says yes before we make any plans. This is scaring me to death."

Sue gave him a kiss on the cheek and said "How could she not want to marry you."

They were drinking there wine and having fun then after a while the television came back with breaking news on there breaking news story. There was a stand off and shooting involving the Phoenix police plus State and Federal agents it had been going on for a good twenty minutes in North Phoenix. After a while it seamed to be over but there was no information coming out of the area that was coordinated off.

It was a good forty five minutes then a spokesman for the Phoenix Police stated there had been three suspects that they had tried to apprehend that opened fire on police and all three had been killed in a shootout and no police officers or bystanders had been hurt. One of the reporters said they had unconfirmed reports that the three men were the suspects that had been mentioned in the morning paper and also involved in the killing of two men earlier that day.

"Will that should handle the people responsible for Ken's Murder but this story and the resulting prosecutions will go on for years."

"I want to thank you for getting the people behind Ken's murder. That came with a kiss.

David said "Call me when you have the wedding plans and I will call as soon as I have an answer."

After David left Sue said "Let's take our wine to the pool and catch up on our kisses."

They spent a good three hours swimming, kissing and laying in the sun. Later Sue and Jim made a nice meal cleaned up then went for a nice walk and talked about the wedding and how much fun it would be with Family and friends.

Tuesday Morning May 11/ 2010 Tucson, Arizona

Jim and Sue were up and running by six. By the end of there run they were walking hand in hand. "Let's go out for breakfast then later get together with Kay and Jan and plan our wedding and get out invitations."

"Why don't we at the same time do all of the financial things with Kay and Jan so Kay can quit at the restaurant. I was thinking you could offer them four thousand a month each plus there benefits of medical a company car and an expense account for stuff they do for the business. Is there anything else you can think of?"

"I am sure they will both be thrilled with that. If Kay is off today would you like to invite them to join us for breakfast?"

"You know I love to have breakfast with a table full of beautiful young ladies."

"Well just remember witch young lady needs most of your attention."

Back at the house Sue called Kay and the arrangements were made. They were all going to the Country Club for breakfast and spring fashions were agreed on. The girls were really having fun with this dressing up; none of them had ever been in a position to dress like that and as Kay had said it was the Cinderella thing.

Jim had called ahead so at the Country Club they were ready and expecting them; the girls always loved that.

Breakfast was fun and Sue officially asked Kay and Jan to come to work for Catalina Consulting and went over her offer as to pay and benefits. The girls were thrilled and Kay had already talked with the Café and they had hired a young lady who Kay was training. On the wedding plans they all had there Blackberries out looking at dates and came up with Sunday afternoon May thirtieth. This was a tentative date till they could contact everyone and get conformations. All in all it was one hell of a breakfast and they all had plans to come over to the house and start making phone calls and arrangements.

Jim took good care of there waitress then it was a short ride back to the house. Everyone was having fun, Sue's first call was to her Mom and asked if they could come out for the graduation then stay for the wedding and as long as they wanted after that because she and Jim would be on there honeymoon. Jim called David and told him of the date and asked if his Mom and Dad would come. David said he would talk with them and he was sure they would want to. David also wanted to meet with Jim and talk. Jim said he would call him back in a few minutes as to when and where. The girls were busy calling friends and talking about who they would use for music. They had the Boys Steve and Frank over and were talking about how they could set up the big meeting room. Steve said the big marble table would come apart and could be moved or stored if they liked. Jim told Sue he was going to meet with David and would call if it was going to be long.

Jim and David met at the Country Club in the bar they got a table and ordered a drink then David said "I am a wreck I want to ask Becky to marry me tonight. I made reservations for dinner and asked her out. I wanted her to help me pick out the rings so I don't have one. What should I do?"

"I am probably not the right person to ask about this but you might think about going over early with the proper flowers and a nice bottle of wine and just tell her the truth that you love her and want to marry her and love her for the rest of your life. Then after she says yes the two of you need to stop at the house and have a toast before you go to dinner. Remember David you're a good man and I can't think of any reason Becky wouldn't marry you. Now no more drinks my friend; just go home and get ready for tonight."

When Jim got home he kissed Sue then told her what David wanted and what he had told him. Sue was immediately excited and wanted to know what time they were coming over. Jim kissed her and said "We will have to wait just like David. But I am happy for him. Now how about we open a bottle of wine and you sit with me on the couch and we watch the news."

"They must be going crazy by now; I sure hope they don't find that Jeff Black."

"We need to keep that name off our guest list."

161

"The girls and I have been working on our guest list and unless you want something different we would like to make it an adult wedding."

"That would be nice and I would also like to keep the reception to only two or three hours; I don't want people getting drunk at our wedding."

"The boys have already talked about that and will nicely handle our guests. They didn't want you beating anyone up." By now Sue was laughing hard.

"Let me get that wine open and turn on the television." Sue was still laughing.

The local news hadn't started yet so Jim went to the Cable News and that was the story they were talking about, it was three of the talking heads that act like they know everything. But in this case they were wondering how someone could have found and compiled all of this evidence without all the resources that law enforcement or the news media would have. In both cases with the paper and the State Police the only name used was Jeff Black and the reporters from the paper stated there source told them the name was a fake. Today the FBI has closed the offices of Valley Electric and Power Corporation. And temporally stopped the trading of there stock. They also have served warrants and sized records at Clifton Financial and the law offices of Sims Brown and Lovitt. The FBI and Justices Department sizing records from a law firm; that in it self should make a lot of people nervous.

Law enforcement wasn't releasing any information on the people that were murdered or the ones killed in the shout out. They also wouldn't comment on any of the information they may or may not have received. But through other sources there are reports of huge amounts of money being withdrawn from many banks both inside and out of the country and it was all done on the same day the news paper article came out. The reports we have heard, but can't verify say the total will be over a billion dollars.

"Do you think there exaggerating the amounts; that sounds like a lot of money."

"I still can't believe how much money you have taken and I am baffled about what you are going to do with it."

"Well it's nothing we need to worry about right now. I have a feeling the right thing will come along and we will be able to recognize it. I know that sounds kind of simple and idealistic, but I think it will be that simple."

"It douse sound silly but I also think you're right. It's like this art thing it will just come together. Also I forgot to tell you Mom and Dad will be here Friday the twenty first again about eleven. It was funny when I called Darlene she said you had already called and wanted her to have Bob fly my parents out just like last time with limousines and everything. You are a funny guy and I do love you."

"Would you like to do something tonight after Dave and Becky leave?"

"How about I fix us something light for dinner then we take a nice bottle of wine and walk up to the upper patio and watch the lights of the city. Then you can come up with some of your own ideas for the rest of the night."

"I think I can do that. Let me shut off the television, turn on some music and we can move this conversation to the pool."

It was almost seven when David called and said he and Becky were on there way over. Jim and Sue were both excited. Jim put two bottles of Champaign on ice and they waited for them to arrive. David had the code for the gate and Jim and Sue went out to the front and sat on the steps waiting for them. It wasn't long and a big black Mercedes came over the hill with Davis and Becky inside. They could hardly wait to tell Jim and Sue that David had proposed and Becky said yes. Jim hugged Becky, kissed her on the cheek and said "Welcome to the family."

Sue also hugged and kissed David as she congregated him. Then hugged and kissed Becky. Jim also hugged David and said "Come in and have a toast and tell us how it all went."

Jim opened and poured the Champaign while Becky was telling them about the proposal and how funny David was. Sue was really excited and happy for the both of them. Jim made a nice toast and asked if they had told any of there other family yet.

David said "We were going to go out to dinner but have decided we would go over and tell Becky's family the news then if it's not too late stop and see my family."

"Well thank you for sharing the good news with us. Now give us another hug then go see you're parents; we do love you."

There were more hugs and kisses and a few tears then David and Becky were gone.

Jim gave Sue a big kiss and said "Let's take that bottle of wine and walk up to the upper patio now; then if you like we can eat something later. Right now I just want to be with you."

Wednesday Morning May 12/ 2010 Tucson, Arizona

Jim and Sue were up and running before sunrise Sue said "This is a beautiful morning and the desert is special but I am feeling a sense of danger and I know you are feeling it also; I need to stop and have you hold me."

Jim did hold her and said "You're right I am feeling it; I know it's not an immediate threat but something is wrong and I can't ignore it. Let's walk back and talk about this."

On the walk back to the house Jim said "We both know for sure that none of this is just a matter of coincidence even the fact that we are together. We both for sure saw it at the Mission. So with that said I believe what ever this is will also be shown to us as this warning was. I don't believe God has gone through this much trouble to bring us this far then drop us in the weeds."

"As crazy as everything you just said is, I have to believe your right. What I am feeling now is close to what I felt at the Mission. So if I am going to believe there is a God then I shouldn't have a problem believing he can reach out to us."

"Each day I ask him to give me the power to do his will then all I have to do is the next right thing. I do know it's not that simple and I don't always know what the next right thing is but I can't just sit and do nothing."

"Take me for a nice breakfast; we never did have dinner last night."

"I will take you to the Congress Street Café and we can have a great breakfast."

While they were at breakfast Jim suggested if Sue had some time they could check out the law firm that Hugh Had mentioned. "I know a law Professor at the University who I could call and ask to recommend a top rated Firm then ask him about the one Hugh mentioned."

"That would be a great help; let's try it."

Sue pulled up his cell Number and got him on the phone. They talked a bit about Ken who was the one that had introduced Sue to the Professor. It was funny after Sue told him what she was looking for he recommended the same law firm that Hugh had. Jim suggested that after breakfast they should just drop by there offices and check them out. Sue started laughing and said "You already know you will get into to see at least one of them; It's like the Police and the bad guys, the lawyers are just part of you're game."

While laughing he kissed her and said "I don't know how you come up with these things; let's pay our bill and go."

Jim looked up there address and it was also in the down town area. There building was an old and large estate that sat on a one acre lot in the middle of the arts district it was a two story structure that had a lot of rod iron and a Mexican tile roof.

Sue said "I like there building they must have gutted the whole structure then rebuilt it to suit there needs."

"Well let's go in and see if we like them."

After a few minutes with there receptionist they were talking with one of the partners Paul Burwell who's main area of practice was Real Estate law. Jim explained the amount of Real Estate they owned and they were planning to expand the amount and they also had three different corporations between them. They now felt they would like to have a diverse law firm on retainer. It took a good half hour to get it all done; they also got to meet with Stewart Walker there criminal attorney. Jim left them a twenty thousand cash retainer then he and Sue were on there way. "I sure hope I don't need any of there services, but incase we do it's already in place. I know none of the information we have given out would lead back to us in any way. The only thing I can think of is someone putting together the fact that I just bought this estate and now this information has come to light."

"I didn't think of that. How can you find out if that's the case?"

"I would like to set up a meeting with Jerry and the boys and go over the security we have in place. I also want to talk to first David by myself; I will call him first. I will also call Hugh and have him notify me of anyone making inquiries on any of my properties."

"What would you like me to do?"

"Just be aware of what is going on around you. I don't expect any problem if anything I believe they just may be curious and want to know all about us. After I talk to everyone I want to I will go back to the computers and search for anyone else in Arizona that is part of this thing. If we are indeed being watched I want to know all about whom it is that is watching us. I can always set them up as the ones who leaked the information on the first bunch."

"You act like this is some huge chess game and you are figuring out your first move even before you know if anyone else is playing."

"You're right on both accounts, but I will try and make sure it doesn't interfere with us having fun. After we get home I will make my calls then meet with David."

Back at the house Jim's calls got made and he was meeting David at the Congress Street Hotel Bar at eleven thirty.

They were both on time and the young bartender Cathy was glad to see them. They got there drinks then found a table with some privacy. David was still on a high about Becky and telling Jim about them telling there parents. The stories were funny and they both he and Becky had a good time. They were going shopping for rings later in the afternoon. After a bit Jim told David what he thought was going on and how he thought it was related to the people he had exposed. They talked about what David would set up with the people from there Barrio. Jim asked him to remind them that everything had to be handled very professionally and quietly. Jim gave David an envelope with a hundred thousand dollars in it to give to them as just good faith money. They finished there drink and were on there way.

Back at the house he and Sue got the boys and Jerry the security guard together for a meeting. Jim went over the possibility of people trying to bypass the security to inter the grounds and install listing devices, also the possibility of some of the workers or delivery people planting a device. He then showed them the scanner he had and what different types of devices it would detect. "I will get each of you one so you can occasionally scan anyplace you think someone would leave a listing device. It won't be hard to detect any of this happening if we just change our prospective about everything going on around us. Now if you do detect anything don't take any action, just write down everything you find and see then let me know. You all have Sue and my cell phone Numbers and if for any reason you can't reach us call David. He has my authority to do what ever needs to be done. I will have a scanner for each of you as soon as I can. Now I am sure you all have questions."

All three of them did have questions and one of the big ones was about who the people might be. Jim explained it could be Federal Law Enforcement or very organized criminals and in either case they would have suffocated equipment. They talked for almost an hour. Sue volunteered to go to the electronic store and have Terry order us five more of the scanners; "I know David like me would like to have one."

"Thank you I will give you the cash before you go."

Jerry went back to the gate and the boys went to check on the theater people who were in the meeting building. Jim gave Sue a kiss and said he would be in the library.

It was after four when Sue came down to the basement and asked if Jim wanted to take a break and have a glass of wine. "I think it's time I shut this all down and pay some attention to you. If you like we could have that wine in the pool."

"My swimsuit is upstairs, but I do have towels down here."

"That sounds perfect to me."

While they were in the pool Sue told Jim that Terry had two of the scanners in stock and he ordered three more for them that should be in Friday or Monday. "Thank you I will give one to the boys and the other to Jerry. While I was searching through some of the CD's I came up with three other corporations in Arizona that are connected to these people and all three of them list Sims, Brown and Lovitt as there attorneys of record and R.C. Rankin as there accountants. Another name that kept showing up in not any big way but was still there is Arizona Senator Russell Tuttle."

"Senator Tuttle! Now that's one hell of a name to show up being connected to these people. He is well respected and very powerful in Congress; how could he be involved in something like this?"

"Remember it takes a lot of money to build and maintain that much power. I still need to do a lot of work before I know how involved he is and if he really knows what they are all about."

"In all this time did you think of something nice that we could do tonight?"

"Actually I did; I went on line and found that you're Theater Company is putting on a preview of the new production tonight, but it is by invitation only. If I can find someone with connections we could go and then have dinner after the show at the Country Club."

"I just happen to have a lot of connections and think it's a wonderful idea."

Sue and Jim dressed the part and the play was fun. They had a great time with the cast and the people putting it together. Sue passed out some cards and offered to be of assistance.

Jim had made reservations so they had a very nice table. Dinner was fun and most of the conversation was about the wedding. It turned out to be a great night.

Thursday Morning May 13/ 2010 Tucson, Arizona

Jim and sue were again up early and went to the gym, they wanted to work out with trainers. When they were done Sue wanted to invite Kay and Jan to breakfast. She called and they decided on the Country Club

Breakfast with the girls is always fun, the talk was about graduation and the weeding Sue and the girls had already arranged transpiration and lodging for the girls family and friends and with the help of the boys they had made plans for a large party in the meeting building with live entertainment. Steve and Frank said they would remove the large marble table and store it in the warehouse where there were enough nice round tables with chairs to set it up to handle up to a hundred people and have a dance floor in the center. There was also a decent size three foot high stage stored in the warehouse that was big enough for a band. They could have there own night club.

After breakfast they were going back to the house where the girls were going to work on all there things while Jim went to the library to work on his things. With a few breaks for drinks and the restroom he worked six hours and went through everything he could on the three Arizona corporations he had found and Senator Tuttle of Arizona. When he was done he shut it all down and locked everything up and came out of the library.

Sue was glad to see him and gave him a nice kiss. Jim had some papers in his hand and said "I would again like to go out of town and call the reporters from the Phoenix Republic. I would like to find out who they are getting heat from about there story. If you like we could drive down to Bisbee Arizona and call from there. In Bisbee they have a great old Hotel called the Copper Queen and they serve a great dinner."

"I would love to go to Bisbee with you. I have only been there once years ago and it also is a great art community."

"It's still early enough let's go now."

The ride was fun and the view and weather were great. They talked about what Sue and the girls and boys were doing and how much fun they all were having. Jim brought Sue up to date on what he had discovered on the three corporations and the good Senator Tuttle. He then explained why he wanted to talk to the reporters Hoyt Segal and Bill Mitchell and find out whom and what agencies of the government have been questioning them about the article and there source.

When Jim called, Hoyt Segal answered right a way and said "We didn't know if we would ever hear from you again. I am sure you know what a zoo it is around here."

"I am sure the two of you are having a ball but I do need to again warn you there are people out there you don't want to meet up with. Remember I told you this is just the tip of a really big story. Now I need some information from the two of you, like what different agencies have been questioning you, who are the agents and what did they want?"

They talked a good twenty minutes and Jim made a lot of notes. Jim did ask them if they have had any contact from Senator Tuttle or any of his people. There was a pause then Bill Mitchell said "I had a call today from one of his people in reference to another story. It was funny because the call didn't make any sense; well maybe it does now."

"I don't have enough to make this a story yet but the information does help. The two of you stay safe and I will call."

"Take me to see some of the galleries here before they close, then at dinner you can tell me what you're thinking."

"Are there any kisses in that?"

The galleries were fun and they did find one original piece of sculpture the both had to have. The Copper Queen Hotel and there dinning room lived up to Jim's description. They started with a drink. Jim said "After everything I looked at today I believe what we both feel is real. I think the amount of information I exposed on the people who had Ken killed has our Senator Tuttle freaked out. I don't think the rest of them are very concerned but the Senator is looking at everything and the fact that I bought the estate just prior to all of this happening he will have people looking at us. Now what I don't know yet is who he will use. It could be federal, state or some of there own people. I will just have to wait and see, now if he becomes a problem I will set it up to where he is a threat to the rest of them. Now on the fun side of this I figured out how you and your corporation can bring in millions of dollars that would fund everyone's salaries, your overhead and give you enough extra income to finance all the projects you want."

"Let's order another drink then you can tell me how I can make all of this money."

The drinks got ordered then Jim said "We will start businesses in different countries around the world then have them make outrages payments to you're consulting company. It would show you're company as consulting on any large cultural, art or entertainment event happing anywhere in the world. The company will pay taxes on it then after expenses it would support art in our country."

By now Sue was laughing really hard and said "You by far are the funniest man I have ever met, but you are right and the government would be happy. Let's order dinner this has turned out to be a great evening."

Dinner was a lot of fun as was the ride home. Sue wanted to take a bottle of wine, two glasses and walk up to the upper patio.

It turned out to be a night to remember.

Friday Morning May 14/ 2010 Tucson, Arizona

Jim was woken by Sue kissing him she said "I had a wonderful time last night. Would you like to go swimming with me; the coffee should be ready by now?"

"I would love to go swimming with you."

The pool was fun and also came with a lot of kisses. After there shower Sue fixed them something light to eat. "If you have time after we do the kitchen, come with me to the basement and let's go through all the spy stuff down there and see what we could use to spy on the people who may be spying on us."

Sue was laughing and said "You make this all like a big game and I know its not. Yet it still is funny to be part of it."

"Remember we call it the juice; and it is catching."

The spy equipment in the basement was light years ahead of what you could buy. There were portable thermal imaging cameras that could work up to a half mile away. There were also starlight scopes that were much more powerful then any thing Jim had. They found not only GPS transmitters but a portable tracking station that would monitor the signal up to three miles. There were six highly suffocated scanning interments. They were probably better then the one Jim had but they were also large and bulky. Jim would stay with what he had. There was also a complete set up for monitoring and recording listing devices and it did include ten of the devices and extra batteries. The instruction booklets said they would have a range of three miles. They also found eight silencers for the hand guns. Sue said "So I guess this makes the two of us spies."

"Let's lock this up and check with Jerry and see if anything abnormal showed up last night on any of our monitoring equipment. They talked with Jerry and the boys and none of them found anything. They had also driven around the estate and checked the fences and equipment; everything looked good. Jim thanked them.

"Let's take a ride; I have a feeling that we will have company."

"If we do, where are we going to go and what are you going to do."

"You will like this, if they are following us we will first call David then we will drive to a nice Mexican restaurant and night club on the south side of town close to our barrio. We will stop and have a drink then when we leave I will have people following them. We can return to the house then when they quit for the night our people will follow them to where they are staying, then later tonight they will go through there car and see if they can find out who they are and who they work for. Then after they leave in the morning our people will go through there Hotel or Motel. They won't take anything but will take pictures of anything they can find."

"You're serious about this. Do you really think it will be that easy to do surveillance on professionals and go through there cars and rooms?"

"That's the funny part of this; these people think they are so covert they would never think that someone is doing surveillance on them. They will be easier then if they were tourist. Tourists for the most part are already paranoid that someone will break into their car or room. Let's go for the ride and see if I am right."

They hadn't gone three miles when Jim said I think there government people there using two cars with two men in each car. There both mid size Fords one is silver and the other one is beige; go ahead and take a look they can't see you with the privacy glass. Let me give David a call."

Jim took his time and stayed on Campbell as long as he could so it would be easy for them to follow. Sue laughing said "You have your own little parade; this really is silly."

They stayed and had lunch, Jim had Sue talk to there manager about having a luncheon for fifteen to twenty people. He said with some notice they would love to do it. Sue left him a card and got one of his. "Now if they check he can tell them why we were here. I am sure two of them are inside and watching us. Now let's take our friends and go back to the house."

Back at the house Jim said "As soon as we are sure of what agency they work for I will use the X computer and see who sent them and what reason they gave to have them look at us. Then we can decide if we need to take any action."

"I wanted a life in the fast lane but with you my love it like being on the freeway. To be honest I think like you and David I am getting hooked on the juice. I know this is dangerous but I am having the time of my life. You need to hug and kiss me."

There were a lot of hugs and kisses then it was time for the sun and pool.

While they were lying in the sun Sue got a call from Todd Butler of the Tucson Art Museum, He wanted to invite her and Jim to attend a cocktail party and showing of three new artists that evening. They were also going to display the six paintings they had loaned them. Both Sue and Jim loved the idea and said they would be there. "Now that was a fun call and I am excited about going. What should I wear?"

"You have some beautiful dresses that you have never worn. Let's pick out some really nice jewelry for you to wear. I love it and you make it look beautiful."

"Give me a kiss then let's go look and see what we can find."

It was only minutes and they were in the basement and had the Jewelry out and they were acting like kids, laughing and having fun. They found a great necklace made of Sapphires and diamonds with ear rings to match. Sue said "I have a beautiful dress this will go with, but do you think it's too much?"

"I don't think so but let's try it with the dress, makeup and hair done. If it is too much I will tell you the truth."

"Thank you now let's go to the shower and make it fun."

When Sue was ready with her hair, nail polish, light makeup she had on a low cut fitted long white dress that had straps going over the shoulders it was very eloquent and sexy. The jewelry didn't over power the look. Sue was stunning and she knew it. The jewelry did work and they were both happy. Kay and Jan came over to see Sue in her dress and jewelry. They both loved it and took a Number of pictures. Jim did manage to be in some of them. The boys had brought up the car. Jim said "Before we leave let's see if they have a tracking device on the car."

Steve used his new scanner and sure enough there was a GPS transmitter under the passenger's side of the car. Steve pulled it off so they could all see it; there only held on by a magnet.

"Let's put it back in place, that way we will have company tonight."

With a few kisses they were on there way to the party. The drive was fun and Sue was excited.

They did have Vale parking and when Sue got out of the car there were a lot of people that were looking at only her. Once inside Cathy was the first to see Sue and loved her dress. Todd came over and thanked them for coming. Sue said "I am so happy you invited us, you know how I love to see the work of new artist" Jim got them both a glass of Champaign. It was fun watching how people were attracted to Sue. It wasn't just the dress and jewelry it was Sue and her smile. The six paintings were displayed well and they had a sign saying they hadn't been viewed in public for over fifty years.

The three artist and there work was well received. Sue and Jim got to talk to all three of them. Sue knew a lot of the people at the showing and passed out a lot of her cards witch Jim had a pocket full of. It was quite a party and a lot of people were there and having fun. When they were on there second glass of Champaign a couple came up to say hello. It was one of there new Lawyers Stewart Walker and his wife, her name was Karen. While they were talking Stewart said "I noticed the six paintings were on loan from your collection. How large is the collection?"

"Sue and I have quite a large collection and like these six pieces most of it has been out of view for over fifty years or longer. If you and Karen would like, it would be fun to have the two of come over and see it."

Karen spoke up saying "I would love to see it, what would be a good time?"

Sue took her hand and said "Why don't the two of you come over this evening then we can have Jim take us out to dinner. It would be fun and we all need to eat."

Stewart was laughing and Karen said "I would love to; are you coming Stewart?"

Now Stewart was laughing really hard and said "I would love to, when you're ready to leave we will follow you."

There were goodbyes to be said then Jim and Sue were on there way home with Stewart and Karen right behind them, Sue was laughing and said "I really do like Karen and she really did want to come over, They seam like a fun couple."

By the time they were at the house and parked out front Karen got out of there car saying "I can't believe this house, it's like something out of a movie or a romance novel.

"Please come in I think you will love it." Sue took them all on a tour of the house and the art. They also went out to the big building. Sue was explaining they were going to be married there on the thirtieth. Karen was really excited and loved all of it. Sue was telling her about the upper patio and watching the sunsets and the lights of the city coming on.

"Stewart said "I can't believe that something like this even exists in Tucson and that it's been here all these years."

Sue told them about the three guest houses, the warehouse, tennis courts and the helicopter landing pad. Back at the pool room Jim opened a bottle of Champaign and said "I made reservation at La Poloma if that's agreeable with everyone."

Karen was looking at the art in the pool room and noticed two of the pieces they had just acquired. "These two look like you and Jim bought them."

"Most of the art in the estate came with it. Jim wants to donate it to museums in and around Tucson. We don't want the house to be a museum so we are slowly replacing the art with things we like. We bought these two pieces in Cuba a few weeks ago."

"The two of you went to Cuba!"

"Jim had us and another couple flown down there and we spent a week at a great hotel on the beach. We had the best time and did everything including taking Salsa lessons. We even went to a great Salsa club in Havana."

They spent a good half hour talking then Stewart and Karen followed them to the Country Club. When Sue walked in wearing that white dress and jewelry the whole staff was excited to see her and it was obvious. The four of them had a really good time and a nice dinner.

On the drive back to the house Sue slid over next to Jim and said "Everyone seamed to like my dress."

Jim laughed and said "Everyone we met tonight fell in love with you. You're not only beautiful, but very charming."

"Are you part of that everyone?"

"Yes I am; I fell in love with you as soon as we met. And since then you have surpassed every fantasy I have ever had. I do love you Sue Taylor."

"After we get these clothes off why don't you open a bottle of Champaign and we will keep this party going in the Jacuzzi."

It turned out to be quite a party they had the music on and they played till after one in the morning.

Saturday Morning May 15/ 2010 Tucson, Arizona

It was almost nine when Sue woke Jim up with kisses and said "Wake up old man and come run with me"

Sue was laughing as he pulled her back into the bed and started kissing her. They did make it to the trails and ran hard. Toward the end they slowed down and Sue said "I am happier then I ever thought I could be and I am so in love with you. Would you like me to cook you something or would you like to go out?"

"I would really like to go to the Congress Street Hotel Café. We could get a paper relax and have a nice breakfast then maybe walk around downtown and look at the shops."

"Actually that sounds like a nice morning; I would love to spend some time with you."

The Café and breakfast was fun. The news paper was still about the big scandal and all the other arrest it was generating as it slowly worked its way down hill. Jim likes the business section and all there different stories and how they are designed to move the public in one direction or the other. Most of what they say is misinformation that supports there advertisers. So when Jim reads it it's with more then a grain of salt.

Jim and Sue were really having fun just walking around down town and looking in the different shops and stores. It was funny but Jim knew a Number of the shop owners from the Café. Jim's phone rang and it was David who told Jim his new friends were from the Justices Department and there were four of them. He gave Jim two names and said I have pictures of what is in there rooms but there was nothing of value. "Now this morning two of them are at the FBI office in the Federal building and two of them are watching you and Sue walking around downtown. If I come up with any more I will call you."

Jim was laughing as he put the phone away. He told Sue what David had told him. She was also laughing.

Back at the house Sue asked if Jim was going to work on the computers.

"Unless you have something you would like to do, I would just like to hang out here with you."

"There is nothing I would like to do more then hang out with you. Let's pick out some nice music."

Sunday Morning May 16/ 2010 Tucson, Arizona

Steve and Frank were going to have a back yard barbecue with there friends Troy and Jared. They invited Kay and Jan then Jim and Sue. Within an hour it was up to twelve people including David and Becky. The party got moved to the big courtyard and pool at Jim's house.

Sunday turned out to be a really fun day and there was no talk about bad guys or federal police. It was mostly about engagements, graduations and weddings and lasted into the evening.

Monday Morning May 17/ 2010 Tucson, Arizona

There morning Shower was so good they ended up back in bed totally wet. "Let me fix us a light breakfast. I know you want to work on you're computers. I will have the boys scan there vehicle then if there clean I will have them pick up the other three scanners and deliver one of them to David. I was thinking just before they leave I will take the government agents shopping with me."

Jim was laughing then kissed Sue and said "What have I created?"

"I am not sure yet, but I am having fun. Now give me one more kiss then get out of bed."

It was a fun start to the morning then Jim took his papers, a container of coffee and went to the basement. Jim started with the justices department and the agents that David and his people had found the names of. After a short amount of time he had the assignment Number the agents were working under, and there supervisor. In his files Jim got there assignment was to do a background and to check for any connection to Clifton Financial or RC Rankin. The request for this was a little harder to trace but in the end it led to Senator Tuttle.

Jim spent over two hours going through everything he could find on the good Senator including a good Number of bank accounts. He even got into his personal computer and searched his files and down loaded a lot of information including all his contacts. Jim was now at the point he could have a section of the X computer go through all the files he had down loaded including all the CD files from the basement he had down loaded. The computer will make millions of cross checks and comparisons of all that information and come back with thousands of different scenarios of things connected to the Senator then print the four most probable.

After less then an hour Jim was sitting with a drink and reading through the first report. Sue came in the library and joined him in reading it. After twenty minutes Sue said "I can't believe you and your computer could find all this information then come up with this scenario. What are you going to do?"

"I don't have enough to even begin to take down this whole organization and don't know if I ever will. Now what I can do is give the reporters enough hints to look in the right places so they can come up with enough to bring down the Senator. The Justices Department will be looking there and not here. That way it will show the story came from investigative reporting rather then an anonymous source."

"That's perfect, but what can you give them that will be big enough to make him really dirty and a threat to the rest of them?"

"I will call the reporters today and tell them what to look for and where; it will quickly link the Senator to Clifton Financial and two other financial corporations and how they have been manipulating energy stocks for years and have stolen hundreds of millions of dollars."

"Well that should keep the government busy and at the same time upset the Senators friends."

"Let me grab some papers then let's drive up to Phoenix and I will call Hoyt Segal and feed him the information he needs to research there story. Then the morning it comes out in the paper I will withdraw most of the Senators money."

The drive to Phoenix was fun, only because of the company. Sue thought it was kind of lonely because Jim left there GPS transmitter back at the house. Jim spent an hour and twenty minutes on the phone with Hoyt and Bill Mitchell and gave them all the information of where and what to look for. He did tell them it was necessary that this time all of this came to light by there research. He asked if possible it would be nice to have the story brake in the Wednesday morning edition. Before he hung up he did tell them this was just another piece of a very large story.

Jim closed the phone, kissed Sue and said "That's one Senator down."

"What are you saying?"

"There is a nice little Cantina close to here that has great Mexican food, let's get a drink and I will tell you who else I found today."

"Ok I will wait, but only because the Mexican food sounds like a good idea."

It was a short drive and right a way they got a drink and were given a basket of great home made corn chips and Salsa. Jim told Sue about the two additional Senators he had found that were directly connected to Senator Tuttle and the stock manipulation and all of the other corporations. Then he took her hand and said "This thing is going to reach out to some of the richest people in the country and they will be willing to do anything to stop this from exposing them. What I am trying to do is make it appear as thou one of the three Senators has rolled over and implicated the others. That should start the whole thing to come apart. I think I can control the rate that this happens."

"If this is as big as we think it is the government couldn't handle all of it at once and it could cause a huge financial crises and recession and that would make the country more unstable then it already is."

"You're right; so we need to be careful. This needs to happen over along period of time. So let's order dinner."

Dinner and the drive back were both fun and there was no talk of bad guys and money.

Tuesday Morning May 18/ 2010 Tucson, Arizona

Jim and Sue spent most of the day in the basement identifying corporations and bank accounts that Senator Tuttle and the other two Senators had common stock in. Then Jim used Senator Tuttle's pass word to remove and move almost all of the money to one of his personal accounts. One hour later Jim showed the Senator closing all of his personal and corporate accounts.

"Well that will start the other two Senators on the war path against our good Senator Russell Tuttle."

"You never said who the other two Senators were."

"I am sorry, I thought I had; well then you will love this. The first Senator is Robert Hawkins of Texas and the second is none other then Senator John Allen of Pennsylvania."

"You're right that is hard to believe. Those two self riches sons of a btches; they both stand up and act like they are personally protecting the common guy on the street. How can they live with them selves?"

"I can't answer that, but I have a pretty good idea of how it will end. Remember they are in partnerships with people who can't let them go to trial."

"I don't like that either, but in there case I don't think it will bother me."

"Let's lock this up grab a nice bottle of wine and go play in the Jacuzzi and pool. Tomorrow will be a busy day; the news paper hits the streets early."

"You pick the music and I will get the wine and towels."

It ended up being a great night.

Wednesday Morning May 19/ 2010 Tucson, Arizona

At six Jim and Sue were out and running. "Let's do breakfast at the Country Club then we can start monitoring the television both local and Cable. It should be quite a story."

"At breakfast I should be the one that gets your attention."

The Country Club was fun they ran into Howard Welt the manager and talked a few minutes, Sue mentioned her parents were coming out for a visit and were bring there golf clubs. Howard said he would be looking forward to meeting them. At breakfast Randy was there waiter and was thrilled to see Sue. They had a nice breakfast and Jim made sure he over tipped.

Back at the house Sue poured them some of the morning coffee she had put in a thermal serving container. Jim turned on the television to the cable news. They were already on continuous coverage of the breaking story of Senator Russell Tuttle of Arizona and the headlines of the Phoenix Republic News Paper accusing him of being involved in the theft of hundreds of millions of dollars from a Number of corporations, stockholders, State and Federal tax payers. The article went on to show how the Senator was also involved with the murder of a young Lawyer named Ken Benton who was the first one to bring this story to light.

The announcer was going on about the amount of details the two reporters Bill Mitchell and Hoyt Segal had found on the Senator all the way to some of the hidden bank accounts he had money in. "All efforts to locate the Senator have come up empty and no one in his office will even respond to any questions. It appears that law enforcement at all levels have been taken by surprise by the morning edition of the Phoenix Republic and none of them are willing to make any comment at this time. We also have made attempts to reach the reporters that wrote the article but they also are not available for comment."

After the commercial break they came back and started telling the Story as they knew it with the accident that killed the young Lawyer Ken Benton and how an investigator for the Arizona State Police named Bruce Tate found the accident was staged to cover up the murder then how the same two reporters broke the story open. They did a good job of retelling the story including the murders and shoot out with the Phoenix police. The only thing they didn't mention was the anonymous source and that was ok with Jim.

"That's quite a story they have there. Why don't we take our coffee and go lay out by the pool and get some sun. Also you never told me how much money you took from our good Senator Tuttle."

Jim started laughing and said "I only got thirty some million from him then I found a numbered account that had a hundred and sixteen million. Now out of the three corporations I got seventy six million. From the other two Senators I took a total of a hundred and sixty some million and moved it to Senator Tuttle's account, then after a while I withdrew that also. I am sure they all will be missing there money soon."

"Why don't you give me some kisses, we can check on them and there story later."

"We need to make sure everything is ready because you're Mom and Dad will be here Friday."

"Mrs. Jacobs like always has the house ready and the boys have arraigned to have flowers delivered Friday morning for all the houses including ours. They also made sure everything they might need, will be there."

"Then should I ask about Graduation and the party?"

"You can if you like, but that also has been handled and we are expecting over sixty people and the boys and girls and I have been having a ball and spent a lot of your money."

"Well then all I have to worry about is how I am going to seduce you."

"For you I am a given, but now you better come up with something Wonderful."

They spent the next hour and a half working on wonderful then Jim opened a bottle of Champaign. They laid out in the sun and talked. Sue kissed Jim and said "Would you like to call David and see if he and Becky would like to go out to dinner tonight."

That does sound like fun. If they can go we can meet them at the Country Club; I don't want David coming over here till I am sure our friends have left. And if I am right that should be today or tomorrow. I think the Justices department will be busy after today."

"If they are going to go, tell David to have Becky call me."

After the arrangements were made for the evening Jim turned on the cable news. They were still into continues coverage in Phoenix with only doing breaks for the regular news. No one had been able to find Senator Tuttle or most of his staff. They reported that the Justices Department had a Federal warrant and five Agents had been seen going into the Phoenix Republic Newspaper. Cable News had a panel of four talking heads going over the Republics story and trying to figure out how Hoyt Segal and Bill Mitchell could have found all the information they had in there story. There were also reports of huge amounts of money being deposited into the Senator's account early in the morning then only hours later the account being Closed by the Senator. "All in all with all the stories about the Senator closing bank accounts that morning the amounts have added up to be in the hundreds of millions."

"What do you think the Senator did with all that money?"

"I am not sure, but if we listen long enough, I am sure the talking heads will tell us; they seam to know more about this then the FBI and Justices Department."

After another hour they shut the television off and went up stars to get ready for there evening with David and Becky.

They met in the bar and both of the girls looked beautiful. After they all said hello and got a drink David said to Sue I was thinking of you and your corporation. I remember you saying you wanted to get yourself and the girls small SUV's. Well today I bought out most of the inventory of a Mercedes dealership that is in receivership. Among the vehicles I got are four brand new Mercedes SUV's and if you like three of them are yours."

"Thank you David they sound great and that is very nice of you, but we may want to talk with Bill Stine, it might be better if my corporation shows that we over paid for them and that would give us a nice deduction. Then you can show the sale as a great profit and pay taxes on it."

"Maybe we should talk to Bill then I can use that money to help support one of your art projects and write that off also."

At dinner David and Becky were talking about looking for a house. They wanted to stay in the same part of town but wanted something with acreage. "Why don't you talk with Hugh and tell him what you both want. If you find the property and the location you want you can always tear down what is already there and build what you want. If you get enough acreage you can also build a garage large enough to have all your car collection at the house."

"Now that's a good idea. I wonder if there are any large plots of land up here by the mountains that are available."

"Our security guard told me that the property to the east of us was for sale for years and they finally took it off the market around eight months ago. He didn't know how big it was or why they took it off the market. You might have Hugh do some research on it."

"That would be nice then after were married Sue and I could go shopping together, with or without sugar daddies."

They were all laughing at that. Dinner was fun and they all seamed to have a good time. Sue suggested that Becky and David come back to house. Becky's eyes lit up right a way so David thought it would be fun.

Back at the house the Champaign got opened and they sat in the pool room. Sue had some nice music on and they were all talking when Becky said "We should have brought our swimsuits so we could sit in the Jacuzzi."

"I have a lot of swim suits that will fit you and I am sure Jim has some to fit David."

"She is right David; let's get the two of you swim suits"

It took only minutes and they moved the party to the Jacuzzi with a second bottle of Champaign and plastic glasses. The girls were talking about the graduation party and the wedding. David and Becky would be at both. It was almost midnight when David and Becky left.

Thursday Morning May 20/ 2010 Tucson, Arizona

Jim and Sue started the day with a nice run and decided they would have a relaxed breakfast at the Country Club. Most of the talk was about tomorrow, Sue's parents would be in about eleven. Steve and Chris had all of the vehicles washed and gassed. They were always looking to see what needed to be done; they didn't wait to be told.

"I have a feeling that when we get home and I scan the car the GPS transmitter will be gone. But I don't want anyone to drop there guard, If anyone does show up I want to know about it. I don't expect that but I didn't expect the Justices Department either. After a week I will break into there files just to find out what they found on us."

"That still amazes me that you can do that and they have no idea that you have been there."

"It's better then that, I can change or add to there files without them knowing it. There is nothing I know of that I can't break into, but the other functions it performs are moor impressive to me. Now more importantly what would you like to do today?"

"Let's enjoy our breakfast then go home and check the news. If there is nothing that needs you're attention lets get together with the boys and girls and make sure everything they need is also handled. I worry they won't tell me if they need something."

"You're right, let's make sure we handle that. You can also tell them about there new SUV's. They should be here by tomorrow."

When they got back to the house Jim was right the GPS transmitter had been removed from his car. They made themselves comfortable and turned on the Cable News. They were again on continuous coverage and had there people in Phoenix. The stories were coming fast and furious. The Justices Department along with the FBI had search warrants and they were at Senator Tuttle's homes and offices in both Phoenix and Washington. They were also talking about the Phoenix Republic and there morning edition where Hoyt Segal and Bill Mitchell's column brought out more charges about the Senator removing large amounts of money from many different accounts to ones he controlled then some time Tuesday morning he closed all of his accounts. After that the money and the Senator have disappeared with out a trace. There article also showed what other Senators he had an alliance with and hinted that this story could be much larger.

The media machine was trying to get statements from any Senator they could find. They also tried to get a statement from the White House. So far all they could get was No Comment. It was the same from any State or Federal law enforcement.

"I have a feeling they may never hear from Senator Tuttle. Senators Hawkins and Allen can't afford to have anyone talk to him."

"These are such horrible people. It's like we all know people like this exist in government, But this gives them a name and makes us all take a good look at it. It's like a reality check."

"Let's turn this off, then why don't you call the girls and boys and invite them over."

It wasn't long and they were all there and Sue had coffee for everyone and the talk was about graduation and family coming in. Both Kay's and Jan's family and two old friends were coming in also Friday morning. While they were all talking David called and said he had the four SUV's in Tucson and would bring them over if the timing was right. Jim told him it was perfect the girls were at the house right then.

The girls wanted to know what that was about. Jim kissed them both on the cheek and said "I will let Sue tell you."

Sue while laughing said "Our corporation is buying three Mercedes Benz SUV's and the two of you can pick out the color you want there are four to choose from and David is bringing them over as we speak. The company will actually own them and will take care of license plates and insurance. Each of you will have company credit cards to handle the gas and any other expenses you have."

Kay and Jan were really excited and couldn't believe Sue got Mercedes for them. It was only a matter of minutes and David arrived with the four SUV"s. Sue told the girls to pick out the ones they wanted then she picked one for herself. Jim asked David if he had another one. He said he did but it had almost five thousand miles on it. Jim turned to the boys and asked if they would like one. They both broke out laughing and said they would love it.

"I will do the same thing as Sue is doing I will have my property company buy them and it will cover license, insurance and the gas can go on your charge cards."

David was laughing and said "I will leave the three of them here and I will go back and have Bill Stine put the three on Catalina Consulting and the other two to Cooper Investments. Then I will bring back the two plus all the temporary plates and insurance binders for the others."

They all thanked David as he left. Sue kissed Jim and "Said should I open some nice wine for everyone?"

"That would be nice because there something I would like to talk about with everyone."

The boys automatically took over opening and pouring the wine. Sue could only laugh. Once everyone had there wine Jim said "There is something else I would like to do for all of you but I would like you to let me explain why I am doing it and the way I would like to do it. This may sound silly but there are reasons. What I would like to do is to give each of you one million dollars in cash and have you put it in a safe deposit box. The reason I would like you to have it is so none of you feel trapped here. Just the fact that you have it will give you the freedom to do the things you want. Sue and I do want you to stay and help with the companies and be part of our family; I think you all know that's a given. Now the reason for the cash and safety deposit boxes is the strange part. I have recently come into a great amount of money and a lot of it is in cash. If any of us deposit a large amount of cash in any one month the bank will notify the government. The guideline is ten thousand in reality it's more like five thousand. Now the government for other reasons has been looking at me trying to find out if I am doing anything illegal. Actually they have been doing surveillance on me. Steve and Frank know about that and you ladies should also."

"So the government thinks you're a crook."

"Actually there is a Senator who was afraid I might have some evidence on him and he was trying to have the Justices Department find something he could use against me. But hopefully that may be over. The Senator was Russell Tuttle."

"Jan and I watch the news so I won't ask anything about you and the Senator."

"Thanks Kay, but I did want the two of you to know."

They all talked about the money then asked the boys to go out and buy four nice sizes inexpensive briefcases.

After the boys left the girls went home and Jim and Sue got the four million out of the basement. It wasn't long and the boys were back and the girls came over and they all put a million in there briefcase. The cars got delivered and all the paper work was put in the proper vehicle. They took Jim's big car so they could all fit into it then it was off to the banks.

Later they all decided they would cook a nice dinner. It was funny the girls were in charge and had no problem telling the boys that fact. Jim and the boys were laughing.

The dinner was great and the boys made sure they told the girls what a good job they did. Jim and the boys did the clean up and took out the garbage. They all had coffee and talked a while but made an early night of it because tomorrow would be a big day and a lot of fun. After everyone left Sue said "We still have time to walk up and watch the sunset if you like."

"Let me put a nice bottle of wine and glasses in the back pack; it sounds like fun."

Friday Morning May 21/ 2010 Tucson, Arizona

It was early when Sue woke up Jim and asked him to go running with her. "I would love to go running with you."

They did a good eight miles they used the outside shower then jumped into the pool. Sue was happy and excited about seeing her parents. "After we shower and dress let's have a nice breakfast at the Country Club and relax, they won't bee here till about eleven."

Sue kissed him and said "You're sweet; let's get ready."

The Country club was a good idea and Sue look really cute in a nice summer dress with the appropriate accessories.

The morning slowed down, breakfast was good and they did relax. Sue asked if Jim wanted a news paper. "No, when we get home I will take a quick look at the cable news."

On the way home Sue asked what she should do with her car. "I am sure you know someone that could use it. When you have time find the title and I will show you what to do."

It was a little past eleven when Jerry called and said the limousine just left the gate. Sue already had coffee ready so they walked to the door and waited till the limousine came around the circle drive. As the door opened Sue and Jim were there to greet them. There were hugs and kisses then Jim and Mike (Sue's Dad) brought there luggage to the house. Once Mike and Helen had freshened up they all went to the pool room. Helen was still amassed how quickly they got from Colorado to the house. Sue served coffee and the conversation was all about Sue's graduation and the wedding. They were having a good time then about two o'clock they helped them take there luggage over to the guest house. Helen again loved the flowers. They were coming back around seven then they were all going out to the Country Club for dinner.

"Would you like to turn on the cable news now, we never did after we got home."

"Thanks, I would."

While Jim turned it on Sue picked out a nice bottle of wine and brought it and two glasses over. No sooner then Jim had it opened his second cell phone rang. It was the one that the two reporters had the number of. Jim looked at Sue then answered it was Hoyt Segal who said the FBI and Justices Department were coming down hard on them. Jim advised them not to have any conversations with any of them unless the two of them were together and had the attorney from the paper also there. "Hoyt this story will reach high into our government and big industry and it may be hard to tell who is playing on what side."

"Shit you're starting to scare me more then they already have."

"Just follow your story and keep you're heads low. I will call when I have something worth printing. For now get rid of the phone your using then I will reach out to you."

When Jim hung up he took the battery out of the phone he was using then broke it. "Let's have our wine and watch the news."

"Do you think they can stand up to all the heat the government will put on them?"

"They're having the time of there lives, this is the biggest story they have ever had and it's the juice to them."

"Well I can understand that. Now give me a kiss then let's watch the news."

Cable news was still going crazy over the story and had on four of there talking heads who were dissecting all the information that was in the article from the paper. They had teams of people trying to find any leads on the Senator's location, the missing money or anyone else that could be connected to the Senator or any of the corporations. They said there were also roomers of some Senators wanting Congressional hearings on all of this.

The four of them were also going over all the different comities Senator Tuttle chaired or was connected with and what other Senators were on those comities. "Well I bet that has your other two Senators a little upset."

"Let's turn them off, take our wine and go swimming. It might be better if we wore swimsuits."

They had fun and most of the talking was about their honeymoon. They had decided to take a week and go to Hawaii. Darlene had found them a luxury hotel on Maui where they could have a private bungalow that was a hundred feet from the surf. They were both excited about going and were only planning on taking casual clothes.

It was funny when Sue's parents came over Helen had completely change her wardrobe and was dressed in a very elegant and sexy dress with all the accessories even her hair was different. "I love it Mom; you look beautiful and a good ten years younger."

"I went shopping with my own sugar daddy. We spent a fortune and had the best time. Even Mike got some great clothes."

"Well it was money well spent both you and Daddy look great and I love it."

Jim opened a bottle of Champaign and they were all having fun listing to Helen tell about her experience of shopping with a sugar daddy. Mike was even tipping the sales girls and telling them the rules of not looking at price tags. They were all laughing and having fun. Jim loved watching Sue's reaction of seeing the wild side of her concretive parents. Before they left for the Country Club Jim gave them there membership cards and told them all the facilities and golf courses would be available to them and there guests. Sue told them she and Jim would introduce them to the general manager Howard Welt.

The Country Club and dinner was fun and Mike and Helen did get to meet Howard Welt who was happy to meet them. Howard told them to call him when they were coming out to play golf and he would take them around and introduce them. Both Mike and Helen were pleased. Sue told them about the graduation party and asked if they would like to invite any of there friends. Helen's eyes got big and told Mike she would like to ask one couple Tom and Patty. Sue remembered them from back when they lived there.

"Why don't you call them now so they can make there plans; you can work out the details tomorrow."

Helen thought that was a good idea and was on her phone right away. Tom and Patty also thought it would be fun and Helen said she would call them in the morning so they could work it all out.

They all had a good time and on the ride home Helen asked if they were all going to have Champaign in the Jacuzzi. Sue and Mike were laughing really hard and Jim said "I for one was really hoping so."

After they got home Mike and Helen went over to there house to change and Jim and Sue went upstairs to change. Sue jumped on Jim laughing and giving him kisses and said "You make my whole world wonderful."

The Jacuzzi and company were great and Sue's parents didn't go back to there house till after eleven.

Saturday Morning May 22/ 2010 Tucson, Arizona

Jim was the first one awake and got to wake Sue with kisses. After all the kisses Sue wanted to start the day with a run then watch the sunrise from the upper patio. While they were watching the sunrise Sue mentioned that she should check with boys about the party. "I talked with them earlier in the week and gave them a budget of ten thousand to make sure the party will be everything you would expect. So let's leave it up to them."

"Ok then let's get Mom and Dad and go out for a nice breakfast."

Sue's Mom wanted to go back to the Congress Street Hotel Café and everyone thought it was a good idea. Sue talked with Kay and Jan and made sure everything was all right with there parents and guests. The girls were both ecstatic and said everything was wonderful and would hopefully see them at the ceremonies or for sure at the party. Sue was laughing when she closed the phone. She kissed Jim and said "You have already made this a wonderful day."

Breakfast was as always great and Helen and Mike were excited about Sue receiving her Masters degree. She also had a degree in business. The other big conversation was the wedding. Helen said they had decided to stay an extra week and leave on Sunday June sixth the day before Jim and Sue got back from there honeymoon.

The morning went fast and soon they were getting ready to go to the university. Sue knew the perfect place to park. They did get to meet Jan and Kay's family and friends. The Graduation was well done and they had the sound system to where you could hear the speakers very well. There were a lot of very happy people there and Sue for sure was one of them. That degree represented a great deal of her life and a lot of work. Like all the other graduates there is almost a sense of loss. School had been what there lives rotated around for years and now it was done.

There had been a lot of hugs, kisses and tears before they returned to the house. The boys again had signs out directing people where to park. Everyone went to there house to freshen up then over to the party.

The boys had outdone themselves; the place looked like a great night club with the stage a band and lots of special effects lighting. There friends Troy and Jared were tending bar and there was a ten foot table with a nice buffet all laid out with glass plates, stainless steel utensils and cloth napkins.

Jim and Sue told Steve and Frank what a great job they had done and they were telling Jim and Sue what fun they have had putting it all together. Sue's parents were the next to show up followed by David and Becky. By the time they all were introduced and had drinks there were another twenty some people there including the girls and there families and friends. Within an hour there was a good eighty people there the boys were playing hoist and the band was playing nice soft rock with a young lady and man doing most of the vocals.

After a lot of handshaking and introductions Jim and David got a second drink and David said "I am sure you haven't seen any of the news today but yesterday morning a private plane crashed in Northern Florida and there was two men killed; there was a third body on board that was already dead and wrapped up a canvas bag along with a Number of steel free weights that weighed eighty pounds. This gets better; the plane had a flight plan that showed it coming out of Virginia Beach and going to a small air strip on the Florida Keys. Today the Florida State Police released the identity of that body as that of our good Senator Russell Tuttle of Arizona."

"Well I am sure that will keep all the federal law enforcement agencies busy for the next month or so. Thanks David; now let's go see if we can get a dance with a pretty girl."

They both must have asked the right girl because in only minutes they were both dancing. The party went on for a good three hours then the band thanked everyone and that kind of ended the party. Within forty five minutes it was down to family and close friends. That lasted another hour then Sue's parents were going out with there friends and the girls and there families were off to there house. Now it was down to Jim, Sue, David and Becky. The boys said they with the help of Troy and Jared would handle the clean up and make sure everything was locked up. Jim thanked them and gave Troy and Jared five hundred each and thanked them.

David and Becky went back to the house with them. Jim told them all to relax and he would put on a pot of coffee. Sue looked exhausted but was happy with how everything worked out. They sat and talked almost an hour then David and Becky said goodnight and left.

"Would you take me to the Jacuzzi? We don't need swimsuits; Mom and Dad won't be back till late and won't be over."

"Let me get the towels and some nice wine."

Sunday Morning May 23/ 2010 Tucson, Arizona

Jim and Sue were up early and out running and having fun. By the end of the run they were walking hand in hand. "Before we go to breakfast I would like to watch the news. We can watch it up stairs while we are getting ready."

"What's the big story you're looking for?"

"Yesterday David told me about a story he watched on cable news that said Friday morning a private plane crashed in Florida killing the two men aboard but there was also a body on board that was wrapped in a canvas bag along with a bunch of steel weights. The plane flew out of Virginia Beach and was in rout to a small air strip on the Florida Keys. They said the body was that of our Senator Tuttle of Arizona."

"I think you're right, we should see that story."

Back at the house they took there coffee up to the master suit and turned on the television and cable news. The story was now huge and they were saying the plane was registered to a corporation in DC and it flew out of a Small private air field in Virginia Beach that was used by many of the Senators and there private staff. They stated that the air field was very secure with both full time security and video. The FBI had the whole place sealed off and no one would make any comment about the plane or who had access to it. it was the same with Florida and all the people who responded to the crash the federal government had them all sequestered and would make no comment on the accident or the identity of any one that was on the plane. The newscaster was saying that all of the media was in the dark.

"Should I shine a little light into some of those dark places?"

"If you can do it without tipping them off about us; then I think they should be exposed. This is scary and these people are worse then the mob. They must have there own little army."

"They call them there security people but in reality they're mercenaries who they can use anywhere in the world. The majority of them are sociopaths who are more into the work then the money and they are very dangerous. We need to make sure that nothing can be traced back to us. I was thinking of having someone in the Senators inner group send the information to Bill Mitchell and Hoyt Segal at the Phoenix Republic."

"Let me get this clear; your telling me you can down load the information into there system then have there system send it to the News paper?"

"I think better than that I can make it appear that the information originated in their computer. We better get our showers and dress, so we can take your parents to breakfast."

The shower was fun and Sue was dressed in a great little summer dress and looked like she just stepped out of a fashion magazine. Jim made sure to tell her how cute she looked.

Sue's Mom was also dressed for the part and looked stunning. Jim did make sure he mentioned it. They went to the Country Club and breakfast was great. They were talking about the Graduation and the party then it again shifted to the wedding. Sue invited her parents to come over and see her dress. She said "Jim has a meeting this morning then he will be working so the three of us can make a day of it."

"Mike you have a set of keys to the sedan, I will take my SUV and Sue has hers but if any of you need me please call."

Once back at the house Jim called David and asked if they could meet. David suggested the bar at the Congress Street Hotel. Jim told Sue and said he would also call Hoyt and Bill with one of the new phones they had bought in Casa Grand and inform them of what will be coming to them and from where it would be coming from.

"Well that should have Hoyt and Bill excited. Just make sure you take care of yourself."

With a couple of nice kisses Jim was on his way to meet David.

Cathy was the bartender and glad to see Jim and had drinks to the table before David got there. Jim told David about the other two Senators Hawkins and Allen and what he had done to them and Senator Tuttle.

"Son of a bitch, you're playing with some bad people who have a lot of power and will use it." David started laughing and said "You took there money and made them think Tuttle took it so then they would take Tuttle out of the picture and off you're back. This is great."

"Well David now I am going to drop a dime on them and hopefully let the government take them out. This information won't come from me but it will end up in the Phoenix Republic. What I need you to do is have our people watching out for anyone with a new interest in me. I think we are at the point I should tell you all of this is just the tip of this thing. There are thousands of these people all around the world and it involves the theft of trillions of dollars."

"I know you well enough that I think you're telling me you're going after all of them."

"I need to do this bunch right now because there a threat to me. The others we will talk about after my honeymoon."

"On a nicer note I talked with Hugh and told him what Becky and I were looking for and he is looking into the property that was for sale close to you. I would like to get in to see it."

"Remember if it is where you want and has enough acreage you don't need to care what it costs, even if you're going to tear it all down and build everything new. David I have billions in banks all over the world and you will always have all you want."

After Jim left the bar he drove over to the federal court house. He wanted the call to come from that cell tower incase it was ever traced. Jim called Hoyt and Bill on the main line of the paper and told the operator it was Jeff Black calling; he got put right through. Jim gave them his new cell Number and got there new cell Number. "The reason I called there is someone who has information on the people behind the murder of Senator Russell Tuttle who's body was to be dropped in the ocean off the keys of Florida. Do the two of you still want to play?"

"You bet we do; what do you need us to do?"

"All I need is a secure E-mail address for you. This is important, what ever they send you and what question you may have, do not try and have any other contact with the sight they send it from. Now to keep yourselves busy while you're waiting for this to happen, you might do some background searches on Senator Robert Hawkins of Texas and Senator John Allen of Pennsylvania."

"Shit; if you're right this will be one hell of a story. This is scary just thinking about it."

"Before you get two excited let's wait and see what they send you."

When Jim returned to the house he fixed himself a good drink then took that and a bottle of water down to the basement where he started on his computers.

It was after five when Sue came down gave him a kiss and asked if he wanted to take a break. Jim locked the library and they went to the pool room. While Sue fixed the drinks she told him her parents were going out with some friends. "Now if you like we can take our drinks to the pool, we have towels there."

The pool was a good idea and they spent a good hour in the water. "Are you going back to you're computers tonight?"

"If you don't mind; I would like to have this all ready and sent from Senator Hawkins DC office some time in the early hours of the morning. This will come from the computer system that can only be accessed by the Senator and his top aids. There system will show it was all created there then stored in a secret file. I will show that someone entered there office but somehow it won't show who's ID they used also there security cameras will be off for the duration of time the person was there E-mailing all the files to the reporters at the Phoenix Republic. Then in the mid morning or early after noon I will empty and close six bank accounts that are controlled by the two Senators. Tuesday morning should be quite a story. I was also considering sending along a list of Senator Hawkins top contributors to his reelection fund. I was thinking it might make interesting reading. What do you think?"

"I think the FBI and Justices department will be going nuts. These people are ruthless and they should all come tumbling down. How about I fix us something to eat and bring it and a bottle of wine down to the basement; we could have a picnic?"

"That does sound like fun; Let me dry off, put on my shorts, T shirt, sandals then go back to work."

The picnic was fun and by one thirty Jim was done. He had showed someone had entered the DC executive office of Senator Hawkins twelve forty A/M but the code Number of ID card that was used was all scrambled. There computer system showed the contents of an unnamed file had been sent by E-mail to a mail box of the Phoenix Republic. The video surveillance cameras had stopped working at twelve thirty then restarted again at one fifteen.

"Well if there security is any good at all by ten o'clock in the morning they should know they had some kind of a break in but I don't think they will find the file and the fact it was E-mailed till some time Tuesday and by then it will be in the news paper."

Monday Morning May 24/ 2010 Tucson, Arizona

Jim woke Sue with kisses and asked her to go running with him. They only did five miles and were walking hand in hand at the end. "Why don't you call you're parents and the girls and see if they would all like to join us for breakfast at the country club. I am going to call the boys and have them check all of the security and fences.

The shower was fun for both of them. Sue called her parents and the girls and they all thought it would be fun and they all talked about what they would wear. Jim talked with Steve and Frank and asked them to take a hard look at all the security and fences. "I don't expect anyone but the possibility is again high. The two of you look out for each other and call if you see anything."

It wasn't long and the six of them were ready. Jim did mention that the ladies all looked like they were going to a fashion show. Mike agreed and didn't even laugh. At the Country Club they were treated as the VIP members and all the girls loved it. All the conversation went to the wedding the guest list was up to about eighty people including David's parents and some of the people from the Barrio. The reception was going to be catered and the band was one that sometimes played at the Congress Street Club. After they finished eating and were down to coffee Jim's phone rang. It was David and he said "Have you been watching the news? The whole country is going nuts."

"We are at breakfast right now but as soon as we get home I will check on it then give you a call."

"Sorry about that, it was David and he needed some figures on a deal we are both involved in."

After they returned home everyone went back to there house and Jim and Sue went to the pool room and turned on the cable news. It was as David said the media machine was going nuts over the story that was the headlines of the Phoenix Republic. The article was accusing both Senator Robert Hawkins of Texas and Senator John Allen of Pennsylvania of being conspirators with the late Senator Russell Tuttle of Arizona in the theft of billions of dollars from the government and thousands of stock holders in many corporations. The article went on to say that when Senator Tuttle was exposed in the thefts and the murder of a young lawyer he not only withdrew Billions from his accounts but also took billions from the other two Senators. The article said that led to the two Senators having Senator Tuttle killed then his body was being flown to a watery grave in the ocean off the Florida Keys. But as luck would have it the plane crashed exposing the plot. The documentation, names, bank records and account numbers that the paper has printed to back up there article is staggering. Again the reporters Hoyt Segal and Bill Mitchell stated that the information and documentation were sent to them by an anonymous source and all there efforts to reach any of the subjects for comments were unsuccessful.

"We must agree with Bill and Hoyt, all of our efforts to contact the Senators, there staff or anyone else in the government or law enforcement, have been met with no comment. Its amazing how the Phoenix Republic was able to sit on this story without any leaks before the paper came out this morning."

"We have just received the information that the FBI and other Government Agencies in Phoenix Arizona have just descended on the Phoenix Republic News Paper with warrants signed by a federal judge. It's not hard to figure out what they want."

Sue with a serious look on her face said "How much more money did you take from the two Senators?"

"I had already gotten the lion's share of there money, but when I was digging around I found a holding company that was owned by the two wife's and it led to four bank accounts that held one point six billion and change. I felt a moral obligation to take all of it; so I did.

Let me call David back."

David told Jim that sense the story broke he had people watching the federal building and court house because that is where Jim had made his last phone call to the paper from. Now about an hour ago a large Number of agents secured the court house not letting anyone in or out. Jim and David were laughing and David said "I hope you got rid of that Cell phone."

"I kept it and took the battery out and will use it when I want to talk with the two of them. I will make sure I call from some exciting places now that I know they are tracing all there incoming calls. Thanks David, have your people be careful and we will see what they come up with."

"You and David seem to be having fun, but these are scary people you're dealing with."

"Well let's not think about them, we have a wedding and honeymoon to think about. We should get a packet from Darleen today with our tickets and itinerary for Hawaii."

Later in the morning Sue's parents were meeting up with some of there friends and going to play golf at the Country Club. Sue had called Becky and she was off today so she talked her and David into coming over and bringing there swim suits. It was going to be a swim party.

Tuesday Morning May 25/ 2010 Tucson, Arizona

Jim and Sue were up and out on the trails early. "Would you take me some wear that we could have a nice and privet breakfast? I love being around our friends and family but I need to be with just you."

"I do know of a nice little restaurant where no one will know us and the food is good."

They quickly showered and dressed. Then Jim quickly cut over to Interstate Ten going south bound then quickly on to Interstate Nineteen then down to the small artist community of Tubac. He said "They have a nice café or we could have breakfast at there Country Club."

"We stopped at the Country Club for a drink the last time we were here. Let's go there for breakfast."

It was early but the Country Club was open and ready; they were seated at a very nice table and coffee and the juice cart was right there. Thank you, I just wanted to be alone with you. I love you very much and do want to marry you."

"I also love you and want to marry you. It's too early to look at the galleries so after breakfast would you like to walk around San Xavier Mission then later we can come back and look at some of the galleries. I think I would like to buy the bronze statue we were looking at the last time we were here."

"I liked it also; let's look at all of the art again now that we know that we will be changing out most of the old masterpieces. This should be fun."

It was after three when they returned to the house and it was nice no one had called them asking where they were. They had brought three pieces of art with them including the bronze statue. There were two larger paintings they would need to send the boys to pick up with the big truck.

"I noticed your parents aren't home so would you like to check and see if there is anything happing at the Arizona Theater Company or the Tucson

Art Museum. If there is would you like to go on a date with me? This would include a nice dinner some where."

"I would love to go on a date with you. If there is nothing happing then we can go dancing."

Wednesday Morning May 26/ 2010 Tucson, Arizona

Jim and Sue were woken by Sue's phone; it was her Mother who was apologizing for her and Sue's Dad being gone all day and not calling. Sue was laughing and invited them to go to breakfast with them.

It wasn't long and they were on there way to the Congress Street Hotel Café that is where Sue's Mom wanted to go. Like Jim and Sue Mike and Helen loved the Café. They were all laughing because Sue's parents spent all of Tuesday and the night with two other couples that were old friends. They had played golf and had a great time with each other. Sue was telling them what a great day she and Jim had. Breakfast was fun but before they left Jim got a call from Steve telling him the security of the estate had been violated last night. Jim told him to just be observant and to hold on to the tapes and he would get with him in a while. After he had closed the phone he said "That was our security who said something had breached the security of the estate last night. Usually it's a mountain lion or a bear that sets off the sensors; I will check with him later."

The drive home was fun and all the talk was about the wedding. Back at the house as soon as Sue's parents went back to there house Sue asked what was going on.

"That call was from Steve and he did say the security was violated last night. I will call him now and we can watch the tapes and hopefully find out what happened and who it was."

Jim called Steve, then he and Sue walked over to the security office in the warehouse. Jerry, Steve and Frank were all there. Jerry showed them where on the property line the breach was based on the sensors then there was video of two men crossing the fence then again the two men showed up coming into the courtyard there were no sensors showing them entering the house. Then only minutes later it showed them leaving by the same rout. Jim just stood there thinking a minute then said "They most likely just planted a listing device. It could also be video but I doubt it; the cameras are small but the equipment to transmit it that distance would be hard to conceal. I will scan the court yard first to make sure there is a device out there but before we do anything I want to locate where they are monitoring it from; it has to be close by."

"Who do you think they are and who sent them?"

"The first thing I need to know is who they are; then I can find out who sent them. For now let's all act as if nothing is wrong. They may have someone up on the mountain watching us. For now the three of you just do what you normally do and I will let you know what I find out."

Back at the house Sue said "This is getting scary. Let's go out to the pool and you can scan the courtyard. This time we can wear swim suits."

Jim was laughing as he gave her a kiss but didn't say anything. It seamed like only minutes and they were in there swim trunks with towels, a scanner and out in the courtyard. It was only a matter of seconds and Jim had a hit on a listing device. Jim and Sue did some roll playing talking about the wedding, caters and the band. Jim then told Sue he needed to go over to the Country Club for a meeting a little later. They swam in the pool for a good twenty minutes then back into the house. It wasn't long and Jim was dressed and on his way to the Country Club. As soon as he was in the parking lot Jim called David on a clean cell phone and asked him to join him for a drink.

Jim ordered a drink and was waiting for David when he noticed two men come in a few minutes apart and try to look as if they fit in. Jim told the waitress he would be right back then went to the rest room and called David and said I have company let's move this to the bar at the Congress Street Hotel. Jim left the rest room to where the men couldn't see him then went out through the hotel and caught a cab and asked to be taken down town Tucson. When they reached the down town area Jim asked to be let out on a street that was close to the Hotel, he paid, tipped and thanked the driver then walked to the hotel bar.

David was sitting in the bar and had a drink there for both of them. The little bar tender was glade to see Jim. Jim said hello to her then went and sat at the table with David who started laughing and said "You seam to make friends Easley."

"This time they came onto the estate and planted a listing device in the court yard. I also believe they have someone up on the mountain watching the estate. As soon as the sun goes down I will try and locate them with my thermal imaging telescope. What I would like you and our people to do is locate there surveillance vehicle that they are using to monitor the listing device. As small as it is they need to be close so all we need to do is position cars and watch for them when they change shifts; we all know what there cars look like. All I need right now is a couple of license Numbers or if you can discreetly find out what branch of the government they are. I brought a map and I believe there are only four possible roads they could use and still be close enough to pick up the transmission."

After a second drink they had located where David would place his people. David said "Give me an hour and everyone will be in place and I do have a clean phone plus the Number you called me from."

"I just want to know what Agency they are from then we will decide what to do about them."

David gave Jim a ride to another hotel then Jim took a cab back to the Country Club got his car and returned to the house. The car did have a GPS transmitter on it.

As Jim walked in Sue greeted him with a kiss and said "We have company." It was her Mom and Dad plus Kay and Jan. "What a pleasant surprise; let me get a glass of that wine and I will join all of you."

Most of the talk was about the graduation and the wedding. Both Kay's and Jan's family and friends had left and they both had a great time with them. They all sat around and talked for a good two hours. Some where Jim invited them all to go to dinner with him and Sue. Now that started a whole new conversation about where they all wanted to go and what they should wear. Jim and Mike were quietly laughing. It wasn't long and everyone went back to there houses and Sue said "let's put on some swim trunks and go in the pool; we can talk on this side of the wall."

Jim was laughing gave her a kiss and said "Let's go change."

Jim poured them both a glass of wine then they got in the pool and he told her what he had David and there people doing. "As soon as I am sure who they are I will break into there computer systems and find out what this is all about. Also later tonight let's use that thermal imaging that is in the basement and see if we can locate there spy on the mountain."

Sue was laughing then asked if she was going to have to invite them to the wedding. "Let's see what there looking for then we can give them something that can keep them busy elsewhere."

They swam for a while and out to the court yard and laid in the sun and made up conversations about a factious real estate deal Jim was working on then swam back into the pool room. Sue started laughing and said "You have your circus back and you're loving it. Don't get me wrong I also love it even thou it scares me. Give me a kiss and we will go up and shower and dress for our guests."

"It's still early, so why don't I call David and see if he and Becky can join us for dinner?"

"That would be wonderful and if they can I will call Becky and tell her what we all are wearing."

Calls and plans were made and the dinner party was now eight people and the Country Club was making the arrangements. The six of them took the big sedan and met David and Becky at the Country Club. They had set up a great round table that would seat eight nicely. While everyone was being seated David quietly said to Jim "The Justices Department".

Jim smiled and said "Good."

Everyone already knew each other so it was an easy and fun dinner. David said that there broker Hugh had set it up for him and Becky to see the property that was to the east of Jim and Sue's estate for ten o'clock in the morning. Everyone was excited for them then David asked if Jim and Sue would come with them.

"You know I would love to and I am sure Sue would also love to see it."

"Yes Sue would love to see it; thank you for asking us."

Becky jumped up ran over and hugged Sue and kissed her on the cheek and said "I really do want you to come with us."

"Oh Becky I am so excited for you and David and this will be fun."

It had been a great dinner and plans were made for the morning.

On the drive home Sue kissed Jim on the cheek and said "You some how knew to ask David and Becky to join us all for dinner tonight."

"I don't know how to respond to that statement but it is true that suddenly it sounded like the right thing to do. What ever the reason I am sure glad I did; they both are excited about finding the right property to have there home."

"You're right they both are nerves about this and I am glad you asked them to dinner."

Back at the house everyone had a glass of wine and talked a good half hour before going to there homes.

"Let's go to the basement, you can get your toys then we can see if we can locate the people that are watching us."

"You little girl are getting hooked on this stuff. Let's change our clothes first."

"If we must but let's hurry."

They were both acting like two kids but did make it to the basement and Jim got out one of the telescopes and a battery pack for it he also got two pairs of starlight binoculars. The binoculars still had enough charge that they still worked, but he needed to plug in the battery pack for the telescope but then it worked great. Jim set the telescope up in the pool room then turned off all the lights and opened one of the large glass doors so they could look without being in the court yard. It didn't take over fifteen minutes and they could see the image of the person up on the mountain just above the cliffs. Sue wanted her turn at looking at them. "What are you going to do about them?"

"I first need to know what they are looking for then I have some fun ideas."

"Shit, you already know who they are. David found them and told you at dinner. Ok now tell me who they are."

Jim was laughing and said "There agents from the Justice Department and will be working out of the Federal Building down town. I would like to go into there system tonight and see what we can find out I think I am the only one in Tucson that has some connection to all these stories and that was only because of our late Senator Tuttle. They never found any connection but now have nowhere else to look."

"Well if this all comes with a bottle of wine and some kisses then I will go with you."

It didn't take long and they were into the file on Jim; it named all the Agents that were assigned to the surveillance. It funny there was no warrant for them to plant a listing device on his property. "There breaking the law, they can't do that."

"Getting all those warrants is just the stuff you see on television and in the movies. Now back to there file they haven't found anything that would connect me to anything except to being rich."

"What are you going to do to send them away?"

Jim started laughing and said "I will make two different calls from the Federal Court house tomorrow to the reporters at the Phoenix Republic and again tell them they will receive an E mail giving them another story that hopefully they can get into Fridays morning edition. I will again tell them they can't respond to the sight the E mail comes from. There is a Federal Judge Harry Kimble that uses his power to constantly go after the Sherriff of Maricopa County because of his politics. That's not the Job of a judge to use his office and power to push people around because of his politics. So I was thinking of having the E mail sent from the computers in his offices. I will again make it look like it was sent at night from a secret file in there computer system. That should give the Judge something to keep him busy and put a cloud over his head for a change."

Sue was laughing really hard and said "You already have the next bunch documented and ready to send out."

"Yes I do and this one will toward the end reach out to some really big names in Tucson, it's not as big as the Senators but involves the theft of billions of dollars and involves hundreds of people and over twenty corporations and a lot of lawyers and accountants both in Arizona and California. You will be shocked when you read the who's who of the names.

Let's shut this all down tonight then tomorrow after we return from breakfast I will have the boys sneak me out of here in the box truck then I will meet David and make my first call from the Federal Court House."

"Would you like to get a bottle of Champaign, some towels and go to the Jacuzzi? Then you can tell me what plans you have for me tonight."

"Trust me there is nothing I would rather do, but you do realize the person on the mountain can see us."

"I do, but from that distance they can only see that we are naked."

Thursday Morning May 27/ 2010 Tucson, Arizona

Jim and Sue were up early and on a run. "Last night was great and it will help hold me over because this will be a busy day for me."

"We still have the shower and I am sure we can make it memorable. Then after we have breakfast with Becky and David we are going to see the property they are interested in. Then after that I am going to spend the day with my parents. But if you need me call."

The shower was wonderful then they went to breakfast at the Country Club so the Justices Department could keep tabs on them. David and Becky met them there and breakfast was fun. David had arranged with Hugh to have them inspect the property at nine o'clock. Jim and Sue were driving with them so the Justices department wouldn't be following them. They followed Hugh up to the property and the entrance was also off of Campbell road close to Jim's driveway. Hugh was pleased to see not only

Becky but also Sue and Jim. The property was over twenty archers and had a beautiful Spanish style home that was over forty two hundred square feet with all the amenities a luxury home would have including a large pool and Jacuzzi. Everything they saw was in pristine condition and both David and Becky loved it. Away from the grounds of the house there was a small barn and ridding arena for horses.

David said "That would be the perfect place to build my garage and warehouse for my cars."

"You could hire a great architect to come up with a Number of different ideas of how it could look and make sure it's exactly what you want."

"Ok Hugh what are they asking for this?"

"David there asking eight million five hundred thousand."

"Do you like it Becky?"

"You are crazy; but yes I love it."

"Let me take Jim and Sue back to the Country Club then I will come over to your office and put in an offer on this thing. I will do eight million two hundred thousand and I want water and mineral rights plus I would like to Close and take possession in two weeks."

"I will have this written up while I am waiting for you."

On the ride back to the Country Club Becky was almost speechless but all over David. Sue was laughing and said "This is going to be so much fun I can hardly wait."

Jim and David had made arrangements to meet at a small bar close to the Tucson art museum.

Back at the house Jim told Jerry he didn't want any visitors including any federal agents. If they had a warrant they should contact his lawyer. Jim gave Jerry the lawyer's business card then smiled. He arranged to have the boys smuggle him off the estate and drop him down town. He told them to stay gone and he would call them in about an hour and a half and tell them where to pick him up.

David was on time and still excited about the property and Becky's reaction to it. "Let's go make a phone call then we can come back here and talk. They drove over to the Federal Building and Courthouse Jim made his first call to the reporters from the Phoenix Republic. Hoyt answered and Jim asked if they were ready to do another story that would bring them more Federal heat. "I don't know how you come up with this stuff but we love it."

"This will again come to you from the source by E mail. Again don't try to have any further contact with the address it comes from. If at all possible it would be nice to have it in the morning edition."

Jim closed the phone and again removed the battery. "Let's go back to that bar have a drink and talk."

Jim explained to David what he was going to do and why. When David found out whose offices the Email was going to be sent from he was laughing so hard he couldn't talk. After about an hour they went back down by the Federal Building and Jim made his second call to the reporters and told them the report would come to there E mail in the next hour. He then again took out the battery before David drove him to meet the boys who would smuggle him back into the house.

Once back at the house Jim fixed himself a nice drink then took it and a bottle of water down to the basement.

It was after five when Sue came down and gave him a kiss and asked if was at the point he could take a break. "Give me five to six minutes and I will."

"I will be in the pool room when you're ready."

When Jim came to the pool room he gave Sue a big kiss and asked how her day went. Sue got a big smile then told him all the things they had done and how much fun it was for each of them. They all knew the next three days would be busy but today gave each of them a chance to say the things that were personal to each other. She kissed Jim again and said "Thank you for that time. I know you are going to say it just worked out that way, but I already know it's you that make things go the way they should. Now if you have time let's get rid of these clothes and go swimming."

Jim did have time and the clothes came off quickly. While they were swimming and fooling around Jim said "I do have more work to do but would like to wait till around midnight."

"Sounds like you're going to take someone's money."

"I am going to take a lot of people's money both in and out of this country. I will let the government take all there corporations, real estate and all the money they can find."

"Well it should be an exciting morning for a lot of people, I will just be happy if were not part of them."

"If they don't have there listing device gone by Saturday night I will take it and turn it off."

"Let's take Mom and Dad to breakfast at the Country Club in the morning then later we can watch the fallout from the morning paper. You don't mind me calling them Mom and Dad do you."

"I do love you, and no I think it's wonderful."

It was a fun night Sue cooked a nice dinner and they both cleaned up and did the dishes. They walked up to the upper patio and watched the sun set then the lights of the city come on for them. Later they went down to the basement and Jim finished up a few things he was working on then started the program he had written to withdraw the monies from two hundred and twenty one different bank accounts and started moving it around the world then it would all end up in forty different Numbered accounts all out of the country. It took a good hour and a half. "How about when you're at the end I go up and open a nice bottle of wine then we can go out to the Jacuzzi with some towels."

After the appropriate Number of kisses in the Jacuzzi Sue asked Jim how much money he had taken. "I took a billion three hundred and fifty two million and change, but I am sure I missed a lot of it. Hopefully the government can find it."

"It's still so weird to hear you say billion."

"Trust me it's still weird to me also. How about one more kiss and we take this up to the bedroom?"

Friday Morning May 28/ 2010 Tucson, Arizona

Jim and Sue slept in till eight o'clock. "Call your parents and ask if they will go to breakfast with us."

Breakfast was set for nine thirty. "Come swim some fast laps with me. I feel the need."

"I would love to swim with you and that beautiful little body of yours."

"Don't start something we don't have time to finish."

"Well we do have to shower."

They spent a good twenty minutes swimming laps and the shower was fun.

When Sue's parents arrived Helen was very sharply dressed and Sue loved it and told her so. "Since I started shopping with a sugar daddy it's a lot more fun and I let him have some input on what I buy. You don't think this is too sexy; do you?"

Sue was laughing really hard, she hugged and kissed them both and said "I love every bit of it. When they left for breakfast Jerry was already at the gate and waived as they left.

Once at the Country Club Sue wanted to check and make sure they would be ready for the rehearsal dinner the next night. She quietly said to Jim "I hope I don't need seating for you're new friends."

Jim was laughing but had nothing to say. Breakfast was all about the wedding and Jim and Mike stayed as quiet as they could then Helen said "The two of you think you're being cute but each of you needs to know your part; so pay attention."

Sue was again laughing and holding her sides. "The two of us should go to the rest room." Sue was still laughing as they left the table.

Mike and Jim were also laughing as the girls left the table then Mike said "While we are alone I need to ask if everything is ok. It would be hard not to notice that between the boys, Jerry, you and Sue that something is going on and it has all of you concerned with the security of the estate."

"Maybe when we get back to the house the four of us should talk about this."

The girls returned to the table and were still having fun. They all finished there coffee and Jim took care of the bill and tip then said "I invited your Mom and Dad to come back to the house so we could all talk about what is going on."

Sue's eyes got big then said "I am not sure what it is were talking about."

"Let's wait till we are at the house."

It didn't take long till they were at the house. Jim said "To start this conversation when we get out of the car I will show you a GPS transmitter the Justices Department has attached to our vehicle so they can track where I go. Maybe Sue would do the honors and scan the car so we can locate it."

Sue with a funny look on her face pulled out her scanner and started to locate where it was located. Jim got on the ground and removed it from the car and showed it to Mike and Helen. He then replaced it and said "That should make it easier to explain the rest."

Once in the pool room Jim again used Sue's scanner and checked for any listing devices. There were none.

"Ok for Helen and Sue's benefit, while the two of you were in the rest room at the restaurant Mike asked me if everything was ok because he noticed how we were all concerned about the security of the estate. Now unless Sue has any objections I think it's time we explain some of what is going on with both Sue and me."

"Whoa! I guess this is going to be a big conversation. Maybe I should open a nice bottle of wine.

"To start with I won't tell you all of this because it would be putting the two of you in more danger then is necessary. This started when Sue's friend Ken Benton the lawyer was murdered and I offered to look into it for her."

Sue brought everyone a glass of wine then sat next to Jim.

"I am sure the both of you have followed to some degree all of the stories that came from the Phoenix Republic News Paper and all the arrest that followed. It included many Senators, lawyers, accountants and CEO's of many corporations. There have been many arrests, killings and hundreds of billions of dollars withdrawn from hundreds of bank accounts both in and out of our country. Now the Federal government for the lack of any one else to look at think maybe I am the source of all this information and have been doing surveillance on us off and on. Now to be truthful I am the source of all these stories and am totally responsible for all the information that is released and who it is released to. Now if it was known that I am the one releasing this information I would be killed. Also I am the one who has stolen the hundreds of Billions of dollars from the bad guys. This is not money we will keep; I already have hundreds of billions of my own. Now to bring this up to date we needed to get rid of the people that are watching us and are listing to us when we are out in the courtyard. Mike why don't you take Sue's scanning device and we can all go out to the court yard and see if you can locate there listing device. Remember we all need to be quiet."

Sue was all smiles while she was showing her Dad how to operate the scanner. Once outside it didn't take Mike over two minutes to locate it then they all went back into the pool room. "I have never seen anything like that. Where did you get that scanner thing?"

"There are a lot of questions you will have but let me go back to me getting rid of these people so they won't be involved in our wedding. Yesterday I gave the reporters of the Phoenix Republic News Paper another story involving billions of stockholders and tax payer's dollars that have been systematically stolen by a number of corporations, accountants, bankers, lawyers and business men. A lot of them are very prominent people in Tucson. I hope none of them are your friends. If you like we can turn on Cable news. And see the story."

Helen suggested that another glass of wine would go well with the story. While Sue was pouring it she gave Jim a small kiss.

Cable news was already on continuous coverage and had one of the talking heads trying to explain all the long term implications the story would have besides all the arrests and closure of many corporations. Two of the corporations each owned huge new car dealerships in both Tucson and California. When they went to commercials Jim said "Now for the part that I am hoping will have the Justices Department looking some where else I had all of this story and the supporting documentation E mailed to the reporters from the offices of Federal Judge Harry Kimble. I know the Justices department is monitoring all incoming and out going calls and E mails the Phoenix Republic sends or receives. They also monitor where those calls originate or are received. So yesterday I made two calls to the reporters on a cell phone while just outside the Federal building."

"Can't they still locate where that cell phone is based on the pings it sends out."

"After I make a call I remove the battery then it can't be traced."

"How can you access a secure government computer system and have it do all of this."

"That is part of my expertise; I can not only access it I downloaded the file into it and created a secret file so it is still in there and I am sure the Justices Department will find it. I shut down the security in there offices late last night and had there system do the E mail then turned it back on a half hour later."

"So why did you chose Judge Kimble?"

"He uses his position as a Judge to go after people that he disagrees with there politics so I figured why not."

Now they were all laughing till Sue said "If any of the information Jim has sheared with you is known both he and I will be killed. As Jim has said all of this is only the tip of this thing and it reaches around the world. So I hope you can see the need for all of this to be private."

They all switched to coffee and talked for another two hours and Jim did explain he couldn't reveal all of the conspiracy because it was still being uncovered.

Helen said "That was one hell of a breakfast but I will try and not worry about the two of you."

Jim's Phone rang and it was David who said the Fed has again sealed off the Federal Building and according our people in Phoenix have said they have also descended on the Phoenix Republic News Paper and so have the television people. "Thanks David I will be in touch later."

Jim was laughing and as he closed his phone he told everyone what the Justices Department and television media were doing. It wasn't long and Helen and Mike went back to there house. Jim called the Boys and Jerry and told them the Fed may be retrieving there listing device some time during the day or night and they should give them a lot of room. The boys thought it was funny but said they would.

"Thank you for telling my parents what was going on, that meant a lot to me." That came with a nice kiss. Now unless you have something you must do let's take off these clothes pour another glass of wine and jump in the pool."

The pool and wine were both a great idea. Later in the afternoon David called all excited and wanted both Jim and Sue to meet him and Becky in the bar at the country Club. Jim said "Give us twenty minutes."

They were both laughing as they got a quick shower and dressed. On the way Jim said "This should give the Government an opportunity to remove there GPS transmitter."

When they got to the bar David and Becky were already there and had ordered Champaign and four glasses. They all shared hugs and David said "We have the property in escrow and should close on it in three weeks. Also when the two of you get back from your honeymoon we all need to start planning our wedding."

They were all having fun and decided to make it a light early dinner there at the bar. David and Becky were spending the evening with her family.

It was almost five when Jim and Sue were on there way back to the house. "Why don't you see if there is something at the Arizona Theater Company this evening and if so maybe you can get us an invitation? Then if there is and you can; we can get all dressed up and go out and play."

"I love it; it's been a while sense we did that."

The calls were made and the Theater Company was excited to have them join them. "Let's go down to the basement and find you something spectacular to wear."

"You are so funny and I love it."

Spectacular it was. Jim picked a diamond and gold necklace with matching earrings and a bracelet. All together it must have been ninety carats or more. "Do you think this is over the top?"

"It just might be but you will make it all beautiful."

Jim shaved and showered first then quickly dressed and gave Sue all the room she needed to put it all together. He went down to the pool room, opened a bottle of Champaign then called Sue's parents and invited them over with there cameras.

When Sue came down the stairs she looked as if she had just stepped out of the pages of Vogue magazine except she had her beautiful smile. Her Mom and Dad were amazed and the diamonds didn't look out of place. Sue was as excited as they were and it all made Jim happy.

They took the sedan and there was no GPS transmitter. When they arrived they have valet parking and as Sue stepped out of the car she had everyone's attention. They got a glass of Champaign and talked with a lot of people before the play started.

It was a Cinderella night for Sue and she loved every bit of it. On the way home she snuggled up next to Jim and said "Thank you for such a wonderful day. Tomorrow is the rehearsal then the dinner. It also will be a fun day."

Saturday Morning May 29/ 2010 Tucson, Arizona

Jim and Sue were up early and on a hard run. "After we shower and dress I would like to watch the news both cable and local. I am feeling as if there is something we need to see."

"Then let's watch the news and I hope it's nothing bad."

The shower included a lot of nice kisses, some groping and a lot of fun. They dressed, got some coffee and went to the pool room with the huge Television. Jim split the screen with both the cable news and a local channel. He could jump the sound back and forth. Cable news had a Number of the talking heads going over the story, all the documentation was so in depth they wondered how anyone could have uncovered it all and then put it all together so it made sense. They were wondering what law enforcement was doing with all of it. The local station was interrupting there news show with a breaking story so Jim switched the sound. They were going live to a local new car dealership where there had been a shooting. The place was covered with police cars and a lot of yellow tape keeping everyone back. The Tucson Police had one lane of traffic shut down on two main intersecting roads that went by the dealership. The News reporter was trying to get anyone that looked like they worked there to comment on what had transpired earlier.

They did say the 911 calls stated there had been multiple gun shots fired in the main office building of the dealership and there were an unknown number of people shot. The police had brought in there tactical squad and vehicle. They broke into that ongoing story to say that the FBI and other Federal agents had closed off the Federal Building and court house and no one was being allowed in. They went on to say that the Federal agents still had a large presence at the Phoenix Republic News Paper. There morning edition stated that they did turn over copies of all the material that had been sent to them as requested by the Federal Government. They again stated they didn't know the identity of who had sent the material or how it had been gathered.

"I think what this is telling us is that we don't need to worry about the government being a nuisance at our wedding. Now would you like to ask Kay and Jan plus your Mom and Dad to join us for breakfast at the Congress Street Hotel?"

"I love it; let me call them right now."

It was funny everyone thought it was the perfect place for breakfast. It wasn't long and the six of them were on there way. Kay and Jan were talking about the rehearsal and they seamed to be more excited then anyone. Sue said "There is going to be another wedding and I believe it will be next month."

Kay said "It must be David and Becky they are perfect for each other. This is all wonderful."

The Café was thrilled to see all of them and arranged the tables as necessary. One couple moved to help accommodate them. Jim thanked them then told the waitress he would also handle there bill and tip.

Breakfast was fun to say the least. Kay said "Steve would be picking up Father Duarte who wanted to be at the rehearsal. And yes he is coming to the rehearsal dinner then after the boys will return him to the mission."

"Thank you Kay; it will be nice to have him join us."

Back at the house everyone went to the pool room and there were a lot of conversations going and a lot of laughing. The wedding rehearsal was set for six that evening. David and Becky were coming over at five. Steve and Frank were having Troy and Jared also come to the rehearsal because they would be helping them keep everything moving along at both the wedding and reception. They were also coming to the rehearsal dinner.

About one o'clock everyone was headed back to there homes. David called and asked Jim if he had been watching the news. "It's getting crazy out there; some of the biggest names in Tucson are shooting each other. Check it out and Becky and I will see the two of you at five."

"David thinks we should watch the television."

The local station was at a loss because the story was breaking out all over town and by its self was more sensational then there normal spin on it would be. One very prominent new car dealer was in Jail accused of killing his business manager and wounding two other people in a shout out at the dealership earlier in the day. There were reports of many other prominent business people just leaving there businesses and disappearing. No one in any branch of law enforcement would make any comment on anything.

"Let's not let their bad day ruin ours. We have time for a swim then we can sit in the sun for a while."

David and Becky came over at five they had coffee and sat and talked in the pool room. It wasn't long and everyone was there including Father Duarte. After a while they all moved to the meeting building then the girls and boys took over explaining how everything would work. Both Jim and Sue were laughing but did as they were directed. It was going to be a simple ceremony and the boys were explaining how the flowers would be arraigned and the cues would prompt Sue and her Dad to start down the aisle. It took a good forty five minutes but everyone knew exactly how the wedding and reception would go.

Sue and Jim were happy and thanked everyone for all the time and work they had put into everything. It wasn't long and they all left for dinner at the Country Club.

Everyone at the Country Club went out of the way to make sure everything was perfect for Sue. It was like she was their Cinderella and they were having fun. Even Father Duarte was having a good time he sat between Sue's Mother and Jan. The four boys sat together next to Kay and Sue's Dad. There was a lot of talk about Hawaii. Sue said she had gone on line and looked at the resort Darleen had picked for them and said they would have there own bungalow no more then a hundred feet from there own private beach. They would be leaving Tucson at eleven thirty Sunday night. Sue leaned over and said to Becky "I will take a lot of pictures and make a lot of notes."

Dinner and the evening was a Cinderella night for Sue and Jim it was after ten when they got back to the house. Sue suggested they opened a bottle of Champaign and go to the Jacuzzi. "Let me scan the court yard and make sure the government removed there listing device."

It was gone so it was Champaign and the Jacuzzi.

Sunday Morning May 30/ 2010 Tucson, Arizona

Jim and Sue were up early and out running. They planed it so they would be at the upper patio to watch the sunrise. As the sun started to come over the edge of the mountains to the east Jim was standing behind Sue with his arms wrapped around her. Sue in quite voice said "Are you having any second thoughts about today."

"Sue I love you more then you can possible imagine and I am the happiest I have ever been. I will do everything in my power to try and make you as happy. So how could I have any second thoughts about today?"

"Kiss me and we will start our lives together today."

When they returned to the house Sue's Parents, Kay, Jan plus Steve and Frank were all there fixing breakfast. Kay handed them both a cup of coffee and told them to quickly get there showers then come down for breakfast. "Remember no time for fooling around up there."

Breakfast was fun and everyone was almost silly. The wedding was to be at three in the afternoon and it was going to get busy fast. Jerry was coming to work at noon and man the gate. The boys with the help of Jan would direct the florist, caterers, band plus the photography and video people. Sue's Mom and Kay would be with her. Jim had moved everything he would need to one of the other bedroom suits so as not to be in the way of the bride getting ready.

The first people to show up were David and Becky they both looked great. David like Jim was wearing a summer tuxedo with the white jacket. Jim and David did wear nicely polished black western boots.

By two thirty more then two hundred people had arrived. The boys had two of there friends directing people where to park. The building where the wedding and reception would be held had been completely transformed and was beautiful. Among all the people that had arrived was Father Duarte with a young lady who had driven him. David's parents Robert and Rose were driven by his older sister Sylvia. Jim was really glad to see them and they got to talk a bit. As the time came near it seamed that everyone they had invited was there.

Jim and David stood up at the front of the room with Farther Duarte. Sue's Mom was seated up front next to Jan. the music started and everyone looked back toward the kitchen in only moments Sue accompanied by her Father came into the room and slowly walked to the center isle. She was not only beautiful but stunning. Her dress was white and fitted at the top with no straps, from the waist down it hung coming all the way to the floor. Her hair was fix differently then Jim had ever seen it and with the vial made her look like the cover of a bridal magazine. The only jewelry she wore was her engagement ring. Everyone including Jim was in awe.

In the ceremony Father Duarte did mention how he got to witness God bringing Jim and Sue together. They both remembered their vows and David had both wedding bands. It was only a matter of minutes and Jim got to kiss his bride.

"Sue you make me complete and I do love you."

The band was ready and started playing softly as soon as the wedding was over. Everyone went through the receiving line then Jan announced the first dance was for the bride and groom. Jan sang and the band kept right with her. Sue was as happy as she could be and the two of them did dance.

The boys and girls had the whole reception planed out; catering and all. Everything went along with ease. Jim and Sue got to talk with everyone. Father Duarte and the young lady that drove him only stayed an hour but Sue and Jim did get to thank him before they left.

At the appropriate time the band quit playing and Steve in a very nice way thanked everyone for coming and being part of the wedding. It was no more then twenty minutes and it was back to the family witch included the Boys, girls, David and Becky. The boys told everyone to go back to the house and they would handle the clean up with the help of Troy and Geared.

Back at the house the girls put on a pot of coffee and everyone found a seat and relaxed. They all drank coffee and talked till almost ten. Jim and Sue already had everything ready and packed for there honeymoon. David reassured Jim everything would be handled while they were gone. All the goodbyes were said and the limousine was on time. Once over the hill and out of sight they were locked in an embrace and a big kiss. They changed planes in Los Angles.

Monday Morning May 31 / 2010 Honolulu, Hawaii

They landed in Honolulu very early in the morning they were met and taken to a small corporate jet that quickly flew them to Kauai. They landed at the Lihue Airport on the Eastern shore. A driver from the Marriott Resort was waiting. Sue was excited by just what she had seen from the plane. They and there luggage wear taken to there bungalow. The bell man told them the dinning room would be open in about twenty minutes. He did ask if there was anything he could get them right now. Jim thanked, tipped and said they would freshen up then go to the dinning room. As soon as the bell man left Sue kissed Jim and said "This is so much more then what the computer showed. What a great place for a honeymoon."

They walked up to the main part of the resort and were thrilled with how beautiful and well kept the grounds were. The swimming pool was the largest that either of them had seen. It was a circular pool ringed by Jacuzzis. They again stopped in the main Lobby and were looking at the brochures of things to do on the inland. Suddenly a young lady from behind the registration counter came over addressing them by name she introduced herself as Heather and said she was aware this was there honeymoon and said "We have already put together a packet of all points of interest and things we think you might want to do. We can tell you all the places on our list have the highest recommendations from our previous guests. If there is some place you would like to go the Hotel car will be available to take you and pick you up again. Also we have luxury rentals also available. So please, what ever your needs are let us know. We are here to help make your stay the best it can be."

Sue and Jim both thanked Heather took there folder and went to the dinning room. Breakfast was fun and the food was good. They decided to put on there swim suits run on the beach a couple of miles then swim in the ocean. The next thing would be to get at least three to four hours of sleep. Sleeping on the plane was not very restful.

Sunday Morning June 06 / 2010 Kauai, Hawaii

Jim and Sue have been having the best time on there honeymoon. They ran on the beach every morning and did a lot of things: swimming, wind surfing, body boarding, snorkeling, helicoptering Kauai they even took an air tour of all the islands. By far the best part was the one on one time they spent with each other. The walked on the beach while watching the sunset and they watched the sunrise while they were on there morning runs.

Jim and Sue had just returned to there bungalow from there morning run and a quick swim in the ocean and were sitting at the small table in there privet patio. Sue was pouring them a cup of coffee witch appears every morning in a thermal pot accompanied by two cups. Also in the evenings a nice bottle of wine and two glasses appear like magic.

Suddenly Jim's cell phone rings. He and Sue look at each other then he answers it. David was on the other end and said "I am sorry to interrupt your honeymoon but you have company in Tucson. There are six of them they got three rental cars and they are staying at the Ramada Inn by the freeway."

"They must have a local connection to get there guns from. If the opportunity comes along lets have our people grab two of them. Our people need to have there faces covered till they can cover there eyes. We would like to know who sent them, where they came from and what there mission is. I don't want them permanently hurt or killed. When they have told your people all they know have them let go out in the desert some where between Tucson and Phoenix and told not to return."

"I have canceled your limousine and I will pick up you and Sue with my driver and a second car."

"Thanks David; if anything changes please call."

After Jim closed the phone Sue asked if he know who sent them. "I don't have any idea but we can rule out the government. Hopefully by the time we get home David will have some answers. He canceled our limousine and he and a second car will pick us up."

"I guess when we get home we will be back in the game. That means we need to have fun today."

Jim kissed her and said "Let's start with a nice breakfast."

Monday Morning June 0 7 / 2010 Honolulu, Hawaii

It was a few minutes after ten and Jim and Sue were aboard there flight that would take them to Los Angeles. "That was a wonderful honeymoon and

I loved Hawaii. I wouldn't want to live there; but it was the perfect place to go."

In Los Angles they didn't need to leave the secured area. They did have time to relax and have a drink before there flight left for Tucson.

Once aboard and in the air they both ordered coffee. "When we reach Tucson and go to pick up our luggage David will be there; you stay with David while I get the bags. I don't expect any problem but would still like to proceeded as if there would be."

"I have a million questions but like you will need to wait and see if David and the others have found any answers."

It was a little past five when they landed and as soon as they cleared the secure area David was there and they said hello. Jim asked David to take his carryon he did as he passed Jim a Glock 40 and an extra clip. Sue said "I brought back nicer gifts then that."

When they reached the baggage area Sue stayed with David with her carryon while Jim went to retrieve the two new suitcases they had bought while in Hawaii. There was no problem and they all walked out to a nice short limousine that had not only a driver but also a second man sitting up front. As soon as they left the arrival area there was a second car with three men inside. David put up the window that separated the rear section from the front. Then he said "We did get the opportunity to grab two of our visitors and gave them the opportunity to answer the questions you had or end up with there heads being displayed on top of a pole out in the middle of the desert. We talked with them separately and they both came up with the same answers one did know a little more. They are both out in the middle of nowhere lost but alive. The six of them are out of the DC area and are x military working as security agents mainly in Pakistan. You definitely are there target and they wanted you debriefed and there was no limit as to what means they needed. In the end you were to be dead. The corporation they work for is called Black Burn and it is located in Richmond Virginia. There contact in Tucson is some dickhead lawyer Tim Shockley. The one in charge of the four that are left here is Joe Ryan."

"Well David it sounds like we have our work cut out for us this week"

"What ever you need, will be there. I still have people watching the other four."

The ride to the house was uneventful. They both thanked David and went into the house with there luggage. "Just leave that I will handle that in the morning. Right now I need some kisses and a drink out in our Jacuzzi.

There were flowers and two notes on the counter one from Kay and Jan welcoming them home and wanting to do breakfast. The other was from Steve and Frank again welcoming them home and stating that nothing had shown up on the security. The drinks got made while Sue found the towels and got undressed. The Jacuzzi was just what the two of them needed and it was the start to a wonderful night.

Tuesday Morning June 08 / 2010 Tucson, Arizona

Sue woke Jim up early and said "Come run with me and we can watch the sunrise from the upper patio."

With the right amount of kisses they were on the path running hard and loving every minute of it. They saw two coyotes and a Number of rabbits. They watched the sunrise with Jim standing behind Sue with his arms around her. The morning was cool but felt good. The days were hot and it was getting close to the monsoon season. "The coffee should be ready I will have a busy day with the computers. How about we start the day with breakfast at the Congress Street Café? We could also invite the girls and the boys."

"I like all of that and you do need to see all of them before you start on the computers. I will spend time with them after we get back to the house."

"I would like to bring David into all of this including the basement. What do you think?"

"You know David better then me so I will leave that up to you. What about Becky?"

"I will ask David to wait till after they are married; but that will be his decision."

"Like I said it's your call; and I trust your instincts."

Breakfast was fun and it was great to see everyone most of the talk was about the honeymoon Sue suggested that the girls should think about a time when they might want to go to Hawaii. "We can make it a business trip and the company could cover everything. I am sure Jim can do the same for you guys and your dates."

The look on all of there faces changed and Jim could see they were all thinking about being in Hawaii. That was about the end of breakfast. As they were leaving Jim told Steve and Frank he would like to see them after they returned to the house. Sue and the girls were going to the Arizona Theater Company in downtown.

Back at the house while the girls went to there house to get ready Jim told Sue that David would have two men in a car following her and the girls. "Thank you for telling me."

"I am going to call David and have him come over here then I will tell and show him what this is all about."

It was only minutes and the boys were at the house. Jim took them to the pool room and explained that there were people that might try and inter the estate. "I don't want the two of you or Jerry to try and stop them. These people are not Law enforcement and are dangerous so please stay out of there way and let me know right a way. I will let the two of you explain this to Jerry."

As soon as the boys left Jim called David and asked him to come to the house. Kay and Jan had returned and the three of them were leaving; Jim did get a kiss. Sue did look great and was happy.

When David arrived he and Jim went to the pool room. Jim made them both a drink and said "I think it's time I told you what this is all about."

They sat and talked a good half hour then they went to the library. Jim locked the doors of the library opened the basement. David couldn't believe it then Jim said "What you see here is worth maybe one to Two hundred million dollars. Now David what you are seeing including the computer system is here just to through off any one from finding what this whole estate was all about."

Jim opened the doors of the big cabinet that held the guns. David said "These people were ready for a war."

Jim removed the one gun and said "Here is the real treasure." As he turned the L shaped bracket. The whole inside of the cabinets started to move exposing the big room, Jim turned on the lights and David just stood there taking it all in then said "What the hell are you into?"

"Something so big it's hard to wrap my mind around it. These people are huge and are all around the world. There the heads of many countries and huge globalised corporations. A lot of them are in our government. The Senators, Lawyers, accountants and big corporation you have seen go down in flames; well all of that's me taking them out. I have stolen trillions of dollars.

Now I think the people you have found that are looking for me are mercenaries being sent out and are trying to find out who or what is exposing there money machine."

"Shit this is like something out of a science fiction movie. How did you ever find all this?"

"When I tell you the answer to that question you will really be entering a different dimension. Before we go into that let's look at the corporation the two men gave to your men the other night. It was Black Burn out of Richmond Virginia. Well look at this David they do exist. Let's go inside there corporation and see who owns them."

"How the hell do you go through there security like that?"

"I have a lot of tricks up my sleeves. Look at the list of stock holders it looks like it came out of Forbs Magazine. Let's look in there personal files for the names the two bad boys gave us here is the one they said was at the top of there list a Mr. Tom Nickels; now let's see if we can find out who had Tom send out the six dummies. Here we go one Terry McClure from Senator Bruce Sysco's office in California. He was the latest Senator caught up in a sex scandal. Let's close this all down and go up and have a drink."

Jim closed everything up and grabbed a million dollars on his way out. They went to the pool room and made up some drinks and talked a bit then Jim said "I would like to make the four men left to think that they have stepped into part of the Mexican Drug Cartel and if they don't quickly get out they will be dead and the Cartel will go after the people who sent them. Let's use the names we have come up with including the Senator and his little stooge. That should do two things: first send them away and secondly make them think they were looking in the wrong direction."

"I can guarantee I wouldn't want to keep looking."

"Ok David let's do that today. I will go with you because like you this is the fun stuff."

Jim did call Sue and told her he was going be playing with David for a while. Sue was laughing and told him and David to be careful.

Within forty five minutes Jim and David were in a warehouse on the west side of down town. Two of the men were in dark suits, the others were well dressed and they were all well armed. Jim explained what he wanted them to do and what he wanted them to tell the four men then take all there guns and tell them to be out of Tucson by night fall. The next one the four men were to visit was the local lawyer Tim Shockley and explain how short of a life he could have if he ever mentioned Jim's name again.

It was a fun afternoon the four bad guys left town within the hour and drove to Phoenix where they caught a flight to Virginia. Jim and David had lunch and talked about what Jim was going to do with all the information he had and when. They did talk about David not telling Becky till after they were married.

Jim arrived home around four and Sue was glad to see him. She suggested they have a glass of wine in the Jacuzzi and they could share about there day. The wine and Jacuzzi were both a good idea they spent a good three hours outside in and out of the Jacuzzi and pool and talked about everything. Sue's day was a lot nicer then Jim's. Sue did ask if he thought that would be the end of them looking at him. "I hope so at least for a while. After things have slowed down I was thinking we could go after some of the money in the Middle East and make them nervous about there American partners; now that should be interesting."

Sue was laughing and gave him a big kiss. Then she said you need to take me out for dinner tonight; I will go shopping tomorrow."

"Let's go to the Country Club; I could use some more pampering."

"Would you like to ask David and Becky?"

"I would just like it to be the two of us. If you like you and Becky figure out a night where we all could do dinner and a play or showing that would be fun."

"I like just the two of us; I will find something fun to wear."

Sue has great taste in clothes. Without over dressing she can look quite elegant and sexy and loves wearing some of the jewelry they have found.

At the Country Club they were again treated like celebrities. To the staff and most of all to the servers in the dinning room: Sue is Cinderella.

Randy again was there waiter; he and Sue were glad to see each other. They started with a nice bottle of wine and Jim asked Sue if she wanted any help with getting her business started. "I would. I am not sure where to start helping people that want to express there idea's on canvas or any other media.

"There are a lot of large old buildings in the downtown area that are sitting empty. I know a couple of people who are working on trying to bring new business to the down town area. Let's have breakfast at the Congress Street Hotel that is where I have met them over the years."

"You know I would love the idea. Now the morning sounds exciting. Let's order our dinner then we can drive around downtown and see what buildings are empty."

"I do love you." Jim motioned for Randy and dinner did get ordered.

Wednesday Morning June 09 / 2010 Tucson, Arizona

Jim and Sue were up early and on a good and fast run. The shower was great as showers go. They both were having fun getting ready. Jim took a small leather book that had room for a small legal pad and a couple of pens.

As soon as they walked into the Café Jim saw two of the men he was talking to Sue about. They stopped at there table and Jim introduced Sue as his wife to Ben Mathews and Bill Baker. They were asked to join them and did. After receiving there coffee and ordering breakfast Jim told them that Sue was looking for a large building or warehouse in the downtown area for her business. Ben asked what kind of business Sue had and she explained it well including the amount of space she would be looking for and again that she would like to be close to the arts district if at all possible. Both Ben and Bill had a Number of possible sights she might be interested in. They also explained that some of them were owned by either the City or the State who would love to get rid of them. Jim made a list of the ones they suggested and said they would drive by them all. Breakfast was fun for the both of them.

"Ok now the work starts. We need to take pictures of each property we are possibly interested in along with all the information we can get."

They spent a good two and a half hours and only came up with two that could work. "Let's call Hugh Hanson and see if he has time for us to come over."

Hugh was excited and said he would be available and would love to see them. It took only minutes and they were sitting in Hugh's office. Hugh said "I have been looking at a lot of real estate, mainly land that I think you might be interested in."

"Well today we have two properties in the downtown area Sue is possibly interested in and we would like to get in and look at them. Sue has the address and a photo of each if you want to down load them."

It took Hugh only minutes and he had the pictures down loaded and printed. The properties were both listed by a company that had all the listings on city properties. Hugh made a call and had someone on the line who said he would meet with them at the first address within twenty minutes. They went in Hugh's car and arrived right on time. Hugh did the introductions and the agent opened the building the interior was in shambles and it was obvious that people had been sleeping in it not too long ago. The building was big but didn't excite either Sue or Jim.

"Let's look at the other one."

The second building was an old warehouse that had its own railroad side track and loading docks behind it. The tracks were no longer attached to main rail line. The building was only three hundred feet deep to the platform but it was two thousand feet long and had been separated into four large warehouses. It was in bad shape with a lot of old equipment inside and it was obvious the entire roof would need to be reinforced and replaced. On the up side it was big enough and was constructed out of reinforced concrete and doubled red brick. Jim said "I would like to have my contractor look at the feasibility of making this usable. But first I need to know what they are asking and how much land comes with it."

They spent the next hour locating the property lines and they showed the whole side of the City block was included and the property extended two hundred feet beyond the railroad track. The City had it listed for one point two million but the property has been vacant for forty seven years so almost any reasonable offer would be entertained. Hugh thanked him and said he would be in touch.

On the drive back to Hugh's office Sue asked Jim what he thought of it. "I think like our house God has had that building sitting there empty waiting for you."

Sue through her arms around his neck kissed him and said "I do love you and I think we are both seeing the same picture of what that can be."

Hugh was laughing and said "I don't know what the two of you are seeing but I know its making the two of you happy."

"Let's forget the contractor for now and make an offer on this when we get back to your office."

They all got some coffee and went into Hugh's office and worked up an offer of nine hundred and seventy thousand dollars under Catalina Consulting. Jim said "I will give you a hundred thousand as earnest money to open up an escrow account. Let me get it out of my trunk."

"You have a hundred thousand dollars cash in your trunk?"

"Actually I have a million in cash in my trunk. Would you like to see it?"

"Of course I do; I have never seen a million dollars in cash."

Sue was laughing and said "I will wait here."

When they came back in Hugh was laughing and said "I can't believe you left that car sitting there with that in the trunk. Let me give you a recite then as soon as I can compose my self I will call Frank and tell him I am bringing an offer over to him. I will call you as soon as I have an answer."

The ride home was fun and Sue was really pumped she said "As weird as it sounds I believe what you said is true, God has a purpose for that building and has arraigned to have us there to be part of his plan what ever that is."

"The neat thing is us knowing we are part of his plan; now for knowing what that plan is; that part is none of our business."

When they got back to the house Jim said "I am going to fix a drink and go to my computers. So why don't you go tell the girls all about the building you put an offer on. If you all go to see it just make sure you're aware of what is going on around you."

Sue kissed him and said "You knew I had to tell them. Keep your phone to where you can hear it."

Jim made his drink and locked the library and went to his computers in the basement. The Black Burn Corporation was huge and provided privet security to many of the corporations and governments in the Middle East that Jim had on the CD's. After looking at all there placements he realized they also protected many of our Embassies in the same countries. That meant they could jeopardize the security of our Ambassadors and there staff and that could affect our foreign policies.

Jim thought about it for a while then started to download many of there files he stayed with it till four o'clock then locked the basement and went to the pool room and was pleased to find Sue and the girls. They were happy to see him and were talking about the building. They had spent over an hour there looking and walking around it. All three of them were really excited about it. They spent a good hour and a half talking about it. Kay and Jan invited Sue and Jim over and they would fix dinner. It was a great idea and they opened some nice wine while they were fixing dinner.

It was after eight when Jim and Sue returned to there house and it was about eighty out side. "Let's open a nice bottle of wine and sit in the Jacuzzi then you can tell me what you found on your computers and why it is bothering you."

"I did find some things that concern me but didn't think it showed."

"Probably didn't show to Kay and Jan but it did to me."

They got the wine, sat in the Jacuzzi and Jim told here what he had found in his research of Black Burn Corporation then explained what his fears were of them putting the Embassies, Ambassadors and there staff in jeopardy and the effect it would have on our war effort and foreign policies if they let something happen to them.

"Shit you really do have a lot to think about; this could affect our whole country and they are only one part of this thing."

"Let's forget about this for tonight and I will think about it in the morning. Tonight we have more important things to take care of."

Thursday Morning June 10 / 2010 Tucson, Arizona

Sue woke Jim up early and asked "Would you run with me? For some reason I feel scared."

He held and kissed her and said "I will love to run with you and as always will do all I can to make sure you are safe."

They ran hard and ended up on the upper patio at the right time to watch the sunrise. Jim held her and said "I love you so much and I believe God has some great plans for us and our family."

"How many children do you think we will have?"

He kissed her and said "As many as he will give us with you still being healthy."

"I hope it's a lot."

The run back to the house was slow and ended with them walking and holding hands. "After breakfast I am going to call David and start looking for a connection in the CIA. I will do a lot of research on him and if I am satisfied he is clean I will see if he will work with me knowing I must stay anonymous."

"Do you think you can do that even thou they also have the same computers you have?"

"Actually it will be easier and a lot more fun. I can give them just enough that they can break into there systems and find the bad guys themselves. He will need to find a trust worthy FBI agent to work with him on the parts of this that are inside the United States."

"This time you are going to have one hell of a circus to keep balanced."

"That's why I need more help then just the news paper. David will always be where I need him that is one thing I never have to worry about."

"While the two of you are playing I will call Becky and see if we can all do dinner and something after."

They did breakfast at the Country Club and it was nice they were getting to know some of the other members. Jim had called David before they left the house and was meeting him later at the dealership.

Once at the dealership Jim asked David if he had something nice to drive that would blend in.

"I have a nice Lincoln I bought last week. Where are we going?"

"Let's start with a drink at the congress street bar."

Jim took his bag of tricks with him it held lots of money, his list of names and numbers, a clean hand gun and a lot of cell phones. On the ride to the bar David was telling him he had given his general manager the authority to run all three of the dealerships. That way he would be available to help Jim and also over see what he and Becky were going to do to the new house.

Cathy the bartender was glad to see the two of them and got there drinks right a way. They sat at a table and Jim brought David up to speed on what he had found out about Black Burn and what he wanted to do about it and why.

"You're talking about being a way out on the edge. On the other hand if we pull it off it will be the best thing we have done sense we were teenagers."

"As soon as we finish these up I want to go over by the courthouse and call the Phoenix newspaper. Another thing do we have a good contractor among our people in the Barrio?"

"Yes Hector Robles and his son Frank who went to school with us. Frank is married and has two kids."

"Great I may have some good work for them. Sue just put an offer in on an old warehouse. It's been empty for forty seven years."

They parked by the court house and Jim called the cell Number for Bill and Hoyt at the Phoenix Republic. Bill answered and said "Hi Jeff, how are you."

"I am great but need some help from the two of you. I need you to use all your connections with other news people and see if you can locate a real straight CIA agent that will go the distance with a big story that could affect our national security and jeopardize the safety of our embassies and troops. I need you guys to do this as quietly and quickly as possible. The people you contact don't need to know the reason why. That information is only for you and Hoyt. Let me give you a Number to call me back at." He gave him the Number then closed the phone.

David was already driving out of the area and heading toward the dealership. He said "I noticed we have lost a Number of the members at the Country Club." They were both laughing as they went to the dealership.

David said "Let me change cars and we can meet at the Country Club for drinks."

Jim left before David and called Sue and told her where he would be. Sue told him she and Becky had made plans for dinner and the theater.

Jim was the first to reach the bar. He got a table and ordered for David and himself. David arrived shortly and told Jim he had received a call from one of there people saying that the Fed had showed up shortly after they left and he was sure they were checking all the surveillance tapes from around the courthouse. Jim said "I need to call Bill and Hoyt through the paper and give them a new cell Number they can call from a different cell phone."

Jim used a clean phone called the Phoenix Republic and asked for Hoyt using a fake name and saying he was from the Maricopa County Sheriffs office. He got right through and gave Hoyt the new cell Number and told him the other two were Toast.

He and David sat and talked a good hour and Jim did tell him the ladies had made plans for the evening. David liked that.

It was after three when Jim returned to the house. He asked Sue if she would like to go for a swim. "I have towels out there if that works for you."

It did and they spent a good two hours in and by the pool and talked of each others day. Sue did ask if Hugh had called "Not yet but I have a lead on a contractor for you."

"Becky and I have reservations for dinner at the Gold Room of the Westward Look Resort then you and David can take Becky and me to a new play at the Arizona Theater Company."

"It sounds like the start to a wonderful night."

Friday Morning June 11 / 2010 Tucson, Arizona

Jim and Sue were up by seven sitting in the Jacuzzi and having coffee. "I really had a fun evening and the play was great. You ladies did a great job."

"Thank you Becky and I really did have fun planning the evening. There house should close hopefully next week. David still hasn't committed on Date for the wedding Becky thinks he is waiting on you and what you are doing."

"I hope that's not the case; I will ask him when the timing is right. Today I am hopping to here from Hugh on your building and hopefully from Hoyt and Bill on a CIA agent. This could be a busy day."

"The girls and I are having a meeting with the Tucson Art museum. What do you want to do with the six paintings we have on loan to them?"

"I talked to Bill Stine about that and he suggested we ask the museum to get us an appraisal on there value then we can donate them. If that is what you would like to do."

"Thank you that's what I would like to do."

"How about the Congress Street Hotel Café for breakfast?"

While they were at breakfast Hugh called Sue and told her the offer on her building was accepted and it should go to closing in two weeks or less. Sue was really excited then asked Jim about the contractor he had found. Jim was laughing then said "I will talk to him and see if he is interested in the job and if so I will have him do a walk through with us after the closing."

"I am sorry but this is so exciting and I am thinking about all the lives this hopefully has a positive affect on. I will need to tell the girls."

It was only minutes and Jim's second phone rang. It was Hoyt Segal from the Phoenix Republic. He told Jim they had a name of a CIA agent who has eighteen years in the CIA and is in middle management. He is not a yes man and that has kept him in middle management he has just returned from Afghanistan and is still in the US. His name is Brian Higgs but no one has a contact Number. "That's a big help; I can get the contact Number. You and Bill stay safe and I just might have one hell of a story for you."

"It sounds like we both will have a busy day. Give me a kiss then let's get out of here."

On the way back to the house Jim called David and asked if he would like to come over and play. David while laughing said he would be there in thirty minutes.

Sue was off to the girl's house and Jim opened the basement and started up the computers and started into the CIA it was fun going into one of the most secure sights there are. It didn't take long and he was into the personal file of one Agent Brian Higgs. Jim didn't want to linger two long so he just printed the whole file then got out of the CIA altogether. Jim put the file together then went out and locked the library while he waited for David to arrive.

It was fun reading Higgs file it showed he was probably a better Agent then he was at kissing anyone's ass. Higgs was single and spent at least half of his carrier oversees. He had been shot once and had received a Number of commendations but none of that ever got him any higher then a senior field agent.

When David arrived Jim said "let's go for a ride I need to make a call to a CIA Agent and I am not sure how it will be received. Let's drive over by the Airport and make the call from there."

On the drive to the airport Jim asked David when the house he and Becky were buying was going to close. David said this next week but he wasn't sure of the day. "Well then have the two of you set a date for the wedding?"

"I was kind of waiting to see what you needed with this stuff."

"David none of this stuff is as important as you and Becky getting married and going on a honeymoon. All of this can wait."

"If that's the case it will be real soon."

Jim had Agent Higgs cell phone Number but he also had his parent's Number witch was a DC Number; He would try that first.

"High Mr. Higgs this is Jeff Black and I was hoping I could catch Brian. ----- Thank you. Agent Higgs you can refer to me as Jeff Black the reason I am contacting you is my research has show you as someone who would use the information I have to first of all protect our Embassies and troops rather then for your self promotion. I have information that will bring down Black Burn Corporation who provides protection to almost all our Embassies in the Middle East they also are the first line of defense to many of our troop compounds. I will also at the same time show how they are allies of the heads of the governments of Afghanistan, Pakistan, Iraq and Iran."

"Well MR. Black why should I believe anything you say. Everything you have said is common information; even my parent's phone Number."

"I am sure even while you were in Afghanistan you heard of all the Senators that have been exposed along with many corporations for stealing trillions of dollars from Americans and our government. Well Agent Higgs they are but just a tip of this thing. Now last week a Mr. Terry McClure of Senator Bruce Sysco's office called a Tom Nickels of Black Burn Corporation and asked him to send out operatives who we know as mercenaries to debrief then kill a citizen in Tucson Arizona. The Senator wanted to know if this person was the source of the information that was bringing down the other Senators like himself. The six men were captured, disarmed, debriefed and sent home alive. Now if you like I will bring down Senator Sysco in a very public way. Is there anything you would like to see to verify it was me who took him down?"

Agent Higgs while laughing said "Weather it is true or not have the story read that this Terry McClure is the one who gave up the Senator."

"I will make sure the story has some funny turns. After you read the headlines you need to decide if you are willing to stick your neck out again. Like the other times you have you probably won't be there favorite agent. So if you want to play I will put the battery back into this phone at ten o'clock mountain time and will leave it in for an hour. So call if you want to play."

When Jim closed the phone David was laughing then said "Are next job is to go back and you put your story together."

"We need to have a drink first; I already have it all laid out I just need to make it to where Terry McClure was the one who gave up the Senator. We should make this story come out on Sunday morning and make sure Cable news gets a copy right a way."

By five o clock Jim and Sue were in the pool the story and all the supporting documents had been E mailed to Hoyt and Bill at the news paper from Terry McClure. The E mail was sent from the Senators office and the file was again in a secret folder hidden in there computer system. Jim had talked with Bill and Hoyt and it was agreed the article would come out in the Sunday morning edition and a copy would be delivered to the CNN local station. Jim would raid all the Senators and his aid's accounts Saturday night.

Sue was telling Jim of her day with the girls at the Tucson Art Museum and of all the fun they had. Kay and Jan had made contact with a lot of people during the week Jim and Sue were on there honeymoon they found one sculptor who had to turn down a project because he didn't have a space large enough to do the piece. "There are a lot of different people that could make use of the space."

"If this contractor is who you want to use the first thing is to make the building and property secure then have the roof reinforced and completely replaced and well insolated. I would suggest starting with one of the four warehouses and get it in operation while he is working on the second. That way you can have him section off the first part as needed. Bill Stine can work up legal agreements that will protect both your company and the artist. This will all just come together."

"I did go shopping today and will fix us dinner then if you like we can walk up to the upper patio and watch the sun set and the lights of the city come on for us."

"I will help you with dinner and clean up afterwards."

"You can help with both."

It turned out to be a wonderful evening.

Saturday Morning June 12 / 2010 Tucson, Arizona

By eight thirty Jim and Sue were having a light breakfast at a coffee house on the west side of downtown. They were meeting Hugh Hanson there Realtor at the remains of a very old house that sat across the street and just North of the Tucson Art museum. It had been for sale a good ten years and the seller was stuck on a price that was at least seventy thousand too high even when Real Estate was at its peak. Jim had Hugh talk with the owner to see if he was now ready to sell the property. Hugh told Jim the seller would drop the price twenty thousand but that was still a way over the market value of the land. There was a fence around the complete property but it was old and there were many places it was open. The three of them walked through what was left of a huge home that was two stories and built in the old Spanish style. It was built in a U shapeand in the center was a large courtyard that was open to the back of the property and an ally. The whole back of the courtyard was all closed off with old rod iron that went from the ground to the top of the second story. The rod iron was beautiful but would need a lot of repair it did have a large gate built into the center of it. There was also a very nice fountain in the center of the court yard that had a lot of damage.

Jim said to Sue "I was thinking this could make a great gallery and the upper floor could be the offices for Catalina Consulting."

Sue was laughing and said "You are serious aren't you?"

"Yes I am, but only if you like the idea."

"I love you and yes I think I can see the whole idea of it. There will be nothing like it in the state at least."

"Ok Hugh you write it up under Catalina Consulting and we will be along in about twenty minutes so Sue can sign the offer and bring you a hundred thousand."

"I assume this again will be cash. Everything will be ready when you get there."

Hugh was on his way and Jim and Sue continued to look around. The house did have a full basement and looked as if it had been built around the turn of the century. They both were having a good time. Sue said "There is an old house on the next street that has been rebuilt in its original style it's the office of some government official. On the way over to Hugh's let's look at it."

They stopped at Hugh's office and she signed the papers and Jim gave Hugh the hundred thousand. The ride home was fun and they decided to invite Kay and Jan over for drinks and the pool. They all had a nice afternoon. Steve and Frank stopped by and said they were going out and didn't expect to be home till mid morning Monday. Jim and Sue told them to have fun. Sue asked Jim if he was going to ask her and the girls out to dinner. Before Jim could answer, Kay said "I want fancy." Now they were all laughing.

"Well then fancy it will be."

Everything was now about what they should wear. Somewhere in conversation Kay said "There is a play at the university tonight that I am sure we can get tickets to."

"Why don't you call and see if we can reserve four good seats. If you can I will plan our dinner around the play."

Kay got the reservations and the play started at seven. Jim in turn made reservations for one of the premier tables at the Gold room at Westward Look Resort For nine thirty. After the girls went to there house Jim asked Sue if she would like to go down to the basement and get a Number of necklaces and earrings so when the girls came over they could find something special to wear tonight. Sue was all over him with kisses and while laughing said "You know I would love to do that. Let's go to the basement."

While Jim and sue were getting ready Sue called over to the girls and told them not to wear any jewelry. She was laughing as she hung up and said to Jim "You sure know how to make us girls happy."

When the girls came over they did look beautiful and better then that, they both looked happy. Sue invited them to the pool room where she had laid out a towel and a large collection of necklaces and matching ear rings.

The two girls were excite and laughing. It took only minutes and they each had picked out a set they liked. Kay put the necklace and ear rings on Jan. Then Jan in return put Kay's on including a kiss.

Jim had opened a bottle of Champaign and poured four glasses. "All three of you young ladies look beautiful and this should be a wonderful evening."

Sue said "I wasn't going to say anything yet, but I will. Today Jim and I found an old two story home in the old arts district of downtown it would need to be totally rebuilt but it would make a great art gallery and the second floor could be the offices of Catalina Consulting. We put an offer in on it today but haven't heard back yet."

Jan said "We have time before the play and it's still light outside, can we at least drive by it?"

"We have lots of time so please finish you're Champaign."

The ride downtown was really fun and the girls had a hundred questions about the house and the warehouse. When Jim pulled up out front of it the girls all got out and just looked at it. "Oh Sue" said Kay "This will be wonderful. It must have been built around the turn of the centaury and was a very prestigious home. I can imagine all of the dinner parties and dances that were held here over the years. What a wonderful building you have found."

"If we do get it and with Jim's help we will again make it a beautiful building."

At the university they did have valet parking. Jim went and picked up there tickets and paid for them. As they went in the ladies did get more then there fair share of attention and loved it. It took a few minutes then a lot of people recognized them and came over to say hello. Sue was introducing Jim as her husband to many of them and Kay was introducing Jan as her partner. All three of the girls were handing out there business cards when it was appropriate.

The seats Kay had reserved were great and the play was good. Intermission was fun and they all had a glass of Champaign.

When they arrived at the Westward Look they were fifteen minutes early but there table was ready for them. Jim was tipping as they went. The Westward Look and the Gold room again lived up to there rating. After dinner they all ordered coffee and the conversation turned to David and Becky's wedding.

Back at the house the girls gave them both kisses and went to there house. Sue kissed Jim and said "You still have work to do."

"It's still early, let's change and go swimming. I want to hold and kiss you in the pool."

Sunday Morning June 13 / 2010 Tucson, Arizona

It was almost one o'clock in the morning by the time Jim and Sue got to the basement and turned on the computers. "This all shouldn't take more then an hour."

They sat and talked about the bad guys and what Jim expected to happen.

Jim and Sue slept in till eight.

"Would you like to go to breakfast with me? I need to be in the downtown area at ten o'clock and wait to see if the CIA Agent Brian Higgs wants to play with us."

"I would love to be your accomplice. Do I get to wear sun glasses?"

"I think you look cute in sun glasses; you can even wear a hat if you like."

"I will, just because I know you love hats on me."

They took there time and went to the Congress Street Café. They had a very light breakfast then drove over to the west side of freeway on Congress Street. Just after you drive under the freeway the Santa Cruse River runs parallel to it and on the North West corner of Congress Street and the river is a grotto that has a life size replica of Jesus and the Last Supper. The sight is always busy on any Sunday. There are many of the Hispanic people in the area that visit the shrine at least once a week. Jim and Sue walked down the stairs to see it. Sue said "I can't believe this has been here all these years and I have never heard about it."

It was ten o'clock so Jim put the battery back in the cell phone that he used to call the CIA agent. He said to Sue "This location uses the same tower as the Federal Courthouse. Let's relax and see if he calls."

They didn't have to wait long the Agent called within ten minutes. "Well that was one hell of a story the Phoenix Republic had this morning. I don't know how you pulled that off but you did what you said you would so it's my turn. Yes I do want to play, so tell me what your fears are about Black Burn."

"I assume you are recording this so I will give you a fast overview. First of all Black Burn is also in partnership with Iraq, Afghanistan, Pakistan, Libya, Iran and Turkey. All of the heads of these governments along with many of there corporations are systematically stealing Trillions of dollars from there countries and ours. I am for reasons of my own going to take down Black Burn Corporation and like I said it may put our interest and people in harms way. What I need you to do is have our government prepared to defend our people and interest. Now the hard part of this is that some of the people in our government and military are also involved."

"So you believe that Black Burn's people will abandon there posts as soon Black Burn is exposed."

"Remember these people are just mercenaries that work for cash, they have no loyalty at all and are well armed. They may well panic and turn into the enemy. The military needs to be in a position to disarm and replace these people. I am sure the CIA can find a way to do this before I dump all the proof of there crimes out for all the people to see."

"Is there something you can give me that I can prove to the powers that be? I will need there help in doing what you suggest."

"How about I give you a list of the last ten people they have killed to protect there on going criminal enterprise. I can give you the list of who, when, where and why. Some of the people are military. I can give you the name of the assassin and the person at the top that gave the order and why. Brian, do you think that will be enough to get you the corporation you need?"

"If that doesn't work then I don't know what will."

"Can you call me tomorrow at the same Number and the same time? If you can I will provide you with that information. I will need a secure E mail address. I will have it sent from Federal Judge Harry Kimble's office in Tucson just for fun."

"I will call you tomorrow at the same time."

Sue was laughing and said "You really don't like that Judge. You better make sure you don't end up standing in front of him."

"Let's go home and watch the television coverage of the morning paper. Then I have some work to do."

Cable news again had gone to continues coverage and had reporters outside the Senators office and home. There were also a lot of police and FBI agents in both places. They must have gotten warrants very quickly. The news casters had circles of talking heads who were discussing the legality of the news paper printing the story before the Justices system had a chance to verify that these crimes had occurred. Sue said "Thy seam to be scared that there names may come up next."

"You might be right on point."

David called and was coming over. Sue asked if Becky was coming with him. After a brief discussion Becky was coming. Sue said "You boys can use the library to talk in if you like."

When David and Becky arrived they were all happy to see each other. Sue suggested they open a nice bottle of wine. Becky was excited she and David had picked a date of Sunday June 27th for there wedding. It would be in the afternoon at the Cathedral in down town Tucson. Both she and David were excited and David told Jim he would be his Best Man. "I would be honored to."

They sat and talked for a while and the girls made a pot of coffee. Jim and David went into the library where they could talk. David said "Southern California seems to be a busy place this morning. I loved the part where Terry McClure was the one who E mailed the documentation to the news paper. Now the big question, did the CIA agent call you?"

"He did and I am going to send him enough evidence so that he can get the backing he needs from the CIA. For them to act on this information they will need to bring in the FBI but before they do that I will ask them to wait then I will give them enough to totally take out Black Burn and all there top management and employees. I need to keep them from again coming after me. I need all of this to happen quickly. I am sure they will quickly or already have seen past the idea that I am protected by the drug cartel. That brings up my second request. I would like our people to keep a look out for any new people coming into town. They will send one or two people and they will be a lot sharper then what we have come up against so far. I would expect them to drive here with there equipment and to keep a low profile."

"It will be in place today and I will keep in touch."

"Let's go see the girls and have a drink."

When they walked into the Pool room Sue jumped up and said "Hugh called and said we are in escrow on the old house. I was just telling Becky about it. Do the two of you have the time so we can all drive by and look at the two properties?"

Jim looked at David and asked if he had time. "I would have to be crazy to say anything but yes."

The drink would have to wait they were on there way to look at both the warehouse and the old house. Sue was telling David all about it and Becky was filling in anything Sue missed. They had a fun two hours.

Back at the house Jim made the drinks while David made a few phone calls. The afternoon went into the evening and the girls cooked a great dinner. David and Becky stayed till eight o'clock.

After they cleaned the kitchen up Jim asked Sue if she wanted to go in the Jacuzzi with him.

"It would be fun, and you can tell me what it is that has you concerned."

"Fair enough I will open the wine and get some plastic glasses."

Once they were in the Jacuzzi and had shared the appropriate amount of kisses Jim poured the wine then told Sue what he was talking to David about. "I can see in you that for some reason you know it is true and that it is immanent."

"You're right and it is so definite that it scares me that I know. It's like a memory of already seeing it. I know it is two men and they are heavily armed and I know how they are coming after us. It is either tonight or tomorrow night."

"What are you going to do?"

"I am going to take them out before they do us. There is a reason I am being given this information. I am sorry about this if you like you and the girls can leave for the night."

"You seam to know it will be tonight so what is it we need to do to be ready for this?"

"Let's get out and dry off I first need to call David then open the basement."

By ten o'clock Jim, Sue and David were ready. David had brought over a dark collard van and Jim had put two dark brown tarps and a roll of duck tape inside of it. David was staying at the house with Sue and two M16 assault rifles and nine mm hand guns. Jim would be out on the estate with a sniper rifle and a M16. He expected them some time after midnight. He and David had two new cell phones with only the others Number in it; they both were on vibrate.

At eleven thirty Jim gave Sue a kiss and slowly worked his way to a position where he would have a commanding view of the area he was sure they would come in from. He had a lot of time to think while he waited and kept watch with his night vision binoculars.

It was almost an hour and a half when he first saw them. It was two well armed men and they also were looking through night vision binoculars and scanning over the estate. They sat and watched a good fifteen minutes then started to make there way toward the House. Jim let them get close to one of the roads the SUV patrol vehicles used then he shot the lead man then as quick as possible shot the second man. The rifle had a silencer and made hardly any noise. Jim watched to see if there was any movement. There wasn't so he slowly worked his way over to where the two men were and checked that they were dead. In both cases they were. Jim called David and asked him to bring the van up. Jim had a small flash light and signaled David so he would know where Jim was.

It was only a matter of minutes and David was there. He and David wrapped each man in a tarp and taped them up while they were wearing gloves. Jim had first removed any papers they had on them. They put them in the van along with there guns and equipment. The guns and equipment were state of the art. They stopped at the house and Jim put all the weapons in the library with the exception of there hand guns. He kissed Sue and told her he would be back in about two hours.

Jim and David drove out to the far west part of the county where they knew of an old abandoned mine shaft that went down a good two hundred feet and was very unstable. They put the two bodies down the shaft then quickly returned to the estate. It took only minutes and they found the car the two men were driving. With gloves on Jim drove it to David's car lot, locked it up then quickly returned to the house. David came in and they all had a drink.

The time came as Jim knew it would when David said "It's time you told me how you knew the two men would be here tonight and everything they would do."

"You're right it is time. I think this all started with the idea of me quitting my job. I can remember, suddenly I knew I didn't want to renew my contract. It was like a force outside of me bring me to that decision. You remember that Monday that is when I met Sue for the first time. I truly believe Sue and I meeting was part of this whole thing. It includes you and Becky, Hugh and Sharon, Kay and Jan even Steve and Frank. This estate was part of it and it brought Sue and me to finding the secrets that were hidden here. Even the murder of Sue's friend Ken Benton was part of this.

Now for me to know that the two men would be here tonight and what they would do that information like a lot of this was just suddenly given to me by something outside of me. Sue and Father Duarte have also seen it. David I believe that God is the one doing this. There are things he wants done and he is arranging things to fit his will. The one thing is he has not taken away our free will. So now you are at the point you can decide if you want to continue."

"That my friend was one hell of an answer. I also have watched this whole thing progress and I do believe what you said. You and I have had a relationship like brothers sense we were kids. Even then my friend I believe you had someone directing what you did. You and I broke a lot of laws but we never just hurt people. We defended ourselves, our Barrio and the people in it. What I am saying is this doesn't seam to be any different; so I will still be at your side."

"Go home my friend we will handle that car tomorrow."

Sue hugged David and gave him a kiss on the cheek as he left. Sue said "Let's hit the shower then go to bed."

Monday Morning June14 / 2010 Tucson, Arizona

Jim and Sue slept in till seven then had there coffee out by the pool. "I know you have a busy morning, but can I come with you?"

"I love having you with me. Let's start with breakfast; I am meeting David at a small café close to his dealership.

David was glad to see Sue with Jim. While they had breakfast Jim told David he needed to keep guns, a scanner, night vision binoculars and extra cell phones with him. After breakfast they were going to clean out the car the bad guys had then drive it over to a chop shop that would have all the good parts removed then the body would be crushed. It would be done before two o'clock that day.

Jim again would put the battery back in the phone at ten o'clock so Agent Brian Higgs could call him.

David and Jim both put on gloves before cleaning out the car. There was a lot of equipment, guns, ammo, papers and money. They put it all in the back of Jim's car then Jim drove that car over to the garage with David and Sue following him. Jim also had the name and the keys to the Hotel the bad guys stayed at. David and one of his men would handle that. It would be like the two men and there car just disappeared.

Jim and Sue went back downtown parked close to the court house then walked around a small plaza and looked at the shops there was a coffee shop in the plaza and Jim had brought his small briefcase. At ten they picked a table that would give them some privacy and ordered coffee. Jim put the battery back into the phone then they talked and waited.

Agent Higgs again called a little after ten. "I have the E mail address you asked for." He gave Jim the Number."

"I will have it E mailed to you within two hours. There is another side to this that the FBI will need to handle. If I am not mistaken there is an FBI Agent you know named Lewis Riley. Do you think Agent Riley would be able and willing to handle the FBI's part of this?"

"You seam to have more information about me and my friends then I am comfortable with."

"I am sorry about that but time is a big factor in this for both my side and our people over sees. Let me go to work on that E mail. See where this goes and if you still want to do this thing call me again tomorrow at the same time."

"Should we go home and make this happen?"

It didn't take over an hour and Jim E mailed it to Agent Higgs from Senator Sysco's office right under the noses of the FBI who had already taken over the offices of the Senator. Jim really liked doing that. "Now let's move all the weapons, equipment and paper work we got down here."

They brought everything down to the basement and laid it all on a table then with gloves on went through every piece of paper they had. The two men had come in from Dallas Texas. Jim ran the two names against the list of employees of Black Burn Corporation and got a hit on both of them. "I need to put an end to Black Burn before they send out more people. If the Government can't move fast enough Then I need to do something myself."

"Why don't you wait and see what Agent Higgs has to say in the morning?"

"Speaking of the morning I would like to take that call from a different location then Tucson. Would you like to have breakfast with me from some where on the coast?"

"You are so funny; yes I would love to have breakfast with you. Should we invite David to come with us?"

"That's a great idea; let me call Bob and see if he is available first and where he would suggest we go so there is no fuss or cameras watching us coming and going."

Calls and arrangements were made and the three of them were meeting Bob the pilot at six in the morning and they would be having breakfast at a nice Country Club over looking the ocean just out side San Clemente California.

"I am sure the government will be tracking where the cell tower is when I answer the call. They can't help themselves."

"You and David make this like a game of chess where you keep forcing them to make the moves you want."

"You're right it is a game; we both want to catch the bad guys but we are both playing by different rules. They really know that they couldn't do what I can do. They even have the same computers but are restricted on how they can use them. To be honest they don't know how to do most of the things the units are capable of doing.

Now what can I do to entertain you this afternoon?"

"Take me to the Tucson Museum of Art then we could also walk through some of the nicer galleries in the downtown area. I am trying to get the picture in my mind of what I would like our Gallery to look like."

"Let me lock this up and we will go."

The afternoon definitely was fun and they talked to a lot of people including people at the University of Arizona Art Museum. They did know Sue and of her company. They stopped and had a light dinner before returning to the house.

"Will you walk with me to the upper patio so we can watch the sunset with some wine?"

"I think you have a very good idea. Let me get the wine and some glasses."

Tuesday Morning June 15 / 2010 Somewhere over California

The three of them were sitting around a table in Bob's Gulf Stream 450 and talking about there security in Tucson and what they might expect when Jim dumped Black Burn out to the government and the News paper. They talked about him giving the material to the Government at least two days before he released it to the Phoenix Republic News Paper. David said he had ten men standing by to do what ever we needed plus all there connections in the Barrio.

Jim thought a minute then said "I don't expect they will have time to think about us but if they do I will be ready to do more then just play defense; I will be ready to strike back at them in a very big and public way."

"you're talking about physically going out after them?"

"It would be the next right thing and I will make it look like one of there new friends did it."

Bob over the PA said "You have fifteen minutes if you want to freshen up."

They took a taxi to the Country Club witch did over look the ocean. They had time to order and eat breakfast before ten o'clock. At ten Jim put the battery back in the phone while finishing his meal. The waitress took the settings and poured them more coffee. At ten after the phone rang. Jim answered it by saying "Hi Brian; did you get my E mail?"

"I did and we can't believe all the facts and information you have in it. We spent all of yesterday and part of last night verifying what you sent us. Now after all the talking heads have gone over it we are in a position we must believe what you are saying. Already all the security at our Embassies and any other insulation that Black Burn has the security for is being replaced by our special forces who will be poised to repeal any siege. This will be completed by tomorrow at noon Eastern time."

"I will today E mail what you need to take down Black Burn Corporation, all of there officers and hundreds of there upper and middle management. Now in forty eight hours from then I will also release the same information to the news media."

"Why release it to the news media?"

"Sorry, but it will assure me no one gets special treatment."

"Ok with me." Then while laughing he said "Actually I think it's a great idea. When do you want me to call you again?"

"How about Friday morning the same time."

"Ok then I will talk to you Friday morning."

Jim was telling Sue and David about Brian laughing and what he said as they finished there coffee. Jim paid and over tipped there waitress then they were on there way.

It was afternoon and they were at the house Sue suggested they take a nice bottle of wine with them to the basement. Jim also thought that was a good idea.

Once the computers were up and running Jim started laughing and said "How about I E mail this from the District Attorney office in San Diego and also leave a secret file in his system containing all of it."

Sue started laughing and said "How do you come up with stuff like this? Your mind works differently then anyone else I have ever met."

"That's only because you're so young."

Sue kissed him and said "That was nice; now let's have some fun with the powers that be."

They spent less then an hour in the basement. On the way out Jim said "Early in the morning I will empty all the bank accounts I have found on these people. Then at the same time I am going to empty and close some of the accounts that were on the original CD's that belong to Muammar Kaddafi and his son's. They stole it from the people of Libya. Another one is Ali Abdullah Saleh of Yemen. Someone should just hang all of them.

"You are thinking they will connect the missing money with Black Burn and its leaders."

"I think they will at least consider it. If they do it would keep them from looking for someone on the outside of there circle. I would like to see there organization fall apart and none of them trusting each other. I think this Robert J Christenson was the one who brought them all together and some how kept them trusting each other for all these years. It would be easier for me to take them out one at a time. We will have to wait and see."

"So Friday afternoon you are giving the same story to the news paper."

"That's the plan. I am sure the government will ask me to give them more time but I won't. I can't be sure how many of them are involved and I don't want to give them any extra time to cover up there involvement. There are people in our government who will kill to protect themselves and there way of life. They have convinced themselves that the people are better off having them running the country."

"Would you like to have something light to eat or we could have an early dinner?"

"It looks like we might have a monsoon thunder storm this afternoon. Would you like to have an early dinner at the Westward Look Resort and sit where we would have a great view of the storm?"

"I love it; you call and make the reservations while I find something special for an early dinner."

The call was made and Jim dressed in tan slacks an off white Oxford dress shirt with button down color no tie but a nice dark blue blazer. When Sue came down the stairs Jim just stood there then said "You look stunning and I love it."

"Well thank you sir" then she gave him a nice kiss.

The people at the Westward Look Resort were also impressed with Young Sue and made it quite evident. They had a great table with a wonderful view of the approaching storm. They started with Champaign and talked of the day's events. It wasn't long and the storm started to come across the valley the thunder and lighting were great when the winds started to hit the restaurant there waiter asked if they would like to move to a different table away from the windows. Jim explained they came in early just to watch the storm. He did thank him.

The storm only lasted twenty minutes then the Sky was like a painting. They ordered dinner and it made a wonderful evening.

Wednesday Morning June 16 / 2010 Tucson, Arizona

Jim and Sue were on an early run and the desert was completely different sense the storm the gullies had been cleaned of all the brush that had grown in them, all the cactus were swollen with the water they had taken in, it was especially evident with the huge saguaro cactus that can take on over a hundred pounds from one rain. Even the rabbits seamed to be happy with the rain.

Jim was going to call the contractor Hector Robles and talk about the building and house Sue had in escrow and see if he would be interested in doing the work of rebuilding them. He asked Sue if she would like to go with him and meet and talk with Hector. Sue said she would love to.

Once back at the house Jim called Hector and talked a bit about old times then Jim asked if Hector and his son could meet him and Sue at the warehouse.

"Frank and I can meet the two of you at eight o'clock if that's not too early for you."

"Eight would be great; see you then."

They showered and dressed and were on there way in plenty of time. Hector and his son had gotten there early, Jim did all the introductions then they all walked around and through the building as Jim explained what he wanted to do and that he didn't want to cut any corners. Frank had some great ideas on the fencing around the building by using a three foot high concrete wall with five feet of rod iron fencing on top of it with gates on either end so trucks could still use the loading docks in the back. Jim gave Hector two thousand cash to get them started on making the plans. They agreed to work on an invoice plus arrangement. After they had an idea of what they were doing Jim asked them to also look at the house Sue was going to have redone as a gallery and offices for her business. Jim explained they were going to have an architect work with them on redesigning the building then maybe he and Frank could be the general contractor and over see the project. "I will guarantee that it will be worth your while so please think and talk about it. They exchanged Numbers with Sue and said they would be in touch.

As they left Jim said "If you let me buy you breakfast at the Tubac Country Club I will look through galleries with you and buy you anything you want."

"You're the only man I know who could and wood make an offer like that; so I accept."

"That's because you have led such a sheltered life my dear."

Breakfast and Tubac was fun and they shopped till after one o'clock and only managed to buy one painting. The ride home also was fun. Sue and the girls were going over to the Arizona Theater Company at two and Jim was going to the basement and work on the next step of the disclosure of information that would bring down some of the other corporations without exposing all of them at once. He would build a file on each of them and all of the people connected to them. It was a lot of work but the files would be ready when the time was right.

Friday Morning June 18 / 2010 Tucson, Arizona

Jim and Sue were on an early morning run. Jim had spent Wednesday afternoon and evening plus all day Thursday working on the computers building Files. Jim had also set up an on line connection where he could be answering his second cell phone and it would show the phone was in Southern California and coming from the cell tower he used in San Clemente.

"After we shower and dress let's start the day with breakfast at the Country Club. I have everything ready to send to the Phoenix Republic. I will call Hoyt and Bill this morning before I E mail it and ask them to try and have it in the Saturday morning paper."

"Are you going to tell them that the government has a copy?"

"Yes I believe that will be an important part of the story I will also give them the names of the two Agents. I will verify with Agent Higgs that he is using FBI Agent Lewis Riley for the part of this that is in our country."

"How can you make them believe that your cell phone is in California?"

"The X computer can do things that seam imposable. I can have the calls come from any cell tower in the country. Actually I can have it use Cell towers in any country. The programs in this thing will do thousands of things that they have no idea it can. When we wrote these programs we only showed the tasks they wanted. Remember it was the government telling us what they wanted."

Sue again looked stunning; she was like an advertisement for summer. Jim did tell her how beautiful she looked.

At the Country Club the servers at the restaurant all wanted to get a look at what Sue was wearing that day. They sat at an outside table the morning was perfect for being outside. It was one of the benefits of living in Tucson.

They returned to the house and waited for Agent Higgs to call. At ten Jim put the battery back in his phone and again in ten minutes the phone rang. Jim answered and said "Hi Brian."

"Hi Jeff we again can't believe the stuff you gave us on Black Burn. We have secured everything of ours that Black Burn was covering. You were right they could have jeopardized a lot of our embassies and a lot of other insulations. Again like you said I brought in FBI Agent Riley. They hopefully will have there warrants today and shut down Black Burn over the weekend."

"As I said I will give this to the media today. Now if there is anything you need to talk about I will put the battery in the phone again tomorrow at the same time. I wish you and Agent Riley good hunting."

Jim turned off the phone then removed the battery. "Ok now let's send a copy of all of this to Bill and Hoyt at the Phoenix Republic. After a few minutes I will call them and make sure they have it. Remember I also ran the program and remove all there money I could."

"That's right you will be spending a lot of money on the rebuilding of our building and gallery."

Jim worked in the basement a good three hours He again sent the entire report from the District Attorney Office in San Diego then shut down all the computers and locked up the basement. Once in the library he again called Bill and Hoyt. They had receive everything and again couldn't believe the depth of all the documentation that came with it and all of the photos of the officers of the corporation. Jim did advise them that the government had received the same file two days earlier so they could replace all the security at there Embassies. He also gave them the names of the Agents that were handling it. "Have fun guys and try and have it in the Saturday morning edition."

"Well I guess Saturday morning will be exciting for a lot of people. Now have you thought of how you would like to spend the rest of today?"

"Would you like to call Becky and see if she and David would like to do something? They should have or are going to close on there new house."

"You're right; let me call her right now."

The girls talked a good half hour and plans were being made. When Sue got off the phone she was laughing and said "They Closed this morning and will have the keys within the hour. Becky will call and we can meet them over there. She said they would have the Champaign so just come over."

"I love it; this should be a fun day. Who knows they may find hidden treasure."

"You are so funny; I do love you."

Saturday Morning June 19 / 2010 Tucson, Arizona

Jim woke Sue with kisses and asked if she would like to run with him. They ran about six miles it was quite humid. "We should have another storm this afternoon or evening."

"Well my love I am sure you have a storm going right now on the television."

"Would you like to shower off outside then we can have our coffee in the pool and watch the news on our huge television in the pool room."

"That sounds like fun let's go."

Sue poured the coffee while Jim turned the television so they could sit on the steps in the pool and watch the news with there coffee. Jim turned it to the Cable News and they were all ready on continuous coverage plus a round table of the talking heads that were looking at all the different areas of security that could have been exposed had the government just shut down the Black Burn Corporation. They were discussing all the other Governments and private corporations that Black Burn provided security for and what they were going to do.

"If nothing else you sure keep the media machine busy."

"I like that; it is a line from Elton John's song Ticking on the Caribou album. I thought I was one of only a few that liked that song. Will maybe you are another of the few."

"I think there are a lot more then a few. Like many of Elton John's songs this one speaks to a social condition most people don't want to talk about. it's another area of our society that could benefit from some of that money you have taken."

"I like that idea. It will take a lot of work to see where it actually would do some good for the people who can't speak for themselves. It could be one of many ongoing projects for your company. I am sure we can find a lot of people more then willing to assist us in this field."

"You're right this Catalina Consulting can be something that can bring together people that want to volunteer there time with the money that will allow them to produce results.

This is a whole different idea of what we can do. This really is exciting."

"let's shower and dress then I will take you to breakfast where ever you would like."

"I would like to dress casually and go to the Congress Street Hotel Café. Your CIA agent is going to call you again and I bet he will also have his FBI friend with him."

"I believe you're right and he will have more questions then I will answer; especially about the bank accounts that are now almost empty. After they call would you like to go and see the insides of the building that is on the next block from the one you bought?"

"Do you think they will let us look around?"

"I can't imagine them not letting you look around. Being Saturday it shouldn't be busy."

"I think we should Shower and dress this is going to be a fun day."

"Do you think there is room in all of this for some kisses?"

"There will be room in the shower for a lot more then just kisses."

The shower was great then it was off to breakfast. The weekend crowd was a lot younger then during the week. Breakfast was fun and they talked about looking at the downtown Galleries after they saw the building.

When they got to the building it was open. Jim explained to the receptionist that he and Sue were buying an old building on the next block and just wanted to walk through there building to get some ideas. The receptionist was excited and explained how they all loved working in there building. She got a young lady from the billing room to give Sue and Jim a tour. They had a great time and loved the building Sue gave both the girls a card and thanked them.

As they left the building it was almost ten o'clock. Jim suggested they again drive over to the grotto where the images of the last supper were.

Again ten minutes after ten Jim's second phone rang and it again was CIA Agent Higgs. He came right to the point and told Jim they have had a taskforce of agents from the CIA, FBI and the Justices Department working on the information he had given them and like he had said they have more questions then he has answers for.

"Just tell them the answers they want are in there files. Remember these people need there lawyers, accountants and Bankers to do just what you have in front of you. This thing is much bigger then what you have seen. Today is the nineteenth so I will put the battery back in the phone on the thirtieth at the same time. You and your people stay safe."

"Was the other agent there?"

"He was but I didn't talk with him. They have more then enough to keep them busy for a while. Now let's go looking for some Art we like."

They bought two pieces of art and had a great time. The whole weekend was low keyed and they spent most of it at home.

Monday Morning June 21/ 2010 Tucson, Arizona

Jim and Sue slept in till seven but still went on a run of a good five miles. On the way back to the house Sue asked Jim to take her to the Country Club for breakfast. "I love taking you to breakfast and you can spend the day with me if you like."

"I first need to talk with Becky and see if she would like me to help her with any of the wedding plans. Remember there wedding is this Sunday."

"After we get home you call her and I will watch the news."

The Country Club was nice and it was amazing how many people they had gotten to know in such a short time. Breakfast was good and Sue as always was the star.

Back at the house Sue quickly had Becky on the phone and was laughing a lot. Jim had cable news on and they had more stories going then they could handle. The Government was shutting down businesses and making arrests faster then the news people could cover. Over sees there were many stories being reported about Black Burn people being disarmed and all there equipment being confiscated. The government was offering a flight back to the United States to those that were citizens. The others were on there own. There was hundreds of video's coming from cell phones showing the military taking over the positions that the Black Burn people had been securing. They also show them disarming them. So far there was nothing mentioned about all the money that was withdrawn from Black Burn, there officers and supporting companies. Jim figured if the government had gotten that far they still wouldn't report it to the media.

When Sue got off the phone she was still laughing while she said "Becky has so much help from both her family and David's she has nothing to do. She also said David is just handing them money and telling them not to cut any corners because money is not a problem. It sounds like there both having a great time. For there honeymoon they are going to some resort in Mexico.

"That's good, David and I are wearing summer tuxedos and black boots; mine are all ready."

"I found something special to wear that I am sure you will like."

"I am sure I will. If you have the time would you like to come out to the Tucson Air and Space museum? A friend of mine said they were trying to raise money to bring a World War Two plane that was donated to the museum from a private collection that is in South Carolina."

"That would be fun; I have never been to that museum."

"To be honest I grew up here and have never been to not only the museum but not even an air show. I just didn't feel the need. As kids David myself and a few friends would break into where they had the old mouth ball fleet of thousands of planes. That was really fun and some times they would realize we were in there and try and catch us. I think they had just as much fun as we did. But in any case we never got caught; You might think of it as early training."

"I guess you could say the training has gone to good use."

"After the Air Museum would you like to stay home and work on the house and decide what things you would like to keep and what you would like to replace. Everything is up for discussion. We also need to hang the Art we bought."

"This could be a fun day; we can make this into our home that reflects us. There are some of the pieces I would like to keep. Well they are pieces we can talk about. there are only a few pieces of furniture I would like to get rid of; but again we can talk about it."

"Let's do the Air Museum now so we can get back here and go to work."

The Air Museum was fun. Jim explained what Catalina Consulting did with cash donations and that Sue had a hundred thousand dollars cash to give to them and then they would Pay Catalina Consulting 5% witch would be five thousand for there services. So Sue gave them the money and her card and asked if they would mail the recite and check to her. They did do a quick tour of the museum on a golf cart with a young lady driving and briefly explained the exhibits to them. They did have fun then quickly returned to the house.

They spent most of the day going from room to room trying to decide what they wanted to keep and what they wanted to get rid of. By late afternoon they were sitting in the Jacuzzi drinking some nice wine. "It looks like we are going to have a monsoon thunder storm. Let's hit the pool and cool off before it starts."

"After the storm I will fix us a nice light supper then if you like we can walk up to the upper patio and watch the Sunset. I will even include a nice bottle of wine."

"I love the idea and will help you fix our supper and clean up after it."

"I like that."

The storm was heavy and fast causing flash flooding in some parts of town. At there home they got a lot of wind and rain but being in the foot hills there is no flooding. Dinner was good and fun as was the walk up to the patio. The desert was anew and the rabbits were out and busy eating.

The sunset and the city lights coming on were like a personal show for just Sue and Jim. While they were drinking the last of the wine Jim said "I been thinking that old guy Christenson would most likely have a safe hidden some where in the master suite for his personal treasure."

"Shit you're not kidding about this are you?"

"It's just a thought, But I don't see him going to all that trouble just to get something out of his safes in the basement."

"You are for sure the wildest man I have ever known. Now you Have me believing you are right. Where do you think he is hiding it?"

"I don't know but when we have some time we should go looking."

"We have the time right now because you knew when you started this that I would have to find it and see what was inside it."

"Remember this is just an idea I had. Now to get me started I would need a lot of kisses."

"I will give you one good one before the treasure hunt."

Now they were both laughing and Sue said "You're as bad as me so let's go back to the house and start looking."

"Ok but let me get that really good one before we go."

Back at the house Sue was like a twelve year old girl on Christmas eve. It wasn't long and they were walking around the bedroom looking for some clue as to where old man Christenson would have hidden a safe. While they were looking Jim found some Numbers written on the inside casing of one of the closets. "I think I have found it. I think it is in this closet. There is what I think is the combination written inside here."

"Let me see. I think your right he didn't want to forget it. where in the closet do you think it is?"

"I am thinking part of the floor comes out and it will be underneath. Let me take you're shoe racks out and we will find out."

It took a bit but Jim finely figured out how to release the section of floor. As soon as it was out there was a fairly large floor safe. Sue was jumping up and down while waiting for Jim to open it. As soon as he had it unlocked he said "I will pull the top off of it then you can see what is inside it."

He pulled the top off and stepped out of the closet so Sue and her small flashlight could go in. "It's full of Jewelry boxes and those canvas bags; there are a lot of them."

"Start pulling them out and hand them to me."

The safe was so deep Sue was lying on the floor to reach the last of them. The last thing she brought out was a small gun. "Should we get a bottle of wine before we open any of them?"

"I will go for the wine and glasses and you get a white towel for the coffee table." Jim was on his way and Sue was laughing as she found a large white towel. Jim poured the wine while Sue brought everything over to the table. With a kiss she opened the first box it was a set of matching diamond earrings, a large diamond necklace that had four very large diamonds that were surrounded by thirty plus smaller diamonds. There was also a matching diamond bracelet in with it. "That will look beautiful on you."

"I can't think of where someone would wear something like that. It is beautiful and I wonder who it was made for."

"It might have been made for you and was sitting here waiting."

"I am scared to open any other boxes."

"I will do the next one. There is one that looks like a man's watch box." It was a watch box. Inside was a gold Rolex that had a diamond inlayed cobalt blue face.

"I love this watch; this I will keep."

They sat on the floor till almost midnight opening boxes of very modern jewelry made with very large stones it was a treasure it's self. Jim kept out a large amount of the matching sets. One that he really liked was a choker made of hundreds of at least ¾ caret diamonds. It was hot looking on Sue. It ended up being quite a night.

Tuesday Morning June 22 / 2010 Tucson, Arizona

Sue woke Jim up early and asked him to go running. They again did a good five miles then showered off out side then right into the pool and swam at least fifteen minutes then sat with there coffee and talked of there day. Jim was going to have the boys move the paintings they had taken down to the warehouse. "Three of them would make a nice showing for the University Museum of Art."

"If you like after breakfast we can take your note book and go over and talk with them. It should be fun."

"I know the Curator Tim Eakins, he is a nice guy and very knowledgeable where it comes to art. Let me get his Number then I will call him before we go over."

"Ok now we have the start of a plan. Let's start with breakfast at the Country Club then you can call Tim after were done. If it is alright we can park downtown and take a cab to the museum; I know there is no place to park."

"That would be a lot easier."

They both dressed very nicely Jim didn't wear a tie but wore a great dark blue blazer with tan slacks and white Oxford shirt with a button down collar. He did wear his new Rolex watch. Sue wore a beautiful summer dress that Jim had never seen she had open toe heals and to put the final touch on it she wore a beautiful set of pearls and matching ear rings.

"I love the whole look. I am sure the whole staff will be out to see this outfit."

"If you like I have the perfect hat to go with this."

"I love you in hats; please wear it."

Sue did look like she was going on a photo shoot and Jim loved every bit of it. At the Country Club they definitely were the couple that was getting everyone's attention. The staff was really excited and loved Sue and the outfit. Breakfast was as always great and a lot of people stopped by to say hello. Before they left Sue called Tim at the University and in the conversation told him she was married and that she and her husband had a fairly large privet collection of art that had been out of circulation for over fifty years and wanted to stop by this morning and talk to him about it. Sue said that they would be there in about forty minutes.

Jim did the bill and tip then he and Sue were on there way. He parked at the train station where he could be there up to four hours then they caught a cab and it took them right to the front steps of the museum. Jim carried the note book and Sue told the lady at the reception desk that Tim was expecting them.

When Tim came out he was at a loss for words when he saw Sue. Sue nicely did the introductions and they went into Tim's office witch was a mess. Tim was making room for the two of them and said "I would like to say it normally looks better then this but as Sue knows that's not the case."

They talked a bit and Sue told Tim that they had loaned six paintings out to the Tucson Art Museum and had three now that they had replaced that would make a nice showing. Jim explained that they eventually wanted to replace most of the art with paintings that meant something to them. They didn't want there home to be a museum. Sue showed Tim the notebook. He slowly went through it with the look of amazement on his face then looked at Jim and asked "Is this collection in Tucson?"

"Yes it's at our house except for the six paintings that are at the other museum. It's a rather large house."

Sue pointed out the three paintings that were available to be loaned out right now. Jim said "If you and some of your staff would like to come out and see the collection we would love to make the arrangements."

"Thank you I would love to and there are three, no make that four people I would love to bring with me. I still can't believe this collection has been in Tucson all these years, and you are right it should be seen."

Sue gave Tim one of her cards and explained a little of what her company did. It wasn't long and Jim called the same cab that had brought them to the University to now pick them up.

Sue was very excited about how well it had all gone. "You do know how to make me happy. Now what would you like to do?"

"When we get back to the car let's call David and see if he and Becky would like to sneak away for a few hours. No business just for some fun."

"I love it and I am sure they will."

As things were meant to be David and Becky did love the idea. They were at there new house and it was arranged that Jim and Sue would pick them up. On the drive to there house Sue was telling Jim how happy she was and how she was starting to see how Catalina Consulting would just come together and be a part of the community.

At David and Becky's house Becky wanted them to check out what they already had started. They had hired a decorator who already had three crews working on the house removing flooring, window coverings and everything in the bath rooms. They were also remolding the master bed room, closets and dressing area. Becky said this and the wedding are like a full time job and David keeps saying money is not an object."

Sue kissed her on the cheek and said "Money is not an object; just make sure they do what you want them to. This is wonderful and the two of you will have a wonderful life and we will have great neighbors."

David said "Let's get out of here and go have some fun."

"Let's go down to the Barrio and have a drink and a light lunch. I am sure we can get a small crowd of the people we love together; then we can introduce the Girls to them."

"I love the idea you Girls have only met a few of them; This will be great."

The afternoon turned out to be a party with over sixty people showing up Jim had the owner just run a tab for both the drinks and food witch he paid before they left.

It was almost five by the time they got back to David's He and Becky were expected at her Mom's later that evening.

"Thank you that was a great afternoon. Should we go home and watch the news?"

"That's a good idea we can spend a nice evening together I surely don't need anything to eat or drink."

The news was all over the people that were stranded over sees and couldn't get any answers from Black Burn Corporation. There are reports that all the corporate founds had been withdrawn only days prior to the government taking over and freezing all of there accounts. There are also reports that the officers and executives had withdrawn almost all of the funds from there personal accounts at the same time. Law enforcement have either arrested or detained all of them they could find. There is no list of the people that the FBI or CIA are looking for. The news went on with all of the other companies that the FBI had shut down and included in that was a huge Law Firm in Washington DC.

"By the time the Feds gets done with this there should be a lot of people in jail."

"What are you going to do with all the other people and corporations that are part of all of this?"

"I have been thinking about that a lot and haven't come up with an answer yet. If I exposed them all at once I don't think law enforcement, the courts and the economy could handle it. But on the other hand every day they are systematically exploiting thousands of there employees and steeling millions of dollars. I need to work on that but not tonight."

"Then shut that off and go for a walk with me; we will talk about nicer things."

While they were walking Jim said "I have been thinking about what room in the house we should use as a nursery."

Sue started laughing then laid a big kiss on him and said "The nursery will be the room next to ours and I have it all planed out in my head. We have a big house to fill up with children."

"Well than that is one less thing I need to be thinking about. We should work on that tonight."

Wednesday Morning June 23 / 2010 Tucson, Arizona

Jim woke Sue with Kisses and said "Thank you for last night; would you like to start our day with a run?"

"A run would be the second thing I would like to start our day with."

They did end up on a run but only went about five miles. At the end they were walking hand in hand. "Let me take you for breakfast. We can go anywhere you want."

"Let's go to the Congress Street Hotel Café. We can act like we are out on a date and have a nice slow breakfast."

"Then we can dress as if were on a date.

They were both having fun and the early crowd had left so they got the same table they had the first time they were there together. They both ordered something different then what they normally did and were laughing and having a great time. Sue's phone rang and it was Tim from the University and he wanted to know if he and his people could come out later that afternoon about two. Jim and Sue thought that would be nice. Sue gave him directions on how to get there.

Breakfast came to the table and they enjoyed what they had ordered. They were having coffee when Jim's second phone rang; it was Hoyt Segal from the Phoenix Republic News Paper. Hoyt said "I am calling you from a phone away from the paper. This morning we got a call from a CIA Agent named Brian Higgs who said he needed to talk to you and it was very important. He left a phone Number."

Jim took the Number and asked Hoyt how he and Bill were doing. They talked about ten minutes. When Jim hung up he told Sue what Hoyt said then decided he would call Brian from the Grotto by the river again. He did the bill and tip then they went for a ride to the river.

When Brian answered he said "I needed to reach out to you and Bill and Hoyt were my only hope. FBI Agent Riley and I have found that there is a contract that has been put out on the people in Tucson. The contract is from a source other then what we have on our list. From what we have been able to find out it went out two days ago and the people who have taken it are very capable and use a team approach. They have been responsible for at least twenty assassinations that we know of. If you will give us the names of the people in Tucson the FBI will have them put into there protective service till we can stop these people."

"Thanks Brian the knowledge is helpful but I can tell you and Agent Riley that the people in Tucson won't go along with that. Hopefully I can talk them into leaving the country for a while. They do have a lot of resources available to them. Remember I told you this thing is much bigger then Black Burn and all the companies linked to them. Brian this is so big that I can't give it all to the government at one time because they couldn't handle it and neither could the country. So I need you and Agent Riley to handle this as fast as possible. I will leave or common connection to Bill and Hoyt open as long as the two of you don't try to capitalize on it. so take care my friend and thank you."

"Well that was one hell of a conversation with just hearing one side of it."

"It was; someone has sent out a contract on us two days ago to a very successful hit firm. The FBI wanted to put us into there protective service. They only know us as the people who Black Burn tried to assassinate. I think we can do a better job of protecting ourselves. Also if we did give them our names then very quickly we would be on everyone's list."

"I think this is moving back from exciting to scary."

"Your right and I am sorry. I need to touch base with a different friend and tell him what is going on, this one I will handle without David. He needs to take care of the wedding and I can do this without him. Would you like to go with me as I set up our people? That way you would know what was happening rather then sitting home worrying about it."

"Thank you; I will change while you call you're...."

The call was made and they arranged to meet for a few minutes in the parking lot near the Barrio.

They met and Jim introduced Sue to Tommy, he explained what was happening and that he wanted David completely out of it and why; Tommy agreed. Jim explained he was still going to be his best man and that he and Sue would be part of the complete wedding.

Jim and Sue next went to the Barrio with Tommy and met up with five of the main people in the gang. Jim explained that the people may have already arrived in town, but he didn't think so, he thought they would fly into Phoenix then rent cars and drive to Tucson. "I believe they will also have a person drive all there weapons and equipment in and set up a base for there operations. I would expect this to be on the north west part of town."

Jim gave them two hundred thousand to spread around to all there connected gangs and other people around town. Tommy the one in charge said they would start right then and would know as soon as they were in Tucson. They were all excited and loved this kind of stuff. Jim did again remind them that he did not want them to make any contact at this time only to call him.

As they drove back to the house Sue said that was kind of unbelievable, you really do have a kind of an army between you're people and there contacts."

"It's even better because we have no rules to get in the way like the police have. We can play the same as the bad guys. Now as soon as I have some information on who these people are and we have eliminated the immediate threat then I will go after there whole little assassination business and destroy them. Before I do that I will use the computer and find out who hired them."

"You're talking like this is personal and you are personally going to put an end to them."

"Sue, this is personal; they are not only coming to kill me but both us and that would include you, the girls and boys, it doesn't get much more personal then that. I know you don't like this but it's real and I need to follow it to its end."

"I don't like it but I will be right next to you all the way and will do all I can to help."

There is a big art type thing happing in Paris on the twelfth of next month. Why don't you send the girls over there tomorrow to check it out and to write up a report on all the different originations that are involved in putting it together? It will first of all get them out of harms way and also give you a lot of companies in France we can show as paying your company huge fees that you can show as income."

Sue was laughing and said "They will love it I can have Darleen set up all there travel and hotels. I will call her as soon as I get home then tell the girls to pack. This will blow there minds."

"Have fun I will talk with Jerry and the boys about security. Also tell the girls not to pack too much I hear the shopping is great there."

Jerry was at the gate so Jim asked if he would come to the security office in about twenty minutes for a meeting with him and the boys.

At the house Sue went to work on her stuff and Jim called the boys and asked if they could all meet in fifteen minutes at the security office.

Once they were all together and hellos were said, Jim quickly told them that there were well armed people who might be coming after him and Sue and if they did get as far as the estate it would be dangerous. He then told them if they liked he would arrange for other people to take over until the threat was gone and they would all have there jobs and his confidence. Starting with Jerry they all said they would stay and do what ever was necessary. Jim thanked them then told them he only wanted them to monitor all the existing systems and to notify him of any breaches no matter how small. "These people are professionals and may well be able to locate our security and overcome it so be careful."

The boys Frank and Steve came back to the house with Jim and the three girls were laughing and having fun. Steve said he and Frank were taking them to the airport at five in the morning. Kay said "Let's have dinner here tonight and use up as much of the perishables we can that we have at our house."

Everyone thought that was a good idea and they should all be in there swim trunks. Now they had a party and it was just what everyone needed including Sue and Jim.

At two o'clock Tim and his four people showed up and like everyone were in awe of the house. Sue knew them all and did the introductions. She invited them in and said she would take them on a tour of the house and the art. Jim stayed behind and set up glasses and a nice selection of wine. It was a good forty minutes before they returned to the pool room. They were all excited and none of them could believe the art collection. They stayed another half an hour and over the wine Jim got Tim's Number and said he would arrange to have the three paintings delivered to the Museum.

As soon as there company left the boys and girls came over. They told Sue and Jim they were overdressed for a swim party. It ended up being a great evening.

By eight o'clock the boys and girls were heading home. The dishes were all done and everything cleaned up. Sue wanted some wine then to sit in the Jacuzzi for a bit. It turned into a nice night.

Thursday Morning June 24 / 2010 Tucson, Arizona

Jim and Sue were up and dressed with coffee made by four o'clock the girls and boys were coming over for coffee and bagels before they left for the airport. There was a lot of laughing and Kay and Jan were really excited and couldn't believe they were really going to Paris. By ten to five they were going down the drive then disappeared over the hill. Sue turned and gave Jim a big kiss and said "I do love you."

They walked back into the house and they both cleaned up the kitchen. "Let's take our coffee out to the Jacuzzi and talk of our day."

At six thirty they were laying in the sun light and Jim's phone rang. It was Tommy and hoped he wasn't calling too early. Jim assured he wasn't. Tommy said the four men flew in last night to Phoenix, rented two cars then drove to Tucson. They rented three rooms at the Ramada Inn by the freeway the fifth man hasn't showed up yet. "They did exactly what you thought they would."

"Good work, now call me if they do anything except get breakfast."

Sue said "So it starts."

"Hopefully it will be over before the rehearsal dinner. I don't want to be looking over my shoulder."

"What can I do to help you?"

"Let's go look at what we have in the basement. I took a lot of nice equipment from the last two people they sent to us, I never took a good look at it."

They both had to leave there cell phones up in the library. There sniper rifles weren't any better then what Jim already had but the AK-47's they had were equipped with silencers and extra long clips. Jim took up two of them and two of the extra clips. He also took up two of the sniper rifles, two of the assault twelve gauge shotguns and ammo for all of them. Jim closed and locked the basement then they went to the pool room got some more coffee and waited.

It was almost two hours when Tommy called and said "They did do breakfast and now the fifth man has arrived in a 4x4 pick up that has a camper shell on the back the five of them unloaded five canvas bags that only looked long enough to hold maybe AK 47's but no long rifles. They took the bags in one room and they are all in there."

"They didn't even bring in any other equipment?" "No nothing else." "Ok then I believe they plan on doing this tonight. They will have two people come out and locate us then figure how to approach the house. if they do that then I will expect them tonight and I will ask you and two of our people to come out and bring only one car. I have guns here for you to use. For now keep an eye on them and call when they leave."

Sue said "You already know there coming tonight. I can see it in your eyes."

"You're right and I think it would be a good idea to have the boys leave till at least noon tomorrow. They don't need to be part of this and I don't want them to be."

"I agree with you they should go for the night. Why don't you go talk with them?"

Jim did go over and talk with them and explained it would be better for him if they left for the night and didn't return till after noon. Jim then went and talked with Jerry and asked him to also leave then and to take tomorrow off with pay. Jerry seamed to understand and said he would see him Monday. Back at the house Jim told Sue if things got bad she was to close her self off in the basement.

"It's strange to watch you; every move you make has a meaning. You already know they are coming tonight and that two of them will come out here and decide the easiest way to break into the house. The only reason you have Tommy and the other men to come out is to watch over me then to help you get rid of the bodies. Then after the wedding you are going to personally destroy the people that sent them. My big fear in this is it will do something to change who you are inside."

"This is not what I wanted and what I was hoping to avoid. As far as changing me this is what I did for the Government and I was very good at it. These people I am going to kill are not innocent, they assonate people for a living and enjoy it. They will die tonight and as you said after the wedding I will destroy the rest of them and the people that hired them. When this is complete I will try and show you I am the same person you married and I do love you."

"I will go in the kitchen and make up some light meals that we can have at your conveyance. Actually a drink would go good right now."

"Your right, this might end up being a long day."

The next time Jim talked to Tommy he asked him to bring a half stick of dynamite, a blasting cap and a foot of fuse. Tommy laughed and said he would have it. when the conversation was over Sue asked what that was all about. Jim explained that he would try and keep what ever happened quiet and privet. And then they would dispose of the bodies in the same place as they had put the others only this time they would cause an explosion that would seal off the mine shaft. We will transport the bodies in there truck then clean out there motel rooms. The truck will go to Mexico and the rental cars will be parked in long term parking at the Phoenix airport. "These people will just disappear."

By nightfall Tommy and his two men were at the house. All three of them were amazed by the house and estate. Two of the five bad guys had checked out the property for almost an hour earlier in the afternoon. They even hiked up one of the neighboring driveways a good half a mile. Jim could see them from the upper patio.

It was almost nine o'clock when Tommy got the call that the five men had left the Motel in the pick up truck. Two of the men were in the back of the truck and they each brought there canvas bags with them. Jim had everyone put there cell phones on vibrate. One of Tommy's men were going up to the top of the hill by the driveway with a set of the starlight binoculars and watch to make sure they didn't try and come in through the main driveway. Jim expected they would come in the same place that the other assassins did. It was by far the most vulnerable area of the estate to attack. Jim gave Sue a loaded Glock and a kiss and told her he would call as soon as it was over. Sue stiffened up and held it together.

The waiting was the hardest part but Jim knew it was as bad for the others. After a good thirty minutes Jim got a glimpse of one of them and they were coming in at the same place as the others. He watched them a good ten minutes and it was all five of them. As they got close to the security trail Jim started to shoot them as fast as he could and they were firing back at him. The whole thing only lasted a matter of seconds but it seamed like a long time. Jim was shot once in the upper left hip just below his belt line. He knew it didn't hit the bone or an artery, he could still walk and the bleeding was light. He slowly worked his way over to check that they were all dead. It was nice they were. He called Tommy and asked him to have his man out by the driveway to locate there truck hot wire it and drive it down to where he was Sue would open the gate for him. Jim put on a pair of latex gloves and went through there pockets and removed everything he also collected there guns and ammo clips. Like last time he shined his flashlight to show where he was. As soon as Tommy and his people got there Jim had them bring out all the canvas bags and all the paper work that was in the truck except the registration and insurance papers. Tommy saw that Jim had been shot and said that there were already tarps and blankets in the back of the truck so they would load the five men and take them to the mine shaft. Tommy knew where it was and he would also handle the motel and moving the cars. Jim said "Then drop me and the canvas bags at the house. I will clean up and go to Mexico to handle this."

It seamed like only minutes and Jim and the bags were at the house and Tommy and his men were gone. Sue was upset but got a towel and wrapped Jim's leg so that he could get to the Shower in one of the down stairs rooms. With bandages and tape he got the wounds covered and all the bleeding stopped. He had Sue wrap it all in clear kitchen wrap so he could take a quick shower. He told her he was going down to Nogales Mexico to have it cleaned and bandaged. "If you like you can come along. Dress very casual and even wear a baseball hat. I will drive one of the small SUV's we have for the security people. We have good people down there who can handle this with no problem. It's not a serious wound."

"I always considered it serious when someone got shot. Of course I didn't grow up in the Barrio."

"One other thing you can't take your gun with us. Mexico gets upset."

Jim made a call to Mexico then they put everything into the library, locked it and the house then were on there way to Mexico.

The little SUV was a Saturn View and it ran and drove very nicely. At the border there was no traffic so it took only minutes to cross. The Clinic they went to was open all night and a Doctor Robles was waiting for them. The one shot was very minor wound and the other Jim was just lucky it missed everything that would have been a problem and went out the back. The doctor cleaned then bandaged both of them; he was showing Sue as he went because she would need to change the bandages. Jim explained the wedding and the rehearsal Saturday. The doctor was laughing as he told Sue how she should bandage it for the services. He then gave Jim a shot of antibiotics and a prescription and a supply of the pills he could take with him. Jim over paid the clinic and tipped the doctor three thousand.

As they drove away Sue asked why the doctor gave him the prescription and the pills.

"To bring the pills across the border you need to show that they were prescribed by a doctor. This makes it legal."

Friday Morning June 25 / 2010 Nogales Senora, Mexico

It was almost one thirty in the morning by the time they cleared customs and were on there way to Tucson and the house. They did have one more border patrol check point then it was clear sailing somewhere before they changed from I-19 to I-10 Sue started laughing and said "You actually got shot in the butt." She was now laughing so hard she was holding her sides. Jim couldn't help himself and was now also laughing. Every time Sue tried to say she was sorry she would start laughing again. It took a good hour and twenty minutes to get home and into the house. Jim made them both a drink and they settled down on the couch and talked of the day. At four o'clock Tommy called and told Jim everything was handled with no problems. Jim said he would call him later in the day and arrange a time to pick up the papers they found in there rooms.

"Let's finish these and go to bed it will be getting light soon."

There were only some kisses then quickly they were a sleep.

It was six thirty and Jim's phone rang and it was David calling and he and Becky wanted to sneak away with Jim and Sue for breakfast before there day got wild. Jim and Sue agreed to meet them at the Country Club at seven thirty. Both Jim and Sue were laughing as they got a shower and dressed. Jim didn't want David to know about what was going on with the bad guys. This was David and Becky's week and they would be gone on there honeymoon by Sunday night. Even Tommy and the other two men from the Barrio knew not to say anything to David.

Breakfast was fun and Becky was funny talking about her family and how they with David's Mom and sisters were taking over the wedding and having so much fun. It was almost nine when David and Becky left. Jim told them he and Sue would see them at the rehearsal and dinner Saturday night. Jim and Sue also left and went back to the house and to bed.

By two o'clock they were up again. The boys hadn't come home yet so hopefully they were having fun. Jim called Tommy who said he would bring all the stuff he had recovered from the motel rooms and the cars over if Jim liked. Jim told him the gate would be open.

When Tommy arrived they went through everything Jim only kept a small amount of paper work then gave Tommy another two hundred thousand for him and his men. Tommy was taking what was left of the belongings and with gloves on dispose of them in a Number of dumpsters.

With Sue's help Jim brought everything from the night before down to the basement. He would leave the guns and equipment alone for now but there was a lot of papers and personal things he needed to go through to try and find the people the assassins worked for. Then hopefully he could find the people who hired them. Sue was going back up and would lock the library so if the Boys returned she could talk with them.

Jim went through each of the men's belongings and three of the five came out of Texas one being the driver of the truck. He also had the rental recites and they were paid on a corporate credit card. That was a big mistake. Jim went after the card and it belonged to a company in El Paso Texas. Jim went to there web sight and it was listed as a security company and there web page was not user friendly. Jim used the X computer and went right through there security witch wasn't much. It was obvious right from the start this wasn't a real company one thing they did have on there computer was a phone list of all of them using there real names. The five men Jim had killed were part of a list of twenty seven names. Jim in his personal phone directory had an old contact in El Paso.

It took a couple of calls to reach his friend but he did. He and Hector talked a bit then Jim asked if Hector would check the address he had and try and confirm that it was a business or what he also gave Hector the first five names on the list and asked if he would find out if they were connected to that address and possibly get a photo of them. Hector wanted ten thousand Jim said he would overnight FED X fifty thousand along with an E mail address to him but wanted Clean and quick work. Hector gave Jim a clean address to send the money to.

Jim locked up the basement then went up to the library then found Sue. She said the boys had returned and said they had a really good time with there friends. She had talked with them for over a half hour. She then said "Let me fix us something nice to eat then we can take a nice walk and make this a quite night."

"I need to Fed-X a package real quick; it won't take a half of an hour."

"Hurry back."

Friday night was quite and nice.

Saturday Morning June 26 / 2010 Tucson, Arizona

Jim woke Sue early and asked her to go running with him. "I love to run with you."

They did a hard and fast eight miles and got to see a lot of rabbits and coyotes. The summer rains had been good and the foothills were beautiful and green. Toward the end of the run they were walking hand in hand the last quarter of a mile. "This will be a fun day and there will be a lot of people to meet."

"I don't think I will be able to conceal a gun on the dress I was going to wear tonight. Do you think I can leave my gun at home?"

"I think they are now only wondering why they haven't heard from there people. I expect by Monday they will be concerned."

"By Monday David and Becky should be in Mexico then you can play with them."

"Where would you like me to take you for breakfast?"

"I was thinking of that and I have a nice summer dress that I have never worn and I think the Country Club crowd will love it."

"It's you they love; the clothes just gives them an excurse to stair at you."

"You sure know how to talk to a girl; let's hurry to that shower."

The shower was great and as Sue called them the Country Club crowd were in awe of her. But to be fair the dress and accessories and jewelry she wore; including the hat were awesome. It looked as if she was a model. The weather was perfect so they sat outside. The young lady that waited on them knew Sue and she was thrilled to see her. Breakfast was fun and it made all that other stuff go away. "When were done here, would you drive me by the warehouse and the other building we are buying?"

"That also sounds like fun. After that would you like to go art shopping?"

The wedding rehearsal was going to be at seven o'clock in the Cathedral in downtown on Sixth Street. It would be casual dress and of course a warm night. Sue and Jim would need to be there early.

David had arranged with some of there people to have valet parking. The Cathedral was again very old and was a paramount part of downtown Tucson; it was beautiful and large with thirty foot high ceilings in the center section. David and Becky were happy to see them. They both looked sharp and happy. Becky loved the jewelry Sue was wearing. Sue looked at Jim and smiled. Jim said to them "Unless Becky already has her hart set on the jewelry she is going wear tomorrow the two of you should stop over to the house after everything is done tonight."

David started laughing kissed Becky and said "This should be fun; we have to do it."

Becky had a stunned look on her face so Sue kissed her on the cheek and said "Come over you will love it."

Parents and brides maids started to arrive with a lot of family. David's family were part of Jim's. As he and now Sue were part of theirs.

The rehearsal was fun and every one with some coaching did there part. Jim's part as best man was easy, as the Priest told him he was not to pass out. Jim would have the rings. The whole thing took no more than an hour and everyone had fun. The next thing was the rehearsal dinner at the Country Club.

David had arraigned to have a separate room set up; there were at least fifty people there. There were a lot Jim and Sue didn't know mostly from David's dealerships.

Dinner as always was excellent and after an hour Jim and Sue said there goodbye's Sue did remind Becky they would be waiting on them.

The ride home was quick and fun. Sue was excited about Becky and the jewelry. Once in the house it didn't take long and they were in the closet then the safe. They spent over half an hour picking out sets of jewelry and things Sue thought Becky might like. Jim said "Not the choker; I would like to keep that for you."

They took the large selection of jewelry down to the pool room. Jim got out some cold Champaign and put it on ice while Sue laid out the jewelry on a large white towel. When she was done she covered it with a second towel while laughing. They shared a few kisses then walked toward the front porch. They sat on the steps and talked while they were waiting.

It wasn't long and David and Becky came over the hill. Jim and Sue walked down to meet them. Both David and Becky were on a high and having a ball. They went to the pool room and Jim opened the Champaign and poured everyone a glass. Sue said to Becky I laid out some jewelry I thought you might like. They walked over to where the towels were and Sue removed the top one. Becky immediately grabbed hold of David and said "Look at this; I have never seen jewelry like this."

Sue said "Becky Jim has been teaching me how to play Indiana Jones; this is just part of what we have found and it would make us happy if you picked out all of it that you would like."

"You're talking about real treasure?"

"Yes and it is as exciting as you can think. This is some of the fun part so let's start going through it."

The four of them were really having fun and by the time it was over Becky had two sets of matching Necklaces, ear rings and Bracelets one in diamonds and sapphires the other in diamonds and rubies. She also with a lot of prompting from Sue got a string of natural pears and four other pieces. Becky said "You guys are by far the wildest people I have ever met."

Jim said "That's only because you're so young."

There were hugs and kisses then David and Becky were on there way. Sue gave Jim a big kiss and said "Take me to bed."

Sunday Morning June 27 / 2010 Tucson, Arizona

Jim and Sue were up early and went for a short and slow run. "This should be a busy and fun day. Would you like to start with breakfast at the Congress Street Hotel Café?"

"You seam to be able to read my mind; I would love that."

They had there coffee in the Jacuzzi then showered and dressed. The wedding was to be at one o'clock then the reception would follow at the Country Club.

At breakfast they talked of many things but Monday and what would happen was not part of it. Sue said "We need to be at the church by twelve o'clock; you know David will be a mess."

"I know that and it is how he should be. David really is a good guy and I am so happy for the two of them. I was also thinking about you're parents and how they are doing."

"I talked to Mom earlier this week and she said they really have been having fun. I think them not having to worry about finances has given both of them a new freedom. I never knew they worried about that before."

"Well than that is one more, nice thing that has come from all of this. As soon as this is all under control it will be fun to have them come out again."

"I don't think you will see them again till fall. Summer in Tucson is not there favorite thing."

"Let's go home and go swimming, we have time."

"would you like to watch the news?"

"Not today; all of that can wait till tomorrow."

"I like that."

Sue looked beautiful in a stunning summer dress with all the proper accessories, Jewelry and a stunning hat. It out did the dress that Julie Roberts wore at the polo match in Pretty Woman. "You by far have surpassed every fantasy I have ever had. You are a beautiful woman and I love the way you dress."

"It's funny but I never thought of dressing like this before I meet you. Some how I feel it's ok to express my feelings. You make me feel free."

Jim kissed her and said "Let's go to the wedding."

They were at the church by twelve. David was there and very happy to see the two of them. He also commented on how beautiful Sue looked. Then he looked at Sue and Jim and said "I know something is going on."

"David the only thing of any importance that is going on is you're and Becky's wedding followed by your honeymoon. I can't wait to see the bride."

"I can't either; they won't let me get close to her. She stayed at her Mom's house last night and my Mother made me stay over at her house; so there wasn't even a drink."

Sue was laughing and gave David a kiss on the cheek. Jim said "In less then an hour you will be married and all grown up in you're Mom's eyes."

They really were having fun and there were a lot of people coming into the church. There was four young men that were part of the two families and were dressed also in summer tuxedos and they were the ushers and seating the people. It wasn't long and both of the families were seated and Sue sat with David's Mom and Dad. His sisters were part of the bride maids. The flowers and decorations were beautiful.

The time was at hand so David and Jim stood up front with the priest and waited for the bride and her Farther to come up the isle. The music started and right on cue, the doors at the front of the church opened and Becky was standing with her arm held by her Dad. Then with big smiles on both of there faces they started slowly coming down the isle everyone was standing and all kind of flash bulbs were going off. Becky looked beautiful and like she just walked off the front page of a bridal magazine. David was almost breathless and was in awe of her.

The ceremony didn't take too long and they both remembered there vows. It was a beautiful weeding. They had a receiving line witch Jim was part of and was also having fun. Then it was off to the Country Club for the reception. Sue was also having fun and on the ride to the Country Club there were a lot of kisses.

David had reserved a large separate building at the club and spared no expense to have it be what they wanted. Jim did a very nice toast to the bride and groom. The food was wonderful and the cake was special and they cut it with grace and class. The band and there music was nice and a lot of people were dancing. The Bride and Groom left a little after six and that was about the end of the party. The family had people there to handle the presents so after a lot of hugs and kisses Jim and Sue left for home. Jim kissed Sue and asked if the Jacuzzi and a bottle of Champaign sounded good to her. "It sounds perfect to me."

Monday Morning June 28 / 2010 Tucson, Arizona

Jim and Sue were on a run and the sky in the east was getting light. "I am going to start working on our new friends after breakfast. Would you like to help me?"

"I would love to. Where do you want to go to breakfast?"

"Let's go to the Congress Street Hotel; I still love to eat there."

Breakfast as always was great and as they were leaving there was a band in the night club setting up there equipment and doing some jamming. Jim and Sue went in and listened a bit then it was back to the house and to work.

While Jim opened everything up Sue made up a thermal pot of coffee and brought that and cups down. When Jim started the computers the first thing he checked was the E-mail on the account he had given Hector in El Paso. There was a detailed report of what they had done along with pictures of four of the men Jim had given them and there corresponding names. There was also photo's of the business and its correct address. At the time of the report they had seen twelve different people around the business. Jim started doing a complete search of each of the top five people, everything from there drivers licenses and the photo's on them then to all of there banking transactions both commercial and private. He also pulled all of there E- mails from there computer both incoming and outgoing. By one thirty Jim had located the company that had sent them an overnight package by UPS. It came out of Hot Springs Arkansas and when Jim checked it was a law firm. Jim printed everything he needed on both companies then asked Sue if she would like to go have a drink as he turned everything off. "I would love to; help me bring the cups and stuff up."

Jim fixed them drinks in plastic glasses and suggested they enjoy them by the pool. It was only minutes and they had changed and had there drinks in the pool. It was over a hundred outside and the water was in the seventies. "I was all ready to go to El Paso and personally take care of these people, but now I am thinking that could be a bad idea for both the situation and for me. I still believe they are a direct threat to us, but one I can handle from here. If I start doing this direct then I am making it too personal and I would be doing it because of my own ego."

"How are you going to do it from here?"

"By now they all know there people have disappeared. I already have all the information I need to take all there money. If I empty there accounts then call a couple of the people at the bottom of there pile and say that they have emptied there bank accounts and are getting ready to split town they may well take care of each other. Then after they are handled we can find out about the new player; the law firm in Arkansas."

"I understand what you are saying and do agree. How about after we are done here I fix us something nice to eat then we can go back to work and do what we need to. Tomorrow you can have Hector in El Paso hide and watch what happens there in the morning."

"If there are any kisses in all that then I think it's a good idea."

There were a lot of kisses and they worked hard in the basement till after eight. After that it was the Jacuzzi and an early night.

Tuesday Morning June 29 / 2010 Tucson, Arizona

"Let's start the day with a run; I feel the need for speed."

"You're on little girl."

By the time they were almost back to the house they were walking and Sue asked if she dressed up real pretty if Jim would take her to the Country Club for breakfast. "I will call first so they will be ready for you."

"I have another hat that I have never worn. I think all of you will like it."

The shower was fun and by the time they were ready Sue did again look beautiful. "What time do you expect Hector to call?"

"He won't call there people till after nine o'clock; it shouldn't be long after that. You do look beautiful; now if you're ready let's go put smiles on all the people at the Country Club."

The morning was perfect for eating outside. And the staff were all happy to see Sue and how she was dressed. While they were eating Jim got a call from Hugh saying he could set the closing on both of Sue's properties for Wednesday Morning if they liked. Jim told him that would be nice and asked the amounts for the checks he would need. Sue was excited and the conversation went to the rebuilding of the properties. Jim thought it was nicer then talking about the bad guys. Breakfast was fun and a Number of people stopped by there table to say hello. "When we leave here would you drive by the buildings?"

"I would love to, we can also stop by the bank and get cashier checks from you're Catalina Consulting account; that is what the property will be titled under."

"We should also photograph each property before we start any work on them."

"We will do that and you should be in the pictures with your hat on. You can also research the Tucson Historic Society and I bet you can get copies of pictures taken in the buildings hay days."

"I love it; we can make an album up of there history."

That was the end of breakfast and they were off to look at the buildings then to the bank.

It was after ten when they returned to the house they stopped and talked with Jerry for a few minutes then to the house and turned on the Cable News. Sue poured them coffee she had put into a thermal pot before they left. They watched the news till a quarter to eleven when Hector Called and said all hell had broken loose in El Paso and there had been a shoot out at the building the bad guys had. He said the police and the FBI were all over it they had taken four people into custody two of them had been wounded. Hector wasn't sure of the Number of people that had been involved in it. He said he would again call when he had any additional information.

Jim was laughing when he hung up. "Ok now tell me everything."

"Hector said there was a gun battle in El Paso this morning. He said they had arrested four and two of them had gun shot wounds, he said the police and the FBI were involved but he didn't have a count of how many people were involved in the shooting."

"Well if the FBI is involved Cable News can't help but to have it on the news."

Sue was right they announced they would be coming back with a breaking news story out of El Paso Texas right after there break. "Well business is business; the commercials come first. I am sure they charge them more if they run there spot before a breaking story."

They came back saying there had been a huge gun battle in an industrial section of El Paso Texas that had left at least eleven people dead, two wounded and another two under arrest. An FBI spokes person stated that an unknown Number of people had left the seen before Police arrived and that there was a short standoff before the last four surrendered. The news reporter stated the business was some kind of high end security company based on what the neighboring businesses told them. "If there count is correct that's fifteen out of twenty two. It will be interesting to see what happens to the rest of them. I should have names by the next two days."

"Do you want to start on the Little Rock law firm?"

"How about you and I take the rest of the day off and I take you and you're pretty clothes and hat some where fun."

"Would you take me back to that little old artist town called Bisbee?"

"I think Bisbee would be fun. Let me use the rest room then I am ready to go."

They took Jim's SUV incase they bought something. The drive was beautiful and the desert was all green from the monsoon storms. "We should get a storm this afternoon or evening. If we do before we leave Bisbee we should watch it from the Copper Queen Hotel; Bisbee sits in a canyon and the storm should be something to see if it hits there."

"Why is it that I am sure you already know it will?"

"I didn't think about that till you mentioned it, but you're right I do know it."

It wasn't long and they were walking through the town and trying to see every gallery. They stopped at a small bar, got a drink and talked with some of the local artist who also happened to be taking a break. They ended up buying one painting and a brass sculpture from the artist that made it. It was a great afternoon. After they put everything into the SUV they drove back to the Copper Queen Hotel ordered a drink and sat out on there front covered patio. The storm was almost upon them. Jim told there waitress they would like to order dinner because the storm should have passed by the time it was ready. Actually it started while they finished ordering. The storm was magnified by being in the canyon. It was something neither of them would forget. As they finished dinner the waitress brought them coffee and Jim's second phone rang. It was again Hoyt Segal from the Phoenix Republic.

Hoyt told Jim that again an FBI agent named Lewis Riley wanted to talk to Jeff Black he left a Number and asked if he would call at any hour. Jim again thanked Hoyt and said "Don't you or Bill go on vacation for the next week and a half."

Jim told Sue who wanted him to call then made the call. Agent Riley answered right a way then started to tell Jeff Black about El Paso and that the people that were killed were part of a sophisticated group of assassins and they were the ones that had a contract to kill the people in Tucson. "We now have an identity of the targets it's a couple named Jim and Sue Cooper who live on the north side of Tucson in a large estate. We believe they are still a target. And people are still after them."

Jim said "Those are not the names I have. The people I know of are out of the country and will be for at least a month so I can't help you with those names. I hope the two of you work that out because I believe by the end of the week you and Agent Higgs will both be busy. Thanks for the call and all of you stay safe."

"Just listing to one side of that conversation it didn't sound good for us."

"You're right but in reality we both knew it was a possibility. They only have us as targets of the bad guys, so I would expect a visit sometime tomorrow."

"Ok then let's go home watch the sunset then have a nice night."

The ride home was fun then it was a nice bottle of wine and sunset.

Wednesday Morning June 30 / 2010 Tucson, Arizona

Jim woke Sue up with kisses then said "We should have a busy day, would you like to start it with a run?"

"A run would be the second thing I would like to start with."

What a morning even the shower was great. "Let's do the Country Club for breakfast then we have the closings. I will tell Jerry we are expecting company, he can call before he lets them in, if were not home he can set an appointment for them. After we are done with them I would like to start with the law office in Little Rock and find the name of there client."

The morning went fast; even the two closings took only forty minutes. On the way home Jerry called and said that two gentlemen from the FBI were there to see him. Jim told Jerry he and Sue were only five minutes out and asked if they would wait.

As Jim and Sue reached the gate house Jerry opened the gate then they followed the FBI car up to the house. As the two agents got out of there car it was obvious they were in awe of the estate. Jim and Sue introduced themselves as did the agents. The one agent was Lewis Riley. Jim invited them in. Sue led the way to the pool room and asked if she could get them anything. They both declined and thanked her.

Once seated Agent Riley got right two it and explained that they have come across evidence in a case they are working that a company of professional hit men had a contract out to assonate the two of them. He went on to explain that the FBI would put them in there protective service. Jim asked Agent Riley why they thought he and Sue were targets. Riley explained that based on the information they had uncovered that someone believed that he was the source of the information that has led to the arrest of all the Senators and the destruction of the criminal syndicates they were part of. Sue and then Jim started laughing then Jim explained he was into buying and selling real estate and he and Sue were just married last month. Jim said "Buying this estate and marring Sue are the biggest things that have happened in my life. Being involved in espionage surely wouldn't be something I would have time for. I don't mean to make light of this and do appreciate you coming out and telling us about it but I must decline you're offer for protection."

Agent Riley said "We have done an extensive back ground check on you and haven't found any thing that would indicate that you do have any information; the only thing that is obvious is that you know your way around the world of espionage as you refer to it and that you are very knowledgeable of computers. Let me leave you my card; for some reason I don't think this will be the last of our conversations"

As agent Riley got up he thanked Sue and Jim for there time and told Sue he loved the estate. As the two agents drove over the hill and out of sight Sue said "I think Agent Riley believes you are the source of all the stories."

"You're right; there was a connection there and he knows."

"What are you going to do?"

"Let's fix a drink then go to work on the law firm in Little Rock; I don't think Agent Riley will be a problem."

"You're thinking he will just sit back and use what Jeff Black gives him."

"I think you saw that in him also."

They worked in the basement till after one o'clock then Jim asked Sue if she would like to call her contractor and see what he had come up with on her warehouse. Sue kissed him and said "It's our warehouse."

They met with Hector and Frank Robles at the warehouse. They had drawings of what they wanted to do about the wall and fence around the property. They were going to make the lot behind the loading docks all concrete and tumbled rose colored brick pavers. They wanted to leave the railroad tracks there just for the aesthetics. Sue and Jim loved all of it. Frank told them he already had the architects and engineer's plans submitted to the city and expected to have the permits by Friday morning. Hector said as long as the sale was completed he would have the property fenced off by the end of the day. Jim and Sue loved it all. Jim gave them fifty thousand so they would be ahead of there billing and not be over extended.

When Jim and Sue left the sight he said "Lets drop in on our lawyers. Paul Burwell may have the name of a good architect that could work with us on planning your Gallery and offices in the old house we just bought. I would also like to talk to Stewart Walked about our new friend Agent Riley. There is nothing for him to do right now but he should be aware of what they are doing."

They got in to see Paul Burwell right a way, he was glad to see them after a few minutes Jim told him what they were looking for and asked if he could help. Paul was excited about the old mansion they were going to rebuild and said the architect they used in redoing the building they were in also did the work on the building that they had walked through that was on the block next to theirs He had also done a lot of the old buildings in the down town area. Paul offered to call him and try and set up a meeting if they liked. Jim thanked him and told him that would be nice. Paul got right through to him then after a moment told Howard what the reason for the call was. Howard knew the building they were talking about and arrangements were made to meet at the property at nine Thursday morning. Before they left Paul's office he called Stewart Walker and told him that Sue and Jim were there and wanted to speak to him for a few minutes. Stewart said he would be right out.

Stewart was also glad to see Sue and Jim and they went into his office right a way. After a bit of conversation Jim told Stewart why they were there and what had transpired. Jim explained that there was nothing Stewart could do at this point but thought he should know what had happened. Stewart made a copy of the FBI Agent's card and put it in Jim's file.

It wasn't long and Jim and Sue were back at the house and in the basement working on the Little Rock law firm there name was Fisher, Banks and Knapp. Jim said "I Know when the bad guys received the UPS package and I am sure it was sent with over night delivery. Let's see if they were dome enough to have one of there people send it from there office. If they did it will show up as an expense charged to the clients account."

"Do you really think they are that stupid?"

"In most cases yes; remember they are driven by there ego's and they believe they are that smart."

It was so easy to find the account that the parcel was billed to. Jim went right into the file; the lawyer handling it was Greg Fisher and his client was another Senator. This time it was Senator Stephan Wetherford from Florida. "That is someone that I haven't come across yet. Let's run Him and Florida through the X computer and see what it comes up with."

The screen was a blur as it went through files and after a good half hour it all came to a stop. Jim looked at what it had come up with and there was nothing to connect the Senator with any of the other people. He never even sat on the same committee with any of them. "Let's take a break, fix a drink and think about this."

He and Sue went up to the pool room and got there drinks Sue put on some good music and sat on the couch with Jim. "There has to be some connection he didn't just come out of the blue and put out a contract to have someone kill us."

"You're right and the only thing I can think of is there are a lot of the files that I haven't seen, so that means the computer also can't scan through them looking for the connection."

"How long will it take you to go through them?"

"It would take weeks to do them all, but what I can do is have the computer scan them one at a time then I will again ask it to look for a connection using all of the files. If he is in any of them it will find him and his connection to all of this. I can have it all in the computer in just a matter of hours."

"Would you like to wait till the morning to do this? You must be tired of looking at that screen."

"You're right, but I will feel better when I have the answers."

"I will come and help you get this done."

It was after eleven by the time they had the last of the files scanned into the computer. Jim looked at Sue smiled then put in the instructions of what he wanted it to do then he pushed the start button. They again watched as it went through all of the files and made hundreds of thousands of checks and cross checks. It was almost an hour before it all came to a stop. Jim looked at it then hit a few keys and it started to print out a good twenty pages then again it stopped, Jim turned everything off and said "Let's lock this up and go fix another drink."

Jim fixed the drinks then they got comfortable on one of the couches and started to read. As Jim finished a page Sue read it. When they finished they both just sat there. Finally Sue said "That is so unbelievable I am at a lost as to what to say. This fucking Senator Steven Wetherford is not only a crook but also a trader who is committing treason on a daily basis. Can you stop him?"

"How about tomorrow after breakfast and our meeting with the architect, you cover the house and what ever needs to happen there while I go to work in the basement. I would like to be to the point that I can have a conversation with both Riley and Higgs so I can give them some advance notice of what will be coming to them Friday." "What about Saudi Arabia and all the money they have stolen from us and plundered from there people."

"I can't bring down there leaders and I can't prove they are directly involved. What I can do is steal a lot of there personal money witch would be in the trillions while I expose there people who are working with our good Senator and his wife's corporate investments. I will also take all there money I can find. This time I will only give the government twenty four hours before the paper puts it into print. Actually I will give it to Bill and Hoyt at the same time and ask that they sit on the story for the twenty four hours."

"Maybe we should leave the country for a while. The shit will surely be hitting the fan."

It ended up being a nice slow night.

Thursday Morning July 01 / 2010 Tucson, Arizona

Jim and Sue were up early and decided to start the day with a nice run. "Let's do breakfast again at the Congress Street Café. We have a lot of time before we meet with the architect."

"We can drive by the warehouse and see what is happening there."

"Do you think they will have already started?"

"I don't think they will waste any time, but we will need to wait and see."

"You know I don't do waiting very well."

Jim kissed her while laughing and said "Let's shower and go to breakfast."

"You shave while I shower." Now Sue was laughing.

Breakfast was fun and it was obvious Sue was anxious about seeing the warehouse. While laughing she said "I think you're just being mean to me."

"You do look beautiful this morning; would you like more coffee after were done."

"Breakfast is over; pay the young lady and take me to the warehouse."

They were both laughing on the way to the car. It was a short drive to the warehouse and when they arrived Sue was astonished at what she saw. All the parking lots had been dug up and the last of the old concrete and pavement was being loaded into dump trucks. At the same time there was a large machine digging the footing for the concrete wall that would surround the back and sides of the building. There was also big trucks backed in toward the front of the building so the men working on the roof could through the old parts into the back of the trucks. Sue said "This is unbelievable I thought they would still be looking at what they wanted to do."

Frank walked over to the car said good morning then said "We have found a lot of old equipment inside this place and we will save all of it then you can see if there is any of it you want incorporate in the studio's. We will also have gas, water and sewers going into each of the four units. Probably by the first of the week we need to decide on the placements of the restrooms."

"Thanks Frank; we will do that Monday morning." Jim and Sue spent over a half an hour walking around looking at all that was going on. Then it was time to drive over to the old house and meet with the architect Andrew Wilson. Andrew was already there and they did there introductions.

Andrew said "I am very filmier with this building. I have had three different clients try and purchase it over the last ten years but the seller wouldn't come up with a reasonable price. I believe this could be one of the nicest buildings in Tucson; I have done a lot of research on it. So what do the two of you have in mind for the building?"

"Sue has a consulting company that is very involved with the arts along with other things. She would like to bring the building back to it's grandeur with the second floor being the offices of Catalina Consulting and the main floor would be a very up scale art gallery."

They talked a good half hour and Andrew said he would be in touch with them some time next week. Sue was excited and couldn't believe how fast things had started. It was now time to go back to the house.

"Have you noticed we have had company all morning?"

"No I didn't. Do you think it's the FBI?"

"Yes it is. I think in part to protect us and I am sure Agent Riley thinks I am possibly Jeff Black. Tomorrow when I call them I will make sure there people have me under surveillance and I will make the call come from a cell tower in Chicago."

"You do love you're games."

Jim worked in the basement till after seven in the evening with only restroom breaks and a couple of drinks. Sue suggested they eat at home then walk up and watch the sunset with a nice bottle of wine. Jim liked all of that and helped her make dinner. On the walk to the upper patio Sue was telling Jim she had talked with Kay and Jan and they were having the time of there lives. "I have them flying home on Wednesday so Thursday should be fun."

Friday Morning July 02 / 2010 Tucson, Arizona

Jim and Sue again started the day with a short run then had there coffee outside by the pool. "Would you like to dress up and I will take you to breakfast at the Country Club? While we are there I will have Jeff Black call agents Riley and Higgs from a cell tower in Chicago. I even have one of those Blue tube devices so I won't need to hold the phone."

Sue was laughing then said "I will even wear a nice summer dress and hat that will get there attention."

As they arrived at the Country Club Jim did see there shadow car also turn in; they were three cars behind Jim. He used the valet parking and talked with one of the young men that parked the cars for a minute just to see if the agents were coming in. They were. On there way to there table Jim put on a tiny ear and microphone peace; it would not be visible from any where over a hundred feet. After they were given coffee and juice and had ordered Jim with a cell phone on his lap made his call to CIA agent Higgs. When Higgs answered Jeff Black explained the reason he called. Jeff started telling Higgs he would be sending him an E mail some time today showing an American Senator who is now and has been for years involved in treason with Saudi Arabia it will also show how he and his wife have been systematically stealing billions of dollars from the government. It will also show how he through a law firm in little rock have contracted the assassination of Americans. "I want to give you and the FBI a heads up because I am also sending this out to the Media. I will ask that they sit on the Story till Sunday morning."

"Do you also have any evidence that names there King Abdullah?"

"Not him but all the way up to his front door. Do you want me to E mail this to the same Number?"

"Yes I will be waiting."

Sue had sat listing as if Jim was talking to her. "Well Mr. Cooper that was quite a conversation. I am assuming you will be taking a lot of money from a lot of people today."

There breakfast came to the table with a lot of smiles. "Well I guess the staff also likes you're outfit today."

Breakfast was fun and Jim removed the device from his ear while they were eating. "I already have everything ready to send this out and also to remove the money I am going after. So is there something you would like to do this morning?"

"Yes, let's take a nice slow drive up to Mt Lemon we could have some coffee or tea up there then drive back to the house its thirty degrees cooler up there and I am sure the FBI will also enjoy the ride."

"I love it; we will go from here after we finish."

By a little after three Jim and Sue were back at the house Jim fixed them both drinks then opened the basement and fired up all of his computers. Before starting he called Hoyt and Bill routing the call again through the Chicago cell tower. Hoyt answered and said "It's been a while; we thought the government may have gotten you."

"Well it's not for the lack of trying. The reason I am calling is I have another story for the two of you. I will E mail a copy to you and the government at the same time but here is the hook. I need the two of to sit on this one till the Sunday morning edition. This is just another part of the same ongoing story, it's a big part but I need to give the government a head start."

"You can count on it, we will hold back till the Sunday morning edition."

"Thanks guys and keep you're heads low." Jim shut the phone.

"Should I again E mail this from the Chicago District Attorneys Office?"

Sue was again laughing and said "Just don't ever get arrested in Chicago."

It took a good two hours but it did get E mailed and again Jim left a copy in a secret file in there computer system, He also disconnected there security while he did the Email then after he was done he restarted it. Now it was time to remove all the money he could from the Senator, his wife, the people in Little Rock, there company and all the partners. The next thing would be the people in Saudi Arabia and as much as he could find from there King Abdullah.

By six o'clock Jim and Sue were out in the pool enjoying themselves. "Do you think The FBI is still watching us?"

"Do you think we should take them out with us tonight? We could do dinner at the Country Club and maybe you can fine us something at the theater or art museum."

"I love it; I will get on the phone as soon as we are done here. I think we could all use some fun tonight."

Sue made her calls and there was a play showing at the Arizona Theater Company that they hadn't seen so Sue arranged the tickets. They showered and dressed and again Sue looked beautiful. Jim had called the Country Club and made arrangements so they could do dinner before the theater.

They had a light dinner and enjoyed each others company. While having there coffee Sue asked Jim what he came up with from the different people and there corporations. Jim laughed and said "From the law firm and there people I got over twelve million. Now the Senator, his wife and her corporations I got over a hundred million, now From Saudi Arabia, the King and his people I took one point two Trillion. I have all of this sitting in four hundred and seventy different Numbered accounts around the world."

"Just hearing you say trillion scares the shit out of me. What do you think will happen?"

"The sad thing is I don't think anything will happen. One point two trillion is just a drop in the bucket. They will be upset and change how they hide there money but the outside world will never hear about it. That money I won't hold and give it back to there country like what I took from Gaddafi and his family. This money I will in time give it to our treasury to pay down our national debt; that way it will help everyone in our country. After all that is who it was stolen from."

"I like that. Now if your ready let's take our FBI friends to the theater." While laughing Jim kissed her and asked for the check.

At the Arizona Theater Company they were happy to see Sue and Jim. Sue was telling some of them about the buildings Catalina consulting had bought and what they would be when they were completed. She did say there would be a grand opening and they all would receive an invitation. The play was very good and both Sue and Jim had a good time but didn't know if the FBI agents did.

Saturday Morning July 03 / 2010 Tucson, Arizona

Sue woke Jim with kisses and said "Let's run up to the patio and watch the sun come up for us."

"One more kiss and I am ready."

At breakfast Jim got a call from the architect Andrew Wilson who wanted them to come by his office and see some of the drawings he had made up over the years for there building. Most of there day was spent with the architect and then the builders Frank and Hector Robles at the sight of the warehouse.

For the whole day and night the subject of the FBI, CIA and the bad guys never came up.

Sunday Morning July 04 / 2010 Tucson, Arizona

Jim and Sue started there day with coffee in the Jacuzzi. "Let's go for a nice breakfast at the Congress Street Hotel and not watch the news till we get home."

At the café they met another couple that Sue had gone to school with and they all had breakfast together. It was nice to meet some of Sue's friends. There names were Phil and Luann and they also had been recently married.

Back at the house Jim turned on the Television to the cable news who was again on continuous coverage of the big story around Senator Waterford of Florida who was the front page and headlines of the Phoenix Republic newspaper. They showed a picture of him and his wife. The story went back to the story of the shoot out at the security company in El Paso Texas June 29th and how it was linked to the law firm in Little Rock Arkansas.

The story also went into how the Senator and his wife were involved with Saudi Arabia and the billions of dollars they stole from our government and the tax payers. The whole article took up a little over four pages of the paper.

"Well Mr. Conner that was one hell of a story; do you think the government can handle all of that?"

"I noticed as we left the café this morning we no longer had our government protection and I am sure if we check our car we also have lost our GPS transmitter. I think the government will need all there agents for other work. Now on the up side of things Tomorrow David and Becky should be back from there honeymoon."

"The girls should be back some time Wednesday night. We should have a party next weekend."

"Your right, we should start a list of the people we want to invite starting with the boys and there dates. They started there list and were having fun. They spent over an hour and had a list of about twenty people. "Let's wait till Becky and David plus the girls are back before we do any more on this."

"You're right, so now would you like to help me work in the basement for a while?"

"Yes I would; then you can tell me where you think this thing is going."

They took a bottle of wine and glasses down with them. Jim turned on all the computers then opened the wine poured two glasses then said "I have been giving this a lot of thought and came up with I think is a double plan. Unless someone comes up as a threat to us I would like to stop all the big stories and try and work with the two agents we have been working with Brian Higgs and Lewis Riley. If they are agreeable I could over a period of time give them a big player and all of his connections, and then after time has passed I could give them another that wasn't connected to the other. They could make it look like it was good police work bringing these people to justices. Now for the foreign leaders, there business people and corporations I was just thinking of taking there money and like Saudi Arabia slowly use it to pay down our national debt. What do you think?"

Sue was laughing so hard she had put down her drink and was holding her sides. After she regained some of her composer she said "Only you would come up with such a simple solution to such a complex problem; I love how you're mind works."

"I know it won't be that simple but I don't want to spend our lives playing policeman for the world. I want to spend my time with you building our lives and having a family. We have billions to try and put to good use and I also don't want any of us to have to worry about our safety. I never expected this would come as close to us as it did. I will promise you that I will do everything in my power to make sure it never does again."

"I love you very much and do know how hard this has been on you. So let's work for a few hours then go play in the pool."

"This is the fourth of July; would you like to have dinner here then watch the fire works with me up on the upper patio?"

"I almost forgot about it being the forth; let's take some nice wine up with us."

It was a wonderful forth of July.

Monday Morning July 05 / 2010 Tucson, Arizona

The morning started with Jim and Sue out for a run they were both happy and excited of the day to come.

The End

287